Heather Ingman has lived in Ireland, France and Ecuador, at present she lives in Yorkshire. She teaches part time at the universities of York and Hull. Heather Ingman's previous novels, *Sara* and *Anna*, reached the bestseller list in Ireland.

For Theo, with great love

"About suffering they were never wrong,
The Old Masters: how well they understood
Its human position; how it takes place
While someone else is eating or opening a window or just
                                        walking dully along . . . "
(WH Auden *Musée des Beaux Arts*).

1990

CHAPTER ONE

THE PRIME MINISTER DROVE, IN TEARS AND A BLUE SUIT, TO Buckingham Palace to inform the Queen of her resignation.

"That's that then."

Grace turned away from the TV screen. She didn't know whether to be glad or sorry. Glad because she'd never agreed with Thatcher's policies. Sorry because it would be a long time, she supposed, before a prime minister would again be referred to as "she". Then she heard Leonard coming down for breakfast and hastily began setting the table.

Leonard strolled into the breakfast room, yawning and scratching his head. He'd been awake for most of the night. At three o'clock in the morning it had suddenly become clear to him that someone was trying to manoeuvre him out of the firm. Why else would the share prices be going up so rapidly? Someone was buying up shares in preparation for a takeover bid. He'd be finished as chairman. He'd only been in the job two months.

"Someone wants me out of the firm," he said, sitting down at the place Grace had laid for him and shaking out cornflakes. He'd gone through yoghurt-covered corn-bites, toffee-coated wheatflakes, coffee-flavoured sugar puffs before deciding his taste buds didn't like so many surprises early on a morning. He'd returned to cornflakes.

Heather Ingman

He glanced up and frowned. The sun was streaming in through the window, making the polished wooden table gleam and striking sparks off the silver cutlery and silver napkin rings. It was also making Leonard's eyes water. He glanced across at his wife, noted her absorption in her paper, sighed and got up to lower the linen blind himself.

Leonard and Grace Napier lived in an elegant four-storey house in the middle of Dulwich Village. The house had a wide, curved front entrance with heavy wrought iron gates. At the back there was a view which normally gave Leonard a great deal of pride and pleasure. This morning not even a country estate would have impressed him.

He sat down again. "Someone wants me out."

"Do they dear?" replied his wife, absentmindedly. She reached for the sugar with one hand and held up the *Guardian* in the other. "That's a pity. Thatcher's gone too."

"What do I care about that? Time she went anyway. She was getting dangerously out of control. No, listen Grace, someone's trying to buy me out of my firm." Lately, Leonard found himself wishing Grace would take more of an interest in his work.

"Can't you do something about it?" she asked, not raising her eyes from the paper.

"Not till they've bought five per cent of the shares. At that point they'll have to declare themselves. But by then it might be too late."

He felt a bout of self-pity coming on. Honestly, you'd think she'd put down the newspaper for a minute. She had all day to read it. And she'd stopped ironing his shirts. He looked down. He'd somehow succeeded in ironing this one in creases.

"I suppose you'd be glad if I was out of a job?" he said dismally.

"Mm? Well, we don't need the money, do we, dear?"

Grace folded up the *Guardian* with a sigh and

2

contemplated her husband. He did look a mess this morning. She'd been against him taking this job. Six months ago, at the age of sixty-three, Leonard had retired as director of a very large oil company. Grace had been looking forward to having lots of free time. She'd made her plans. They'd be able to travel, go to the theatre without fear of having to cancel at the last minute, stay long weekends in the country with friends without having to dash back for Monday morning. She'd counted on being finished with working as unpaid secretary, entertaining wives and providing one, or sometimes two, freshly ironed shirts each day. For a short, blissful while it had been like that. Then, two months ago, Leonard had come back home and announced he'd been offered the chairmanship of a small electronics company. He'd always wanted to be chairman of something. It was only a three day a week job, but tying, nonetheless. Grace had put her foot down and refused to iron any more shirts or entertain any more wives. Hence Leonard's creased shirt.

Glumly Leonard returned his wife's gaze. Ever since he'd started in this new job Grace had been behaving oddly. She'd begun buying the *Guardian* regularly, for instance, and reading bits out to him about women's rights, women in the City, all that sort of thing. She was no longer so particular about the dusting, he'd noticed. Her hair was looking odd too, straighter than usual. Had she given up going to the hairdresser's?

"Damn!" she exclaimed suddenly.

For a second, Leonard's eyes brightened. At last. A bit of sympathy coming his way.

"I've put sugar on my egg."

She got up and threw it into the bin.

Leonard felt a headache coming on. He decided to get his own back.

"You've remembered Clive's coming to dinner tonight?"

He permitted himself a small, malicious smile. Grace loathed his brother Clive.

She groaned and began buttering a piece of toast. "I've remembered. He's bringing a doctor friend of his. A medical researcher from Cambridge. I don't know where he finds these people."

"And Jean, of course."

"And Jean."

It was easy to overlook Jean. It was Grace's private opinion that a dose of the *Guardian*'s women's page would do her sister-in-law a power of good. She was a slave to the house, her three children and Clive's meals. I used to be like that. Grace munched her toast. Spending my time, when I wasn't hanging around the school gate, making jams and juices for the village fete, driving Senior Citizens to collect their pensions, fund-raising for the local picture gallery.

Recently rebellion, simmering for years, had finally come to a head. All the time she'd been at home potty training her children, encouraging them to make messes with poster paints and play, other women had been working as company directors, or starting up their own businesses, or making a killing as financial whizzkids on the Stock Market. Whilst she'd been intent on turning her daughters into civilised human beings, other women had been running the country. One evening Grace had sat up and thought, there must be more to life than a well-polished house and nicely mannered children. She was secretly looking round for a job.

There has to be something I can do, even at my age, she'd thought (she was fifty-one). She heard her mother's voice, "Children need their mother at home. And men are great children too. They have to be looked after." But her daughters were at boarding school and Leonard wasn't a child, he was an adult. If he wasn't capable of getting the odd meal for himself, well, it was high time he learned. She'd begun training him in.

"I don't know why you have such a down on Clive," remarked Leonard, clearing away the breakfast things (this was one of his new duties).

"He's a flirt, Leonard." Grace retrieved the knife he'd dropped on the floor. "A sexist flirt, what's more. A sexist, Conservative flirt. We all know about the Conservative Party and sex," she added darkly.

"Grace! What *are* you suggesting?"

"Nothing perverted. Clive wouldn't have the imagination. Only your brother doesn't always behave as if he was a safely married man, I've observed."

Leonard smirked. "Clive did sow some wild, liberal oats in his youth, I believe."

"Ah, ha!"

"Yes, hung around with some arty types when he was at college. He told me about it once when we got a bit loaded together. Almost bohemian it sounded."

"Arty? How interesting. And he's such a great supporter of Thatcher. Or was. I wonder if he'll change his tune now?" Grace began to reorganise Clive in her mind. After a few moments, she said, "And what did you confess?"

"What?" Leonard stared fixedly at the toast rack.

"Well, if Clive confessed to that, you must have confessed something too."

There was a pause. "Darling, you know you know everything about my past." He flashed her a smile and began loading pots into the dishwasher. "By the way," he continued hurriedly, "I think this machine is going to pack up soon."

"Mm, I've ordered a new one." She picked up the *Guardian* again.

"What?"

"That's all right, darling, I'll pay for it. I sold some shares recently."

"You what? Ouch!" Leonard, straightening up rather suddenly, felt a twinge in his back.

Grace peered round the corner of her newspaper. "I sold some of those shares Daddy left me."

"Naturally, Grace, you have a perfect right to do whatever you wish with your own shares," he said, hurt. "However, if you'd told me you were selling them, I could have advised you when to do it."

"I got a good price for them. Just under two pounds a share."

He whistled. "Not bad."

"I know."

"You were lucky."

"Not at all. I know what I'm doing. You always underestimate me."

"That bloody woman's page!" He growled and bent down to the dishwasher.

Grace settled back to her paper, grinning to herself.

Ever since her mother had died two years ago, giving rise to a week of mourning in Ireland, she'd been nothing but trouble to Jade. Interfering in her thoughts, distracting her attention at inconvenient moments, confusing her tongue.

On the morning of Thatcher's resignation, Jade woke up and said, "All right, mother, you win."

Which was exactly what her mother wanted.

"I'm thinking of making a film," said Jade to Lallie, over breakfast.

"Of course you are." Lallie helped herself to muesli.

In the eight years Lallie had lived with Jade, the latter had made four short history films for Channel Four, three training videos for oil companies and countless marketing films. Lallie, who had a Masters from the Warburg Institute, had done the research for the history films.

"Yes, but . . . I mean a different sort of film. Part fiction." Jade hesitated. Or was her mother's life wholly fictional?

"Oh?" Lallie's cool blue eyes fixed on her.

"About my mother."

"Your mother?!" Lallie's hand, reaching for the carton of soya milk, halted in mid-air.

"Yes, you know the sort of thing. Famous Irish actress. Sketches of Irish society in the fifties. Should be easy enough to get some sort of backing for it, maybe even a grant."

"Your mother?" repeated Lallie. There was a pause. She ran her fingers through her short black hair. "You hated your mother."

"Precisely. I want to finish her off, fix her for good on celluloid and get her out of my mind. It's time I was free of them, Lallie, free of the whole wretched lot."

Lallie didn't need it explained to her that by this Jade meant her family. "Wretched" was an adjective that suited them particularly well. Lallie poured the soya milk over her muesli and ate a spoonful. "Libel actions."

Jade rested her elbows on the table. "I've thought of that. I'll end the film with my mother on the brink of being discovered. Everyone knows about her public life as an actress. There was that RTE documentary a few years ago. It's the early part of her life that interests me – and most of the people connected with that are dead now, or live abroad. I don't think we'll have any problems."

Lallie looked across the table at Jade. She was wearing a pink tracksuit. Her blonde hair was done up in a ponytail and her tanned face glowed with health. Jade was always optimistic at the start of a new film.

"It's to be a family thing, then? Personal?"

"Yes." Jade's long, brown fingers touched the edge of the tablecloth, nervously.

"All of them?"

"Yes." Jade glanced down. It had to be all of them, only in that way would she be purged of her memories.

Lallie's blue eyes rested gently on her lover's bent head for a moment. "It's a dangerous occupation, raking over the past. You might find more than you bargained for."

Jade looked up. "I want a clean break, Lallie. I want to be free of them."

A lesser woman would have had tears in her eyes. But Jade was the least sentimental person Lallie had ever met.

"Well," she said, adopting Jade's matter-of-fact manner, "make a list and we'll get to work."

Joachim stepped off the plane. Ireland. Even the air smelled fresher here, after Munich. One by one, invisible chains fell away from him. Some day he'd come to live here permanently, make a clean break with his country and its past. He'd live on his farm, thinking only of his wheat and barley, the milk yield and how to save the local church. He'd forget all about Germany, that sick and soulless society.

Paddy was at Dublin airport to meet him and, as they bumped their way down to Bannon in the old Land Rover, he recounted to Joachim the events of the past three weeks. Joachim half listened. He'd go over everything in detail later with Alan, his farm manager. Looking out of the window he was struck, as always on his return from Germany, by the dilapidated state of the houses in north Dublin, the amount of rubbish left lying around on the streets. People said the Irish were a slovenly race, but to anyone who'd ever visited a concentration camp (and Joachim had visited three), Germany's cleanliness had something suspect about it.

They cleared the sprawling Dublin suburbs and were out in the countryside, flat green fields, spoiled only by the Spanish hacienda style bungalows that had sprung up in the last twenty years and the pretentious red brick mock-Georgian mansions which were a more recent innovation.

"Fergus's ailing again," said Paddy, changing gear. "Slipped outside his back door and did his ankle in."

"Oh dear. I must go and see him. How's he managing for meals?"

"Molly's been popping in most days. He can get about

with a stick but he can't make it down to the shops. He'll not last the winter here."

Fergus lived in the lodge by the front gate. In the old days, he'd been the estate gardener. He was retired now and hadn't been replaced. There was no money to spare for luxuries. Paddy did what he could when he could be spared from the farm, but the gardens were getting more and more overgrown. It was lucky in a way that Fergus was too infirm nowadays to make it down the long front avenue; it would have broken his heart to see the weeds in the flower beds, the moss and dandelions on the lawns he'd faithfully tended for so many years.

They were passing the front entrance now. The huge gates were shut up and never used, except by Fergus. They drove parallel to the crumbling estate wall and turned in through a side entrance. They passed a couple of nondescript modern bungalows where the dairy workers lived and then the castle with its fantastic Gothic towers, all of different heights, came into view. Joachim felt a surge of pride, a feeling that had nothing to do with ownership (his family were relative newcomers to Ireland) but with the whole history of the place.

His father had bought the estate in the sixties when it had been fashionable for wealthy Germans, fearing their country was about to be overrun by Russia, to buy land in Ireland. His father's friends had looked on Ireland with condescension, as a delightfully old-fashioned country where the pace of life was charmingly slow, but where they wouldn't want their sons educated. Joachim, sixteen when the estate had been purchased, had stayed on in Germany to finish his studies. Ireland had been a holiday place till his father had died seven years ago, leaving Joachim with the problem of what to do with the farm. Katrin, his wife, had been in favour of selling it, but already Joachim had begun to feel there might come a time when he'd need a refuge, not from the Russians, but from his life in Germany.

They drove into the courtyard.

"There's a bit of beef and suchlike laid out for you in the kitchen." Paddy switched off the engine. "Molly was in earlier."

"Great, Paddy. Thank her for me." Joachim stepped down from the Land Rover.

"Sure, it was no trouble at all." Paddy grinned. "I'll see you in the morning then, please God." He gave a wave and crossed the courtyard to the cottage where he'd lived for twenty years with his wife, Molly and their five children.

In the kitchen Joachim went to the fridge, took out a can of beer and sat down to his supper of cold beef and salad. When he'd finished, he put the dishes into the sink and wandered down the corridor into the central hall. His footsteps echoed hollowly on the cold, cracked flagstones. He pushed open a heavy oak door leading off from the hall and went into the library where Molly had laid out his letters on his desk. Ignoring them, he went over to one of the tall windows and unfastened the shutters. They swung back with a creak to reveal a velvet black sky.

He opened the window and breathed in the cool night air. In the distance he heard the grunts of rutting stags, like giant frogs in the night, deep, bestial, eerie. The muscles in his shoulders relaxed. His face slackened into a smile. This feeling of homecoming was the nearest to earthly happiness he would ever get. His love of the land was so sharp it sometimes caused him physical pain. Walking through the streets of Munich or listening to a concert on the radio, he'd feel a stab of hunger to be back in Ireland.

He closed the window. Tomorrow he'd go round and see Cornelius Fry. This was his second piece of earthly happiness. No, third. His sons came before Cornelius. But only just, because with them, inevitably, came their mother.

CHAPTER TWO

CORNELIUS FRY LIVED ON THE OUTSKIRTS OF BANNON, IN AN eighteenth-century manor house he'd inherited from an aunt and which caused him horrendous financial problems as bits of it kept falling off and had to be put back again. He worked in Dublin, as a lecturer in European Studies at UCD, specialising in the history of the Jews in sixteenth-century France. The fact that the Jews had been officially expelled from France in 1392 would have worried a lesser man than Cornelius Fry. He viewed the problem with the same equanimity as he viewed the tiles which fell off his roof.

Joachim decided to walk over the fields to Cornelius's house. Freshly ploughed, they looked like bales of new, brown corduroy. In the distance his lake shimmered silver in the pale November sun. At the edge of a thicket a fox stood and stared boldly at him. Joachim didn't approve of foxhunts, nor of shooting parties.

Cornelius, dressed in baggy cords and a maroon jumper with a hole in the elbow, was leaning on his garden gate. His wiry black hair stuck out at odd angles and his cheeks glowed pink from the sharpness of the autumn air. He looked like an enthusiastic schoolboy, a studious, enthusiastic schoolboy, amended Joachim, taking in Cornelius's thick spectacles. An alsatian sniffed around Cornelius's ankles.

"Hello Cornelius!" shouted Joachim, from several yards away.

"You'll have to come nearer, whoever you are," Cornelius

shouted back in his rather high-pitched voice. "I'm terribly short-sighted. And mind the dog, he's quite savage."

Joachim was not deceived by the warning, nor by Cornelius's pretence of restraining his dog. Cornelius had chosen as guard dog the cowardliest alsatian in the country. He had to grab him whenever strangers approached to prevent him from running away. He was called Diogenes, after the Cynic philosopher who lived in a barrel.

With his long legs Joachim rapidly covered the distance between himself and his friend.

"Oh it's you." Cornelius let go of Diogenes who immediately slunk across the lawn into the house. Cornelius opened the gate and, being several inches shorter than Joachim, steered him by the elbow towards the house. "Come in, come in. Elizabeth's in the kitchen making pies."

Conventional and Georgian on the outside, in the inside Cornelius's house was quite extraordinary. Like a cross between a Gothic cathedral and an Oriental despot's harem. Joachim believed Cornelius added a bit whenever he got bored. He blinked as he stepped inside the dark, oak panelled hall.

Portraits of earlier Frys hung on the walls and two huge Chinese vases stood on either side of the door leading into the drawing-room. This door, of heavy oak carved with violent Old Testament scenes, was Cornelius's pride and joy. Too good for a church, he'd thought when he saw it and immediately set about bullying the local parish priest into giving it to him. "You need a new church door, Father. All this slaying and pillaging puts people off. I'll start a subscription." And the parish priest, sniffing the possibility of a new parishioner, had been reluctant to dissuade him. Consequently, the Catholic church in Bannon had a garish red door and Cornelius's hall had this beautifully carved one. Cornelius hadn't been near the church since.

In the kitchen they found Elizabeth rolling out pastry. She

looked up as they came through the door, pushed back a strand of faded red hair and smiled. "Hello, Joachim."

"Is the kettle on?" enquired Cornelius, peering through his glasses.

"No, but you could put it on," replied Elizabeth and winked at Joachim.

"Darling, what is Joachim doing here at this time of day? Why isn't he coming to dinner tonight? Would you like to come to dinner tonight, Joachim?" Cornelius turned to his friend.

"Well, I . . ." Joachim spread out his hands and looked at Elizabeth.

"I didn't know you were coming this weekend else I certainly would have invited you," she replied, brushing flour off her nose.

"That's settled then." Cornelius measured out Nescafé.

Joachim, more aware than his friend of catering difficulties, raised an enquiring eyebrow at Elizabeth.

She nodded. "It's OK."

"Come on then," said Cornelius impatiently. "Let's take our coffees into the study, away from this hive of activity."

Elizabeth made a gargoyle face at him. "Take Diogenes with you, please. He keeps following me around sighing and moaning."

"He's in love," said Cornelius. "An unrequited love is a very sad thing for a dog. Isn't that so, Diogenes?" He patted the alsatian.

"Anyone we know?" asked Joachim, following Cornelius down the corridor to his study.

"Mrs Dart's fox terrier. A totally unsuitable match. Poor old Diogenes."

Cornelius settled himself in a huge leather armchair and Diogenes flopped down at his feet. Joachim sat on the window seat. The study had a wood panelled ceiling and was lined with books from top to bottom. In one corner stood a carved oak pew "borrowed" from the local Protestant church. Beside it was a sort of pulpit affair at which Cornelius stood to write his learned articles for academic journals. Above this hung a large portrait of Erasmus, a copy of the painting by Quentin Metsys. The study looked out onto the back garden. In the centre of the garden was a fountain around which nymphs and dryads cavorted in a variety of erotic poses, to the scandal of the inhabitants of Bannon. Joachim glanced at the spines of the books heaped on Cornelius's desk. *Witchcraft in Medieval England, Exorcisms in Sixteenth-Century France, A Short History of Alchemy.* Cornelius's interests became more eccentric by the day.

"So," began Cornelius, stirring his coffee, "how was the harvest this year?"

Cornelius knew nothing about farming but he'd lived long enough in the country to be able to fit his questions to the seasons.

Joachim grimaced. "The wheat was wet. I'll be going over the figures with Alan later today but I shouldn't think we'll have got anything like a good price for it." He sighed. "I don't know how long we'll be able to stagger on like this, short of a miracle . . . Speaking of which, what do you think of this moving statue?"

He was referring to recent events in a small Irish town where people claimed to have seen a statue of the Virgin Mary raise her arms in blessing. Thousands had flocked from all over Ireland to view this miracle. There'd even been reports of healings.

"I advise extreme caution," answered Cornelius. "If you stare at anything long enough it appears to move or otherwise do odd things. It's my belief it's all a plot by the banks to distract people's attention whilst they raise charges yet again and double their already obscene profits."

Cornelius was a fanatic on the subject of the enormous

profits made by banks and other financial institutions. He had a huge overdraft and had changed banks twice already that year. Bank managers had been known to creep out the back door when they saw him coming. Elizabeth claimed he dreamed about banks, muttering things like "Nationalise them" in his sleep.

"Incidentally," he continued, "I've a plan to make you some money."

"Yes?" said Joachim, without much hope.

"You borrow a short-term loan from one bank to pay off a long-term loan in another bank. Then you take out another long-term loan and pay off the short-term loan. Foolproof."

"It's illegal."

"My dear fellow!" Cornelius rocked in his armchair. "The way the banks treat us they deserve all they get."

"And besides, everything's computerised nowadays. The banks have lists of everyone who takes out a loan."

"But you'd be borrowing from different banks – how would anyone find out?"

"They would, believe me."

"Oh." Cornelius looked crestfallen. "Never mind, it was just a thought."

"Thank you, Cornelius."

"Keep your spirits up. Pessimism is such a waste of time, isn't it? Speaking of which, how's your wife?"

"The same," replied Joachim gloomily.

"Poor boy." Cornelius was fond of calling Joachim "boy" despite the fact that, at forty-two, he was only two years older than Joachim.

"The less said about her the better, Cornelius. Who's coming tonight?"

"Ha! An interesting little party!" Cornelius rubbed his hands. "I've invited the Reverend Sam Cleary, a couple of Jewish friends (Elizabeth had a fit – she'd bought a leg of pork), and, I ought to warn you, Plod will be here."

Joachim groaned. Plod was Cornelius's name for the Protestant Bishop of Meath.

"Come on, Joachim, he's not a bad old sod. He can't help being Low Church. He'd never have been made bishop if he'd been anything else."

"He's so Low he'll disappear through the floor of his cathedral one day."

"And you're so High you'll fly through the roof," retorted Cornelius, from the smug vantage point of a sceptic. "Yes, it should be interesting – there's Plod who's Low Church, you a German Lutheran turned High Church Anglican, Sam Cleary who used to be moderate in his views till you encouraged him to chuck incense around and camp it up in front of the altar in little red numbers . . ."

"Cornelius!"

"It's well-known that the High Church section of the Anglican church is the cradle of camp. Can't think what two confirmed heterosexuals like you and Sam are doing in it. Then there's me – a Catholic atheist . . ."

"I beg your pardon?"

"Culturally I'm Catholic. I can't get away from my upbringing. Even if I have lost my faith, I've lost it in a peculiarly Catholic way. As Elizabeth says, I will keep going on about it. *She* is a part-time Catholic, that is to say, she believes in God when something awful happens like the fire in York Minster. Quite a lot of people turned bonkers over that, didn't they? Yes, it will be quite a little symposium. We might even have a freemason among us, who knows? The Protestant church in this country is said to be riddled with masonry. Perhaps Plod's a mason . . . By the way, would you mind just putting your two thumbs between the first and second fingers of each hand?" Joachim set down his coffee cup and complied with his friend's request. "Ah yes, I see. Thanks. There's a sixteenth-century dialogue, you know, set at a dinner table . . ."

"Excuse me, Cornelius," interrupted Joachim, "would you mind telling me what all that was in aid of?"

"What?"

"That business with the thumbs."

"Oh." He shrugged. "It's a secret obscene gesture supposed to have been made by witches at the elevation of the host. It was one of the charges brought against them by the Inquisition. I wanted to know what it looked like."

"I see."

"Anyway, this dialogue has seven people of different faiths debating theological points. I thought it would be fun to recreate it in a twentieth-century setting. Unfortunately, I've been rather hampered by being unable to locate any Muslims in Bannon. You don't know of any, do you?"

"No."

"Pity. Since pork's already off the menu it would have been handy to have had them at the same time."

"Well, Cornelius, fascinating as this all is, some of us live in the real world." Joachim glanced at his watch. "I have to be off to do my shopping."

"I thought you had slaves to do that for you?" Cornelius was in the habit of teasing his friend about living in a castle.

"Ha, ha. What time does this jamboree start then?"

"Half seven for eight. I never know what's meant by that so I enjoy saying it to other people. I mean, are you supposed to arrive the polite ten minutes after seven thirty or after eight? I'm always hoping my guests will solve it for me."

Joachim collected the coffee cups and took them back to the kitchen where he stopped to have a chat with Elizabeth. As he was leaving, he popped his fair head round the study door. "See you at seven thirty then." He thought for a moment. "Or is it eight?"

"See," said Cornelius, "confusing, isn't it?"

When Joachim had gone, Cornelius picked up one of the books lying on his desk. He'd been reading an account of an exorcism where the victim, a young girl believed to be under the devil's influence, was said to have uttered profanities with her black and swollen tongue hanging out of her mouth. She'd been miraculously "cured" by some Catholic priests and as a result quite a number of Protestants had converted.

Cornelius stuck out his tongue and tried speaking to Diogenes. As he'd thought, it was impossible to say anything sensible with one's tongue hanging out of one's mouth. Either the devil knew something he didn't or they'd had a Catholic priest hidden somewhere to fake the responses. He bent excitedly over his books.

"Another triumph for rationalism," he murmured.

Diogenes blew gently on his paws.

In the centre of Bannon, Joachim met Reverend Sam Cleary driving down the street on his lawnmower. He waved to Joachim and came to a halt in front of him.

"Look what my diocese bought me," he said proudly. Sam, who was humble enough to believe he'd never be made bishop, always referred to his small country parish as a diocese. "Handy, isn't it?"

Joachim nodded. "Very."

"Plod's visiting."

"I know. We're all dining at Cornelius's tonight."

"You've been roped in too? Better play down the bells and smells tomorrow then hadn't we? We can have candles of course but they're no fun now they're legal. Well, see you tonight. Is it half seven or eight? I forget."

"Both," replied Joachim.

With a wave Sam continued down the main street on his mower. Joachim smiled after him. Sam was fanatical about any kind of machine. The previous summer Joachim had bought him a diesel hedge trimmer. Sam had been so delighted with it that he'd trimmed all the hedges for miles around, much to their owners' annoyance. "There should be an eleventh commandment," he'd said sadly once, after losing money on a car. "Thou shalt not lust after cars, nor word processors, nor video recorders, nor any sort of new machine."

After Joachim had made his few purchases he walked up to the grey stone Protestant church at the top of the street. Inside he found Mrs Dart doing the flowers.

"I'm making a special effort for the Bishop," she explained. "It's only we High Church people who really know about flowers."

Joachim put his bags down on a pew. "How are you keeping, Mrs Dart? How's the family?"

"Grand, thank you, sir. Though our Eugene still hasn't found a job."

"The bread round fell through then?"

"Sure, it's no wonder. Doesn't everyone get it from the supermarket nowadays?"

"And your feet?"

"All cleared up now. Thanks be to God."

Yes, thought Joachim. He'd prayed for Mrs Dart's bunions. He glanced up at the ceiling. More plaster had fallen off since his last visit. He wondered how much longer they'd be allowed to keep it open. It was the only High Protestant church outside Dublin. It had taken Sam, heavily prompted by Joachim, several years to accustom the congregation to incense and vestments and though, in the end, they weren't the most important part of a service, they added dignity and mystery and it would be a shame to have to give them up.

"Look, sir. Come and look at this," shouted Mrs Dart from the front of the church.

Joachim walked up the aisle to inspect. The altar was sticky with honey. There were several dead bees lying about.

"There must be a bees' nest somewhere up in the roof," said Mrs Dart. "Kind of symbolic, isn't it, honey on the altar?

After all, honey plays quite a large part in the bible, doesn't it?"

"I suppose it does, Mrs Dart."

"I'll clear it away before the Bishop comes. The kind of services he's used to, he wouldn't recognise a symbol if one leapt up and hit him in the eye, would he, sir?"

Joachim smiled.

"I went to my sister's church over in Longford last week. Such a plain service. No vestments or incense. Not even a candle on the altar. I don't know how folks put up with it, I really don't." Mrs Dart who, until Sam Cleary had taken over as rector of Bannon, hadn't so much as sniffed a stick of incense, shook her head over the deprivations of the Longford congregation. "The rector was saying the Bishop's come to look at the roof. I hope he gives us the money for it, else I don't know what will happen. Do you think he will, sir?"

"I don't know, Mrs Dart."

Joachim sighed. Everything in his life seemed to boil down to money. Or lack of it. If he'd had enough money, he would have paid for the repairs to the roof himself. In the old days, this had been the church attached to his castle and though it was now owned by the Church of Ireland, Joachim still felt a special responsibility towards it. If only the harvest hadn't been so bad this year.

The door at the back of the church creaked. Miss Connolly waddled in to rehearse her organ playing for Sunday. She smiled round at them rather vacantly. She was growing increasingly deaf in her old age and was a bit of a trial to Sam who hadn't, however, the heart to dismiss her.

Joachim sat down in a pew, stretched out his long legs, listened to Miss Connolly's hit and miss organ playing and watched Mrs Dart clear away the bees from the altar and polish the lectern. For him church, particularly this church, was the place where time and eternity intersected, a moment both in and out of time. He loved the quiet dignity of the Anglican service, the ritual that carried with it a period of self-emptying, a sharing in the ashes and the glory of Christ. At such moments he had intimations of immortality, like snatches of music dimly heard, faint echoes from a far-off land. Far-off because, as he was aware, there was a shadow over his relationship with God.

On his way home Joachim called in to see Fergus. He was sitting by the stove in his tiny kitchen, his foot propped up on a stool.

"I shan't last another winter here, indeed I won't," he said, shaking his head.

"Is there anything I can get for you, Fergus?"

"Thank you, sir. I'm very comfortable here, indeed I am."

Joachim, looking around the cramped kitchen with its formica topped table and its two hard chairs, thought that Fergus lacked most of the things that people required nowadays to be "comfortable." Tears pricked the back of his eyelids. He gritted his teeth and, as always when he wanted to stop himself getting sentimental, thought of his wife. It never failed to work. He cleared his throat and said, "I wish we could have made you more comfortable, Fergus. But you know how things are . . . "

"Sure, didn't your father and you give me a free home here all these years? What more could I want?"

"Have you any plans, Fergus?" Joachim said hastily.

"My brother's in St Colm's. Sister Benedict said they would make room for me whenever I decide it's too much for me here."

Joachim stifled a groan. He'd visited St Colm's once. There were eighty beds to a ward. The nuns were kind, but there was no privacy. You couldn't even undress in private. All your worldly goods were reduced to what you could get into a locker. He'd have liked to have discussed with his wife ways of helping Fergus, but Katrin was coldly unsympathetic to Ireland and the Irish.

"There're fruit drops in the cupboard," said Fergus. "Help yourself."

"Thanks."

Irish country folk, Joachim reflected, were never so poor that they didn't have something to offer guests, be it only a cup of tea or a sweet. He took a fruit drop and handed the paper bag to Fergus.

"Will your wife be over this summer?"

"I don't know. She finds Ireland . . . wet."

"Pity. That lovely house. How's the garden looking these days?"

"Not too bad, Fergus." Joachim crossed his fingers. "Not like it was in your day, of course."

"Those were grand times, weren't they, sir?" He grinned and shook his head. "Remember the day I kicked up stink because the cattle got onto the front lawn?"

"I do indeed, Fergus. You put the living daylights into the men!"

The old man was on to his favourite pastime, reminiscing about the olden days. But those days were well and truly over, Joachim realised, as he went through the accounts later that afternoon with Alan. The figures were even worse than he'd anticipated. The wheat had been wetter, the milk yield lower.

Alan frowned. "It looks bad."

Joachim contemplated him. He was young, bright, straight from agricultural college. He was enthusiastic about the job, but he had a wife and child to support. Joachim knew that if the figures didn't improve soon, Alan would be looking around for another post. He couldn't take risks with his family.

Joachim attempted to put a brave face on things. "We've pulled through before after a bad harvest. We'll just have to hope the heifers bring in some money."

"But will farmers be able to afford the prices we need?" replied Alan. "It's been a bad year for everyone."

"Grace, darling! Ravishing as usual!" Clive kissed her.

She winced and stepped backwards. She looked past Clive to a small, balding man with glasses and past the small, balding man to . . . darkness.

"Clive, where's Jean?"

"You haven't met professor Weinbaum, have you, Grace? Professor Weinbaum – Grace, my sister-in-law."

The little man jerked his head downwards in a sort of salute. "Call me Carl," he said, with an Eastern European accent.

"Pleased to meet you, professor – Carl. Clive, where's Jean?"

"Carl brought his two children with him. We've dumped them on Jean. It's no use you looking like that, Grace," he added, as Grace raised her eyes heavenwards, "Jean loves children."

"I expect she'd like a break from them now and then like everyone else. You could have got a babysitter, Clive."

"Nonsense. What would be the point? Jean's perfectly happy. She was settling down to watch *Dumbo* with them when we left."

"Well, don't stand there getting cold, you'd better come in," said Grace, a shade reluctantly.

She ushered them into the drawing-room at the front of the house. It was spacious and tastefully decorated with a cream carpet and dark blue wallpaper. Red and navy Liberty curtains hung at the windows. The double doors leading through into the dining-room stood open, revealing a large oval table set for five.

"Jean's had to babysit," she informed Leonard, after introductions had been performed for the second time.

"Oh?" he said, his mind on the drinks. "Oh good." He

turned back to the drinks table and missed the venomous look his wife shot him.

"Well, Leonard. Elder brother. How's tricks?"

Clive sat down in an armchair, gin and tonic in hand, yawned and dangled one leg over the arm of the chair. Make yourself at home, thought Grace, irritably. Do.

Clive was dressed in a lightweight grey Italian suit ("Made to measure?" wondered Grace), with a red silk tie and cutely matching red handkerchief. He still had a tan left over from his summer holiday in the Caribbean. Beside him Leonard, who never cared what he wore, and the professor, who was pale and podgy from too many hours spent hunched over a microscope in the laboratory, looked decidedly shabby. Grace herself was wearing a linen suit she'd picked up in Simpson's sale. Her fine brown hair was cut experimentally in a bob. She was trying to reduce her trips to the hairdressers in preparation for having a job. Anyway perms were out of fashion these days, even for middle-aged women. It was all body waves and finger drying.

"Someone's buying up shares like crazy," said Leonard gloomily, in response to Clive's question. "If it goes on like this I'll be out of a job."

Which is worse, wondered Grace, to be about to lose a job which you don't really need, or never to have had one? She got up to see to the duck casserole. There was too much of it, now that Jean hadn't come. She jabbed at it crossly with a fork, wishing it was Clive.

Grace had few illusions about Clive. He'd been trying to get her into bed ever since marriage to Leonard had brought her within his orbit. Leonard, bless him, never noticed a thing.

By now she could have written an in-depth biography of her brother-in-law, complete with Freudian analysis. The late child of elderly parents (he was seven years younger than Leonard), Clive had been, unlike Leonard, dreadfully spoiled.

He'd had an expensive education at a rather silly public school (Leonard had gone to the local grammar school). Clive had learned nothing at school, so far as Grace could see, apart from the importance of having contacts and of dressing correctly. Turned down by Oxford and Cambridge, he'd gone to Trinity College, Dublin to study law. He worked in the City and always insisted on the best of everything. Beside him Jean, trailing around in her cotton skirts and long cardigans, looked positively dowdy, though before her marriage she'd been considered quite a catch. Clearly life with Clive had got the better of her.

Grace suspected, without proof, that Clive had affairs. She was sure that if he saw a woman he wanted he'd set out to get her, just as he had to have the latest gadget for his car, or the most up-to-date video equipment for his house. But he knew which side his bread was buttered. He'd stay with Jean who was warm and domesticated and knew how to create a comfortable home for him. Sickening. Grace drained the potatoes and stood them on the hot plate.

It all went to prove that children should never be spoiled. Her own two (Emma (17) and Carolyn (15)) had been brought up at home till they were thirteen. They were both away at school now, but at a sensible, co-educational school where all the meals were vegetarian. What were Emma and Carolyn having to eat this evening? She poked about at the salad. She'd sneaked in a few dandelion leaves. She hoped Leonard wouldn't notice, he wasn't keen on health food.

Refreshed by once again having fixed (impaled) Clive in her mind she returned to the drawing-room, retrieved her sherry and sat down on the sofa beside Carl.

"I was explaining to your husband," Carl said, turning to her, "that my wife, who's head of a PR firm, has had to fly to New York unexpectedly this weekend on business. So I had to bring the children with me."

"Head of a PR firm," echoed Grace. She looked

meaningfully at Leonard who shifted his gaze to the ceiling. "Aren't women doing marvellous things these days?"

"I wouldn't feel comfortable with Jean working," said Clive. "Leonard and I were brought up to believe that children need their mothers at home."

A saying of her mother's popped into Grace's mind. "Different spheres, but equal. A woman's work may be in the home, Grace, but never think it's on that account less valuable than a man's." But it was less valuable; society saw to that. It gave mothers a ridiculously short period of maternity leave, no help with childcare and put financial considerations before a father's right to stay at home and bond with his baby. Lately Grace had begun to think that the only way to get society to value the task of childrearing was if mothers were paid to bring up their children. Or if the task was shared equally between men and women. She gazed at Leonard. But then men would have to be trained. Had she been trained? No. One moment she'd been childless, the next moment the baby had been there and she'd been expected to get on with it, expected to know what to do simply because she was a woman. Well, she hadn't known what to do, she'd learnt as she went along. Surely men could do the same? Then they'd see how infinitely more precious and valuable the work of childrearing was compared with whatever went on at the office. And then firms would change their working patterns to accommodate parents of young children. And then society would learn to value its children. And then . . . Grace's imagination took off, as it was wont to do, into a fantasy of a brave new world organised along lines determined by herself. It was several minutes before she could bring herself to pay attention to the conversation.

"It's not as if we need the money," Clive was saying, as if that clinched the argument as far as *his* wife was concerned. "I suppose it's different on a professor's salary."

"Yes, indeed," agreed Carl amiably. "Every little bit helps.

In fact, with us, it's the other way round. Natalie earns twice as much as I do."

"Gosh!" said Grace, envious. "Surely that would tempt you, Clive?"

"We manage well enough," replied Clive vaguely and, from Grace's point of view, unsatisfactorily.

In all the years Grace had known Clive, she'd never quite been able to work out what he did for a living. He'd qualified as a solicitor but that wouldn't account for the large sums of money he seemed to lavish on his sports, his cars, his clothes, his three children and, occasionally, on Jean. How Clive earned his money was one of the best-kept secrets Grace knew of. Even Jean, when pumped for information, didn't seem to know the whole story.

She decided they weren't going to be let in on the secret of Clive's finances tonight. She stood up. "Let's eat, shall we?" She led the way into the dining-room and pointedly removed the setting for Jean.

Leonard glanced approvingly at the table. It was looking particularly nice this evening, he thought, with its gleaming silver cutlery, crystal glasses and linen napkins. In the centre stood a bowl of late roses from the garden. The wine bottle clinked as he took it out of the cooler. He smiled across at his wife. Perhaps straighter hair did suit her, after all, made her look younger.

Grace was also looking at the table and wondering where her afternoon had gone to and whether it had been well spent. Why weren't they eating in the kitchen, using cutlery and glasses that could be put into the dishwasher and paper napkins that didn't have to be washed and ironed afterwards? My damnable upbringing, she thought, not for the first time.

Over the avocado dip, they discussed politics, economics and Thatcher's resignation.

"A crying shame," declared Clive. "Who will they get to

replace her? The men in her Cabinet are a lily-livered lot. That woman's put this country on its feet."

So much for mothers staying at home, thought Grace. Did Denis need the money? I imagine not.

Aloud, she said, "Thatcher's ruined this country. She's sold off all our assets and plunged us into the deepest recession since the thirties. High time she went before she does any more damage."

"It's a complex matter," put in Leonard hastily. "In some areas, Thatcher's policies were obviously a mistake – like selling off National Gas, for instance. But she's done some good for people wanting to start up small businesses."

"Men," said Grace.

"What?"

"Men who want to start up small businesses. Women haven't been helped particularly. There's been no talk of state nursery provision or after-school clubs."

Leonard sighed. "All right then, men."

"Seriously though, Leonard, you must admit that people like you and me have never had it so good as under Thatcher. Tax cuts, incentives, falling interest rates, reduction of trade union power, deregulation . . . " Clive spooned in the avocado.

"Agreed. She did all that. But she's had her day. What we need now is somebody moderate. Someone who'll consolidate her gains but operate a more consensus style of government. I see this as a turning point. Thatcherism may have worked for you, Clive." Leonard took a sip of his wine. "But you know she never listened to us industrialists. Took no notice of what we had to say. And taxes have got so complicated lately that my firm's accountants have to spend all their time looking for legal tax loopholes."

Have to? wondered Grace. There were times, usually when Clive was present, when she almost disliked Leonard.

"What I can't understand," she said, "is how she's got

away with giving a hundred pounds a week rise to top people like judges and generals and chairmen of privatised industries whilst ordinary working people are called greedy if they ask for a one per cent pay rise."

Is it disloyal to attack another woman, she wondered. After all, Thatcher was a role model. Or was she? Wasn't she simply upholding a system which had been bad for so many women for so long? It was all very confusing. Grace felt a headache coming on.

"We have to pay our top men," Clive said, in reply to Grace's question, "otherwise they'd be off to the States."

"Then they've no loyalty." Grace began noisily gathering up the plates. "If our leaders are greedy what can be expected of the rest of us?"

"Am I correct in thinking, Leonard, that your wife is turning into a bit of a Red?" Clive enquired, giving one of his most charming smiles.

"I'm tired of the Tories." Grace banged down a spoon. "They've been in power too long. They're getting corrupt. A change at the next election would do this country no harm at all."

Clive laughed. "Who do you have in mind, Grace? Labour with that Welsh windbag in charge is unelectable and you can hardly be thinking of the Social Democrats, can you?"

Grace fumed off to the kitchen.

Over the duck casserole, recalled to her duties as hostess by a glance from Leonard, Grace made an effort and asked Carl about his work. He was engaged in medical research at Cambridge.

"We're hoping for a breakthrough pretty soon. We're developing a new drug. A pain-killer for people suffering from rheumatoid-arthritis. Your brother-in-law has been most helpful in getting us financial backing for our research."

"Has he?" Grace smiled winningly at Clive.

He smiled back, volunteering none of the information Grace had been hoping for. He *was* irritating.

"We're trying out the drug at the moment on student volunteers," Carl went on. "They get free meals for a week and pocket money so we're never short of volunteers. There're a few side-effects still (weight gain, hair loss, diminished vision) but we're working to eradicate those."

"They must be pretty short of money to volunteer for that sort of thing," Leonard remarked. "At their age one of my big worries was that I'd go bald before I was twenty-one like Dad."

Carl looked puzzled. "We don't tell the students about the side-effects. As I say we've almost eradicated them and anyway we'd never get any volunteers if we did."

"No," murmured Leonard. "No, I suppose not."

"But surely you *ought* to tell them," put in Grace.

"My dear." Clive reached across the table and patted her hand. "You're being at your most delightful tonight."

"I suppose, strictly speaking, we should inform them of the possible dangers," said Carl slowly. "But the risk is really very slight. One in a thousand at most. And think of the countless numbers of sufferers who'll be helped if the drug's put on the market. Surely it's worth a risk or two for the sake of progress?"

"Progress!" exclaimed Grace. "We hear too much nowadays about progress. There's no such thing as society, we're told. Only individuals devoted to self-betterment, which they must be allowed to do completely untrammelled so that we can have progress. We go on pouring money into developing new technology, giving us luxuries we don't need, whilst we cut back on our children's education, on the national health service and the welfare state which deal in the necessities of life . . . "

"The welfare state *is* a luxury," muttered Clive. "I'm with the Tories on that one."

"Technology has run riot." Grace ploughed on recklessly, ignoring Leonard's warning glance. "Science has advanced too quickly for our consciences. I read an article in the *Guardian* recently," (Leonard groaned) "arguing that our inventions should be kept in cold storage for several decades until our moral capacities have caught up with our intellects . . . " She petered out feeling rather foolish.

"Well, well, well," murmured Clive. "Standing for Dulwich East, are we?"

"I'm sure Grace didn't mean to imply . . . " began Leonard, looking embarrassed.

"As a matter of fact," Carl brushed his apology aside, "in some areas, nuclear weapons for instance, I happen to agree with your wife. Allow research, yes, you can't stop the human race experimenting, but its practical application must be strictly controlled. In my own field of medical research, though, it's vital to apply the new inventions we come up with."

"Yes," agreed Grace reluctantly. "Yes, I suppose it is." She put her head in her hands. She needed practice in this. She needed training. For, somewhere along the line, she'd lost the thread of her argument.

"Heaven knows why I spend all afternoon in the kitchen cooking for your guests just to be insulted by them!" she growled crossly, after Clive and Carl had eaten their strawberry pavlova and drunk their brandies and departed.

"You weren't insulted," said Leonard reasonably. "You embarked emotionally on an argument you hadn't a hope in hell of winning. The professor's probably had the same argument put to him hundreds of times. He must have become adept by now at outmanoeuvring Greens, homeopathists, anti-vivisectionists, all sorts of cranks."

"I'm *not* a crank." Grace scraped dandelion leaves from Leonard's plate into the bin. "That professor Carl is a speciality idiot. The kind of person who becomes so immersed in his subject he loses touch with ordinary human beings. Think of his poor students being exploited like that!"

"All right, all right! I agree with you!" Leonard threw up his hands.

Grace ran fresh water to wash the pans. "Look at the Victorians, look at the social and political reforms they bequeathed us. And what have we to hand on to the twenty-first century? Technology and computers. New machinery but no new wisdom." She banged pans around in the sink. "Sometimes I wish computers would just go away."

Leonard picked up a dish towel. "If you're going to praise the Victorians, there Clive would agree with you. He thoroughly approves of them, self-help and all that."

"Oh well, *Clive.*"

Finishing with the pans, Grace dried her hands. She put out the milk bottles and they went upstairs.

"I sometimes think, Grace, you don't treat my brother with the respect he deserves," said Leonard, in an ironic tone of voice.

"I would treat him well if he treated Jean better. Fancy not bringing her here tonight! . . . Leonard," she added, when they were in bed, "where does Clive get his money from?"

"Contacts in the City. Lucky devil," murmured Leonard, half-asleep. "By the way, remind me to cancel our subscription to the *Guardian.* I don't see why I should pay for it to give me indigestion."

"No chance, darling." Grace leaned over and switched off the light. "If you do that, I'll take it out of my housekeeping money instead."

Leonard groaned.

Cornelius's dinner was turning out to be everything he'd hoped. He was enjoying himself tremendously. There'd already been barbed comments exchanged between the Reverend Sam Cleary (High Church) and the Bishop of Meath (Low Church) over drinks in the study.

"Well, Sam." Bishop Masterson took a swig of sherry. "No moving statues yet in this part of the world?"

"Not yet, my Lord. If a statue moved in my church I'd throw a cassock over it and lock it in a cupboard."

"Really, Sam? I'd have thought a bit of statue worship would be right up your street."

"Come, come, my Lord."

"The Bishop's in fine form tonight, isn't he?" whispered Cornelius gleefully, as he refilled Sam's glass.

"Much as usual I thought," muttered Sam.

The two Jews, Simon and Ben, sat on the windowseat looking glum and left out.

"Sam," Joachim attempted to act as peacemaker, "have you noticed the honey leaking onto the altar in your church? Symbolic, isn't it, in a way?"

Sam grunted. "I could do without the symbolism. Soon it'll be rain and snow on the altar and the church will have to be deconsecrated and shut up through lack of funds."

He frowned in the direction of the Bishop who, not being so hard of hearing as he sometimes pretended, turned and said, "Sam, you bring your services down a few notches to make at least a pretence of conforming to the Canons of the Church of Ireland and I'll consider allocating some money for that roof of yours."

"Dinner's ready," announced Elizabeth, appearing in the doorway with a pair of oven gloves over her arm.

She led the way into the dining-room. Cornelius had been responsible for the decor here and the walls were covered in rich red damask.

"What an erotic colour!" exclaimed Ben. The Bishop glanced at him repressively.

At one end of the room stood two tall Corinthian columns. The heavy walnut dining table had feet carved in the shape of devils' heads. The sideboard was elaborately inlaid with stars of David, a seven-branched candelabra, a rose, a crescent and several fishes. On top of it, next to the cheese, sat a smiling Buddha.

"The perfect setting," murmured Cornelius.

Disorientated by the decor, his guests fell into some confusion over grace. The Bishop clearly expected to be asked to say it, but Sam had forgotten whether Jews said grace or not and Cornelius, playing out his role of sceptic, didn't feel moved to ask him either. In the end Ben and Cornelius sat down straightaway and began digging into their salmon mousse whilst the others mumbled a variety of things to themselves and crossed themselves or not, as the case may be.

"Money troubles everywhere," began Cornelius cheerily, through a mouthful of mousse. "You with your roof, Sam. Joachim and his wet wheat. Did it turn out to be as wet as you expected?"

"Wetter," replied Joachim dismally.

"In the sixteenth century, you'd have been able to accuse your local witch of putting a curse on it, dragged her before the magistrates and had her burned. That would make you feel better, wouldn't it?"

"Not particularly," muttered Joachim. He shifted his chair away from the table and tucked his legs to one side. Either Ben or Simon was trying to play footsie with him.

While Elizabeth cleared away the plates and brought in the lamb Cornelius, feeling the Christians had had a good innings, decided to shift the conversation round to Judaism.

"We were going to have pork," he explained, starting to carve, "but we changed it at the last minute."

"Cornelius!" hissed Elizabeth.

"You needn't have bothered for us, my dear," said Ben, flashing his rings and his teeth at the same time, "we're not strictly Orthodox."

"Oh." Cornelius's face fell.

"Though we do try to keep Passover, Shavuoth, Sukkoth

and Purim," put in Simon, the younger one. "There's something beautiful about the idea of a life hedged round by obedience to God, don't you agree? The Law has kept Jews together for centuries."

"Can't think how you Christians manage," added Ben.

Cornelius brightened, perceptibly.

"We do have the Ten Commandments," said Sam, a little stiffly. "Christ said . . . "

"Let's not talk about him or we'll never get anywhere," Simon interrupted. "An impostor, a charlatan, an inferior magician performing second-rate miracles easily surpassed by his contemporaries. Simon Magus could fly, you know."

Behind his thick glasses, Cornelius's eyes gleamed. "Pity about the Muslim," he murmured.

"Doesn't it say somewhere that Christ was transported up to the top of a mountain?" began Sam vaguely.

"By the devil," Bishop Masterson put in firmly. "That hardly helps our argument."

Under the table, Diogenes yawned and scratched himself noisily.

"It's arguable Christ never intended to break with Judaism," said Joachim, in an attempt at reconciliation. "You know what he said: 'Think not that I have come to abolish the law and the prophets; I have not come to abolish them but to fulfil them.' It was Paul who took Christianity out of its Jewish context."

He felt justified in getting in a dig at Saint Paul. He was due to read the epistle in church the next day – some rubbish from *Romans*. He often thought that if he could have his way, Paul would be out of the bible altogether.

"And so preserved the uniqueness of the Christian religion." The Bishop pursed his lips. "We owe everything to Paul."

Joachim decided not to give Cornelius the pleasure of watching another bout of theological squabbling.

"Coward!" whispered Cornelius.

"If I may say so, monotheism seems much the most sensible doctrine." Ben waved a fork at the Bishop. "The Trinity is so complicated, m'dear, and so unnecessary. Why have three gods when you can have one?"

"It doesn't mean three Gods," replied the Bishop, through gritted teeth, "but three Gods in One."

"I see." Ben looked vague.

"More sauce anyone?" asked Elizabeth brightly. She was not unaware of the high degree of tension Cornelius was stirring up around the table. Her dinner parties often turned out like this. It was one of the hazards of being Cornelius's wife.

"Good heavens!" Sam exclaimed suddenly, pointing at his plate. He'd eaten enough of his lamb and brussels sprouts to reveal part of the design on the plate beneath. He'd uncovered one plump, pink buttock and a well rounded breast with a particularly rosy nipple.

"Like it?" Cornelius grinned. "There's two of them. You've got the other one," he informed Ben. "I found them in a second-hand shop in London. Pornographic pottery."

"The expression playing with one's food suddenly takes on a whole new meaning," murmured Ben, starting to eat with alacrity. "My dear, just look at that splendid organ. Totally out of proportion to the rest of . . . "

"Must be very uncomfortable, for all sorts of reasons, to be built like that," replied Simon with a grimace, looking over his shoulder. "Be thankful for small mercies, that's what I say."

"Don't be bitchy, dear."

The Bishop of Meath looked as if he wished he was several hundred miles away. Sam coughed discreetly.

"Sorry, Sam," said Ben. "Conversation getting too blue?"

"Just a little." Sam fingered his collar and shot an anxious glance at the Bishop.

"Talking of blue," said Elizabeth hastily, "would anyone like cheese?"

"Honestly, Cornelius," Joachim whispered as they retired to his study for brandy and cigars, "do you intend everyone to go home offended?"

Cornelius raised one finger and whispered, "You underestimate me, my friend. The climax of the evening is yet to come. I think you'll approve of this."

"I doubt it."

Cornelius poured out brandies for the Bishop, Sam, Joachim, Simon and himself, but not for Ben who suffered "dreadfully from hangovers m'dear." Not for Elizabeth either – she was in the kitchen doing the washing up.

"I heard you were in Greece recently, Bishop." Cornelius settled himself comfortably in an armchair. "A retreat, was it?"

"Yes, indeed, Cornelius. A retreat in a monastery at the top of Mount Athos. The monks were most kind."

"I've heard they're very hospitable." Cornelius took off his spectacles and polished them excitedly. Joachim glanced at him suspiciously.

"Yes, they even gave me a parting gift, a tiny statue of Saint Andrew. Very appropriate." The Bishop nodded towards Simon and Ben. "You see, besides being a saint in the Orthodox church, Saint Andrew is the patron saint of Scotland and I'm Scottish on my mother's side. As a matter of fact I think I have the statue on me."

He rummaged in his voluminous pockets and proudly produced the little statue. He passed it to Ben who took it fastidiously between his thumb and first finger and handed it on quickly to Cornelius.

"You know," said the latter, "I've seen one of these before. It's probably unscrewable. Oh yes." He nodded as the Bishop looked surprised. "I think you'll find that its head unscrews."

"Well, well." The Bishop put down his glass and got up

to look. He took the statue from Cornelius and began twisting the head. After three turns, it fell off. The Bishop bent to pick it up. "Good Lord!" he exclaimed. "There's something inside." He held up a small piece of wood. "What is it, do you think?"

"It's a relic," said Cornelius, with a straight face. "They always put one in, I've been told."

Sam grinned into his brandy glass.

Cornelius took the piece of wood from the Bishop and examined it. "Looks like a fragment of the Sacred Cross to me."

The Bishop turned pale.

"You Christians are always so ghoulish!" murmured Ben.

"You've been carrying around a holy relic, my Lord," said Sam, still grinning. "I'm surprised at you. My dioc . . . parish will be pleased and touched by this. So you've come over to our side at last, have you?"

The Bishop groaned. "How much do I have to give you to hush this thing up, Sam?"

Sam laughed. "A small donation for repairs to the roof would come in handy. A few bring and buy sales opened by your Lordship might do the trick."

The Bishop shuddered. "Where's your Christian forgiveness, Sam?"

"It's not at all certain that Christians have the monopoly on forgiveness they like to claim for themselves," put in Simon sternly, making everyone jump. "I think you'd find that the God of the Jews is quite forgiving too."

"Yes, yes, of course, I didn't mean to imply . . . " began the Bishop, by now thoroughly demoralised. "It was just a figure of speech. Well, not exactly a figure of speech, for of course Christians are supposed to forgive, but . . . "

"Figures of speech." Simon scowled. "Jewish avarice, Jewish pride, Jewish pigs – the war taught us where they lead."

"Now, now dear. Don't go upsetting yourself." Ben patted his hand.

"My God!" whispered Cornelius. "Things are getting out of control. Do something, Joachim!"

"I visited a concentration camp once," said Joachim. "It was silent as death. Not a blade of grass anywhere, not a bird in the sky. It was the emptiest place in the world."

"You're German?" said Simon, with a flash of recognition.

Joachim slowly nodded, reluctant, as always, to be identified with his country of birth.

"My grandfather was a rabbi," Simon began. Joachim's heart sank. He could guess what was coming next. "He swapped his bread for two lumps of sugar every mealtime during Passover. He spent five Passovers in Auschwitz. Then he was gassed."

Joachim bowed his head.

"My uncle who was let out at the end of the war weighing seven stones has a habit of eating up all the leftovers, right down to the breadcrumbs on the tablecloth. His nerves are shot to pieces. He flies into rages over nothing. Yet they say, before the war, he was a cheerful, placid sort of man."

Joachim waited in silence for the blow to fall. This was what he hated about being German.

"There's an eternal bond now between Jew and German," continued Simon. Joachim looked up in surprise. "Oh yes, the French can go on being as anti-Semitic as they ever were – and the English reverted to it pretty quickly too, after the first shock of the concentration camps had passed. But the Germans have a blood tie with the Jews that can never be washed away. And they turned the sword upon themselves," he added quietly.

Joachim nodded. He remembered the photograph he'd seen in Dachau of a prisoner, a German, who'd hung himself. A life-size photograph suspended from the ceiling.

There'd been no anguish on his face, no expression of any kind. Treated like an object, he'd become one. His face hadn't registered even despair, he'd been beyond it. Yes, to know that Germans had suffered too took away some of the guilt, but only for those of his countrymen who'd been on the right side.

There was silence in the room. The fire crackled. Someone coughed. Cornelius shuffled his feet. Elizabeth came in.

"We can't blame the Germans entirely," Cornelius said at last. "Such camps exist in other parts of the world. The English did something similar in Kenya, I believe," he muttered.

"You must excuse my husband," said Elizabeth, not quite knowing what had happened, but sure something had. "He was born with a lung disease and spent the first six months of his life in an incubator. He tends to be a little detached from people."

Soon after this, Cornelius's party broke up.

CHAPTER THREE

"OUT OF A TOTAL OF NINETY FAMILIES LIVING IN A TOWER BLOCK IN Middlesbrough, only five men are in employment," Lallie read out to Jade at breakfast.

Jade grunted.

"Many unemployed people are taking unpaid work – running theatres, organising five-a-side football matches, cutting pensioners' hedges," Grace read out to Leonard from the same paper.

"Good idea, dear. The hedge could do with a cut," replied her husband, not lifting his eyes from the business section.

"It's terrible what's happening in the north. Thank God I got out in time." Lallie turned to the arts pages. "They're putting on a new production of *The Cherry Orchard* at the National. I'll get tickets."

"My mother acted in that once. Chekhov was right up her street. She was fond of tragic parts."

Whilst my mother really was tragic, thought Lallie. She folded up the paper. "I'm going out for a run."

"You're supposed to run before breakfast, not after," Jade remarked.

"It's better than not running at all," replied Lallie, with a smile.

"I run around enough at work sorting out people's problems. Unlike you, I'm not privileged enough to sit on my bum in libraries all day."

No and would you want to? thought Lallie.

"By the way," Jade looked up from her paper, "are we having lunch?"

"I think a cheese sandwich and a pint down the pub will do, don't you?"

"Good." Jade yawned, pulled her silk kimono more tightly around herself and turned back to the paper. "I wonder if anyone ever bothers with Sunday lunch nowadays?"

"I'll have your dinner ready when you come back from church," Molly called across the yard as Joachim was leaving.

The service wasn't a success. The Bishop arrived late and had difficulty getting the chasuble over his head. The choir, that is, the Ryan brothers, who usually could be relied upon, arrived even later than the Bishop with the excuse that they'd been feeding nuts to their bullocks. Joachim read mutinously from *Romans*. Miss Connolly on the organ began playing the Gloria too soon.

"It's the Kyries, you silly old bitch," muttered Sam, giving her stool a kick. His normally genial face looked flustered. "I've suddenly lost interest in the whole thing," he whispered to Joachim who was serving at the altar.

"Now, now, Father," Joachim whispered back. "I expect Christ found the Resurrection wasn't all plain sailing either."

The Bishop, having another church to go to, left quickly after the service. Joachim and Sam had already started to disrobe when Jimmy Ryan came rushing over to them.

"Father, Father, there's a plateful of wafers on the table beside the altar."

Sam went to look.

"Oh dear." He scratched his head. "Do you think they're consecrated?"

Jimmy looked doubtful. "I don't know, Father. What would they be doing here if they weren't?"

"We'd better consume them, in case. Here, you have half," Sam said to the unfortunate Jimmy.

They stood in a corner of the church, surreptitiously munching wafers.

"The Bishop must have expected a bigger turn out," said Sam dismally.

On his way home he met Cornelius loitering at the gate, a bundle of newspapers under his arm and Diogenes on the lead. Cornelius often hung around church on a Sunday to check up that things were carrying on as usual. "It's to my advantage that the churches remain as backward as possible," he'd explained once to Joachim. "It reinforces the position of us sceptics. Let's hope you never decide to have women bishops."

"Congregation falling off, Sam?" he said cheerily as Diogenes, no respecter of persons or places, cocked his leg against the gatepost. "I counted ten less than usual."

"There's a bad bout of flu going round," lied Sam. God forgive me, he added to himself. "I wouldn't stand there if I were you. You might catch something."

"What you need, vicar," said Cornelius, hurrying after him, "is a good exorcism. They were great tourist attractions in the sixteenth century."

"We in the Church of Ireland," replied Sam stiffly, "have never been much in favour of exorcism. We have generally left an interest in the diabolic phenomena to the Romans."

"No, seriously, all you need is a stage, a priest hidden beneath it, a young girl prone to having epileptic fits and you'd be made. You might even entice some worshippers away from the Romans. That would be a coup, wouldn't it? Exorcisms were very effective religious propaganda in the sixteenth century."

"Stop teasing Sam, Cornelius," whispered Joachim, joining them at that moment.

"The trouble with the Church," Cornelius stared after

Sam's retreating back, "is that it's run by people who have no imagination."

Joachim went for a ramble through his estate to walk off the effects of Molly's lunch. He walked up the front avenue. It was overgrown with weeds and pitted with potholes. On either side were fields of winter wheat. On his right the fields stretched towards Bannon; on his left ahead was the hill, the highest part of the estate, indeed the highest point for miles around in this flat Irish midlands. He kept it in sight as he walked. There were always a thousand colours on that hill – browns and purples, orange, burnt ochre, amber – his vocabulary didn't extend far enough to describe all the different shades.

He veered round the foot of the hill and through the wood where he disturbed a herd of deer. Beside the path the damp bracken shone like polished copper. A pheasant rose suddenly in front of him with a whirring of wings. He noted with approval that the trees he'd marked for thinning on his previous visit had been felled. He crushed some pine needles in his hand and sniffed them. The almost unbearable poignancy of their scent seemed to contain within it the sum of all his wishes for the estate. To hand it on to his sons and his sons' sons down the ages. To create something that would last. He walked on, his brisk pace serving to keep away troublesome thoughts.

He passed two stone crosses marking the graves of former owners. One was a suicide who'd been denied burial in consecrated land, the other his brother who'd asked to be buried alongside him out of loyalty. It had been Joachim's wish to be buried somewhere on this estate. Now? He hurried on, not wanting to face these thoughts.

He cleared the woods and saw the lake below him, glinting in the pale winter sun. He looked around. In the distance was Bannon wrapped in a silver mist. The twin towers of the Catholic church rose majestically through the mist and beside them, the single, shorter steeple of the Protestant church. He made out the hospital, the convent, the asylum. But it was the lake that drew him. He searched for one of the overgrown paths that led down to it and began fighting his way through the brambles and bracken.

He sat down on a rock by the shores of the lake. His wellingtons, splashing in the water, made the little fishes scurry away. Across the other side two swans sailed sedately. He gazed down into the clear water and thought of the estate. Only a miracle could save it now. He believed in miracles, he'd seen them happen quite often. Mrs Dart's bunions, for example, didn't get healed by themselves. He'd prayed and his prayer had been answered.

But was it right to pray for a miracle in this case? If he sold the estate the next owner might be just as attached to the land, would have money to make all the necessary improvements, a family to pass it on to. Had he the right to keep it ticking over from year to year like this? Didn't the farm deserve a better owner, one who lived here all the time? It was undoubtedly selfish to pray. Nevertheless, he prayed.

"Good heavens!" exclaimed Lallie, sitting up on her knees. She and Jade had been over to the pub on the corner for a pint and a sandwich and had returned to finish the Sunday papers before going on to a concert at the Festival Hall. As was her habit, Lallie had spread the paper out on the living-room carpet and had been sprawled on her stomach reading.

"Mm?" muttered Jade, from behind the review section.

"A girl I was at school with. Ruth Martin. She's interviewed here in that article about unemployment in the north. She's got five children. Five! Can you imagine! And her husband's been made redundant. Christ!"

Jade grunted. "I see Neil Jordan's got another film coming

out. Hollywood backing too. Don't know how he does it. Sod!" She continued with the reviews.

Lallie looked around their living-room. It was decorated in pink and grey. Pale grey carpet, grey walls, pink curtains and low, square dusty pink armchairs. A couple of black and white photographs by Karsh hung on the walls. Over the bamboo coffee table hung an oil painting of an empty whitewashed room lit through blinds by bright Mediterranean sunlight. It was a jewel of a flat, on the edge of Kensington, before it runs off into Notting Hill Gate.

She stood up and went across to the window. Opposite was a yellow brick building – a Unitarian church where she and Jade had ventured one Sunday and a man in a brown suit had read from Camus and talked in a large-minded way about the predicament of modern man. Presumably he'd done so again that morning but they'd never been back. Next to the church was a restaurant run by a Vietnamese and a bookshop. Philosophy, books and food. It was conveniently situated. If anyone had told her when she was younger that she'd find herself living in a place like this, she'd have laughed at them. It was a far cry from the shabby northern semi-detached in which she'd been brought up. And yet she'd done it. She'd persevered and come south where the books, the music, the art, lay waiting for her.

She went over to the mirror and surveyed herself. She was thirty-three. In certain African countries and parts of Glasgow, she'd be an old woman by now. She was lucky. She'd had a long youth. No husband or child to worry about, just the gradual accumulation of knowledge. She thought of Ruth Martin with a husband and five children to feed, on how much did it say? Seventy pounds, was it? She, Jade and a film executive had recently spent that amount and more on dinner in Covent Garden. She shivered.

"I've been lucky," she murmured.

"Lucky? Rubbish!" Jade put down her paper. "You're

talented and you've worked hard. You've earned your success."

She came over to Lallie, put her hands on her shoulders and stroked the back of her neck beneath the close cropped black hair.

"Have I?" said Lallie. "Earned it, I mean?"

Jade frowned.

"Now, snuggler, don't you come over with that northern Protestant work ethic of yours. You work harder than anyone I know."

She kissed Lallie's shoulder and flopped sideways into an armchair, her legs dangling over the arm. "And to stop you feeling guilty I've work for you to do. We'll need to read through all the press cuttings about my mother. I've a couple of scrapbooks but she was too scatty to keep them in any systematic way. That means a trip to Colindale for you. And then there's Stefan. We'll need the lowdown on him. I've an idea there was a book published a while back, but whether it's a study of his poetry or a biography, I don't know."

Lallie turned away from the mirror. "You're including Stefan? Is he still alive?"

"Living in South America, I believe."

Lallie chewed a fingernail. "I'm worried about libel."

"He must be over seventy by now. He won't bother us, even if he does hear of the film, which is highly unlikely."

"From what you've told me about him, he sounds exactly the sort of guy to try and screw a few thousand pounds out of you."

"Depends what we dig up on him. If his career's in the doldrums, as I expect it is, he might be flattered at getting some free publicity. At any rate, he's crucial," said Jade firmly. "I see the film as a sort of portrait of an actress. I want to show those early years when she lived alone with her father in that huge barn of a place outside Bannon. I don't know whether it's still standing," she added, in response to a glance from Lallie, "or if we'd be allowed to film there. It would be nice if we could. Her father was a bit of a bully, from what I could gather. She had a succession of governesses who came and went rather quickly. There was something sinister about my grandfather which frightened them away. She lived in a kind of time-warp, with a nanny she'd long outgrown, till she got married at the age of eighteen, a marriage arranged for her by her father, or so she always said. The marriage lasted a year and then she met Stefan. It was after that relationship broke up that she started on her career as an actress. Stefan must have been pivotal in some way. I want you to find out as much as you can about him."

Lallie sat down in the armchair opposite. "And how far will you take the film?"

"Until the point where she began to establish herself as an actress. We'll include the birth of Diana, I think."

"Oh. And yours?"

"That would be difficult to portray, wouldn't it?" replied Jade dryly. "Since we don't know, perhaps my mother even didn't know, which one of her myriad admirers was my father." She gave a short laugh. "Odd, isn't it? Somewhere out there is my father and I wouldn't recognise him if we passed on the street. I don't know whether he's a hero or a roadsweeper."

"Or both."

"Or both . . . Anyway, be a darling and do some research for me. There must be plenty of old cuttings about my mother in the early days."

And perhaps somewhere amongst them is the name of your father, thought Lallie. Was that what Jade was really asking her to look for?

CHAPTER FOUR

GRACE REHEARSED THE SENTENCE TO HERSELF. "LEONARD, I'M GOING to see about a job today." No, too blunt. "Leonard, I saw this advertisement in the paper. They want volunteers." Or why not be honest? "Leonard, I'm thinking of doing some social work."

"Leonard," she bent down to unload the dishwasher, "I'm going to the hairdresser's this morning."

"Good idea, love. I'll stroll down and meet you for coffee afterwards."

She groaned silently. She'd forgotten it was his day off. "No, it's all right. I don't know what time I'll be finished and I may want to do some shopping and . . . and so on."

He looked at her suspiciously. Why did women suddenly change? What made them become secretive, indifferent about the housework, experimental in their appearance? An icy feeling ran down his spine. Grace was having an affair! That was it! After all these years! Oh God, what should he do? He looked at her in dismay.

What advice did people hand out in these circumstances? He'd once listened to a phone-in programme on the car radio about people's reactions to discovering that their spouse (or was partner the word they'd used?) had been unfaithful. He couldn't remember now what they'd said, indeed hadn't paid much attention, thinking it could never apply to him. One thing was for sure, he shouldn't just blurt out his suspicions. No, he'd proceed by silence and stealth.

"I'll do a spot of gardening then," he said dismally. "Will you be back for lunch?"

"Probably."

Probably! He fiddled sadly with a ball of twine.

"Remember to put on the alarm if you go out," called Grace from half-way up their curving staircase. She went into their bedroom and stood in front of the mirror. No, too smart. She threw off her jacket and put on a jumper she used for doing the housework in. Better.

She's even got changed for him, thought Leonard, watching her leave. He jabbed viciously at the hard earth with his spade.

Armed with notebook and pen Lallie set out for the British Museum. Taking the Central line from Notting Hill Gate to Tottenham Court Road she arrived just after nine and waved her reader's ticket to get her past the little knot of tourists hanging around outside the gates.

She sprinted up the steps and into the Museum. The uniformed security guard squinted at her ticket and let her pass into the warm, womb-like atmosphere of the library with its huge glass dome and blue and gold paint. She chose her favourite seat (F9), pushed aside the blotting pad and switched on the reading light. She rested her head on her hands, trying to cut out her neighbour's sniffs, the early morning clearing of throats, the murmur of voices behind her, the thud of catalogues being opened up, the squeak of the book trolley doing its rounds. Whoever said libraries were quiet places, she thought crossly.

Where should she begin? Perhaps with Stefan. The Russian Jew and minor poet who, Jade believed, had changed her mother's life in some crucial way. She went to look up his name in the catalogue and then in the microfiche. There was a short biography of him published ten years ago at a time when his fame (if poets can properly be said to have fame) peaked. It was something, at any rate. The start of a research project was always frightening, like facing a blank page or an unpainted room. She filled out a docket for the biography and went off to an Italian coffee shop nearby to drink a cappuccino and read the newspaper. She glanced at her watch. It was nine thirty.

At nine thirty German time Joachim stepped off the plane in Munich and felt his stomach contract. It was always so in Germany. He felt his senses close up, his strength ebb, his very body shrink in on itself. He became like all the rest, a machine for making money.

The address was in a road Grace had never seen before, though it was only ten minutes' walk from her house. A row of tiny terraced houses which used to be council and had now been sold off. Each had its own separate front gate and pocket-handkerchief-sized front lawn. The meeting was in the fourth house along. As she drew near Grace saw a young girl in a leather jacket and leggings knock on the door and be admitted. A very young girl. Perhaps this wasn't going to be her sort of thing then. Grace began to wish she'd talked it over with Leonard. But she'd been afraid he'd disapprove and she'd let herself be talked out of it – for she only half-approved herself.

The door opened and a bright-eyed young woman of around thirty said,

"Hello, I'm Sally. Come in."

Grace shook hands and stepped inside the tiny hall.

"In here."

Sally gestured to a door by Grace's left elbow and Grace found herself in a living-room, which obviously served as an eating room too. About twenty people were packed into it. On the sofa, perched on the arms of chairs, on the floor. A youth in denims stood up to give Grace his seat.

"No, it's all right," she replied, a little flustered. "I can sit on the floor. I'm quite used to it," she lied. She squeezed down beside a plump, curly-haired woman with a baby asleep on her lap.

"I don't know how long this'll last," whispered the woman, pointing to her sleeping child, "but I thought I'd give it a try. I'd got my childcare all sorted out and then I was made redundant. Just like that. I've been chewing the carpets at home. It's great to see some grown-up people for a change."

Grace took a peep at the sleeping infant. "She's a lovely baby. She must keep you busy."

'Too right she does. But I need to get out of the house once in a while, do something different. Not always changing nappies and warming bottles."

"Quite right."

Grace had always admired mothers who were able to do several things at once. She herself had only ever been able to concentrate on one job at a time. A mistake. It had limited her possibilities. "Motherhood's a full-time job," all the experts had said. Was it though? Or wasn't it better for children to have mothers who felt busy and fulfilled and led independent lives? It wasn't as though these new career mums were disgorging thousands of vagrants and serial killers onto the streets, was it? Now, according to the newspapers, researchers were even saying that young children did better with several different caretakers. She felt obscurely conned.

She glanced round the room. It was tastefully, if cheaply, decorated with canvas chairs, beanbags and paper lampshades. Just the kind of thing her daughters would like. One entire wall was lined with books and there were books and papers heaped up on the table beside the typewriter. It was quite a different sort of house inside from its council house exterior. She'd never have guessed they could be made so nice.

"We may as well begin." Sally moved some books to one side and perched on the edge of the table, swinging her legs. "I said ten o'clock and it's now ten fifteen. I expect some of you will have to dash off at twelve to collect children from school."

There were several nods around the room. Grace realised uncomfortably that she must be one of the oldest people present.

"I know some of you, but not all," continued Sally. "So I'll introduce myself. I'm Dr Roberts and I put the notice in the newspaper. Please call me Sally. The 'Doctor', incidentally, in case you're thinking it may come in useful, is related to Social Studies (I lecture at the Poly). So if you have a headache, don't come to me. I can only give you statistics on unemployment."

There was a ripple of laughter around the room. Grace scolded herself for having expected "Dr Roberts" to be a middle-aged man.

"I'll come to the point. There's a project to start up a hostel for the homeless in this area and they're looking for volunteers. Now my work and my daughter don't leave me much spare time, as you can imagine, but when I heard about it, it occurred to me there might be others in the same position as myself, with some experience of social work and some regular spare hours. It doesn't matter how few, just so long as it's on a regular basis so that we can get up a rota."

Experience! Grace gazed down at her lap. The fatal word for a woman like me.

Joachim strode through the cool, grey courtyards of the Residenz on his way to meet a client. If he walked fast enough he might escape the evils that lurked in every corner of this scarred city.

Lallie read that Stefan Chertkov, born in Latvia in 1915, had been a popular poet in his youth, drawing large crowds to his poetry readings. Temporarily banished to a labour camp under Stalin, he'd managed to get out of Russia in 1950 and escape with his mother to Israel where his poetry had a following amongst Russian emigres. His father, a journalist, had stayed behind in Russia and died a few years later.

Realising, after some months in Israel, that he needed a wider audience for his poetry and tiring of his mother's fervent Zionism, Stefan moved to England. He was drawn to that country through his reading of Shakespeare and Dickens and schoolboy tales about the English "gentleman" and his notions of fair play and tolerance. Indeed Stefan's English, when he'd first arrived in London, had had a distinctly Shakespearian flavour. He'd rapidly become disillusioned, however, with the English gentleman's crassness and indifference to poetry and from London he'd moved to Dublin where he found the atmosphere more congenial for a writer.

He'd had a relationship for three years, the book said, with Rachel McKenna who went on to become a well-known Irish actress and who bore him one child, Diana, now a promising poet.

Soon after the birth of his daughter, Stefan left Dublin and went to South America. He'd wandered through Mexico and Argentina, finally settling in Chile where he married a wealthy Jewess who bore him three daughters. There the preface ended and the book went on to discuss Stefan's poetry: political in Russia, religious in Israel, wordy in Dublin, sensual in South America. 1963 was the date of his last collection of poems though, according to the bibliography at the end of the book, since then he'd published several translations of South American poets and edited an anthology for English readers. He occasionally leaves Chile to go on lecture tours of the States, the book concluded. Surely not any longer, thought Lallie, but then

Russians go on being active for so long. She peered at the small, blurred photograph on the inside of the dust wrapper. He was a short, squat man, with broad shoulders. Tough-looking. Probably had bad teeth, like all Russians.

She skimmed through the few collections of his poems in the library but they revealed nothing about his relationship with Rachel. Only one poem was directly addressed to her and it was wrapped in such a veil of symbolism that the real woman was lost, had turned into a mythical figure stepping through cornfields in a long petticoat in a way in which a real woman would be very unlikely to, Lallie thought.

At twenty to five the bell rang. She closed the book with a bang. Tomorrow she'd go to Colindale and begin her inspection of back copies of Irish newspapers.

"Experience?" stammered Grace. She hastily discarded her long years of nursing aged parents, her cordon bleu course, her flower arranging, her French evening classes, as being of no relevance. "I can type a little." She'd sometimes typed a letter for Leonard when his secretary was off sick. "But I've never done this sort of work before."

Sally beamed at her. "Don't worry, there're training courses for people like you. I'll give you some bumpf. You can look through it at home and decide when you want to enrol."

It was going to be more difficult than she'd expected. Perhaps, after all, she was only fit to stay at home and do the cooking.

Cornelius Fry, pausing in his perusal of an account of a witchtrial in Kilkenny, wondered what could be done for Joachim.

"Sure it's no life at all for a young man," he mused. "Tied to that old harridan in Germany and to a job he hates. Something must be done," he told Diogenes sternly.

When Joachim, operating an hour ahead of the rest, returned from his day of meetings and writing reports, he found a note from his wife requesting him to call round when he got back from Ireland. He pulled a face and decided to go at once. It must be urgent. Katrin hardly ever asked to see him.

Sitting crosslegged on the pink sofa reading through the notes Lallie had made, Jade tried to push all thoughts of the mother she'd known out of her mind. The self-centred actress with a carefully preserved Irish lilt and a sense of what was due to her. The adroit self-publicist who gave interviews to journalists dressed in black lace, with an orchid pinned to her breast. The imperious middle-aged mother flashing her rings impatiently at her daughters, neither of whom was beautiful or talented enough for her. All this must go.

She must think of Rachel as a shy country girl of nineteen meeting Stefan, sixteen years older than herself and already a well-known poet. He must have seemed remote. Exotic. A Russian Jew and a poet, the kind of person she'd only read about in books. Rachel had rarely spoken of Stefan to her daughters and when she had, it'd always been with a note of pain in her voice. Genuine pain, not the kind she used to such effect with journalists. Once she'd said, "He changed my life. Without Stefan, I'd never have been an actress. Only a little girl daydreaming."

This was what Jade wanted her film to show – the awkward young girl turning into an artist.

She took out a small black and white photo of Stefan which had been in Diana's possession and after her death had passed to Jade. She looked at the thick brows, the black hair brushed upwards from his forehead, the dark eyes sneering into the camera. He was an extremely ugly man. Yes, it was an unpleasant face, with its thin lips and wide, flared nose. What on earth had attracted Rachel to him? Her mother had always said that Diana had nothing of Stefan about her except the way she moved, graceful and swift as a gazelle. That must have been striking in a man. "He was ugly," Rachel had said, "but so masculine-looking, so essentially male, that he became almost beautiful. To me."

Jade had in mind David McGregor for the part. A fierce Scotsman, he was a pain in the arse to work with; but if he could be persuaded to transfer some of his bad temper to the screen he'd be perfect.

Lallie, piling dishes into the dishwasher in their small green and white kitchen with built-in hob and eye-level grill, raised her head from her task and thought of her schoolfriend, Ruth Martin, cutting fish fingers into two to make them go round, spreading margarine as thinly as possible on her children's bread, eating nothing herself. Whilst she'd spent the day comfortably in the British Museum, then come home and prepared a meal of home made soup, pasta and salad. Whose life was more real?

Lallie looked round their neat and shiny kitchen. She'd made her life with Jade so comfortable and safe. Even if she were to be struck down with cancer (the only thing she really dreaded), death would come in a bright, efficient hospital in some fashionable part of town. Or in a hospice where she'd be tended by nuns. She could afford, just about, to surround her life, and even her dying, with dignity; to protect herself in a way her parents, for example, had never been able to.

"Thinking?"

Jade stood in the doorway smiling ironically at her.

"Yes, you know, about trivial things." Lallie straightened up, closed the dishwasher door with a bang and brushed her hands down her jeans. "Have I packed the dishes right, is there enough soap in the machine, is the life we lead real?"

"God, Lallie! What's come over you recently? Life's only real if it involves hard work and suffering. All the rest is self-indulgence, according to you." Jade turned back into the living-room. "One of these days, you'll see it's not a sin to do work you enjoy, to be able to afford holidays and good food."

"Perhaps," murmured Lallie, wondering what in the world she'd done to deserve Jade's tone of exasperation.

That evening Grace wrote to her elder daughter, Emma, that she was thinking of doing some social work. In the middle of writing this she hesitated, looked down at the words on the page, then tore up the letter and began again. After all, she hadn't even told Leonard yet.

"Your hair doesn't seem very different," he'd remarked when she got back from Sally's meeting. "What are we paying for here?"

"Body. They've given it body. It's a new process," she'd replied. "Took ages."

She laid down her pen. Lying to one's husband. Where did that lead?

"Hello," said Katrin frostily. "Come in."

He stepped into the hallway of the apartment where he'd lived for ten years with Katrin and where Werner, his younger son, had been born. His heart gave a lurch, as always, to be back.

"New wallpaper?"

"Yes."

"I like it."

Katrin said nothing. She glanced pointedly at the carpet.

Joachim sighed and wiped his feet. She led the way into the small back room which had once been his study and which now seemed to belong to the boys. His heart tightened again as he noticed Peter's jumper tossed over a chair.

"Ach! The boys are so messy." Katrin bundled the pullover out of sight. "I leave them to it in here. I don't come in."

Joachim, correctly, understood this to mean that she'd no interest in this room because, more than any other room in the apartment, it had been his.

Katrin indicated the armchair and took the hard back chair for herself. Joachim felt this was to be seen as symbolic – and he knew exactly in what way.

"Has something happened to one of the boys?"

He could hardly bear the suspense. If anything ever happened to them . . . but he must be careful, he mustn't show he was vulnerable, for there were still ways Katrin could harm him.

"How's Werner settling down?" he continued, more calmly. Their younger son was in his first term as a weekly boarder.

"Very well. I never have problems with the boys," she replied, emphasising the last word.

Knowing his unruly sons, Joachim doubted this, but he let it pass.

Katrin continued. "I'll come straight to the point. I'm planning to spend the summer in Sweden and I want you to take Peter and Werner."

Joachim could hardly have been more astonished if she'd leapt into his arms screaming she loved him. Katrin guarded her sons jealously, allowing them to spend with him the number of weekends laid down by the court at the time of their separation, and no more.

"I'll be in Ireland for part of the summer," he warned. "Seeing about the farm."

"That's all right. It will be good for their English."

Another surprise. Katrin usually objected to the boys spending time in Ireland. She wanted them to be German through and through. And businessmen rather than farmers.

"Is it a job that takes you to Sweden?" he asked hopefully.

"I don't have to tell you anything," she replied stiffly. "It is not, however, a job."

"Holiday?" he enquired, knowing he was pushing his luck.

She gave him a withering look which he interpreted,

again correctly, as meaning where would I get the money to go on such a long holiday from the tiny allowance you give me? As a matter of fact, in his view, it wasn't a tiny allowance – but that was just one of the many points on which he and Katrin differed.

He looked at her, a small, neat figure sitting upright in the hard chair, not a hair of her tight black curls out of place. She was dressed immaculately, if conventionally, in a navy blue dress. There was a string of pearls around her neck, not given by him, they'd belonged to her mother. She never now wore, at least to his knowledge, any of the jewellery he'd given her.

He suddenly felt afraid for her, sitting there rigid with hate for him and pity for herself. She saw him as selfish and uncaring. No doubt he was. He'd been unfaithful to her and she was making him pay. No doubt that was right. But she was exacting a price from herself too. God knows he was content to be forever in the wrong. But she was hurting herself, had walled herself into a kind of living death. She had to be the perfect mother, the efficient hausfrau, the wronged wife. They were lonely and demanding roles to play. And they didn't seem to have brought her happiness.

"I'll gladly have the boys. For as long as you wish," he continued, more gently. "It'll do you good to have a break."

"Someone's had to provide them with a stable home these past three years," she snapped.

He raised an eyebrow. "I'm not up to providing stability, aren't I?" he queried, then immediately regretted it.

"I suppose, now they're older, they can be left. They've learned to judge for themselves how things are. In Ireland, with Molly around, you won't be able to carry on so much."

"I don't know what you imagine is the kind of life I lead, Katrin, but – "

"I assure you I never ever think about your life. However I've a duty to protect my sons from bad influences."

I'm not a bad influence, I'm their father, he felt like screaming. He stayed silent. He knew from experience how bitter the scene would get if he attempted to argue back. One short-lived passion when the cracks in their marriage had already begun to show and she'd made him pay for three long years. He bowed his head. She wouldn't believe him if he told her he'd not slept with a woman since, Christabel having killed in him the desire for other women. It seemed to give Katrin some sort of bitter satisfaction to picture him as incurably promiscuous.

He stood up. "That's settled then. Let them spend the summer on the farm. If I still have it, that is."

"I don't know why you don't sell that place. You can't afford to do it up. Half of it is unfurnished. And it takes you away from your job here. It's a millstone round your neck."

He went away with the taste of ashes in his mouth. She was a tight, unforgiving woman, buttoned up with misery and resentment and wounded pride. She'd succeeded, as usual, in making him feel his life had been one long failure. His job in which (she was right about this) he hadn't progressed as far as he should have. The farm, which got deeper into debt every year. His marriage. But why did she always make him feel his failures had wrecked her life?

He clenched his fists and beat on the steering-wheel. "Dear God!" he groaned. "Is she right? Am I as selfish and callous as she thinks? Did I trample on her life?" And why, why wouldn't she forgive?

But before she could forgive him, she had to learn to forgive herself; forgive herself for having let her husband slip through her fingers. Yes, he knew the way her mind worked. She reproached herself for his infidelity which seemed to prove to her that she'd been a less than perfect wife. Katrin had no notion of muddling through life. Everything she did, had to be done to perfection. Her father had been a hero and dangled on the end of a butcher's hook for his part in the 1944 plot against Hitler. She expected similar standards from herself and from others, which was a little hard at times on his sons. Not to mention himself. If only she'd give a little, yield a little to life. He let out the clutch, promising himself that the next bar he saw he'd stop for a cognac. My God, he thought, I wish Cornelius was here.

He swallowed the cognac and felt in his pocket for coins. He went to phone Gunter, the only one of his colleagues he socialised with. He was out. He returned to his seat, ordered another cognac and thought of Christabel. Christabel, the laughing, tempting siren with blonde hair tumbling down her back like a golden waterfall. A mad artist who danced down the streets barefoot handing out roses to passers-by. She'd looked at Joachim in a bar one day with that beguilingly astigmatic stare of hers and he'd been lost. Her voice was like the sound of a mountain stream. She moved like a dancer. He'd been mad to be in the light of her strange personality.

For two months he'd lived at an intensity he'd never known before. Walking through the streets of Munich at night, talking, laughing, drinking in bars. Making love till dawn so that he arrived in the office feeling dull and hungover and counting the hours till he'd see her again. She laughed at his stuffy old job. Told him to throw it over and take a risk for once in his life. She was completely free, careless about money and possessions, giving them away to anyone who asked. She was fickle too. And she lied. What did she do all day while he was at the office? Where did she go? Who did she meet? He'd wanted to take her back to Ireland, to live with her there. Perhaps he'd wanted to tame her?

On the morning they'd been due to leave, he'd overslept and woke to find her gone. Nothing but a note propped up against the mirror, telling him to take care. If it hadn't been for that note (he had it still, carried it around in his wallet) and for his wife's frozen face when he returned home, he'd have thought he'd dreamed the whole thing. And for the ache in his heart . . . He'd never been able to trace her. By now she'd probably left Munich, perhaps even Germany. Though sometimes he thought he glimpsed her in the street and ran after her. But he was always mistaken.

He finished his cognac and ordered another.

CHAPTER FIVE

CORNELIUS WAS WALKING DIOGENES DOWN THE MAIN STREET IN Bannon when the Reverend Sam Cleary drew up alongside him on his lawnmower.

"Are you on for a coffee, Cornelius?"

Cornelius looked at his watch. "Eleven o'clock. All right, you've caught me at a good time."

"A good time?" queried Sam, parking his mower.

"Yes. In the early part of the morning, I feel emotional, so I take Diogenes for a walk. Around eleven, my critical faculties begin to assert themselves. Between two and three, I get drowsy – "

"And then?" asked Sam with interest, as they walked towards the hotel.

"Then I feel angry."

"Ah yes." Sam pushed open the door. "A common condition among atheists."

"Huh," said Cornelius rudely. "What about some of your lot? Saint Jerome, for instance. He seems to have been in a constant state of irritability and sexual frustration."

"True," acknowledged Sam.

"'Morning, Father," chorused a trio of Roman Catholic nuns as Sam and Cornelius took the table next to them. Sam nodded across.

"That's interesting," murmured Cornelius. "They think you're one of them."

"It's the collar," Sam explained. "No different from a Roman one."

"You should think seriously about going over to the Romans, Sam. You're getting very High."

"I know." Sam looked at his watch. "In fifty minutes I'll be celebrating Mass. Joachim's persuaded me to introduce a mid-week service. I'm afraid there'll be a split in the congregation soon. Some of them hold to Queen Victoria's belief that taking communion more than twice a year is simply greedy." He broke off as the waitress came up and ordered coffee and a jam doughnut.

"Nothing like a quick fast before Mass, eh Father?" said Cornelius, with a wink to the waitress.

"Now Sam," he said, when the coffees had been brought, "what's to be done about Joachim?"

"Done? In what sense?" Sam bit into his doughnut.

"He has a perfectly nice farm here which, with a bit of effort, could be put on a paying basis. He hates his job in Germany. He doesn't get on with his wife . . . Can't you persuade him that the right thing to do is to move over here?"

"Persuade him?" Sam looked doubtful. "How could I persuade him? Rather than you, I mean?"

"Because he thinks he has a moral obligation to stay in Germany and earn lots of money so that that old hag can go on living in the style to which she thinks she should be accustomed and her sons train to be wealthy businessmen."

"Bugger morality!" said Sam firmly. The nuns at the next table glanced up, their habits quivering with excitement. "Sorry, sisters."

Cornelius grinned. "You know, Sam, there may be hope for you after all."

Lallie sat in the caféteria at Colindale letting the sun's rays warm her. She'd spent the morning reading through back copies of Irish newspapers. Rachel McKenna was starting to become real for her. The small oval face with its huge dark eyes stared out at her from photograph after photograph taken during the fifties and sixties. This was Rachel in the early days, before she'd become plump and comfortable and absorbed into the establishment. In those early days she'd gone about dressed in long skirts and old fur coats and been the scandal of Dublin with her two illegitimate daughters.

Lallie went back upstairs, studied again the picture of the slight, fragile looking girl and wondered where all that strength to rebel had come from. She'd found, in the local Westmeath paper dated 1949, a photograph of the wedding between Miss Rachel McKenna, daughter of Frank McKenna, and Mr Nicholas Johnson, a solicitor in Bannon. She scrutinised the tall, slender, fair-haired man in top hat and tails but the photograph gave away no clues to his personality. He was smiling politely into the camera. Rachel leant on his arm, an expression of anxiety on her face. She hadn't yet learned to disguise her feelings from the cameras.

Lallie thought over the facts. Born 1931 in a large house outside Bannon. Mother died when she was four. Brought up by a loyal nanny and a succession of governesses. Lived in virtual seclusion in her father's house until she was eighteen. Married Nicholas Johnson. No children. A year later, met Stefan Chertkov. Lived with him, on and off, for three years, till shortly before the birth of Diana. There was a strange thing – what kind of a father would walk out before the birth of his child? After Stefan's departure, in order to make ends meet, Rachel had got a job selling tickets in a tiny Dublin theatre run on a shoestring in a mews. From there she'd graduated to stage management and then to acting. Wilde, Shaw, Yeats. She was an astonishing overnight success. "A natural" raved the headlines.

In 1956 a second daughter, Jade, had been born (father unknown). Later Rachel had gone over to London where she'd acted in Shakespeare and Chekhov and got parts in several films. Another strange thing: why had she never sought a divorce? It wasn't of course permitted in the Republic but there were ways round it for the really desperate. In the eyes of the law, then, Nicholas Johnson was the father of both Diana and Jade.

But as to Jade's real father it would be impossible, surely, to trace him after all these years. The men Rachel had been photographed with around the time of Jade's birth were colleagues, other actors, theatre directors. Jade's father could have been any one of those – or, more likely, someone else entirely whom Rachel had taken care to keep out of the papers. She'd never been photographed with Stefan, for instance.

Lallie rested her elbows on the table. After all these years, would it really help to uncover the name? Jade idealised her unknown father, imagining him to be quite different from her mother. Calm, efficient, unselfish, someone whom she could be proud of. He'd achieved almost mythical status for her, unfairly, Lallie thought, for Jade had reasons to be proud of her mother. But perhaps it would be better not to disturb the picture Jade had built up?

Well, now she had the facts. A life on paper. Though what could facts tell you about a person? It was only the skeleton. Someone would have to fill in the emotions.

Joachim stumbled through the city clutching his aching head. He had a hangover. He was going to be late for work. He was cross. Groups of tourists stood around admiring the beauty of the baroque churches. The rococo facades. The Altes and Neues Rathaus. Later, no doubt, they'd go on to gape at the works of art in the Alte Pinakothek. But he could tell them that behind the glories of the post-war reconstructions lurked corruption.

The dates were burned into his memory. 1348: Jews were massacred by the citizens of Munich who accused them of practising ritual murder and starting a plague. 1527: twenty-nine Baptists who'd refused to recant were burned by the Catholic hierarchy. Even before Hitler's arrival the city had been a breeding-ground for extremists. Then, in 1920, the monster had come, rallying his troops in the Hofbrauhaus. June 1938: the central Jewish synagogue had been ransacked, five months before the rest of Germany followed suit during Kristallnacht. September 1938: scene of the ignominious appeasement. Munich had become the headquarters of the Nazi party. Some of their buildings were still standing, grim, concrete affairs. And the murder hadn't ceased with the ending of the war. In 1972, twelve Israeli athletes had been killed by Palestinian terrorists.

The stench of blood seemed to rise up from the very pavements, sickening him.

In the hamlet of Dulwich, Grace went out through the iron gates and turned right, in the direction of the shops. Leonard, lifting his head from pruning the roses, wondered where she was off to now. He frowned to himself.

Grace walked along the neat little path edged by white posts and went into the grocery. There she purchased a tin of lobster bisque soup and some wholemeal bread. Remembering that a button was missing from one of Leonard's shirts, she picked up a card of buttons. She'd been reading about these in the newspaper. Some woman, an immigrant probably, would have strung them on at the rate of thirty pence an hour. She threw them down in disgust and hurriedly left the shop. Ten minutes later she returned and bought two dozen cards. For a fall in demand would put some homeworker out of a job, which would be worse (wouldn't it?) than being exploited.

"This will never do," she thought. "I'm totally confused. Perhaps I should try something less ambitious than social work."

Meanwhile Leonard, watching her come and go,

suspected she was trying to ring her lover from the call box at the end of the village. Pride, however, forbade him to follow her.

How much longer can I bear working here? Joachim stared out of his office window onto the factory site below which resembled, in the rain, some weird city out of a science fiction movie. Tall lean smoke stacks reared up towards the sky. Thick cooling towers squatted like giant egg timers. One of these days, these monstrosities erected by man would come to life, advance on human beings and destroy them.

He was roused from this fantasy by the persistent bleep of the telephone. One hand shot up to his aching head whilst the other reached for the receiver.

"Gunter here," said the voice on the other end. "Fancy a drink after work tonight?"

Joachim was fond of Gunter. A thin, angular man with a sharp brain, Gunter possessed a fund of funny stories. He was a good sailor too. They'd sometimes gone sailing together on Ammersee. He was several years younger than Joachim who'd acted in a kind of fatherly way towards him. It had been partly on Joachim's recommendation that Gunter had been appointed to the division board.

Over recent months they'd developed an unspoken understanding that they'd cover for one another at meetings, defend one another's patch. It had been Joachim who'd guided Gunter through the web of unspoken tensions at his first board meetings, who'd tipped him off as to each member's foibles, vanities and grudges. The board was riven by hostilities going back ten, fifteen years. Joachim hated to see a decent man like Gunter defeated through ignorance of the ground rules. He felt an absurd desire to protect him. Perhaps it was because he didn't see enough of his sons. His paternal feelings were underused.

"Drink?" he said. "Good idea."

With a bit of luck, his life might develop into one long drinking session.

"Nicholas Johnson."

Jade and Lallie were sipping gin in the foyer of the National Theatre.

"We'll start with him. My mother never talked about him. Shut him away as she shut away all that part of her life." Jade rolled a lump of ice around her mouth. "Interesting, isn't it? None of the articles I've read about her deal with that early part of her life – and yet that's what's intriguing. What made her become an actress? It was so unlikely, given her background. And then there's the feminist angle." She tilted her chair back. "She went from a life that was like something out of a nineteenth-century novel, governesses and so on, to being a thoroughly modern woman, a single mother with a career of her own and numerous love affairs, in the space of three years. The years she spent with Stefan. Maybe Nicholas Johnson would be able to help me account for it. What do you think? He must have noticed something during those early years, seen something in her that pointed to the actress she was to become."

"It's amazing how detached you can be about her." Lallie set down her glass as the bell for the performance rang. "You're treating your mother as if she was simply another subject for a film."

Jade shrugged her shoulders. "So she is." She stood up. "After all, what do I know about her early life except what other people have written? Even when we were children, Di and I didn't see much of her. She was always sleeping or rehearsing or on stage or at a party. I've a memory of a ravishingly beautiful woman trailing scarves and perfume, hugging us and telling us to be happy. And then dashing away. Or arriving home at odd hours laden with presents for us. A piece of jewellery or some toy she'd picked up in the market. It was as if she was playing a role, even for us. But as to what she was really like . . . "

They went into the play.

Lying in bed later that night, Jade said, "For as long as I can remember I was the one who had to pick up the pieces. My mother had no grasp at all of what are called 'the realities' of life. And Di had a trick of disappearing whenever a crisis was brewing. If I could only get free of my memories I could start living again."

"We could all say that," commented Lallie, dryly.

"Don't mock. I want this film to bring about my rebirth. From the womb."

Lallie was silent. She turned over the scenes in her mind. Where Jade saw neglect, Lallie saw freedom. What wouldn't she have given to have grown up surrounded by people who talked of Shakespeare and Yeats as naturally as her own parents had discussed the price of bread? She sometimes thought her deepest bond with Jade lay in their mutual dissatisfaction at their childhoods, the very different sorts of misery they'd each endured during those years, the burden of their mothers they each had carried, and carried still, separately.

"Well," Jade turned over decisively into her sleeping position, "I'm going to fly to Dublin, make contact with Nicholas Johnson, if he's still alive, and see whether the house where my mother was brought up is suitable for filming. You know, it's an odd thing," she looked over at Lallie, "that Johnson fellow is legally my father."

"I'd figured that out too."

"I hope he lives up to it. Terrible if he turns out to be a creep. Still, he's not my real father. I imagine him as someone practical and efficient, full of commonsense. After all I must get my practicality, and all the other things, from somebody. There's nothing of my mother in me." She glanced at Lallie. "It's like half the jigsaw's missing. Sometimes I think I can see how the pieces might fit. But how can I be sure?"

Again the cry for her father. Louder this time.

Lallie shook her head. "What can you find out from newspapers?"

"How's life?" Gunter bent over his beer till his sharp chin almost touched the rim of his glass.

"So-so. I saw Katrin last night."

"I bet that was fun, eh?"

Joachim wove an amusing tale of their encounter for him.

"Home is the place where, when you have to go there, they have to take you in," commented Gunter. "As Robert Frost said."

"Katrin didn't feel under any obligation to take me in. Rather the opposite, she didn't even offer me a drink."

They chatted for a while about inconsequential matters, discussed the possibility of going sailing again on Ammersee. As they were leaving the bar, Joachim said,

"Gunter, we've forgotten that report. Weren't we supposed to prepare comments on it for tomorrow's meeting?"

"Er . . . it's at home. Look, I'll make some notes on it when I get back and you can check them over tomorrow before the meeting."

"OK."

It was slightly unorthodox since this was meant to be a joint operation. But perhaps Gunter felt he owed him a favour. Too late to do anything about it now. Joachim shrugged his shoulders as he got into his car. It was a minor matter.

When he looked for Gunter the next morning, he was nowhere to be found. Joachim went to the boardroom early hoping to have a word with him before the meeting began but Gunter slid into his seat a couple of seconds before the chairman arrived and there was no opportunity.

Hans Wedelmeier, the chairman, began by running through the minutes of the previous meeting. Joachim permitted his attention to wander. He looked around the room. Opposite sat Hermann, the newest member of the division board. This was only his second board meeting and he was pink with anticipation. If that was his style, he wouldn't last long. Next came Wolfgang, a tall, gangling man in his mid-fifties. He'd been on the board eight years and wouldn't get any further. People were already whispering that he should step down and give a younger man a chance.

The most talented of them all was James, the monetarist whizz kid enticed over from England by a fat salary. Cool and unperturbed, James put forward the first item on the agenda, his scheme to "rationalise" the factory at Essen which was losing money. He proposed phasing out part of the workforce over the next three years by a series of carefully planned redundancies. There were several nods of approval around the table.

Here we all are, thought Joachim, poring over the figures in front of us, adding them up, making tidy sums, never once raising our heads to take a look at the men outside whose livelihoods we're so calmly smashing. And there's no proof these policies work, he thought gloomily. It came to him suddenly: he had nothing in common with these people, their aims were not his aims.

With difficulty, he focused his attention on Wedelmeier. He was asking Gunter about the report he and Joachim had been supposed to comment on.

"I haven't prepared anything on it. Have you, Joachim?" Gunter shot Joachim a glance from his small, very blue eyes.

Joachim was conscious of his eyebrows shooting up and his eyes widening. He was conscious that he was looking slightly ridiculous. Gunter turned his head aside so that Joachim could only half see the malicious smile that played around Gunter's lips. And he saw, in that split second, a side of Gunter he'd never noticed before. His malice, his envy, his determination to get to the top at any price.

"No. I haven't prepared anything either," he replied quietly.

Wedelmeier looked down at his blotter, no doubt sensing that something was amiss but unable to untangle the unspoken tensions.

"Well," he said finally, "it's not urgent. We'll hold that item over for the next meeting."

He moved on to other business. Joachim found it hard to concentrate. What had motivated Gunter to land him in it like that? Had he slighted him in some way? Gunter was notoriously touchy, having come up the hard way, working night shifts in order to support himself at college, which was partly why Joachim had been fond of him and encouraged him. All the other board members came from comfortably-off middle-class families. Their rise had been predictable. Had there perhaps been something condescending in his attitude? Had he offended Gunter?

But perhaps it wasn't that at all. Perhaps Gunter had only been friendly with Joachim so long as it had been in his interest, long enough to get onto the board and establish himself there. Perhaps he really thought Joachim a tiresome old bastard? Gunter was planning to move on and this was the first sign. He'd realised Joachim wasn't the best person to help him up the next rung of the ladder. Yes, as Joachim watched, Gunter did seem to be agreeing rather warmly to proposals put forward by Wedelmeier and James. No doubt he'd pinpointed those two as the men of influence. And no doubt he was right. A wave of disillusionment swept over Joachim. He felt he would welcome oblivion.

CHAPTER SIX

CLIVE AND JEAN LIVED IN A NEW HOUSE BUILT TO CLIVE'S specifications (i.e. large, lots of glass, white columned veranda, built-in barbecue set, three en suite bathrooms), on the other side of the park from Grace and Leonard. When Grace called round one afternoon Jean was ironing, as indeed Grace could have predicted.

"Clive's shirts?" she enquired, plomping her shopping basket on one chair and herself on another.

Jean nodded.

"I make Leonard iron his own now."

"I don't think I could get Clive to do that." Jean brushed back a loose strand of hair. Before her marriage she'd walked with a spring in her step and turned heads in the street. Nowadays in her long skirts and shapeless cardigans, she looked frail and tired. Her hair which had used to glow chestnut had faded to a dull brown colour. For all of this, Grace blamed Clive.

"You look done in, Jean. What's the matter?"

"I am rather tired. Carl's children turned out to be a bit of a handful. I was glad to see the back of them." She paused in her ironing and looked out fondly at Jill and Graham playing in the garden. "Bless them!" She opened the window. "Aunt Grace is here. Come in and say hello."

"It doesn't matter. Don't disturb them."

"It's good for them. I don't want them to grow up hooligans. Wipe your feet," she added as the twins trooped in.

"They are sweet." Grace gave them each a kiss on the cheek. "They take after you."

"I don't know about that," said Jean modestly.

I do, thought Grace, watching Jill and Graham sit side by side on the bench peaceably sharing a can of Coke. "Where's Leonie?" she asked. Leonie was her goddaughter.

"Up in her bedroom sulking. She spends a lot of time doing that when Clive's not here. She's turning out to be one of those daughters who hate their mother all through adolescence," Jean added ruefully. "I won't call her. It'll only provoke a crisis."

They chatted for a while over their tea.

"I'm thinking of looking for a job," said Grace suddenly. She had to tell someone. She wanted to hear herself say those words out loud. She wanted to see other people's reactions. Encouragement. Approval. Surprise. She hoped not surprise.

"A job?" Jean looked surprised. "You mean outside the home? Don't you need experience for that?"

"Surely I should be able to do something." It annoyed Grace to hear Jean echo her own doubts. "I mean I've run a household, organised three other lives for over twenty years, and before that I nursed my parents. Surely that qualifies me for something?"

"I don't think they quite see it like that, somehow," said Jean hesitantly. "In the outside world."

"I'm going to have a shot at it."

"What does Leonard say about it?"

"Mm, well – "

Jean sighed. "They were both brought up so badly, weren't they? Especially Clive. I've always thought Leonard was more understanding. Clive expects everything to be done for him. He'd ask me to brush his teeth if he thought he could get away with it. Sometimes I could just curse my mother-in-law. What about going on one of those courses the Poly runs for women returning to work?"

"They cost money. And I'd have to tell Leonard."

"Oh. So you haven't told him?"

"No."

"Bloody mothers-in-law."

The doorbell rang. It was Clive. Grace glanced at her watch. Four o'clock. What *did* Clive do for a living?

"Hello, Clive. You're home early."

"Yes," replied Clive shortly. There was a smug expression on his face, as if he guessed at Grace's curiosity.

He *was* irritating.

"Daddy!" Leonie burst into the kitchen, a tangle of blonde hair and long legs.

"Hello, darling." Clive rumpled her hair. "How's my favourite girl today?"

"Fine, Daddy." Leonie beamed at him. Jean raised her eyes heavenwards. Jill and Graham crept back out into the garden. "Daddy, are you taking me swimming this afternoon?" She entwined her hand in his. Grace watched her. She was going to be a stunner when she grew up.

Clive looked at his watch. "Yes honey, I might just have time. Jean, is there a clean shirt ready? I'm dining out tonight with clients."

Jean gestured to the pile of clean shirts.

Well! thought Grace. "I make Leonard iron his own shirts now."

Clive turned his gaze on her. "That, if I may say so, doesn't surprise me in the least."

Well! thought Grace.

Waiting outside Nicholas Johnson's Dublin office, Jade became aware of an odd sensation in the pit of her stomach. She realised with surprise that she was feeling extremely nervous. Her hands were damp. She wiped them on her corduroy skirt. She'd thought this would be an interview like any other; but how could it be? After all, due to this curious quirk in Irish law Nicholas Johnson was legally her father. She swallowed. Her throat felt prickly and dry.

The door opened and a silver-haired, slightly stooped man came over and shook her by the hand.

"Miss McKenna? I'm Nicholas Johnson. So you're Jade . . . I've seen one or two of your films."

She met his gaze and saw her curiosity reflected in his eyes.

"Well er . . . come in." He showed her into his office, a lawyer's office with a large leather topped desk covered in papers and a glass case full of bound legal tomes. He pulled out an armchair for her and instead of sitting behind his desk took the chair next to hers.

"Off-duty for a bit." He smiled. His voice held a soft Irish lilt. His manner was gentle and rather melancholy. "So you're Jade. You don't look like your mother."

"No, everyone says that. I suppose it's my blonde hair. She thought I was going to have black hair like herself, that's why she chose the name Jade. A mistake from the start." She laughed. "It's possible I take after my father."

He studied her. "Your eyes have a look of old Frank McKenna about them. Probing." He winced slightly.

"I never met my grandfather." Pushing down the emotions that threatened to rise to the surface, Jade assumed her most professional manner. "I've come because, as I mentioned on the phone, I'm planning to make a film about my mother's early life."

"Portrait of the actress as young woman?" He raised a quizzical eyebrow.

"Amongst other things. I feel I have a duty to her. And then I'll be free of her."

"Hard being Rachel McKenna's daughter, eh?"

"Yes," she replied shortly. "One of us didn't make it."

A look of pain flashed across his face. "Ah yes. Diana. I read about her death in the papers. You blame your mother?"

"Partly," she replied, wondering what had caused, after so many years, that expression of pain.

"Maybe you shouldn't blame her. There was a streak of violence in that family usually, though not always, self-inflicted."

She leant forward eagerly. "That's what I want to talk to you about. Her father, the nanny, the governesses – her whole life at that time. She spoke so little about it."

"She had good reason." He was silent for a moment, gazing down at his carefully pressed trousers. He made a small, involuntary movement with his hands. "And I? Am I to be in this film of yours?" He shot her a half amused, half ironical glance. She was beginning to like him very much indeed.

"I'd like to put you on screen, in a minor part."

"A minor part." Again the ironical smile, just skirting the edge of bitterness. "Yes, that's me. Your mother now, she went for the big one. Always."

How well he knows her, she thought. Aloud, she said, "Will it cause you problems? I mean, with your practice?"

"I'm a lawyer, remember. I know the libel laws inside out." He grinned suddenly and relaxed. "My clients aren't the type to go and see well-made, low budget films. I don't suppose you'll do me any harm." He thought for a moment. "Look, if you want me to dredge up my memories I'll need a more congenial setting. Why don't I invite you to dinner tonight? There's a reasonable little restaurant in Dun Laoghaire, overlooking the bay. I'll book a table for eight o'clock, shall I?"

"I should invite you," she protested. "You're doing me the favour."

He waved away her objections and stood up.

"What kind of a 'father' am I if I can't buy my 'daughter' dinner at least once in her life?"

She stared at him. So he *had* thought about it. The past weighed with him then, even after all these years. He held open the door for her. He seemed old-fashioned and rather kind. But shrewd – he obviously had definite opinions about Rachel and her family. It would be worth finding out what they were. He was stylish and distinguished. He'd have done for a father, she thought.

In the outer office she passed a man and a dog.

"Good morning, Cornelius. The litigious mood come over you again?" called Nicholas cheerfully.

"I shouldn't complain if I were you," answered Cornelius, tipping his hat to Jade in an oddly quaint way. "We all know what huge profits you lawyers make."

"Actually," he continued, following Nicholas into his office, "it's not about myself that I've come. I was out in this direction bringing Diogenes to his guard dog training classes" (Diogenes gave a snort), "and I thought I'd pop in and have a word with you about the divorce laws in Germany. What are they like, do you know?"

"Ah, Cornelius, almost anything is easier to get into than out of. And that particularly applies to marriage. I wouldn't do it if I were you."

"But I'm not," protested Cornelius. "It's for a friend."

"Oh yes." Nicholas sat down behind his desk and reverted to his professional manner. "Could you tell me a bit more about your – I mean your 'friend's' – situation?"

That'll teach him to bring me up to Dublin and make me jump through hoops. Diogenes rolled on his back and kicked his legs up in the air in a quite un-guard dog-like way.

Joachim lay in bed, sweating and clenching his fists as wave after wave of anger swept over him. He must be going mad. Where was all this hatred coming from? What had Gunter done? A minor piece of careering, a tiny act of self-interest, and he was raising it to epic proportions.

He tried to concentrate on Gunter's good points, the pleasant times they'd had together, sailing and drinking. It was no use. Between Gunter then and Gunter as he was now, always with that malicious grin on his face, the gap was unbridgeable. The images were broken, irreconcilable. He felt the burden of his hate. Was this how Katrin had felt when she'd found out about Christabel? Had he smashed everything up for her? God forgive me, he thought sadly.

"We more or less grew up together." Nicholas took a sip of wine and nodded to the waiter. "My father, like his father before him, was the McKenna family lawyer. The two families had been linked as far back as anyone could remember. Our . . . marriage merely formalised the bond."

She noted his slight hesitation before the word marriage. It was understandable. He must have long ago ceased to think of himself as married.

"Yes, my father got a lot of work through Frank McKenna." He finished his soup and sat back in his chair. "He was always in and out of the courts, quarrelling with his neighbours about rights of way and other matters."

"What do you remember about my mother in those days?"

"I remember she used to bite her nails." He smiled to himself. "I don't suppose you've ever bitten your nails in your life?"

"Only at previews." She laughed. "Funny – my memory is that my mother was quite particular about her nails. I remember them as beautifully long and tapered, with dark red polish on them."

"That was later. As a small girl she was in the habit of biting them down to the skin till they bled. She was a nervous child. There was always a little frightened look about her. She resembled her mother in that. I was three years older. I suppose I sort of took her under my wing. We played together. She loved make-believe games. She'd escape into her own world for hours at a time. She was an obsessive reader – Dickens, the Brontës, *Little Women*, film magazines – anything she could lay her hands on. She lived each book as she read it. We'd act out scenes from them. Her nanny lent us bits of old curtain, tablecloths, discarded bedspreads, to dress up in. Rachel was always obsessed with her looks." Jade nodded. "She'd spend hours posing in front of the mirror. Once a week she went to dance classes in Bannon. Ballet, tap, she loved all that stuff. She became a different child when she was dancing or dressing up. All her nervousness disappeared."

The waiter took away their plates and served the main course. Jade began tackling her lobster. "You said she resembled her mother. What was my grandmother like?"

He shook his head. "I must have been eight when she died. Rachel was about four or five. I've vague memories of a small, thin woman always half a step behind her husband." He slit open his steak and oyster pie. "Later I remember hearing gossip that he beat her. And then there was her death. So sudden. It was never clearly explained."

"Oh?"

He shrugged. "Gossip. You know country Ireland."

"No, I don't. I grew up in Dublin and now I live in London. I dislike the country."

"Pity. Anyway, there were rumours. That he'd beaten her once too often, that sort of thing. She was an excessively frail-looking woman."

"Like my mother?" suggested Jade.

"No." He waved his fork in the air. "Your mother may have looked frail but she had a will of iron which only became apparent later on."

"Yes." Jade's eyes gleamed. He had the measure of her mother all right. How strange. Perhaps they were the only two people in the world not to have been taken in by her butterfly exterior. She swallowed another mouthful of lobster. "You said there was violence in the family. Do you mean her father?"

"Partly, yes."

She noticed his hand shook slightly as he reached for his glass. Was it old age? Or did he have a drink problem?

"Was he violent to Rachel?" For a second, she actually felt a twinge of pity for her mother, for her mother as a young girl.

"Not physically, no. I don't believe he ever raised a hand to her."

"Mentally?"

He glanced down. "Mentally, yes. Your grandfather was a bully." He pushed away his plate and took another sip of wine. "He'd shout at her for hours on end. Over all sorts of things. Stupidity. Clumsiness. When I knew her, she wasn't yet the graceful actress. And of course his shouting made her all the more clumsy. He'd swear at her too, yelling his disappointment that she wasn't a son, lacked intelligence, daydreamed . . . "

"Why didn't he marry again if he wanted a son so badly?"

"All he needed was someone to act as punchbag for his foul temper. Rachel fitted the bill perfectly. She was trapped there in that big house with no relatives to intercede for her, no money of her own, governesses who came and went very quickly . . . Then at other times, he could be charming to her, taking her to the cinema, which she loved, or watching her act in plays put on in the town hall. In those days, there was an amateur company in Bannon, Rachel sometimes got small parts."

He broke off as the waiter came up to their table. Jade

ordered a lemon sorbet. He refused dessert but ordered brandies for both of them and a cigar for himself.

"Let me give you an example of his bullying. One day he was taking us both out to Brittas Bay in the car. Rachel clambered into the back first and I followed. The wind made the car door swing against my leg. I'm afraid I howled with pain. He turned round – to this day I've not forgotten the rage on his face – and roared at Rachel. 'You did that on purpose. Don't bother to deny it, I saw you. Don't you ever do that again.' I can see the scene still – Rachel sitting there, too stunned for tears." He lit his cigar. "McKenna was afraid. A bully is always a coward at heart. He was afraid something serious had happened to me and he'd be blamed. Or sued."

Jade was silent. She looked out over the bay at the lights of the night ferry twinkling in the blackness. Inside the restaurant a tape of Mozart softly played.

"I hadn't realised there was so much cruelty in her childhood," she murmured.

He nodded. "She was a thin, frightened waif when I married her. She married me to get away from her father, I've no illusions about that. Well, perhaps she did feel a bit of tenderness towards me. I was practically her only friend in the world. There was a cowed look in her eyes in those days, like a dog that's been beaten and kicked . . . "

"And you, what was there in it for you?"

"Tenderness, a feeling of protectiveness towards her." He smiled wryly. "And to prove certain things. I was beginning to have doubts about myself, you see." He held Jade's gaze and, as she continued to look puzzled, added with a trace of irritation, "Come on, you've lived in London."

Suddenly she realised what he was saying and it all slotted into place – the absence of a second wife, of rancour, even, over Rachel's desertion.

"I hope you won't use that piece of information in your

film. I give it to you as 'daughter' rather than film maker. People suspect, but no one can prove. I'd prefer to keep it that way. I have my practice to think of. My clients mostly come from the narrower-minded sections of the population." He paused. "I'm hoping to pass the practice onto my nephew. I might have thought of you, if your interests had lain in the law. I've followed your career with curiosity, you know, over the years."

She smiled and felt tears prick the back of her eyelids. It was the first fatherly gesture anyone had ever made towards her. She felt she owed him something in return.

"I'd never exploit what you've just told me. I know what it's like to be gay. Yes, I live with a woman. I have to say it's probably easier for women. Lallie and I are perfectly open about our relationship but still people don't always twig."

He stared at her, astonished. Then gave a short laugh. "Strange how life repeats itself. Your mother wouldn't have approved."

"She didn't."

"Not that she knew what homosexuality was in those days. You know what Ireland was like then. And your mother was so naive . . . Strange thing was, our marriage was never properly consummated. We could easily have got an annulment but neither of us bothered. I know why in my case. It was a useful cover. But I often expected to find a solicitor's letter requesting an end to the marriage to arrive in the post. Well," he came to a sudden halt in his reminiscences, "I've told you a lot about the past. More than I meant to. In fact, I've been hopelessly indiscreet. I hope you'll use the information wisely."

"I'll do my best."

He signalled for the bill and helped her on with her jacket. We really might be father and daughter, she thought, to anyone looking.

"I'm going to try to get permission to film in the house where my mother grew up," she said, as they made their way down the stairs and into the street. "Will it be possible, do you think?"

"The house outside Bannon? No. It was a fine Georgian mansion but when Frank McKenna died and your mother sold it, it was taken over by a consortium of businessmen who were only interested in the land. They allowed the house to fall into ruin. Three years ago, the roof had to be taken off. A great pity." He unlocked his car.

"Why do the Irish allow their heritage to decay in this way? It's so irresponsible."

"Lack of money and the fact, I suppose, that what's thought of as beautiful architecture is bound up for us with painful history."

She got into the passenger seat. As he started up the car, she glanced across at him. There was one more question she wanted to ask. She hesitated. He'd already told her a great deal. Temperament, circumstances and his profession combined to make him normally a reticent man, she guessed. Nevertheless, for the sake of her film, and because she too was a professional, she had to ask.

"I was wondering whether you'd ever met Stefan Chertkov?"

There was an uneasy silence. He ran a hand over his eyes.

"No," he said shortly. "I never met him."

"I see."

They drove in silence for several minutes. She was wondering where to take the conversation from here when he continued,

"I saw Rachel only once after she left me. We met in a café. By then she was living with Stefan and I had the impression she was in a hurry to get back to him. She looked thinner than when I'd last seen her and there was a bruise on the side of her face. When I asked her about it, she said she'd fallen. I must say I didn't believe her. I thought she was going the way of her mother. There are some women who attract violent men – I've seen enough of that in my profession . . . I gave her a bottle of perfume. There were tears in her eyes as she took it, almost snatched it from me, like a child starved of affection. I asked her to have dinner with me that night. She accepted. I cooked coq au vin which was about all I could manage in those days. She never came. In the middle of the night I got a phone call from her. She sounded scared, said she was sorry for not turning up. That's the last time we ever spoke. Over the next few years, I caught sight of her from time to time in the distance – I'd begun spending the occasional day in our Dublin office. I think I may even have seen you with her once." He smiled. "Then she moved to London and I never saw her again. I didn't go to her funeral. It was cowardly, I know, but the press were out in force and I'd no wish to court publicity. I sent white roses, anonymously."

"Did you ever see her act in the theatre?"

He shook his head. "Never. It would have brought back too many memories."

She hesitated. She was treading on thin ice here. "You said that if I'd shown any talents that way, you'd have considered leaving the practice to me. Would you have done the same for Diana?"

"Stefan's daughter? No."

She wondered how much bitterness lay behind that "no." And how far could she trust his account of their marriage? Perhaps he'd been more in love with Rachel than he wanted to admit?

They drew up outside her hotel.

Jade leaned across. "Thanks for your help. And for a

lovely evening." She kissed him lightly on the cheek and got out of the car.

He flushed slightly and wound down the window. "You've your mother's charm." He smiled at her. "I hope you'll keep in touch, now that we've met up at last."

"I will," she promised, waving him off.

Turning into the hotel she reflected that it was the first time anyone had ever compared her to her mother. But I'm not like her, she thought. Not at all.

"Leonard," said Grace, that night in bed, "you don't think there's something fishy about Clive, do you?"

"Fishy? In what way?" muttered Leonard, absorbed in his One Minute Manager book.

"You know how he goes on with Leonie? He scarcely takes any notice of the twins but he and Leonie are always hanging around each other. Take the other day. It was Leonie he kissed and cuddled when he came home from work, not Jean. Don't you think that's rather odd?"

Leonard put down his book and took off his glasses.

"For heaven's sake, Grace, what are you trying to say?"

"I . . . well, nothing really . . . only I was listening to this radio programme about child abuse and they were saying how we all must be vigilant and keep our eyes open and – and so on. There were some real horror stories about children who'd been abused by their fathers for years without anyone realising."

"Grace! Do you mean to tell me you're accusing Clive of incest! With his own daughter?"

"No, no. Not really . . . " she stammered, alarmed by the glint in Leonard's eye.

"Grace, I don't know what's got into you lately. All these books and newspapers are filling your head with rubbish. For God's sake get a grip on yourself. We're the middle classes. Incest doesn't happen to people like us. I strongly advise you not to read any more of this kind of thing until you can learn to take a more objective attitude towards it. And that goes for the radio too."

"All right," said Grace, thoroughly humbled.

"And you should set your own house in order," mumbled Leonard, turning over and preparing for sleep, "before you start throwing stones at other people."

What did he mean? She switched off the light feeling troubled.

While Jade was away Lallie spent her days in the British Museum, researching the social history of Ireland during the thirties and forties when Rachel was growing up. She found her thoughts constantly turning to her own childhood for comparisons. This was a nuisance. She'd thought she was finished with all that, thought she'd succeeded in making a fresh start after her mother's death. And now, suddenly, she found herself overtaken by an explosion of memory.

She was back in the north-east. A schoolgirl. She felt the hard floor beneath her knees during school prayers, the splinters that snagged at her woollen stockings when she stood up. She heard the dreary voices with their flat Teesside accents telling her to walk, not run, in the corridor, to sit up straight, not to pull faces. She clenched her fists not wanting to become bitter. Only by erasing memory would she be able to avoid the slow corrosion of the soul that bitterness brings.

Nevertheless, walking to the tube station or wandering aimlessly about the empty flat, small scenes would suddenly flash into her mind and she'd have to pause to catch her breath. It was all there still, then. It hadn't gone away. Simply been overlaid by her years of success in London, first as a history undergraduate, then at the Warburg and finally, as Jade's researcher, lover and friend.

Lallie never discussed with Jade her years in the north. It wasn't that she feared Jade wouldn't understand but that, on the contrary, she'd understand too well. Understand the whole humiliating struggle on which her youth had been spent. Besides, Jade got irritated whenever Lallie started to dwell on the past. The grinding drabness of lower middle class life in Stockton, a small northern town on the edge of a huge industrial site, wasn't the stuff out of which films could be made. And now that industry which had sucked in whole families, fathers, sons and daughters through its greedy jaws, had spat them out again, closed up its jaws and gone away leaving, if pictures on the television were anything to go by, houses boarded up, shops closed, entire communities devastated.

It had been one huge con job. About a hundred years ago industrialists had moved into the area bearing gifts and bribes. They'd taken the local people into their factories and heaped them with material goods to keep them there. But no one thought of bringing in art and theatre and music to lift the people's spirits. No – beer and darts were good enough for them. If they wanted more, they could move down south (but it was well-known that northerners were an ignorant, backward lot – even their churches were grimy, red brick affairs).

And when, one by one, the factories closed down and the rich industrialists had moved to better parts, the material things began to dry up too. Soon there was nothing left for the inhabitants of Stockton but drink and gaming parlours and a vague sense of camaraderie. Not that they protested much about this. It wasn't in their nature.

Lallie thought of the teachers in her school. Her mother had had romantic notions of training her daughter to be a lady and so she'd gone, with the help of her eleven plus, to a private day school for girls and been taught by a series of spinsters, some gently faded, some sad, some sarcastic, one a bully. Almost all of them ignorant, or if not ignorant and cheerful, then defeated, which was worse. Not even despairing. No. That would be too strong a word, too tragic. Rather, they were resigned to defeat, it was woven into the texture of daily life up there. Their most characteristic gesture, a sad smile and a gentle shrug of the shoulders. Their only means of escape, bee keeping, or tapestry work, or a quiet tipple in rented rooms.

When she'd told them she wanted to write books, the English teacher had laughed dryly and said, "I wanted to do that too, once." Everywhere in Stockton there was a general acknowledgement that one would never do the things one wanted, never have the things one desired. Lallie had sometimes imagined she could smell defeat in the air. It hung around the town, as unpleasant and corroding as the evil-smelling smog that on fine days drifted over from the factories on the coast, blocking out the sun.

It had been a strange aim in that rough town, to turn girls into ladies. Much better to have taught them some useful trade, educated them about strikes, politics, the economy. They'd learned nothing in depth, neither music, nor art, nor science which took place in a leaking prefab in the schoolyard. And so her youth had been largely robbed from her, stolen and spent in the hard, dull process of educating herself from books, since the teachers hardly sufficed. She remembered long summer evenings spent poring over maths tables and grammar books, laboriously translating by herself every word of a Molière play because the teacher said it was too difficult for the rest of the class. Whilst from outside her window came the laughter of children playing hopscotch in the street or the shouts of her classmates on the way to the pub.

How could she explain all this to Jade who'd grown up to the sound of Fauré and Brahms, to people around her discussing Joyce and Synge? It wasn't Jade who'd stepped inside an art gallery for the first time at nineteen and felt her stomach tighten in panic as she realised her ignorance.

There were other memories too, more appalling than these. Lallie succeeded, for the present, in keeping them at bay. By the time Jade arrived back from Ireland, she'd managed to reason herself onto an even keel.

CHAPTER SEVEN

ON JADE'S FIRST EVENING HOME THEY WENT OUT FOR A MEAL, sauntering arm in arm down Kensington Church Street. Past the antique shops with their black cherub clocks and glass chandeliers. Past a shop with a bible open in the window and another with a sign saying "ironer wanted." They paused to look at a pair of green Chinese dragons and saw themselves reflected in the shop window. Jade with her blonde ponytail, Armani jeans and leather jacket, her collar turned up against the November chill. Lallie with her cropped black hair and pale blue eyes, in loose yellow trousers and striped jacket. They smiled at themselves and walked on past the laundrette and the delicatessen to the small French restaurant halfway down the street.

There, at a table covered with a pink cloth and decorated with a couple of carnations in a Perrier bottle, they ate salmon mousse and vegetarian lasagne, and Jade told Lallie about her meeting with Nicholas Johnson.

"I've struck gold with him. I'm beginning to build up a picture of Rachel's childhood. There should be a certain amount of mystery in the film. My grandmother's death, for instance. And violence – my grandfather's bullying which forced Rachel to retreat into a world of make-believe (I'm beginning to understand now why she always preferred to live in a fantasy world). And yet I'm still convinced the film has to hinge on Stefan. It was he who taught my mother to turn her fears and her dreams into art. But how?"

"I've an idea," Lallie said, when they were drinking their

coffee. "Why don't you leave it with me for a while? I'd like to try and write something around that Stefan episode. There're similarities between your mother's life and mine."

Jade looked surprised. "Such as?"

"Struggle. That's something she and I have in common. It was different for you. You were born in the right place."

"I doubt if my mother thought so." Jade pulled a face. "She always made it quite clear I was a mistake."

Lallie glanced at her. "Will you let me do this? Write about your mother, I mean? It might," she hesitated, "it might help me understand things about myself."

Jade shrugged. "All right. If you like." She reached across the table and took Lallie's hand. "Come on, snuggler, I'm sick of talking about the past. Let's go home to bed. I've missed you."

In the early morning in Munich Joachim sat in a bar drinking coffee, thinking confusedly of Christabel and Gunter. He'd got drunk again last night and now his head ached. He glanced around at the other breakfasters, sallow and sickly-looking beneath the harsh lights. Ezekiel's valley of dry bones.

His nerves were on edge. The least sound jarred on him and filled him with loathing for his fellow human beings. The girl behind the counter was banging plates about. A desire to scream rose up inside him. He felt an urge to go over to her, seize her by the shoulders and shake her. Kick her. Knock her head against the counter till she bled all over her face. Then the banging stopped, his anger ebbed and a feeling of shame flowed in to take its place.

"Our civilisation is cracking," Cornelius had said. "Our endless quest for material comforts masks the emptiness of our lives. Look at the increase in violent crimes, in armed robbery, in rape. And those appalling video nasties children seem to enjoy so much. Our philosophy has come to a dead end. Our language is disintegrating. Soon we'll be communicating in grunts. Western civilisation is in decay. We've lost all belief in ourselves."

Cornelius is right. Joachim bent his steps towards work. We're living in decadent times. No man can trust his neighbour. Christ is being crucified all over again. He thought of the Maundy Thursday service which for him always summed up the end of the world. The church in darkness, the altar stripped, the fleeing figures of the apostles.

I am becoming apocalyptic, he thought. Something is surely about to happen.

Lallie felt the past begin to take her over. On the tube, in the library, in the supermarket, images from her life in Stockton flashed into her mind. She found it difficult to concentrate, became increasingly absentminded. At the same time she was trying to work out a convincing account of Rachel's relationship with Stefan.

One night she had a dream. It convinced her Proust had been quite wrong about memory. There are some things that are indelibly burned into our consciousness and have no need of madeleines to bring them back.

In her dream she'd attended a class reunion. Quite by chance. They hadn't invited her. She'd happened to come out of a meeting and bumped into a couple of her old schoolfriends in the hotel foyer. Embarrassed, they'd said, "Your invitation must have gone astray in the post" and they'd led her into a room.

There they all were. Fatter, greyer, heavily made up. She went round them all saying hello. She received a few surprises. Wendy, a big, blonde woman in a tweed suit, had married a divorced dentist with an eleven year old son and had since produced four of her own. A remarkable feat, thought Lallie, for someone who'd planned to marry a rich old man and never ever have children. There was ginger-haired Clare who'd been captain of games and was now games mistress back at the old school. There was Sandra, the dark-haired sexpot never without a boyfriend from the age of twelve. She'd married straight from school, was living on a council estate somewhere in Hardwick and going out mornings cutting hair. Her eldest boy was well into his teens and had already been nicked for joyriding.

The only one she hugged was Jenny. They'd played together from the age of four, fought and separated at twelve, come together again after a year and were inseparable till they reached fifteen and found they hadn't the energy left to go on arguing the toss. One Monday morning Jenny had simply stopped speaking to her.

It was Jenny who'd instilled in Lallie what courage she possessed. Knowing that if she fell off the tree or refused a dare, Jenny would be watching, contempt on her face. With Jenny she'd learned that friendship had to be earned. When they were still quite small Jenny'd planned that they should creep out of their houses at midnight and meet up on a patch of wasteland on the edge of the town for a feast. Lallie hadn't dared back out. She was terrified of the dark but more terrified of losing Jenny's respect. She remembered the overwhelming sense of relief when Jenny had phoned at four to call it off.

There'd been moments of sweetness too. Falling off the wall bars in the gym and the second before she lapsed into unconsciousness hearing Jenny scream her name from across the room and realising she still cared even though, by this time, they hadn't spoken for eighteen months. Yes, Jenny had been her first real love. She'd since then had one or two loves like that (always with women), where she'd felt tied to the other person by a bond so deep it seemed to reach back beyond birth. Yet living with them for any length of time had proved impossible . . . until Jade.

In her dream she'd asked where Robina was. There was a silence. Someone giggled nervously. It was like being back at school.

"Haven't you heard?" said Jenny. She'd always had the courage to withstand group pressure. "She died last year. Cancer."

Lallie turned away. The shock had brought tears to her eyes. Only Jenny noticed. The others immediately began talking of something else.

"But you weren't particularly close, were you?" said Jenny, laying a hand on her shoulder.

"No, but . . . " How could she explain? Robina had been her idol. Not a friend, like Jenny, but someone to be worshipped from afar. In a school of beautiful girls, of beautiful middle-class girls filling in their adolescence before marriage, Robina took your breath away. She had long black hair and brown skin. Almond shaped eyes. A solemn face, with a broad, smooth forehead. She'd been Lallie's ideal of beauty in a woman.

"But it wasn't her physical beauty that fascinated me during those years at school," said Lallie, recounting her dream to Jade the next day, "so much as the air of tragedy that clung to her. She resembled those nineteenth-century paintings of Jewesses. In fact, for all anyone knew, she may have been Jewish. She'd been adopted as a baby by an elderly couple, together with her sister who was three years older and not actually related to her. 'Any one of you could be my real sister,' she'd said one day, looking around at us all, a small girl trying to come to terms with the mystery of her birth. We glanced at one another sheepishly. It was highly unlikely. Our faded and exhausted mothers could hardly have had that kind of past. We thought it terrible not to know who one's real parents were. I began to see Robina as tragic. She didn't get on with her adoptive family. Her elderly parents were dull. Her sister took up with a bad crowd, started smoking and drinking and left school at sixteen, pregnant. She was sent away to have her baby. For me, her sister's fate increased the aura of tragedy round Robina. Though she laughed and joked with the others, for me, she was always a haunted figure."

Jade leant forward, resting her elbows on the table. "What happened to her after she left school?"

Lallie shrugged. "Nothing very remarkable. She told us she was going on a catering course. Then I came south and never saw her again. Except that once, back up visiting my mother, I bumped into Clare who told me Robina had put on weight, which I found unlikely."

"How did the dream end?" asked Jade.

"I can't remember very clearly. It didn't have a definite ending. It faded away as dreams often do. Mine, anyway." There was a silence. "I thought I'd done with the past but it, apparently, hasn't finished with me."

"I wonder if she ever tried to discover who her real parents were?" mused Jade. "You know," she stood up and began clearing away the breakfast things, "I don't believe that dream had anything to do with your past. Don't you see? The child without parents, that's me. No one knows who my father was and you've been helping me rediscover my mother. Your mind has been working overtime and made a link, in your dream, between your childhood idol and me. Life has repeated itself for you."

How selfish you are, thought Lallie. You turn everything back to yourself. It was *my* dream, *my* past. Then she felt foolish for wasn't it precisely her past she was trying to avoid? Close behind that dream stood her mother. So far, Lallie had managed to suppress the memories of her but she felt them edge daily closer to the surface. For safety's sake she immersed herself in inventing scenes between Rachel and Stefan.

"Stupid!" exclaimed Joachim. "Stupid, self-absorbed idiot!"

Shoppers in the pedestrian precinct stopped and stared at him. He continued his argument with himself in silence. So someone betrayed you, what does that matter? It's happened to bigger men than you. It happened to God, if you believe Christ was God, he added, aware of his doubts on that subject. What did God do? He went on loving. I must love, love, love, he thought gloomily. I must not become like Katrin. He clenched his fists and walked on fast. The possibility of ever again loving Gunter seemed remote.

The world's becoming a dry place. Dry and dull. All because of a friend's treachery. And my job. And my wife. I've lost my passion. He gazed with unseeing eyes at the woman opposite. Christabel, where are you? I'm dead without you.

It was no use. Grace finished reading her way through the pile of information on social work Sally Roberts had sent her. They were too young and too committed. She sighed. She'd do it the old-fashioned way, her mother's way. She'd ask the vicar on Sunday if he knew of anyone in the parish who'd like a visit. A nice old age pensioner who needed her shopping done for her. Nothing too ambitious. She heard her mother's voice. "That's right, dear. A spot of charity work's a good thing for a woman your age. So long as it doesn't take away too much time from the family."

She grimaced. Life seemed to be settling itself down into a familiar pattern. Were all daughters doomed to repeat their mothers' lives? If so, God help Emma and Carolyn.

"What are you reading?" enquired Leonard, coming into the drawing-room at that moment and observing his wife on the sofa surrounded by leaflets.

"Odds and ends." Grace hurriedly gathered up her leaflets. "It's amazing what comes through our letterbox."

He caught sight of a title: *Bringing up a Family on the Dole*. He wasn't encouraged.

"By the way, I was going to ask you," she continued, deftly changing the subject, "how are the shares going? Is that anonymous buyer still snapping them up?"

"He seems to have stopped, deliberately and sneakily, at four point nine per cent, so we still don't know who he is." He tried another peek at the leaflets. Grace stuffed them down the side of the sofa. He sighed. "Perhaps I'll ask Clive. He knows a lot of dubious characters in the business world." He flopped down into an armchair. "Why?"

"I thought I might buy a share or two myself," she said airily. "Then I could come to your meetings."

"What for?"

"To protest about various matters. For instance, the lawn outside the factory gates needs cutting. I noticed that the other day."

Leonard raised his eyes to the ceiling.

"And then there's the South African question. I hope you haven't got business there, Leonard."

He shifted around in his chair. "Only a small sales outlet," he replied cautiously. "About five per cent of our turnover."

"There you are," she said triumphantly. "I could protest about that."

Her boyfriend's a leftie. He plucked sadly at the arm of his chair. He's encouraging her to sabotage my firm. She's preparing herself for life on the dole when I go out of business. If it comes to a divorce, will the girls take my side?

Poor Leonard, she thought, it isn't his fault. I expect lots of firms have links with South Africa. I just happen to know about his. This is what comes of having no occupation, I latch on to my husband's. I've got to do something of my own. I'll tackle the vicar on Sunday.

Jade received a letter from Nicholas Johnson. She handed it to Lallie.

"Here, take a look at this. It might help you."

Lallie spread the letter out on the table in their flat, which was where she was mainly working these days, drafting scenes between Rachel and Stefan and tearing them up.

"There's a kind of dishonesty in silence," the letter ran. "That evening in Dun Laoghaire I felt you were pressing me to tell you more about Stefan. I kept silent out of resentment, partly, and partly out of fear that, if I once started talking about him, things would get out of control and the picture would become distorted.

"However, you asked about the past and I feel an obligation not to withhold anything that may be of help. Evidence may be falsified as much by what is not said as by what is. I find it easier to write down what I feel about Stefan than to discuss him with you, face to face. Writing has always been my favourite medium of expression; it's easier to censor if one's emotions get out of hand.

"Stefan had all the worst faults: cruelty, dishonesty, indolence." There was a line drawn through this sentence. "There, you see, the censorship has already begun. I've crossed that line out, yet not so heavily that you can't read it. Still, it's crossed out, my conscience is salved. Let me begin again.

Stefan was one of those people who believe love should be absolute. He persuaded Rachel that our 'love', based on years of friendship, was a paltry thing . . . I suppose what I objected to most was his tactics. He broke up her life and tried to reshape it to suit his own ideas of what a woman's life should be. You say you want to show the point at which the girl turned into the actress. But Stefan was never interested in Rachel becoming an artist. He couldn't bear rivals. No, he wanted to mould her for his own convenience. And she very nearly let him.

"He played on her worst fears. At the best of times she'd wake up in the morning panic-stricken, full of nameless terrors at what the day would bring. She'd have been destroyed, I'm convinced, if she'd stayed with him. He confused her, muddled her emotions, told her she was trivial and conventional. She lost her centre, that core each of us are supposed to have, that keeps us stable.

"When she finally left him, something had broken in her forever. What shall I call it? The capacity for a gentle, settled happiness . . . Yes, I expect you've guessed by now, I tried to get Rachel back after she left Stefan. She refused me. Stefan had done his work well. He'd succeeded in implanting in her a fear of me, a fear that with me, she'd become ordinary again, a woman without passion, a little girl looking through the window at life.

"But perhaps I'm biased. Why blame Stefan? She was a mother by then and quite well able to make up her own mind. Why blame him for her rejection of me?

"I leave you to draw your own conclusions, my dear. I see Stefan as a dangerous and destructive man, but maybe you'll think that mere prejudice on my part. It's up to you to weigh the evidence. At any rate, I felt I had to complete my side of the story. Be a credible witness, so to speak. You must be the jury.

Best Wishes,
Nicholas Johnson."

It was an odd letter. Formal in tone and hedged round with a lawyer's qualifications. Nevertheless, at the heart of it, was an honesty that was beyond question.

Lallie put down the letter. Now she understood.

Rachel's illumination, her flight to freedom, hadn't come step by painful step, as in her own case, but in one fell swoop, in the shape of Stefan. Only someone as brutal and cruel as he could have peeled off the layers from the nervous, awkward girl to reveal the artist beneath. He'd set her free, though that had never been his intention. As Nicholas had said, his aim had been to educate her into understanding himself. But in doing that he'd shown her the way for an artist to be; he'd taught her to take her gift seriously. And Lallie didn't doubt that for Rachel every painful minute of the three years she'd spent with him had turned out to be a small price to pay. With Stefan she'd been deprived of all she'd loved. Husband, friends, father (who was scandalised and refused to have anything more to do with her). She'd come out of those years strong and fierce and independent. No wonder she'd refused Nicholas.

Yes, thought Lallie, they were perfectly matched, Rachel and Stefan. Sadist and victim. Rachel must have lived every one of those days with Stefan in fear and trembling. Trembling that she'd lose him and so lose the small flame, the best part of herself, which was beginning to flicker into life. Fear that he'd demand too much of her, find her too trivial or unworthy, and she'd run back to Nicholas and so lose herself forever. There were times when she must really have believed God was speaking to her through this Jew, Stefan. The dark, wrathful God of the Old Testament, chiding her, reproaching her, giving her one last chance to set her life in order.

It was a situation familiar to Lallie. The bully and the bullied. She'd encountered it once or twice in her own life. Not that Jade bullied her. No, that was too strong a word. All the same, cracks were starting to appear. Small differences as yet. But she could foresee the day when one of them would have to compromise – and she didn't think compromise was in Jade's nature. She was like Stefan in that. She'd protect her work and her vision, even against those who loved her best.

Lallie fingered Nicholas's letter and began to see a way round her problem. After all, what was fiction but an enlargement of life?

The end of the Sunday service found Grace hovering nervously in the porch. If she was honest with herself, she had to admit she didn't much like Father Keogh. He was a stout, gruff Northern Irishman with a manner she found decidedly blunt. If not downright rude. As when he'd suggested that five per cent of his parishioners' income would be a suitable contribution to parish funds or when he'd criticised those who came to church twice a year and then expected him to marry them and bury them.

"Could I have a word with you, vicar?" Oh gosh, he liked to be called Father.

Father Keogh glanced at his watch. "I should have been at another service three miles away five minutes ago. Is it very urgent? Could you pop round to the vicarage some time during the week, Mrs er . . . er?"

"Napier," she replied, well aware that this was his favourite technique for emphasising a parishioner's less than satisfactory attendance at his services. The man got above himself.

Nevertheless, on Tuesday, she went round to the vicarage. It was in a row of rather nasty terraced houses in the poorer part of the parish. The house next door to it was boarded up. The vicarage gate was rusty and almost came off its hinges when she pushed it open. Father Keogh opened the door himself.

"Hello Mrs er . . . er . . . Napier. Come in."

From somewhere up at the top of the house came the sound of a flute. She'd heard the Keoghs took in lodgers. It had been the subject of some contention in the parish. He led the way across the threadbare hall carpet to his study. It was heaped with books stacked up on the floor, packed into cardboard boxes, or lying strewn across his desk. It was also extremely cold. A single bar electric fire seemed to be the only source of heat. He offered her a sagging armchair. She sat down.

"I won't ask you to take off your coat." He grinned.

"I thought the parish had arranged for central heating to be put in?" Where was her money was going to then? She stared at Father Keogh's stout frame. Did he have a drink problem?

"They put in oil. We can only afford to run it a couple of hours a day."

"Oh."

She flushed bright red. She must double her Easter contribution.

He glanced at her. "What can I do for you, Mrs Napier? Would you like a cup of coffee?"

"Yes, please," she replied and then immediately regretted it for he went out and made it himself.

"I didn't realise your wife worked," she remarked as he came back carrying a tray with a kettle, a jar of Nescafé and a carton of milk. "Or is she out shopping?"

"She does supply teaching in some of the schools around here. The money comes in useful. Is that enough coffee? I don't want to be stingy but we try not to go mad with it."

He handed her a cup, took two sips from his own and then sat back waiting for her to announce the reason for her visit.

She gazed at him rather blankly. Why did people ask to see their vicar? Weddings, funerals, the summer fête, spiritual problems? Did people still have spiritual problems? She pulled herself together, explained that she had time on her hands now her daughters were away at school and was there something she could do in the parish?

To her surprise, far from jumping at her offer, Father Keogh began questioning her rather closely about her training (none), previous experience (none).

"Have you never been in paid employment at all?" he asked, looking at her, she thought, as if she was some relic left over from the Stone Age.

"I did start to train as a nurse but my father got sick. It was a long illness. I went home to help my mother. Then shortly after he died, my mother got ill too. After her death I met my husband. So you see, till now, there's never been time."

"Mm." He looked at her with a shade more sympathy. He sat back, pressed the tips of his fingers together and considered her for a few moments. Then apparently he came to a decision.

"I don't know if you're aware, Mrs Napier, living where you do, that in this part of the parish there are many families who barely manage to survive. Who live in fact below the poverty line." He paused and glanced at her.

Yes, all right, she thought. It's not my fault I live in a big house. It's just worked out that way.

He went on. "And a number of elderly people living on their own who need a bit of shopping done for them or even just someone to chat to now and then. The cuts have meant that social services don't bother much with the mobile elderly now. They have their hands full with the infirm."

Shopping and a chat, that sounds my line, thought Grace. She was about to say as much when he rushed on,

"Then there are the single mothers, the homeless and Sedgefield Estate. Nearly all the families on that estate are deprived in some way or other. Very often they need someone to fight their battles for them with the DHSS. Someone who can fill in a form correctly and who speaks with a middle class accent. Oh yes, it helps," he added, as Grace looked shocked. "But to be really useful, you'd have to understand how the social services operate. Why don't you go home and read up about it? In the meantime I'll give you the address of one or two people you might visit in the parish." He got up, went over to his desk and shifted a few books around.

"I've the name of a girl here. She's homeless and living in a bed and breakfast place with her two babies until the council gets round to rehousing her. She lacks an older person, a woman, to advise her. You have daughters, I believe? There may be something you can do for her."

He handed her the address.

"Debbie Jackson she's called. She comes from a large family living on Sedgefield Estate. You could visit them too, perhaps." He smirked slightly. "But I'd start with the girl."

CHAPTER EIGHT

"I'M LEAVING! I'M LEAVING! I'M LEAVING!" RACHEL SCREAMS.

"OK. Go." Stefan's thin lips curl. "Without me, you'll be nothing. Go back to your stupid husband and your comfortable Familienleben. I need a woman who knows how to be strong."

"Don't say that!" She sobs. "I've done my best. I've tried to change."

He looks thoughtful. "I doubt whether anyone can really change their personality. I was wrong to encourage you to try. You lack the necessary moral courage."

She buries her head in her hands, oblivious to the stares of passers-by (they're sitting on a bench in Phoenix Park). "I need more time," she murmurs. "Give me more time, Stefan. Please."

He crosses his legs and lights a cigarette. "I need a woman who'll support me in my work. Stand with me against society. A woman who knows how to subordinate her own ambitions, her life, her very self, to me. Quite frankly, I don't think you're up to it, Rachel. If I was an ordinary man, like your husband, it wouldn't matter. But I'm a poet. Poets have been ruined by their women. You ask me to be pleasant to other people. Pleasant!" He spits out the word. "I don't aim to be pleasant. I despise pleasantness. Why can't you be more like Shaw's wife? She protects him from people instead of asking him to be pleasant to them."

She gives a little moan. "Don't leave me, Stefan, not yet. I know you will in the end. But not yet."

Slowly and deliberately he grinds his cigarette under his heel. He turns to her and takes her hands in his. They make an odd couple, sitting here on the bench. The small, shabby man with his thick black hair and scuffed shoes and the young girl in pink cotton dress and white socks and sandals. Even the most superficial of observers can see at once they don't fit.

"Rachel," he says more gently, "I can't afford to give you any more time. I need to concentrate on my poetry. I'm tired of explaining to you things I shouldn't have to explain. Taking you to films, choosing books for you, trying to educate you. If we stay together, you'll have to do all this for yourself. I need proof you love me enough to do it."

And Rachel, accustomed by life with her old bully of a father to equate love with pain, murmurs, "I do love you enough, Stefan, I do."

He leans across and kisses her hair, then turns her face towards him and kisses her long and fiercely on the lips.

"Stay with me," he murmurs. "I will set you free. You'll be destroyed if you go back to your old life."

They rise from the bench and walk, arm in arm, to a secret spot they know of in amongst the trees and there make love.

Lallie paused, her eyes filling with tears. There'd been a time when she and Jade had rowed and made love afterwards. Now they just rowed, or not even rowed . . . their quarrels had degenerated into half-hearted bickering, each moving her arguments along well-worn grooves.

She turned her thoughts back to Rachel. She'd have met Stefan at a poetry reading or perhaps in a café – that Bewley's Jade sometimes talked about. It would be obvious that Stefan wasn't unused to chatting up pretty girls, that in fact it was one of his specialities. They'd stay talking for hours. He'd speak of his life in Russia, his poetry. And listening, Rachel would realise that here was a man who could make her dreams come real.

Lallie rose from the table. Yes, this is what she'd felt, meeting Jade for the first time. She'd spent years up in Stockton reading about artists' lives whilst Jade had actually lived among them, been part, from the very beginning, of a charmed circle of writers and theatre folk. She went across to the window and stood looking out at the yellow building opposite. Too late now for bitterness. Too late to wonder whether the long hard years of study had crushed the creative spark from her; whether, born in a different place, she too might have been an artist . . .

Rachel left the safety of marriage with Nicholas and moved in with Stefan. In Ireland in the 1950s it was a scandalous thing to do. Her father disowned her, as did most of her friends. "Stefan is cruel, selfish and he tells lies," she wrote to her nanny, in an attempt to hang onto her approval at least. "He's wicked, I know, but beyond that is something else, something pure, not recognised by the world and which surpasses its conventional standards of good and bad." (Here, Lallie saw Jade tossing her head and saying, "What do I care about ordinary people?"). "Poppycock!" Rachel's nanny wrote back.

Another scene . . . A room serving as bedroom, study and kitchen. A single bed stands along one wall. It is covered with some dirty-looking sheets and blankets. In the corner is a cracked sink and beside it, a small gas ring. In the centre, in front of the grimy window, stands a table heaped with books and papers and a typewriter. A thick film of dust lies over everything.

Beneath the grubby sheets Stefan sleeps. It's eleven o'clock in the morning. The door of the tiny bedsit opens and Rachel comes in carrying two rounds of egg sandwiches. Stefan's breakfast, purchased at a nearby café. The room smells of stale cigarette smoke. An empty bottle of wine stands on the floor. Stefan stayed up writing into the early morning. Rachel goes over to the sink and fills a pan to make his coffee. He drinks it in a glass, thick and black, with four spoonfuls of sugar. When it's ready she brings the coffee and the sandwiches over to him.

"Stefan," she whispers. "Stefan, I've made your breakfast."

He grunts, opens his eyes and gropes around for his watch. Looks at the time and groans again. "I need more sleep. Leave it on the table. I hope you've remembered my cigarettes?"

She nods and puts the tray down on the table, balancing it on top of some books. She hesitates.

"Stefan, I – I'm going out for a walk. I'll be back in a little while."

He opens one eye. "Remember we're going to see that film at one. Don't be late." He disapproves of walks. "Have you finished that book on Shaw yet?"

"No."

"Make sure you get back in time to finish it before we leave. It's simply sloppy to see a film before reading the book."

"Yes, Stefan."

He rolls over onto his stomach. "Ugh! My head feels so heavy. I smoked too many cigarettes last night. You must stop me smoking so much."

She picks up a jumper and a shirt lying on the floor and folds them. Stefan hates disorder and Rachel, brought up in her father's huge house, with a housekeeper and a nanny, has never learned to be tidy. It's a constant source of friction between them.

She creeps softly down the stairs and opens and closes the front door without a sound. She's living here illegally with Stefan. Their landlord occupies the basement flat. She suffers tortures every time she has to go in or out, but they're too poor to move.

She walks rapidly down the road, over the bridge and into Lower Leeson Street. She crosses the canal and hurries towards Stephen's Green. Every few minutes she looks at her watch. She told Stefan she was going for a walk but in fact she's hurrying to meet Nicholas. The first time she's seen him in six months. She feels choked with anticipation. Her heart's beating fast and there's a tightness across her chest. She tries to walk more quickly but her legs have turned to cotton wool.

When she enters Bewley's she sees Nick straightaway, sitting at a table in the corner, a cup and a jug of coffee in front of him. She hesitates, then walks slowly towards him and stands before his chair. He raises his head and smiles. Rachel is surprised to find her eyes filling with tears.

She swallows. "You look thinner."

He stands up, touches her arm in greeting, then pulls out a chair for her. Moved by his gentle courtesy (how could she have forgotten that?), she sits down. He beckons to the waitress to fetch another cup and saucer.

"How are you?"

"Fine." She smiles, rather wanly.

The waitress brings a cup and he pours her some coffee.

"Still one sugar?"

She nods, pleased he's remembered.

"Are you hungry? Do you want to eat something?"

She's about to say no when she remembers she hasn't had any breakfast and that if she eats now she'll save money on lunch.

"I wouldn't mind a sandwich," she says. Then feels bad. It's Stefan who's taught her to eat at other people's expense, pointing out that otherwise they'd often have gone without a meal. Nevertheless, it feels wrong. Nevertheless, she eats the sandwich.

"I've got something for you." He draws out a small package from his jacket and hands it to her.

She unwraps it with the eagerness of someone unused to receiving presents. It's a bottle of perfume. She turns it over in her hand delightedly. "My favourite. You remembered." She unscrews the top, sniffs it, then dabs some on her neck and wrists. As she does so, she hears Stefan's voice scoffing, "Perfume! How trite!" She puts down the bottle hurriedly and shivers. He's stolen all my happiness, she thinks.

"Thank you, Nick." Her voice sounds hollow.

"All right for money?" he asks, playing with his spoon, not looking at her.

"Yes. Thanks." She's glad now that she's put on her best skirt. Her clothes are getting decidedly shabby but Nick mustn't know that. "I'm looking for a job," she adds.

"You shouldn't have to."

"I want to. It'll make me more independent. Give me a chance to stand on my own two feet for a change. It will be good for me." Too many excuses? she wonders. The truth is, Stefan's broke.

"What will you do? You're not trained for anything."

"I've one or two ideas." The vagueness is deliberate. She intends waitressing, but Nick would consider that beneath her.

Suddenly, he reaches over and gently touches the side of her face. "What's that bruise on your cheek?"

"Nothing," she replies hastily. "I – I fell."

He gazes at her with so much feeling in his eyes that she has to look away. He takes her hand. She stiffens. "Rachel, I'm in the Dublin office for the next few days learning the ropes. I've borrowed a friend's flat. Why don't you come round tonight and I'll cook you a meal?"

Dinner with her husband. How warm and safe it sounds. No arguments, no reprimands. Just a pleasant chat about old times. She feels a sudden yearning to retreat from the frightening new world into which Stefan has led her, a world of complicated choices and terrible decisions.

"Yes, Nick, I'll come." She looks at her watch and almost gasps. She's going to be horribly late. "I have to go."

He releases her hand. "Have to?" he queries.

She tightens her lips.

He pays the bill and helps her on with her jacket.

"See you at eight then," he says outside the café.

She nods, knowing that she won't be free to come and that even if she is, Stefan has taught her to distrust the kind of safe, easy happiness Nick's offering. She watches Nick turn up his coat collar, smile and walk away. She watches till he turns the corner and she can see him no more. This is the last time she ever sees her husband.

She runs all the way back. Their landlord is pottering in the front garden. She nods in the direction of his stubbornly turned back. It's a quarter to one. Guests are allowed during the day.

She enters the room in a rush. Stefan, writing at the table, turns round as she comes in.

"Where the hell have you been?" he snaps, his black brows drawn together.

"Out." She turns her face away. "For a walk. I told you."

"A long walk," he says suspiciously.

"Yes."

"We'll have to hurry or we'll miss the start of the film and that'll be your fault."

He makes her run all the way to the cinema. She sinks into her seat feeling dizzy.

"It's stupid and sloppy," he hisses, "not finishing that book."

Bloody Shaw, she thinks, and bloodier Shaw's wife.

Afterwards they meet up with some of Stefan's friends in a café to discuss the film. When the café closes they drift on to a pub where Stefan in a loud voice expounds his theories on aesthetics to a group of young admirers in shabby jumpers who keep buying him drinks.

From time to time, he turns to Rachel and says, "Have you understood? Pay attention now. This is serious." Once he puts his arm around her and says, "This is Rachel. I'm remaking her." For that's what he's attempting: her transformation from the shallow, trivial, morally confused girl he believes her to be, into a woman whom it will not humiliate him to love.

However, for most of the evening he ignores her. She thinks of Nick waiting and waiting for her, the meal cooked, a bottle of wine cooling in the fridge. How comfortable it would have been . . . On and on he goes, rasping out sentences in his harsh Russian accent. She scarcely understands a word he's saying but his groupies do. Some of them even take notes. Pain and anger rise up inside her. She has to make him stop. She has to make him notice her. She interrupts him:

"No women of genius? What about Virginia Woolf? She put into words feelings that had never been described before."

"She adapted Joyce's technique. Anyway, she was a snob." He smiles. "Rachel thinks (though in her case, thinking is an overstatement) that women . . . "

Summoning up her last reserves of courage she slaps him. Right then and there, in the middle of the pub. For a moment there's silence. Some of the groupies look embarrassed, others irritated or even anxious. She wonders whether he's going to hit her back. Then he laughs.

"Well," he says, clapping an arm around her shoulders, "perhaps I deserved that."

He's that strong. She realises again how much he fascinates her. For he too lives on dreams. Only his dreams are cruel dreams. They harm everyone but himself.

They make love when they get home, slowly and silently, till she thinks she will drown in passion. Utterly satisfied she falls asleep with his arms around her. At two, she wakes to find him out of bed and writing at the table. She pushes back the bedclothes and pads over to him.

"What is it?" she whispers.

"Shaw's dead. They've announced it on the radio. I'm writing a poem."

Half asleep though she is, she feels the news pierce her like a knife. Dead! The man she's been told to admire, whose works she's been reading for weeks, whose wife she's learned to hate and envy. Suddenly she thinks of Nick and in her blurred sleepy state confuses the two events.

He's been waiting for her all evening. She has to speak to him. She rummages in her bag for coins. Throwing her coat over her shoulders, she slips down to the pay phone in the hall. He answers on the second ring. Has he been waiting up for her then?

"Nick, it's me. I'm sorry, I couldn't come round. Something turned up."

"It's OK. Are you all right? I was worried about you."

She suddenly longs to tell him everything about her life with Stefan. Is she mad to stay with him? In the past it's always been Nick she's turned to for advice. But she's cut herself off from the past. Besides she knows what he'd say.

"Yes, Nick, I'm all right."

"I love you very much."

"I know. I'm sorry." Is that the landlord moving around in the basement? "I have to go now."

She replaces the receiver and creeps back upstairs.

He's finished writing and is sitting on the edge of the bed, smoking a cigarette.

"What were you doing?"

"Phoning Nick," she answers, too sleepy to invent an excuse.

He glowers. "I tell you that Shaw is dead and I begin a poem, perhaps a very great poem, and your response is to go and phone your stupid husband."

She stands in her coat in the middle of the room biting her nails.

"We're both wasting our time, Rachel. You'll never change. You're as shallow and trivial as when I first met you. I was beginning to think there were some signs of hope, but I can't blind myself any longer. My love for you humiliates me as an artist and a man." He inhales fiercely.

"Please Stefan, I had to phone."

Smoke curls out through his nostrils.

"Whenever I speak with anyone else, I have the feeling of discussing things which are important, but when I talk with you, Rachel, I find myself immersed in absolute trivia. As usual this conversation we're having now will turn out to be morally degrading, intellectually humiliating and artistically disastrous."

"Stefan, please. I'm trying to change. You said yourself I was making progress."

He stands up and begins pacing the room. Now and then ash from his cigarette drops onto the carpet.

"Yes, and then you go and phone that idiotic husband of yours. For all I know, you may be preparing to go back to him."

"I'm not, I'm not. I promise. That's all finished. I panicked when you said Shaw was dead. I don't know why."

"So you ran to your husband for comfort? A nice touch, that." He runs his fingers through his hair and lights another cigarette.

"I swear I don't care about Nick any more. I only care whether you leave me or not. You're going to, I know. I know." She sinks down on to the carpet and crouches against the foot of the bed.

He comes to a halt in front of her.

"Listen Rachel, I don't think I was wrong when I saw in you sensitivity and intelligence. I rarely make mistakes of that kind. But you have to prove it to me. I can't go on arguing about trivialities – money, your husband, what the landlord will say. It'll ruin me as a poet. I need a strong, confident woman who knows how to make sacrifices. I see none of this in you."

"I can do it. I can. I can learn to be all those things." She cradles her head in her hands and rocks on her knees from side to side.

There's a knock on the door. They look at each other in alarm.

"Hide," he hisses.

"Where?" There isn't even a wardrobe.

The knocks become louder and more insistent.

Stefan goes to the door. "Who's there?"

"Mr Raftery."

Stefan groans. The landlord. He opens the door. Mr Raftery is being dignified in dressing gown and badly fitting toupee.

"Mr Chertkov, I thought I heard voices. Ah yes." He looks past Stefan to Rachel, shivering beneath her coat. "As I thought. You realise it's now three o'clock in the morning? Overnight guests, particularly of the opposite sex, are strictly forbidden." He folds his short arms across his voluminous dressing gown. "I must ask you to vacate these premises by nine o'clock tomorrow morning."

"Now listen Mr Raftery . . . " begins Stefan, then stops as Rachel comes up beside him and touches his arm.

"I'm so sorry, Mr Raftery." She flashes him a charming smile. "I'm Stefan's cousin. I live in Rathfarnham and missed the last bus home. He kindly said I could sleep on his floor for the night. I'm so sorry we disturbed you." She gazes at him in appeal from beneath her dark lashes.

"Cousin, eh?" His small, suspicious eyes dart from one to the other. Rachel flashes him another smile. "Very well, Miss. You can stay. Just this once, mind. And don't go letting on to the other tenants. And you, Mr Chertkov," he looks at Stefan severely, "should not make a young lady sleep on the floor. The gentlemanly thing would be to offer her your bed."

"I certainly will, sir," replies Stefan, irony in his eyes. He gives a slight bow.

Mr Raftery marches back down the stairs, one hand on his slipping toupee.

"Rachel, you were wonderful. I love you." Stefan grabs her by the waist and waltzes her around the room. "You should be an actress," he jokes.

"Maybe. But first I'm going to be a waitress and earn money for us both," she says firmly.

The next day she gets a job in a coffee bar. Eventually they're able to move out of Mr Raftery's house and rent a small flat to themselves. There, amidst quarrels and reconciliations, Diana is conceived. By the time the baby is due, Stefan has walked out, come back and walked out again. He blames Rachel's carelessness for the pregnancy and is scared fatherhood will make demands on him incompatible with being a poet.

Approaching motherhood gives Rachel new courage. Whilst she mightn't fight for herself, she will for her child. She's no longer so willing to endure Stefan's tantrums, his habit of keeping her awake till dawn telling her about the poems he's written and is going to write, the women he's had and is going to have, the faults she must get rid of. When Stefan comes back the second time, he finds her changed and falls in love with her all over again. But she knows he'll always expect to be put before the child and that it will be impossible to live with them both. It's a choice between Stefan and her unborn child. She chooses the child . . .

After Diana's birth, Rachel scrapes a living as best she can, cleaning houses, looking after other people's children. She and Diana are very poor. Once or twice they almost starve. She buys clothes for herself and the child at jumble sales. Then she moves in with some theatre people, to help look after their children. They rope her in to sell tickets in the small mews theatre that's just opened in Dublin. She graduates from that to helping out backstage. One night the girl who's playing the maid comes down with flu and Rachel takes over her part.

The rest's well known. On stage Rachel's shyness and fear falls from her. She loses herself in her roles. The safe, enclosed world of the theatre, with its rituals, its traditions, its cosy superstitions, becomes the mother she's never had. Her lack of formal education is no disadvantage. She knows the lines of all the parts she wants to play – Ophelia, Rose, Pegeen – before they're offered to her. The silent years of reading in her father's library pay off when she steps onto the stage. She brings with her, too, all the pain and humiliation of life with her father and with Stefan. She's brilliant in Tennessee Williams.

She escapes them in the end, those two men who tried to shape her to their desires. Her life takes off. She's much in demand in Dublin and London. The press begin to report the most mundane incidents of her life.

But all this was irrelevant to Jade's film. Lallie laid down her pen, exhausted. Had she written the truth about Rachel, or simply invented a story?

That evening she handed Jade the scenes she'd written.

"This is my picture of your mother. I've written it as a story. You'll have to get a scriptwriter to put it together properly. If you like it, that is."

She paced up and down the sitting-room, biting her nails, as Jade read the story. From time to time Jade paused, grunted and went back over pages she'd already read. After what seemed like a lifetime, she threw down the manuscript and came over to give Lallie a hug.

"Yes. It works. You've begun to make a character out of her. It's not the mother I knew. But then the mother I knew would never have let herself be bullied by anyone, let alone by the second-rate poet Stefan turned out to be. You've understood her as a girl better than I could have done. I wonder why you've understood her so well?"

"I've a certain sympathy for people who've had difficult childhoods," replied Lallie, in the dry tone she adopted when she wanted to be self-protective.

"The bleakness and frustration of life in the north-east?" mocked Jade. She rubbed the back of Lallie's neck. "I detected traces of myself here. Stefan . . . he's me, isn't he? And my mother is you. Just like her – she always took the best parts for herself."

Lallie jerked her head away. "Not quite like Rachel. I'm not a famous actress, am I? Merely a historian. A chronicler of other people's lives."

"Good enough," said Jade, more softly. She sat down on the arm of Lallie's chair.

"I wonder? Oh I don't mean I've ambitions suddenly to become an artist," she went on hastily, as Jade frowned. "It's just that, well, I spend my life amongst books, in libraries, or on film sets with you. It all seems so . . . privileged, so cosy, compared with the life of someone like Ruth Martin, for instance, with her five children and a husband out of work."

Jade moved across to the other side of the room. She sat down in an armchair. "Delving into books is what you're good at. Leave social consciences to people who haven't your talent. Look at Diana. She squandered her gifts on the hopeless. Don't become like her."

It was an argument Lallie had frequently used on herself. It never convinced her.

"They think she's a saint," she said. "Those people Diana helped think she's a saint."

"The dividing line between the saint and the clinically insane is extremely thin," replied Jade, flicking on the television. She disliked speaking of her sister.

CHAPTER NINE

TO SLIDE DOWNWARDS INTO DEATH, LIKE SLIDING DOWN INTO WATER. To let the waves lap over him, warm and voluptuous . . .

The telephone rang.

"Seefeldt? Wedelmeier here. I'd like a word with you."

"Sure," replied Joachim in his "I'm-awfully-busy-but-I-could-squeeze-you-in-if-necessary" voice. He disliked his job a lot, but he disliked it somewhat less on the days his boss wasn't there and the disagreeable sensation of being watched by that great brooding presence in the office down the corridor was lifted.

"Ah, Seefeldt. Come in. Sit down."

From behind his huge mahogany desk Hans Wedelmeier pointed to an uncomfortable-looking swivel chair. For a fraction of a second Joachim wondered whether to be subversive and take the armchair. He decided against it. His position in the firm wasn't that secure.

Hans Wedelmeier's office was furnished with a couple of paintings by local artists, what Joachim supposed was a drinks cabinet (he'd never been offered a drink), and two thick dictionaries. Joachim sniggered inwardly. He'd been reliably informed by Wedelmeier's successive secretaries that his boss couldn't spell.

With studied carelessness Hans Wedelmeier flung down his pen, rested his elbows on his desk and attempted what could only be described as a smile.

"I'll come straight to the point, Seefeldt. We had a meeting of the management board yesterday and the first subject on the agenda was our paints factory in Dortmund," he paused, "and the fact that it has failed to make anything approaching a profit, indeed has been losing out substantially to our competitors, over the last four years." He paused again.

"Ah," said Joachim helpfully.

"We recognise that these, er, substantial losses aren't due to any particular inefficiency on your part or on the part of your men. We realise they're the result of a drop in demand, market forces . . . " He went off into a series of technical explanations. "So yesterday the board took the painful decision to close down the factory altogether. Naturally, this will be a delicate operation and we'd like you to be in charge of it since, as division director, this particular factory falls under your aegis."

Spell that, thought Joachim.

"We're hoping the men will be persuaded to take early retirement or accept transfer to one of our other factories . . . "

"The nearest one is eighty miles away."

"Quite so. We'd contribute towards removal expenses, of course."

He knows as well as I do, thought Joachim, that whereas managers are prepared to move around for jobs, workers rarely are.

"What I want you to do, Seefeldt, is to work out a schedule for closing the factory down, and a list of redundancy payments. You know the men better than anyone on the board. I'm sure you'll find the most tactful way of managing this painful process. And Seefeldt," he added, "I can't stress enough the absolute need for secrecy. This closure must be kept from the men till the last possible moment. We don't want rumours flying around and strikes on our hands."

Dejectedly, Joachim went back to his office. The men in Dortmund had been working hard over the past year to

Survival

increase productivity fearing just such an outcome as this. But increased productivity hadn't meant increased profits, or indeed any profit at all. His men were trapped by economic forces outside their control.

In her council flat in Camberwell, Pat Jackson lifted the lid off the tea caddy. Jaysus! The last frigging fifty pence gone. That thieving sod Jimmy. She'd give him what for when she caught up with him.

Then she remembered that her eldest son was six foot tall and had recently been inside for assaulting a police officer. He was long past the age when she could give him a clip round the earhole. He was likely to retaliate by punching her in the stomach. There was nothing for it but to trek round to the Mammy's and cadge a few pounds off her and maybe a pound of butter and a couple of tea bags. It was about the Mammy's turn anyhow. Pat rotated her debts between various members of her family – her mother, her two older sisters and, occasionally, her brother. He was the one that could best afford it but his wife had a way of looking down her nose at you. Not that she could talk, with her eldest on remand.

She turned round in time to catch Dave stabbing two-year-old Sal with a pencil.

"You little sod! Stop that!" She grabbed the pencil off him and belted him. He started howling. Sal silently examined the red weal on her arm. A girl of about ten, dressed in jeans and a dirty T-shirt, appeared in the doorway.

"Where were you when you're wanted?" snapped Pat. The girl merely glowered. "Look after these two and see they don't get up to any more mischief while I'm gone. I'm off to the Mammy's to get us some tea."

"Don't see why I should," said the girl sullenly. "Why can't Marie look after Sal? She's her kid."

"Listen you." Pat went over to her daughter Penny and

123

shook her. "Do as you're told for once. Marie isn't back from her cleaning yet. She's the only one brings in any money around here so we got to help her out, see?"

The girl sniffed and sat down on a chair. Apart from this hard chair and one other like it, the room was sparsely furnished with just a rickety formica-topped table and an old black and white television set. A scuffed piece of lino served instead of carpet.

Pat sighed, flung on her coat which failed to cover her shapeless woollen skirt, and made her way down the five flights of concrete stairs. She'd given up using the lift except when she'd heavy shopping to carry. The kids were always stopping it between floors or pissing in it. Once she'd got in and found the walls smeared with shit. It was a dump this place. Unfit for human habitation, she'd call it. Damp streamed down the walls in the winter. In the summer piles of stinking garbage lay for days by the chutes. The whole building was plastered with graffiti. She passed some now. "Thatcher's a cunt." "Feel like a fuck?" (with phone number). How could you be expected to bring up kids properly in this place?

Now that Da had died the Mammy lived by herself in a block of flats at the Elephant and Castle. Pat knew she could count on her being in. The Mammy was afraid to go out after dark. She walked all the way down Walworth Road to the Elephant. God willing, she'd get thirty pence off the Mammy for the fare back. The Mammy was the only one in their family who was able to get by decently. When everything else had been cut, pensions had been increased. Pat vaguely thought it must be something to do with votes. She hadn't time for politics, being much too taken up with the ordinary difficulties of day-to-day living.

The Mammy was sat in a hard chair by the two-bar electric fire, a blanket round her shoulders.

Pat shivered. She'd been looking forward to a bit of warmth after her long walk. "What's up with the paraffin?"

"Shut it off for a bit. Couldn't stand the smell. How's the kids?"

Pat sat down in the chair opposite and laughed.

There were too many kids in her life for her liking. She'd been married twice. To Sean who'd caught emphi-what's-it (she could never pronounce it) from working on the hospital boilers. He'd been sick for years and years. She'd had to go out to work as a machinist in a clothing factory in order to feed her kids – Jimmy, Marie, Debbie and Joe. They'd lived in a proper house then, with two bedrooms. Damp, though. The wallpaper was grey and where it wasn't grey, it had peeled off. Unsafe as well. You took your life in your hands every time you went upstairs. Later it had been condemned. Later still, pulled down. She'd preferred it, though, to the flat they were in now.

Then Sean had died. All she'd felt was, one less mouth to feed. He'd never been the same since he'd lost his job. Hanging around the house all day, moaning. He'd never got used to the fact she was the one going out to work whilst he had to look after the kids. Sometimes he'd imagine she was having it off with some fella at work and he'd rough her up a bit when she got home.

She'd met Mick, her second husband, down at the local Irish club. He was an out of work fitter. But he had plans. They'd moved into the flat on Sedgefield Estate and she'd had two more children. Penny, the ten-year-old girl and Dave, six now. By the time Dave was born, she'd realised Mick's plans would never lead to a job, not a legal one at any rate. Those two, Penny and Dave, took after their father. Right little fuckers. In the end Mick had buggered off. She hadn't been too bothered about that, either. Many's the time he'd robbed her of the housekeeping.

So there they all were, packed into the three-bedroom flat. Marie and her kid Sal in one room, she and Penny in another, Joe and Dave in the third. Jimmy slept on the floor in the lounge when he came home. Debbie, who was eighteen, had gone homeless with her two six months ago. She was in a bed and breakfast place waiting to be rehoused. So that had got them out of the way. Before that, she and her kids had been sleeping with the neighbours, on and off.

All the same, how could she be expected to manage? She'd never had a penny from either of her husbands since the day Sean started to get sick. She got her Giro on Friday and by Wednesday, she'd run out and had to borrow till Friday came round again. She was permanently in debt. How could you be expected to live on one pound sixty a day? There was child benefit, but that only got deducted from the rest. The settee had been repossessed recently and it was all she could do to hang on to the fridge. "A luxury," the social worker had called it. Fucking cow. Catch her going without a fridge! Last year the electric had been off for three months. It'd got so miserable, sitting there night after night by candlelight, with the kids shivering and bored out of their skulls because the telly was off, that she'd got Jimmy to reconnect it. That way she'd more of a chance of making ends meet. So long as the neighbours didn't shop her.

"Want a fag?" offered her mother, recognising signs of strain. She'd brought up eight of her own.

"Thanks, Mammy." Pat got up to look for the matches. The Mammy was getting forgetful.

Social security didn't care a monkey's (she continued airing her grievances to some imaginary listener). They just stared at her and passed her on to another department. Stingy sods. You'd think the money was coming out of their own pockets. Once they'd asked her why she'd had so many children. She hadn't known what to answer. She was Irish. The Irish liked children and before Sean's illness they'd seemed set to be comfortably off. By the time they'd diagnosed emphi-what's-it from the asbestos on the boilers, she'd already had three and Joe was on the way. And Mick, well, it was natural he'd want kids of his own. It's never the same with someone else's.

Children used to be an insurance policy against old age. She retrieved the matches from under a cushion and lit up. Fat fucking chance of that. None of her children had regular jobs, nor were likely to, as far as she could see. Marie did the odd bit of cleaning or babysitting, which was handy because there was no need to declare it. Joe was on a Youth Training course for twelve weeks. That'd be coming to an end soon and then he'd be back on the dole, sleeping in till lunchtime. She was afraid he'd start going with Jimmy. She didn't see much of a future for any of her children. They wanted GCSEs nowadays even to work in a shop. Well, there'd be no more. After Dave she'd got herself sterilised on the National Health. Not that there was much opportunity for that kind of thing nowadays, with the kids all around her and not a bit of privacy.

The Mammy leaned forward and tapped her on the knee.

"I hear there's a job of work going. Home work. Overlocking and machining. You wouldn't have to declare it."

"Oh Ma, I'm not starting that again. They dump you as soon as they don't need you any longer. Or refuse to pay up. And there's not a thing you can do about it, having no cards. Besides, it give me pains in me shoulders hunched up over that machine all day long. And the neighbours kicking up stink about the noise."

The Mammy sniffed. "God helps them as . . . " she began, in her rich Dublin accent. Ma was the only one of her family who spoke with an Irish accent. For that matter, she was the only one who still went to Mass. Pat had given up going to Mass after Sean fell sick. That Father Keogh was a good sort. But he was a Prod. It was never the same somehow.

Pat often wondered why the Mammy and Da had come over. Life back in Ireland surely couldn't be worse than over here. She'd never seen the country though she counted herself Irish. It was her dream to go there one day. And likely to stay a dream, too, she thought sourly.

"I've got Marie's Sal to look after now," she said, in response to her mother. "I can't be working an eighty hour week. Anyways I'm doing a bit – glueing pearls onto earrings. Penny helps out when she's in the mood."

"How much?" The Mammy's eyes gleamed. She'd become greedy in her old age.

"Fifty pence an hour it works out at."

"Huh! You won't get fat on that." There was a silence. Pat savoured her cigarette. "Have you heard from housing yet?" Pat was applying for a transfer.

"I've got the form here." She rummaged in her bag. "They tried to make out I didn't have enough points but I created such a fuss they ended up giving me the form anyway. I can't stick that flat no longer. The bath takes two days to empty and you never can get them to come and repair it." She spread the form out on her knees. "It's that long. I've read it over twice and I can't make head nor tail of it." She frowned. "I wish Di was here. She'd have known how to fill it in. She always helped me with the forms. And they took notice of her down the DHSS because she talked posh. Us they think they can kick around like effin' dogs. She got me that one pound twenty diet allowance when I was poorly with the ulcer."

The Mammy sighed. "Yes, Di would have known what to do."

Jade, going out to book tickets for their flight to Ireland saw, with a sudden stab of pain, her sister's face clearly before her. She slipped into St Mary Abbot's and sat down on a pew. My sister, my child, she thought, as she rarely allowed herself to think. Cursed by the drugs that broke your body, damaged your mind and silenced your poems for ever.

She put her head on her knees, clenched her fists and saw two little girls huddled together in one bed for comfort whilst their mother was out. Two sisters who'd stood up for each other, fought each other's battles at school. And then had drifted apart. For they hadn't been alike, not really, coming as they did from different fathers. Though there were certain things. A tilt of the chin, meaning pride. A glance sideways – embarrassment. Yes, she thought, to my dying day I will carry this of you in me, my sister. You were here before me and you have gone ahead to prepare the way. And that is right for you were the forger and I the mender. And when we meet again, as we surely will, it will be once more as in the days of our childhood and it will be as if all the rotten intervening years had never happened.

Jade unclenched her fists and looked up. Someone at the front of the church was playing the organ, practising for Sunday. In the pew along from hers sat a tramp surrounded by plastic bags. He nodded to her. Ignoring him she got up and resumed her walk down Church Street.

For as long as she could remember she'd been sorting out problems for her mother and her sister, smoothing things over, acting as a bulwark between them and the outside world. They'd lived in a fantasy world. It had been Jade who'd learned early on to handle the bills, get men in to fix the fridge or mend the roof.

Well, now they no longer needed her. Either of them. Beautiful and fragile as the butterflies on her mother's walls, their wings were broken, their flying ended. She'd live with them again for eight weeks or so – as long as it took to shoot the film – and then she'd be free of them. Free of their voices in her head. She'd have paid her debt. She quickened her step towards the ticket office.

"Tell me the rest of the story," said Lallie that evening, as they were finishing supper.

"The rest of the story?"

"After the film ends."

Jade reached for an orange and began peeling it.

"When Rachel's acting started to take off she gave up looking after other people's children and rented a basement flat in Rathmines. It had three rooms and a bathroom. She painted the bedrooms dull pink and the living-room dark green. She hung paper butterflies on the walls, draped Indian shawls over the sagging armchairs. A door led out of the green room, I remember, into a tiny rock garden which my mother filled with old English flowers which grew without order or discipline, a confusion of colours and scents." Jade divided her orange into segments. "That garden seemed to me to express her personality which was always made up of whatever parts she'd recently been playing.

"Anyway, here we lived, the three of us, for all of my childhood and most of my adolescence, till Frank McKenna died and with the proceeds from the sale of his house, my mother bought a house in Rathgar – the one from which she gave interviews in later years dressed in that ridiculous black lace." Jade grimaced.

"Diana and I were left pretty much on our own when we were growing up. Rachel's life was made up of rehearsals, first nights and celebrations in McDaid's. She flitted in and out of our basement flat wearing an assortment of second-hand clothes, twenties style dresses, motheaten furs. Always with an admirer or two in tow. She took us to parties, leaving us to sleep amongst the fur coats and the shawls. She made half-hearted attempts to get nannies, au pairs, babysitters for us, but they never lasted long. None of them could put up with our chaotic way of life. We were left to fend for ourselves. Nowadays, we'd be called latch-key kids." She sliced through the Brie.

"I can't remember her ever advising us on anything. When we asked her what we should do in life, she said, 'Do what feels right. Do something you believe in. And start using face cream before you're twenty.' Di left school at sixteen without any qualifications, unless you include a burning desire to be a poet. She worked as a waitress by day and wrote poetry at night . . .

"Rachel came over to London to act for a few months (Shaw, I think it was) and brought Di with her. Di never went back to Ireland. She made friends and moved into a squat in Little Venice. She continued writing poetry and started taking drugs. She moved around from squat to squat and got busted several times for drugs. My mother always bailed her out. She began giving poetry readings in pubs around south London. She was published regularly in worthy literary magazines with tiny circulations." Jade paused and stared down at her plate.

"Go on," said Lallie gently, aware she mightn't get another chance to hear this story.

"If you want me to tell you about my sister, I'll need a whiskey."

Jade got up and poured them both a glass. They moved from the table to the armchairs. Jade sat sideways, dangling her legs over the arm.

"Di wrote once to her father in Chile, enclosing some of her poems. I was there when she received Stefan's reply. He'd sent some of his own poems and returned hers, with corrections. 'Keep trying,' he wrote. 'One day you may be a poet.' I watched her burn the letter. She never referred to him again. I don't know what she'd been hoping for – praise, encouragement, an invitation to stay, perhaps. I'd always envied her for knowing who her father was. At that moment, I pitied her.

"I returned to Dublin and began studying film production. I got that job at RTE. Even when I moved over to London, Di and I hardly ever met. We moved in different circles. I thought she was ruining her life. She thought that, because I was successful in finding backers for my films, I'd sold out to the establishment. But my ideas were never hers." She shrugged. "If they had been, I'd never have got a single film made . . . What I know about her after that comes mainly from her poetry. Oh yes, I used to read it," she added, as Lallie glanced across in surprise. "Though the left wing magazines she published in were often hard to find."

She got up to pour herself another whiskey.

"Want another? No? When Thatcher came to power, Di's life took on a new intensity. She was living among people who were directly affected by Thatcher's policies, who were having their rents increased, their benefits cut, services eroded, all to provide tax cuts for the rich middle classes – at least that's how Di saw it. She moved in with Philip, a social worker."

She couldn't have put more disapproval into her voice if she'd tried, thought Lallie.

"Her poetry became more and more political. She wrote about a mother who killed herself and her two babies on Christmas Eve because she'd no money to buy toys; about the man who went without food for three days because his Giro had got lost in the post; about the riots, desperate people on the streets of Brixton and Toxteth."

Jade drained her glass.

"She wrote, but few people listened. The newspapers refused to print reviews of her books. One national newspaper was going to carry a profile of her but it was suppressed at the last moment by the proprietor. And after all, why should people have listened? She was only a junkie . . . "

There was a silence.

"It wasn't drugs that destroyed her poetry, it was politics," Jade burst out. "She should have left all that to journalists. The eighties were a time when English writers were making a name for themselves with exquisite analyses of human relationships in carefully crafted novels. That's what readers wanted, an escape from the economic crisis and the violence on the streets. When they picked up a book of poetry, they didn't want to be reminded that people were starving in Brixton and Liverpool. Politics killed her poetry and then drugs killed her body. You remember I got that call on Christmas Eve? Di had been admitted to hospital suffering from pneumonia and heart failure. She died three days later."

"I remember you going to her funeral," said Lallie softly. She resisted the temptation to go over and put her arms around Jade and comfort her. Lately Jade had shied away from her embraces, as if she found something claustrophobic in them. "You wouldn't let me go with you."

"Why should you have gone? I hadn't seen Diana for years. You'd never met her." Jade fingered her glass. "Two funerals in one year. First my mother's, all pomp and circumstance. Then Di's, a hole in the corner affair, attended by the people she'd surrounded herself with over the past few years. Tramps, squatters, shabby women trailing dirty children." Jade shuddered. "I was glad to get home . . . Stefan wrote a lament for her, you know. It found its way into the *TLS*. One of his better poems, I thought, though there was nothing of Di in it. Hardly surprising since he'd never known her. It was like him to make literary capital out of her death." She fell silent.

"Perhaps that's it?" said Lallie slowly.

"What?"

"That's what Diana was rebelling against – exploiting others for the sake of art. She'd seen too much of it in her own father. And maybe your mother. She chose compassion instead. It's becoming a buzz word. She was ahead of her time."

Jade shrugged. "Perhaps. She was my sister. I knew her too well to make a saint out of her. At any rate, her death won't be exploited by me. She'll appear in the film as she was when she was a small child – with our mother's dark eyes and black hair, and so paternally deprived that she'd wander up and stroke the hand of any man who visited us."

There was a silence. Lallie wasn't satisfied. It seemed to her that Jade dismissed Diana too readily.

"You've never felt tempted to . . . take up where Diana left off?" she began, hesitantly.

Jade stared at her. "No, why should I? I'm a film maker, not a social worker. Let the hopeless help the hopeless." She frowned. "Anyway, why all this social concern all of a sudden? What's got into you? These people have always been there. Why have you suddenly started noticing them?"

"I guess everyone goes through a period of questioning what they do for a living," murmured Lallie.

"The difference between us," remarked Jade "is that you don't believe in art like I do. Without my art I'd be nothing."

"Yes, I know, you quite despise people who aren't creative, don't you?" snapped Lallie, hurt at the small importance given to their relationship in Jade's scheme of things.

"Not despise, no." Jade glanced at her fingernails. "Despise would be too strong a word."

"So why do you stay with me?" Lallie got up and began pacing the room. "I never create anything. All I do is uncover facts and order them."

"You help me." Jade held out a hand. Lallie ignored it. "Where would I be without you? You give my life a stability it's never had before. You mother me. Besides I doubt I could live with another creative person."

"So you put up with me because I'm no threat. Is that it?" said Lallie, stung. "Good old staid uncreative Lallie."

"That's not what I meant. Stop shouting, you're being perfectly ridiculous. I love you." She held out her hand again. "Come on, snuggler, come and sit down here."

Lallie sat on the carpet by Jade's feet. Jade stroked her hair. "Why do we keep on arguing like this?" Jade sighed.

"Something's happened to you, Lallie. You're changing, questioning things you've never questioned before. Why?" She began massaging Lallie's shoulders.

Lallie plucked at the carpet.

"I feel . . . dissatisfied with myself. A short while ago I was congratulating myself on having escaped from the north. Now, all of a sudden I feel guilty about it, as if I've lost my way somewhere along the line. Working on your mother's life seems to have woken things in me."

"It's a phase." Jade bent to kiss the back of her neck. "It'll pass." She straightened up. "Meanwhile, before we go over to Ireland, you could pay a visit to Philip, that guy my sister lived with. I still have his address somewhere. Di may have told him things about my mother that I don't know. She was closer to Rachel than I was. Rachel and I couldn't be two minutes in the same room without bickering."

"Don't you want to go and see him yourself?"

"No. Philip and I took an instant dislike to one another." She grimaced. "And then," she continued, "you could go and see the kind of people Di lived amongst. That should fulfil your urge to do social work."

Or cure it, she thought to herself. Yes, a dose of Di's "people" would swiftly reconcile Lallie to her present way of life. She'd see there was nothing to be done for them, these down and outs, these lost souls of Thatcher's, and now Major's, England. She thought again of the funeral and shuddered. All those wretched people looking at her as though they'd expected her to step into Di's shoes.

"All right," said Lallie. "I'll go and visit them." She had a feeling, though, that her dissatisfaction with herself wouldn't be so easily cured.

Jade breathed a sigh of relief. When Lallie had done that, they'd fly off to Ireland to look for a suitable location to film. Then there'd be all the business of raising money, casting, hiring a scriptwriter. Lallie's scenes would have to be properly worked out and added to. Not every detail though. She liked there to be a few surprises, some magic that would only reveal itself when the cameras were turning.

Jade felt her spirits rise, as they always did, at the prospect of hard work. When the film was under way Lallie would have no time to brood over her problems. Jade would be able to rely on her again. The quarrels which had clouded their love recently would be forgotten and they'd work together, the harmonious, efficient team they'd always been.

Over the course of several days Joachim wrote, and tore up, six different schemes for closing down the Dortmund paints factory. Coincidentally he had to pay a routine visit to that particular factory, speak encouraging words to the men and congratulate the managers on the introduction of a new safety scheme. He came away feeling a bastard. Three thousand workers were about to lose their jobs. There was no way the region could provide employment for even a quarter of that number.

On Wednesday he had dinner with a friend of his, Franz Schmidt. Franz was industrial affairs correspondent for a national newspaper.

"There's a rumour going round that should please you," Franz remarked, over beer and noodles.

"Yes?" said Joachim. He wasn't really attending to his friend. He was weighing up in his mind whether to risk leaking news of the Dortmund closure. Franz would never betray his source. Wedelmeier wouldn't be able to prove where the leak had come from. It might be worth it. Set the cat among the pigeons a bit. Give his men a fighting chance. Then his attention was caught by something Franz was saying.

"And one of your rivals, HFW the paints firm, is going

down the tubes. I've been slipped a preview of their end-of-year accounts." Franz made the thumbs down sign.

Joachim laid down his fork. "How long have they got?"

"Six months. At the outside."

"Hum."

"That's not a smile appearing on your face is it? I thought you'd forgotten how to. Of course this puts you lot in a pretty strong position."

"Yes." Joachim grinned. "Yes it does." He raised his beer glass. "Cheers."

He worked till four in the morning drawing up a set of figures that would make staying in business in Dortmund attractive to the management board. He was in his office by seven thirty. At eight, he was speaking to Wedelmeier.

"With HFW out of the running we'll have only one other big competitor to worry about." He handed Wedelmeier a copy of the figures. "If we manage to get HFW's share of the market, we'll be making a profit by the end of the year."

Hans Wedelmeier coughed, looked at the figures and coughed again.

"What you say may well be true, my dear Seefeldt," he said slowly. "But it's still a risk. There's no guarantee we would in fact pick up HFW's business."

Joachim tapped the figures impatiently. "With three thousand jobs at stake surely it's a risk worth taking. Think of all the adverse publicity we're going to get if the closure goes ahead," he added, shamelessly playing on one of his boss's fears.

"There's another factor in all this. I may as well let you in on it now, though you'll understand it has to be kept top secret." Wedelmeier paused, at his most pompous. "The management board plans to open a new paints factory in the new year, outside Munich. So you see," he continued smoothly, "the failure of one of our competitors doesn't alter our decision to resite this particular factory – though it will undoubtedly boost the profits of our other factories in paints division."

"I see," said Joachim stonily. He swept the sheets of figures off Wedelmeier's desk and left the office without another word.

So it wasn't a straightforward closure due to falling profits, as Wedelmeier had at first given him to understand. It was a tactical resiting. The reasoning behind the move from Dortmund to Munich was obvious. Bavaria, with its conservative, capitalist government, was an industry-friendly region. It handed out grants and subsidies to firms moving into the area, unlike the socialist government of North Rhine-Westphalia, where the factory was located at present. And the workforce was likely to be more amenable too. There'd been a couple of strikes at the Dortmund factory in the past two years. Nothing serious. Mainly due to management incompetence. In both cases Joachim had sorted out the problem quickly enough. But the management board had obviously taken fright and decided to make a fresh start elsewhere.

It was a deliberate, callous withdrawal of jobs from an already hard-hit area to a much richer one. Shops would close, people would move away, houses would be boarded up. His workers would become deskilled. A community would be destroyed. The empty factory would lie idle, its machinery rusting away. The area around it would become a wasteland.

Oh, this country, he thought. This empty, hollow country, where materialism's pursued for its own sake by a people afraid to look over their shoulders at the past. This was Hitler's legacy. They were a frightened generation.

He could resign of course. But there were the boys to think of. All those long years of schooling and college ahead. If only the farm was making instead of losing money. And if he did resign they might appoint a director

(Gunter, for instance), who'd be ruthless in pushing through the closure. Wouldn't it be better to stay and fight for the best terms for his men? Or was this only an excuse? Had he too been sucked in by his country's materialism? When it came to the crunch wasn't he the same as everyone else, unwilling to sacrifice his standard of living for a principle?

He got through the day on auto pilot. At four thirty he looked at his watch and decided to leave early.

On his way home he stopped at a bar and had a whiskey. Then another. Then another. He bought an evening paper to check what was on at the cinema. An old Fassbinder. He decided to see it anyway. But when he got there he found he'd drunk too much whiskey and couldn't concentrate. Halfway through he closed his eyes and fell asleep. He was woken by bright lights and people pushing past him. In his crumpled suit and smelling of alcohol they probably had him down as some kind of tramp. What a hell of a day, he thought. What a hell of a day. Thank God tomorrow's Friday.

He'd get his secretary to book an afternoon flight. He'd go over to Ireland for the weekend, maybe even take Monday off. He needed to get out of Germany, get a different perspective on the idea of making three thousand men redundant. He needed, above all, to talk with Cornelius.

He stumbled out of the cinema and was about to hail a taxi when he caught sight of a long-haired woman walking on the other side of the street. He began waving frantically at her.

"Wait! Wait!"

He weaved in and out of the traffic. A car slammed on its brakes. Drivers leaned out of their windows cursing him. Joachim ignored them. The woman turned the corner. Joachim ran after her. But when he turned into the street it was empty. He wandered up and down it for several minutes, peering into dark alleyways, examining the name plates on the doors of the apartment blocks. Finally he collapsed on a bench and put his head in his hands.

"Christabel," he muttered. "Where are you? I need you. Come and save me."

CHAPTER TEN

LALLIE CAUGHT THE 68 BUS AT RUSSELL SQUARE. IT STOPPED AND started all the way down the Strand, jerked past King's College and Somerset House, picked up speed over Waterloo Bridge, slowed down again at the Elephant and Castle. A sign welcomed her to Lambeth, a nuclear-free zone.

She peered out through grimy windows at the tall blocks of flats scattered amongst the office buildings and scarcely distinguishable from them except for the lines of washing slung across their balconies. Where did the children play? The only patches of green in sight were roundabouts and they could hardly play on those.

They jolted down the Walworth Road. It swarmed with people waiting for buses, queuing outside a Citizens' Advice Bureau or just hanging around eating food out of cartons. They were in Southwark now, also a nuclear-free zone. It didn't seem to have done much for the vegetation though. She glanced at the stick-like trees lining the road. They were clearly losing the battle against traffic pollution. They passed a small park with wooden horses and wooden slides and a sign saying "GLC. Working for London's recreation." Someone must have forgotten to take it down. A café advertised "Egg Bacon Bubble." What did that mean? She felt as if she was entering a different culture, yet it was only another part of the city.

She got off at Camberwell Green and walked up the hill, past Kennedy's pie shop and King's Hospital. A giant cardboard thermometer hung suspended against the wall. "Save King's Scanner," it said. An Indian went past shaking his head furiously from side to side. "Fucking shit. Fucking shit," he muttered. They'd been told the community was taking care of people like him. She hoped it was, but it didn't look like it.

She arrived at the address Philip had given her: a six-storey block of council flats set in a square facing another, similar block. Separating them was a tiny strip of green. "No ball games," a sign said. Where did they play? She looked up. She could hear children's voices coming from a balcony somewhere above her head. Several of the windows in the block were boarded up. At others dirty net curtains hung limply from their wires. Nearly all the window frames were unpainted and looked rotten. She swallowed hard and went inside.

Rejecting the stinking lift, she walked up the five flights of stairs to the Jackson residence. Her nostrils were assailed by a sickly mixture of curry, hamburger, onions, fried fish and cake. On her left she passed the "Thatcher is a cunt" graffiti, now joined by "Major is an arsehole". Several other scrawls stated their desire to give or receive sexual gratification, with telephone numbers.

"If you want to see the kind of people Di wrote about, go and visit the Jacksons," Philip had told Lallie. He'd refused to discuss Di with her. Their life together was private, no concern of anyone else's. He'd heard enough about Jade to distrust her motives.

At the top of the stairs Lallie found herself in a long windowless corridor lit by strip lighting. At one end was a rubbish chute, half open where an oversize plastic bag had been jammed into it. The bag had split and some of its contents (egg shells, tins, cabbage leaves) were strewn around the floor. It reeked.

She knocked on the door of the Jacksons' flat. A dirty-faced girl edged open the door and stared sullenly at her through the crack. She would have slammed the door shut again if Lallie hadn't wedged her foot against it. Philip had warned her she might have difficulty getting into the flat.

"Ma!" shrieked the girl. "Ma! It's the electric!"

A weary-faced woman with lank dyed blonde hair appeared at the door, a dish towel in her hand. She shoved Penny out of the way.

"Well?" she said impatiently. "What is it?"

"I'm not from the Electricity Board," said Lallie. "I'm a friend of Diana's," she explained, giving herself a certain amount of licence. Pat Jackson continued to eye her suspiciously. "Philip Scott gave me your address. You can phone him and check if you like."

"We ain't got no phone," said Pat dully. "OK, I believe you. Come in. I was just doing the dishes. Here you," she threw the cloth at Penny, "you finish them. I'll keep an eye on the kids."

She opened the door wider and Lallie stepped into a narrow hall, about three feet across. It resembled the corridor of a train, with doors leading off. From behind one of the doors came the sound of screaming. Pat led the way towards it and they entered the living-room to find Dave had got Sal in a half-nelson.

"Let go of her, you little sod." Pat cuffed him. "Can't take my eyes off you for a second, can I? Trouble is," she explained to Lallie, "they're bored stiff, the pair of them, cooped up in 'ere all day long. But what can you do? I can't let them out. Cars rush though this estate at sixty miles an hour. There was one kid got himself killed last year."

"Is there nowhere for them to play?"

"There's a playground round the back. Hasn't been seen to for years. Dead dangerous it is. All the swings are rotting. It ought to be shut up." Her eyes narrowed. "You sure you're not from the DHSS?"

Lallie shook her head.

"Last time the woman was here she caught me clipping

Dave. Said the next time I did that, she'd take him off me. But what can you do? They're little sods, the pair of them. Here you two, watch telly for a bit."

She switched it on. Sal stopped crying and crouched down on the floor at a safe distance from Dave who stood moodily against the wall chipping away at the plaster with his thumb.

"Might as well take the weight off your feet." Pat pulled out a chair and sat on the other one herself. "So you're a friend of Di's?" She stared Lallie up and down, taking in her expensively-cut jeans and silk shirt.

"Yes. We – a friend of mine is making a film about Di's mother. There's going to be a bit in it about Diana herself. I'm the researcher. I wanted to find out about her. What kind of a person she was."

Pat sat back and lit a cigarette. She offered one to Lallie.

"Don't smoke? Wise girl. I wish I could kick it. It's the nerves." She shoved the packet back into the pocket of her skirt. "Diana McKenna was one of the best friends this family ever had." She inhaled deeply. "Films? That'd be her sister, wouldn't it? Didn't take to her. Stuck-up looking bitch at the funeral. Di was all right though. No side to her, if you know what I mean."

"Yes," lied Lallie.

"Diana – " Pat was interrupted by the sound of a car engine being revved up. "Fuck it, he's started again."

She went over to the window to look.

"Bloody Paki. He was at it for over an hour this morning, trying to get the fucking thing started. Why doesn't he call it a write-off and have done? Bloody wogs. Mick always said they don't know their arse from their elbow when it comes to mechanics."

She turned round.

"Listen, since you're here, can you help me write a letter and fill in a form? Perhaps you'll know how to put it so that those bastards down at housing will read it instead of chucking it into the bin. You speak their language. I don't. I just get raging and that gets me nowhere. I thought if I went next time with a properly written letter they'd fucking sit up and take notice. They always did when Di wrote."

She looked at Lallie.

"I can try," began Lallie. "I don't have much experience at this sort of thing."

"Don't need experience." Pat rummaged in a corner for some writing paper. She produced an old exercise book of Penny's. "You're their class. You've had schooling. They'll listen to you." She spread out the form on the table. "I don't understand the half of it, so how will I know if I'm filling it in right? They say I haven't enough points. But where could I live that'd be worse than this dump?" The front door slammed. "Penny." She sighed. "Off God knows where."

Lallie pulled her chair up to the table and began reading through the form and the notes at the end.

"Hang on." Pat turned the television down. "Can't hear myself think with all this sodding racket." The noise from the revved up car engine stopped. "Not before time," she remarked.

As she sat at the table trying to frame Pat's grievances into the kind of bureaucratese she guessed would be acceptable to a housing department, Lallie began to realise how very cold it was in the flat. Having no carpet on the floor didn't help. She shivered and glanced over at the paraffin heater standing in the corner.

"Daren't on account of the kids," said Pat, noticing her glance. "I sometimes have it on of an evening, when the young 'uns are in bed."

Lallie looked around. "Is that the only heating you have?"

"The whole block was built with underfloor electric heating. Bloody crazy idea. Too fucking expensive. People got behind with their payments, so they shut it off. You can still see the ducts over there."

"Oh yes. What's she doing?"

Sal had been poking around inside one of the ducts. As Lallie spoke Sal put her fingers one by one into her mouth and licked them.

Pat gave a shout. "Christ! The insecticide! I had it down in the ducts to kill them ants." She swooped down on Sal. Frightened, the child took her hands out of her mouth and burst into tears. Pat inspected the ducts. "My God, she's swallowed nearly the whole fucking lot! Jaysus! What did I tell you? Can't take your eyes off them for a minute. Brats!"

Lallie sprang up. "I'll phone for a doctor." Then she remembered they hadn't a phone.

"There's a call box down the road. On the left hand side, near the pub. Here's his number." Clutching the howling Sal, Pat scrawled on a scrap of paper and handed it to Lallie. Dave leant against the wall, looking smug.

Pat began dragging Sal out of the room. "I'm going to try to make her sick up."

Lallie headed out of the door. Holding her breath and praying she wouldn't get stuck between floors, she stepped into the lift. She ran all the way to the pay phone only to find there was a queue. Two elderly women and a Rastafarian. Inside, a girl with braided pink and yellow hair was having a lively conversation with a friend.

"Been on quarter of an hour, she has," complained one of the women.

Lallie waited a few seconds, then wrenched open the door and said, "Please, I've got to phone a doctor. It's an emergency. A child's sick."

"That's what they all say."

"But . . . "

"Sod off!" replied the girl, turning her back.

Lallie slammed the door in disgust.

"Little cow," said the elderly woman sympathetically. "There's another phone about ten minutes away, too far for me to get with my legs. Down that road." She pointed.

"It's bust," put in the Rastafarian. "I just tried it. Go that way." He pointed in the opposite direction.

"Thanks." Lallie set off at a run but it was fifteen minutes before she found a phone that worked, by which time it was out of surgery hours. An answering machine gave her the doctor's home number.

"I'm sorry to bother you, doctor. A child's just swallowed some poison. Can you come round?"

"Yes, I'll come immediately. Where is it?" enquired a clipped, middle-class voice.

"Sedgefield Estate."

He groaned.

"It's the Jackson family."

"Are they patients of mine?"

"Yes."

"Don't tell me. Insecticide to kill the ants."

"Yes. Can you come? The little girl seems to have swallowed rather a lot."

"Listen, Miss, if I was to turn out for every case on that estate of an infant who swallowed something, or burnt itself on a heater, or tore its leg on a rusty nail, I'd have no time for anything else. Now listen carefully, I'm going to tell you what to do." He gave details. "If that doesn't work get her mother to bring her round to surgery at six. If she's really bad when you get back, take her to casualty." He rang off.

"Didn't think he'd bother himself," said Pat when Lallie returned. "Anyway, she's been sick and seems right as rain now. If she turns poorly again, I'll get Marie to take her round to surgery when she comes in."

"He should have come out. She might have been poisoned. It's his job."

Pat stared at her. "Sure it's his fuckin' job. And if we'd given a middle-class address he'd have been there like a shot. This kind of thing happens all the time around here. He's not a bad man," she added. "Just overworked. There aren't many doctors that'll start up in this area. Not enough private patients – " She was interrupted by the sound of scuffling in the hallway. "What the . . . ?"

The living-room door opened and a tall, thin lad with a bad case of acne came in, dragging Penny by the scruff of her neck. She was screaming and kicking out at him.

"Joe! What the hell are you doing? Leave her be, for Christ's sake," said Pat.

Joe let go of Penny's collar but continued holding on to her arm, as if he was afraid she'd run off again.

"I caught this one down in the sheds sniffing glue," he said.

"I warn't Ma! Honest! I war jus' watching," yelled Penny.

"Sniffing glue! You'll wreck what little brain you have, my girl. Go to your room," ordered Pat and, as Penny continued to scream, she gave her a slap. Penny slunk off down the hall. Dave and Sal watched wide-eyed, Sal sucking her thumb. Pat nodded after her daughter. "That one'll go to the bad, mark my words."

Lallie arrived home with a splitting headache and found Jade in the kitchen, frying steak. "Well," she said, "find out anything interesting?"

"Um. I'll, er, make some notes for you," replied Lallie, guiltily. She'd been so swept along by events at the Jacksons' that she'd forgotten the real purpose of her visit had been to gather material for Jade's film. Instead of notes, she'd come away with Pat Jackson's form and the rough draft of a letter to the housing department.

She wandered into the living-room. The central heating was on and Chopin's *Preludes* was playing. From the kitchen came the smell of steak. A bottle of Cabernet Sauvignon stood open on the table. She sank down onto the thick carpet. Hard to believe she and Pat Jackson lived in the same country, let alone the same city and only a few miles apart.

The difference in their way of life seemed unbridgeable, even with a lifetime of effort.

"Food!" called Jade from the kitchen. She arrived in the living-room bearing two plates of steak. Lallie looked at them.

"Do you know there are people in this country who haven't enough to eat?"

Jade glanced at her, then set the plates on the table. "Eat, will you?"

Lallie got up off the floor. They sat at the table in stony silence.

Jade cut into her steak. "As a matter of fact, yes, I do know there are children who go to school with a packet of crisps in their lunch box and nothing else. I do know that in parts of London there are pregnant women whose calorie intake is less than the average intake in Ethiopia. What do you expect me to do about it?"

"I don't know," said Lallie miserably. "But surely something should be done? We're supposed to be living in a welfare state, for God's sake. What's happened to it?" She laid down her fork.

"Recession plus monetarism." Jade poured out the wine. "Thatcher believed everyone should stand on their own two feet. And Major, for all his supposed softer touch, apparently thinks the same. His government is looking less and less like the turning point everyone predicted and more like the same old thing in a minor and less efficient key."

"What if they can't look after themselves? Some people can't, you know."

"There's a safety net for the worst off."

"It seems pretty minimal," remarked Lallie, thinking of the Jacksons' bare flat.

"Look, are you going to eat that steak, or not? It's getting cold. I put a lot of effort into cooking it."

"Yes, OK. Sorry." Lallie took up her fork again.

"Most of these people's problems are caused by the fact

that their families are too large. Why do they insist on having so many children if they can't afford to feed them? People earning less than ten thousand a year should be forced to restrict their families to one child."

"With penalties for every extra child?"

"Why not? It might focus their minds." Jade jabbed at her meat. "They might remember to take the pill if, instead of more child allowances and more housing points, they were penalised for getting pregnant."

"China operates that system very well, I believe. You're in favour of communism then, are you?"

Jade slammed down her fork. "Listen, I asked you to find out about Di, not throw her words back at me. Every argument you've put forward I've heard a hundred times from her. If my own sister couldn't convince me, nobody can."

"Oh," said Lallie, hurt to discover that after all she came behind Diana in Jade's affections.

"I'm a film maker, not a social worker. I can't afford to get tangled up with these people. Nor can you. They're hopeless, believe me. They drag you down. Look what happened to Di." Jade was pacing up and down the room now. "I feel sorry for them, of course. But there's nothing I can do for them."

"It's too easy. It's too easy to say there's nothing we can do. There must be something."

"There isn't, believe me. What difference did Di make? Oh, I'm sick of all this. Lallie, listen." Jade came and stood behind her chair. She placed her hands on Lallie's shoulders. "We're going over to Ireland soon. Let's have a real holiday there. No more arguments." She bent down and kissed Lallie's head.

Lallie nodded.

But that night, lying awake beside Jade, she knew it was no good. She'd smelled it today in the Jacksons' flat, that smell of failure and powerlessness and humiliation she'd thought she'd put behind her for ever. Her memories of home were about to come flooding back and there wasn't a thing she could do about it.

Debbie Jackson lived in the end house of a crumbling Victorian terrace. In the garden was a sign: Green Park Hotel. Everything about that sign was a lie. It wasn't a hotel, there wasn't a park and there wasn't a patch of green in sight. What had been grass was ruined by litter and broken glass. A mangy-looking alsatian sniffed around a plastic bag filled with rubbish. Finding something to its liking it began tearing the bag open with its teeth. Grace skirted round the dog, looked for the bell, failed to find one and pushed against the front door. It gave way with a groan.

Inside was a din of televisions and children running up and down corridors, drumming on the bare floorboards with their heels. Debbie lived in room 16B. On her way up the three flights of stairs Grace glimpsed, through a half open door, a room packed with beds and clothes and furniture. An Indian woman in a sari came out of it carrying a baby under one arm and a pile of dirty washing under the other. She stared at Grace.

With sinking heart (never had she seen a house like this), Grace knocked on the door of 16B. She'd half thought of bringing with her some of the girls' baby clothes, but she wasn't sure what size Debbie's children would be. Besides, it might have smacked too much of charity.

A pale-faced girl with long brown hair opened the door. She was wearing boots, a pair of patched jeans and an old jumper with holes at the elbows.

"'Ullo," she said sullenly. "What you want?"

"I'm, er, Grace. Grace Napier. Father Keogh sent me." She hesitated. It suddenly seemed as if it was all going to be much more difficult than she'd imagined. There was a little hard look about the girl, whereas Grace had pictured her as rather tearful and sad and in need of mothering.

"'E'd no fucking business givin' out my address." She glowered. "You're not from the DHSS, I 'ope?"

"No, I'm not. Certainly not. He gave me your address because he thought I might be able to . . . " What? Help? It sounded a bit patronising. "Have a little chat with you," she ended lamely.

"You've not come round to lecture me 'ave you? An old cow from the Mothers' Union came round the other day 'anding out contraceptives to everyone. Fucking disgusting it was."

"No. I . . . I'm a journalist."

"Tabloids?" For a second, Debbie's eyes gleamed. Sharper than her mother, Debbie was like the Mammy in always being on the look-out for ways of making a quick buck.

"Er, no. *Guardian.*"

Debbie's face fell.

"I'm doing an article on the homeless and I'd like to talk to you. I understand you're waiting to be rehoused by the council."

"Rehoused? 'uh! That's a laugh." She sniffed. "Not enough 'ouses to go round, are there? You may as well come in, then. If you can get in."

She let go of the door. It swung back against a large double bed which practically filled the room. On top of it two children, of nine months and two and a half years respectively, were playing with a grubby towel. Debbie squatted down beside them on the bed. "You can 'ave the chair," she said.

Grace stepped inside the room, closed the door and squeezed past the bed to the chair. She sat down and looked around. Apart from the bed and the chair, there was a wardrobe, a cracked wash basin and a huge black and white television set. The room, dark even in the daytime, was lit by a naked light bulb. A curtain of faded blue material hung limply at the window. On the windowsill was a pot of plastic flowers, grey with dust. Grace glanced up at the ceiling. It was covered, unevenly, with polystyrene tiles, some of which had come unstuck. On the wall above the bed was a large patch of damp. She looked down again. There was about three feet between the chair and the bed. Not enough room even for a table to eat on. Clothes and nappies spilled out of the wardrobe. On top of the television set was a teapot, a bag of sugar and a tub of margarine.

"How long have you been here?"

"Six months. I was living with me ma but there weren't enough room and her kid and Marie's were always fighting mine. So I went 'omeless and the council put me in 'ere. I was supposed to've been rehoused three months ago but like I said, there ain't enough 'ouses to go round."

"Surely with two young children you must get priority? It can't be good for them cooped up like this." She looked at the two pale-faced little mites crawling around on the bed.

Debbie stared at her. "'Course it's not fuckin' good for 'em. But what does the council care? They don't give a monkey's. They give away all the 'ouses to wogs 'cos they're afraid of what the papers'll say if they don't. You should know that, seeing as 'ow you're a journalist yourself."

"Hm. Yes." Grace's eyes swept round the room again.

"Well," said Debbie, sitting cross-legged on the bed. "Aren't you going to ask me questions and write them down in a notebook?" She eyed Grace suspiciously. "That's what journalists do, isn't it? Or 'ave you brought a tape recorder?"

"Notebook," said Grace hastily. She ferreted in her handbag and brought out the pad she used for her shopping lists and a pencil. She hoped she looked even a bit convincing. "Now then. Do you mind if I ask your age?"

"Nineteen next March."

Grace gave a start of surprise. She'd taken Debbie to be in her mid-twenties at least. She was only a year older than Emma then. Emma, whose letters home were filled with accounts of rock concerts and anxieties about her mocks.

"I 'ad Jill when I was sixteen. Me ma couldn't throw me out 'cos Marie, that's my eldest sister, 'ad already 'ad one an' ma'd tried to throw her out but she'd always come back looking for a bed. Anyway Ma likes kids really. Stop fighting, you two." She separated the children, putting one on either side of her. "They're always at it. Drives me fucking crazy. It's being stuck in 'ere. No place for Jill to run around. 'Ere, shut up for a bit." She stuck a dummy in each of their mouths. "I suppose I should've been more careful after Jill but you don't think, do you?"

Oh God, Emma take care, thought Grace.

"I mean you can't plan these things. They just 'appen. I guess I must be specially what-d'you-call-it – fertile, cos it was first time unlucky for me."

Debbie picked up the baby who was getting fretful and rocked her on her knee.

"After Lyn, I wanted the doctor to sterilise me but he wouldn't, the sod. As if I'd ever want another! Can't afford these two as it is."

She looked at her. Grace pretended to scribble something on her pad.

"What do you live on?"

"Supplementary benefit plus child benefit. I could get the single parent benefit for Jill but it's not worth claiming that. They'd only take it off supplementary benefit. I get all the clothes for me and the kids from jumble sales. Father Keogh's very good. He always lets me know when there's one on."

Grace felt she was being told about life on a different planet.

"Where do you wash and cook?"

"There's the sink there and a toilet round the corner. All of us share that. There's no bath. There's a room downstairs with a stove in it. It's open a couple of hours every day. I do my cooking there. Usually egg and chips or a can of soup.

Nothing fancy." She laughed. "I miss me ma's cooking, though that's nothing to write 'ome about either. Shopping's not too bad. There's a shop on the corner. It's getting there with the kids that's the problem. Ma lent me a buggy but the wheel fell off and I've nothing to mend it with."

"Perhaps I could mend it?" suggested Grace, meaning she'd get Leonard to have a look at it. "Or better still, I've an old pram . . . But I suppose it'd be too big. You haven't anywhere to store things?"

"No."

"Well . . . er . . . "

Overcome by the hopelessness of Debbie's situation, Grace ran out of inspiration.

"Look, you're not a real journalist, are you?"

"No," confessed Grace, shutting up her notebook. "I'm not."

"You shouldn't tell lies." Debbie looked severely at her.

"Sorry," replied Grace meekly.

Debbie sniffed. "I suppose you're one of those middle class do-gooders." Lyn started to scream. Her dummy fell out of her mouth. "Oh Christ. Hungry." She picked up the bottle that was lying on the bed and stuck it in Lyn's mouth. She glanced across at Grace. "If you really want to do something useful, you could slip out to the shop on the corner for a can of soup for me and Jill. By the time I'm through feeding this one, I won't 'ave time to get there and back before they lock up the kitchen again."

"Lock it! Why on earth do they do that?"

Debbie shrugged. "Dunno. Another one of the landlord's little rules. 'E's a real sod, 'e is. If you haven't got the rent on time 'e turns nasty. I'm all right, I get mine paid direct by the council. But there's one girl, two floors down, 'er cheque from 'er old man didn't arrive one week. Quick as a flash the landlord was round, knocking on 'er door at twelve o'clock at night, threatening to chuck 'er and 'er kid out on to the streets. Called 'er all sorts of names. Practically raped 'er, filthy bugger. I suppose 'is wife isn't giving it 'im any more so 'e comes round 'ere, trying to blackmail us into 'aving sex with 'im, dirty ol' sod. Pity you aren't a journalist. I could tell you things would make your hair stand on end."

It already is, thought Grace. "Can't you go to the police?" she asked.

Debbie looked scornful. "Think they'd believe us? It's our word 'gainst 'is and 'e talks posh. Anyway the landlord's not the real bastard. 'E only looks after the place. It's the owner of this fucking dump I'd like to get me 'ands on." She glanced up at the damp patch above her bed.

There were bars on the windows of the corner shop. Grace thought at first that it must be closed; but it wasn't. She bought five cans of soup, two loaves of bread, some fresh fruit and a box of tea bags. The prices were a few pence higher than at her own supermarket, she noticed.

"Thanks," said Debbie as Grace unloaded the food onto the bed. "You needn't have bothered buying two loaves though, one'll go off before we can eat it."

"It's an expensive shop, Debbie. Why don't you try Sainsbury's or Tesco's? I find them very economical. It's worth shopping around a bit."

Debbie gave her a withering look. "Yes, and 'ow am I to manage on the buses with these two? Besides they sell everything in large packets in those shops and as you can see," she gestured ironically around the room, "the fridge 'asn't arrived yet."

"Oh," said Grace, embarrassed.

"Look, you don't mind if I chuck you out now, do you? I got to cook our tea before the kitchen closes."

Grace watched as Debbie gathered up her two children and a can of soup. "Can I come and visit you again?"

Debbie shrugged. "If you want."

"And can I take the buggy? I might be able to get it mended."

"'Elp yourself. It's under the bed." She waved the can of soup. "Don't bother bringing it back if you can't fix it. It's bleedin' useless like it is."

"I'll get it fixed," said Grace firmly. She had great faith in Leonard's fixing abilities.

As visits went, it hadn't been half as successful as Grace had hoped, but she supposed she had to start somewhere. She dragged the buggy down three flights of stairs. When she got to the bottom and glanced up, she saw three pale faces staring down at her. One of them gave a brief smile before all three disappeared. Lonely, thought Grace. No transport. No friends her own age. Probably hardly ever gets to see her family.

She put the buggy into the boot of the car and drove home. On the way she had a stern talk with Major on the subject of council housing and his failure to provide enough to go round.

Leonard, spying from an upstairs window, observed his wife surreptitiously remove what looked suspiciously like a child's buggy from the boot of her car and carry it into the garage. Going down later to investigate, whilst Grace was busy in the kitchen, he discovered the buggy, clumsily covered up by a piece of old curtain. This called for direct action. He marched back into the house.

"Grace, I came across a child's buggy in the garage just now when I was looking for my er – spanner. There isn't anything you'd like to tell me, is there?" He twiddled anxiously with a fork.

Grace turned round from stirring something on the cooker. "Darling! I'm not pregnant if that's what you mean. It'd be practically an impossibility at my age. Unless I went over to that nice man in Italy who gives nature a helping hand." She turned back to the cooker. "The buggy belongs to a . . . a friend of mine. I said I'd ask you if you'd have a go at mending it for them."

Her clever disguise of the gender of the word "friend"

157

wasn't lost on Leonard. Grace was going out with a married man. Or perhaps he was a single parent. At any rate, he had children. And a buggy. That made his children very young indeed. My God! She was in love with a younger man. He sat down on a chair and stared at his wife. That was it. She was in love with a young leftie who was hopelessly impractical at the things he, Leonard, was good at. Like mending buggies. He didn't derive much satisfaction from this picture. Most likely the young man gave rousing political speeches. Or took her to left wing rallies and held her hand.

She must think I'm fearfully dull and past it. He looked gloomily down at his baggy corduroy trousers. Should he buy some new clothes? And a bottle of that stuff that covered up grey hairs? (The trouble was, he had so many). Oh dear, he needed help. His rival had youth and enthusiasm and political commitment on his side. And children. Grace'd always loved small children. He wished his daughters were at home. They'd have been able to advise him on clothes at least. He wondered whether those foolish magazines they read gave any help with this sort of thing.

"Leonard." His wife's voice broke into his thoughts. "Are you all right? You're looking a bit peaky. You're not ill, are you?"

"Ill? Not at all." He leapt out of his chair and began striding up and down the room. "You know me, Grace. Fit as fiddle. Never had a day's illness in my life. Fitter than many chaps ten years younger. Twenty years younger. Half my age," he added, to be on the safe side.

Grace raised her eyebrows in surprise. She was remembering several occasions when Leonard had used the excuse of a slight cold to retire to bed and be waited on hand and foot. She turned back to her soup.

"Grace," he said, after a while, "you do love me, don't you? I mean I do have some good qualities, don't I? I'm thoughtful, practical, neat about the house . . ."

Grace laughed and stirred the soup. "Darling, you've been reading your CV again."

Now was that the reaction of a woman who loved him?

Lallie sat on the floor of the living-room, rested her head on her knees and was wafted back, amidst strains of *Fire and Water*, to the north of England and to the time when people called her Lillie and pitied her on account of her mother.

Lillie stood at the foot of the bed. "Come on, mother. You have to get up."

"You don't understand," her mother moaned, from beneath the bedclothes. "I can't get up. You don't know what it feels like."

Lillie sighed. She went round the side of the huge iron bedstead and reached across for her mother's breakfast tray. She'd nibbled at a slice of toast and sipped half a cup of tea. The cup wobbled precariously on its saucer. Lillie put her knee up against the bed to steady the tray.

"If you don't get up, you won't get any dinner," she said firmly. "I'm not bringing it up to you. The doctor said I wasn't to."

"A man! What does he know?" Her mother sniffed and burrowed further down the bed.

Lillie went out of the room, placed the tray on the carpet and closed the bedroom door. Then she picked up the tray and went downstairs. Her mother was beginning to answer back. Things were looking up. Lillie calculated that in another couple of days she'd be able to get back to school.

She put the tray down beside the sink, tied an apron over her red and white kilt and quickly did the washing up. Then she returned to her books which were strewn over the kitchen table. A hardback copy of *Prester John*, a maths exercise book and a French grammar. She could count on a bit of peace till it was time to get the dinner ready for Tom, her younger brother. Even if her mother did manage to drag herself out of bed she wouldn't have the energy to cook dinner. They'd have fish fingers and peas and custard with jam in it. That would please Tom. He hated it when their mother was ill, he didn't understand.

"Your mother's got multiple sclerosis," the doctor had said. "You must make sure she does her exercises every day."

Lillie had looked up "multiple sclerosis" in the school dictionary. "A wasting disease," it had said. "It is incurable and often goes on for years." She had closed the book with a bang. A sick mother and a helpless father. She'd have to make her own way in the world.

"She could go into hospital," the doctor suggested.

"No, no!" screamed her mother. "Don't let them take me away. I might never get out again."

This was more than her father could bear. So Lillie took over. There were days when her mother would hardly speak, hardly eat. She stumbled over chairs, dropped things, lurched awkwardly about the house like a drunk, frightening Tom. Then, quite suddenly, her symptoms would quieten down again. Her mother would jump out of bed one morning, begin spring cleaning the house from top to bottom, rearrange the furniture, start knitting them all new jumpers. She'd follow them about the house, chatting ten to the dozen about what she'd been doing while Lillie and Tom were at school. Lillie who, like her father, was fond of peace and quiet, found her mother's readjustments to health only slightly less wearing than her illnesses. She'd grown up loving her mother, feeling fiercely protective of her, yet resenting her demands. One time, coming out of a particularly long bout of sickness, her mother had put her arms round her daughter and said, "You know, you're the only one who can save me." Lillie had felt it was too great a burden to put on anyone.

When she was fifteen, she'd looked up her mother again in the dictionary. A medical dictionary this time. She came across the word obsessional. It fitted her mother perfectly. She was obsessed – about muddy footprints on the clean linoleum, about spots on the furniture, about keeping doors and windows locked. Nightly the house shook as her mother went back again and again to check that the front door was securely locked. Lillie often wondered whom she expected to break in. They lived in a semi-detached with two bedrooms and a boxroom. The covers on the sofa were worn and darned. The curtains, though clean, didn't quite reach down to the windowsill. They possessed nothing of value.

Because of her mother's illness they rarely had callers. Lillie hadn't invited friends round since the day she'd brought Jenny back and her friend had sat all through tea staring at her mother's hands which were red and swollen and bled at the knuckles.

"When I married her, Florence was known as the most fashionable woman in Stockton," Lillie's father would say, shaking his head. Ron was deeply in love with his tall, thin, beautiful wife. But he didn't know how to help her. Also, he was a little in awe of her. Florence's father, Lillie's grandfather, had earned money out in Africa. Enough to give his daughter dreams of being a lady but not enough to satisfy them. Nevertheless, Florence's family was regarded as a cut above Ron's. Ron was a foreman in ICI. At half past six every morning, the works bus would pick him up from the end of their road and take him the twenty odd miles to the factory site. He wore cloth caps and a satchel slung across his chest.

On summer weekends, when their mother was well, they'd take the bus to the seaside and Lillie and Tom would build sandcastles and paddle in the sea which swirled blackly around their legs because of the coal. They'd walk for miles across deserted expanses of sand and their mother, her coat collar turned up against the wind, would tell them about the time when this seaside resort had been visited by the cream of southern society. Ladies and gentlemen who'd stayed at the huge hotels, now crumbling and derelict along the sea promenade.

"This was a smart town then," she'd say. "Full of elegant people."

"You're elegant, Florence," Lillie's father would reply.

And her mother would laugh and toss her head. "Get along with you, Ron."

In moments such as these, Lillie caught glimpses of what life could have been like if her mother had never got sick. Beauty and elegance. Her mother had wanted to surround their lives with these. She wore tailored suits and pencil skirts that emphasised her height and slimness. She had, when she was well, sparkling brown eyes and thickly curling brown hair. Her face was rather long and angular and she had long, narrow hands with perfect nails. Her clothes were all browns or black, with the occasional cream blouse. She wore no colour, ever, except a dash of red on her lips. Occasionally, she made a concession to propriety by cramming a brown felt hat on her head. She had style, which her husband had not.

She yearned to be mistress of some country house and pour tea from a silver pot and nod graciously to the maid to clear away. And since she couldn't have these things, she wished them for her children, for Lillie in particular. Polished furniture, a laden table, sweet-smelling linen – these were Florence's goals. They shored her up against the periods of sickness when she lay in bed not wanting to go on.

Not many of the fathers down their street bothered with their children but Ron was different. Leaving their mother resting in bed, Ron would take Lillie and Tom off to Middleton-One-Row to walk down by the river and wrinkle their noses at the pungent smell of stinging nettles and wild garlic. Or the three of them would spend the whole day tramping the moors. Mile after mile of tough heather, springy ferns and peat, with the wind tossing their hair and only the sheep for company. She and her father would stride along discussing trade unions, books, art, whilst Tom trudged behind them, stalwart, his hands in his pockets. For lunch they'd light a fire and roast sausages and marshmallows. Osmotherly, Sheepwash, Black Hambleton, Chop Gate. The places of her childhood had quaint and mysterious names.

He'd been a strange man in many ways, her father. Timid and unpractical. Always living out some fantasy from the latest book he'd been reading. He devoured biographies of great men. If they shot and hunted, he wanted to do the same and would stride off into their tiny backyard to shoot at pigeons with an air gun. After reading a life of Gauguin, he bought a box of watercolours and tried his hand at painting. Another time it was music. He borrowed Tom's recorder and taught himself to play.

He'd left school at fourteen and always regretted his lack of education. At the end of every week Tom and Lillie had to give an account of what they'd learned at school and if there was something he didn't know about, he borrowed their school books and read it up. When Lillie started French, he went to evening classes to learn the language, until he was put on night shifts (after one of these shifts, he was brought home with his leg badly burned from an explosion). To the end of his life, he was convinced there was something he would excel at if only he could find out what it was. At work these aspirations counted for nothing and what with that, and his wife's illnesses, he didn't progress nearly as far as he should have done. He remained on the shop floor all his working life.

He encouraged Lillie to try for university.

"But how will you manage when mother gets ill?"

"We'll manage. You go for it, girl."

They hadn't had to manage for long. Ron had died of pneumonia during Lillie's first term at London. Lillie suspected his lungs had got polluted at work but of course it was impossible to prove a thing like that. She worried about what would become of her mother and in fact, shortly after the funeral, Florence collapsed. Lillie took a year out from university to go home and try to get her mother back on an even keel. It wasn't easy. By this time, Florence was confined to a wheelchair and her sight was going. She missed Ron dreadfully. Lillie had decided to give up university altogether when a letter from her tutor arrived saying she was the best student he'd had for years, it would be a crime if she gave up her course and couldn't something be worked out? Lillie spent the rest of the year up in Stockton, torn between resentment and fear. She went behind her mother's back and contacted distant relations who'd never been told of Florence's illness. With money they supplied, she arranged for a nurse to pop in daily. She returned to university.

In her second term, by now a year behind, Lillie was once again summoned home by Tom. She was shocked at what she found. Florence had deteriorated badly. Day after day she sat in her wheelchair in the front room, immobile, almost blind, definitely incontinent. Now the dialogue went: "I'm a burden to you, Lillie." "No, mother. You're not." "I am. You should be getting on with your studies, not looking after me." "Don't worry about that now. Concentrate on getting well. I'll think up something." Lillie wrote to the university to ask for another term off. Before she'd received their reply, she went into her mother's bedroom one morning and found her dead in her bed.

The doctor said it was inevitable, her kidneys had become infected. The day before she died, as if foreseeing her own death, Florence had said to Lillie. "You've done the most any daughter could do. And more. Don't blame yourself, my Lillie. It's this horrible disease." Lillie did blame herself. For the next few years she woke every morning to face the fact she'd failed to keep her mother alive. At night she dreamt of people dying, of her mother sitting up in her coffin at the funeral and reproaching Lillie for not looking after her better . . .

Tom became manager of a furniture shop in Middlesbrough. He married a typist. They'd been going to live in the family home but when they showed her round, Evie had wrinkled up her petite nose and said, "It's that small and dingy. It smells of boiled meat." And Tom and Lillie had looked down at the dull brown carpet in the living room and seen their mother sitting there in her wheelchair. They'd sold the house and divided the proceeds. Lillie and Tom sent each other cards at Christmas. Tom had two little girls now. The family had disintegrated. "Perhaps it never worked very well," thought Lillie. "Perhaps it's better this way."

She'd completed her undergraduate studies and progressed, with the aid of a grant, to the Warburg Institute to study history. During these years she made many interesting discoveries. One of them was that she preferred women to men. At a party she met Jade. "Don't you have any other name but Lillie?" Jade had asked on their second evening out. Lillie shook her head. Jade thought for a moment. "I knew an American girl once – her name was Lallie. Lillie sounds like a century ago."

So Lillie became Lallie and felt all ties with the north had finally been broken. And was glad.

Later someone told her that the Jews change a person's name to invest their life with new significance or herald a change of fortune or, in the case of a very sick person, to mislead the angel of death. Which fitted. For in her new-found happiness with Jade, Lallie had been able to suppress all memory of her mother.

And now those memories had come flooding back. The newspaper article about Ruth Martin, her absurd dream of Robina, they'd been brought together and summed up in the smell of hopelessness that had clung to the Jacksons and their miserable flat. She remembered the anger she'd felt at her mother's death. The outrageousness of having been made to suffer as Florence had.

Lallie banged her head violently against her knees several times and stood up. Ridiculous to go on like this. Her mother had been dead for over ten years. Yet she saw her as clearly as if it had been yesterday, sitting rigid in her wheelchair, her gnarled hands clutching awkwardly at the arms.

She kicked the table and went out for a walk.

"You don't know what it's like to live in a country that's rotten to the core. Where everyone talks of progress all the time so they don't have to look over their shoulders at the past."

Joachim clenched his fists and paced the floor in Cornelius's study.

Cornelius shook his head. "Germany has her past greatnesses like any other country. Goethe, Beethoven, Rilke, Brecht. You can't dismiss those names."

Joachim paused and looked at him. "What other western country has systematically tried to destroy one section of its population in the way the Nazis tried to destroy the Jews?" He resumed his pacing.

Cornelius sat back in his armchair, his slippers on, smoking his pipe and observing his friend. "You know," he said, taking his pipe out of his mouth, "such things have happened before – and in countries other than Germany. Think of those great witchhunts of the sixteenth and seventeenth centuries. Thousands of innocent women burned all across Europe, victims of a huge delusion on the part of the authorities. The Nazis can't be seen as an isolated case. The urge to purify the world by annihilating one group of human beings thought to be agents of evil runs very deep in us."

He knocked his pipe against the hearth.

"Incidentally, did you know?" he continued, warming to his theme, "Ireland has a famous witchcraft case. Alice Kyteler of Kilkenny. She was accused in the fourteenth century of killing off her three husbands by sorcery. Pity it's died out really," he added, "you could have accused Katrin of being a witch and solved one of your problems. They used torture so even Katrin would be bound to confess to the most lurid crimes in the end."

"Cornelius!"

"And of course most of the accusations were brought by people who had a guilty conscience towards their victims."

"Cornelius!" Joachim came to a halt in front of the armchair. "I don't have a guilty conscience about Katrin."

His friend looked up at him quizzically.

"OK. I feel slightly guilty about Katrin," he conceded. "But," he turned on his heel and continued his pacing, "that has nothing to do with the factory closure, which is what we're supposed to be discussing. For heaven's sake, step out of the sixteenth century for a second. I need your advice."

"I wouldn't hope for much from a man who sits up in bed reading with a colander on his head," remarked Elizabeth, bringing in a tray of coffee and biscuits. Diogenes lolloped along at her heels.

"A colander?"

"I find it extremely convenient," Cornelius explained. "It shades my eyes from the bright bedside lamp Elizabeth insists on having and it keeps off the flies."

"There aren't any flies," retorted Elizabeth, going out of the room and closing the door behind her.

"Anyway," Cornelius poured out the coffee, "I thought the factory closure and your marital problems were intimately linked. If Katrin didn't demand such large sums of money from you or if she tried to earn some money herself, you wouldn't have to keep on with a job you not only detest, but which you're now beginning to disapprove of."

Joachim looked at him sharply. But Cornelius's expression, as he handed him a coffee cup, was at its most impenetrable. The silence in the room was broken only by the crackle of the fire and soft moans from Diogenes chasing rabbits in his sleep.

"You think I should give up the job?" said Joachim eventually. "But even if we set aside Katrin, what about the boys? There's their education to think of."

"The boys, the boys," grumbled Cornelius. "There're scholarships and grants. You could even sell a field or two. Don't you think your sons deserve to see you happy once in a while?" He glanced up at Joachim. "You haven't been happy for a long time, have you?"

"I . . . " He was startled by the suddenness of Cornelius's remark. He went over to the window and stood looking out at the long-haired nymphs and dryads dancing around Cornelius's fountain. "No," he said finally.

There was a hiss from the hearth. Cornelius leant across and threw the smouldering twig back into the fire.

"I thought I saw her the other day," Joachim murmured. "For the most fleeting of seconds I thought I saw her."

He had no need to specify who he was talking about. Cornelius understood.

"Why don't you advertise in the newspaper?"

"Christabel never reads the papers."

"On the radio then. One of these phone-in programmes. I'm sure they must have them in Germany too."

"Yes." Joachim swung the curtain cord to and fro. "But she doesn't want to see me. I know that. I'm easy enough to find if she did." He let go of the cord. It fell back against the window with a clatter. "Oh, what does happiness matter? Who's happy these days? Is anyone?"

But later, walking back over the fields to his castle, Christabel danced once more into his mind and he thought that maybe happiness did matter, a little. He'd felt alive with her. That was surely better than this dull closing up of the senses, this slow retreat from life upon which he seemed engaged. He felt like some sort of octopus. Every time he put out a tentacle, life dropped a brick on it. Soon he'd stop bothering altogether and stay curled up in a corner refusing to get involved.

He caught sight of Mrs Dart out in the fields gathering tansey and dandelions. Mrs Dart knew a cure for jaundice. It had been handed down through her family from mother to daughter. It appealed to Joachim's sense of interlocking generations. Waving to her, he wondered what his sons were doing at that moment and whether he'd have something to hand on to them which they'd want.

He wandered into the castle gardens and stood looking at the grassy terraces. The gravel paths that used to run between the terraces were hidden now. Everything was overgrown. Below him he could dimly discern the outline of a tennis court, long fallen into disuse. This way of life was doomed. In the Waltons' time they'd have had half a dozen gardeners. The castle had been built for the Walton family in the eighteenth century. Remnants of the eighteenth-century landscape lingered on in the copper beeches and evergreen oaks that stood in the fields around the castle, in the rhododendron bushes by the lake, in the curve of the wood sweeping up the hill.

The Waltons had taken it all for granted. A dull family they'd been, judging from the books in the library. They'd administered their estates, sent their sons to Harrow, taken care over their daughters' marriages and died fighting for England. They'd had shooting parties, hunt balls and maids to light fires in their bedrooms. In fine weather the ladies went in carriages for picnics by the lake. When it rained they got horribly bored.

Nowadays it would be thought a wicked way of life. He threw away the piece of grass he'd been nibbling and walked in the direction of the castle. That wasn't what he wanted for his sons, not that they should turn the estate into a vast pleasure ground and reap profits from tenants. No, a solid life of farming was what he pictured for them. Working the land, providing jobs for local people, preserving the castle which was part of Ireland's heritage.

He crossed the courtyard and stood looking up at the grey towers where crows were circling. Would it be possible after all, as Cornelius had suggested, to settle here?

He pushed open the kitchen door and went up the back stairs to the first floor. He walked along the corridor to the couple of rooms he kept for himself. The rest of this floor and the one above it were unaltered since his father's time. All of it badly needed replastering. He fished a beetle out of the old stone bath and turned on the tap. It took a good ten minutes for hot water to get up to this part of the castle.

He went into the bedroom and started to undress. There was no central heating above ground floor level but storage heaters took the chill off the air. He was used to it, though his sons always complained of the cold when they came and, to prove the point, spent a lot of their time in bed.

He stepped into the bath, his cold flesh becoming pimply under the impact of the hot water. He lay there soaking and looking up at the ceiling. Paint was flaking off in several places. To live here. To live here and teach his sons to love the land, to care for the people who worked it, not to mind the cold, the lack of comfort, the absence of carpets on the floor. To teach them to measure their lives by the rhythm of the seasons, the ripening of the barley, the cutting of the silage. Was it such an impossible dream?

He stood up in the bath and reached for a towel. He must begin at once, plant the idea in their minds this summer. They'd been with their mother too long. He had rights too. And, goodness knows, in these times how lucky they were to have jobs waiting for them.

He went downstairs and collected the cold supper Molly had left for him in the kitchen. He took it into the yellow sitting-room, poured himself a glass of whiskey and switched on the television.

"It's no life for a married man, sure it's not," muttered Molly, glancing across the courtyard later and seeing Joachim at the sink washing up his dishes.

And Joachim, lying in bed thinking that if he took it very slowly maybe he could piece together Christabel (start with her legs, long, perfectly shaped, her rather large wide feet with the skin rubbed hard on the soles from going barefoot in the summer), would have agreed.

Grace was in the breakfast room writing to her daughter Emma. She'd written that she'd started doing a little social work. (Though, really, could you call it that?) She'd met Debbie, a single mother living in a hostel with her two young children, and would Emma like to come with her to visit them next time she was home from school? Debbie might be glad to see someone her own age.

"Hullo." Leonard appeared in the doorway.

"Oh. Hello, dear." Grace hurriedly laid down her pen and placed a blank sheet of paper over the letter she'd been writing, an action which did not escape Leonard's notice. Intrigue, he thought. Plots and conspiracies wherever I look.

Grace turned round. "What on earth . . . ?" she began.

Leonard stepped into the room. He was wearing a pair of bright red trousers. "Do you like them? They're all the rage, I've been told," he said proudly. He did a twirl for her benefit. The trousers rustled a little.

"Very nice, dear," said Grace weakly. "Almost like a pop star."

"You know me, Grace. I like to move with the times."

She stared at him.

"After all, I'm not in my bathchair yet," he added meaningfully.

"No dear, I never supposed you were."

That shook her, thought Leonard, rustling out into the garden.

Grace added a postscript to her letter to Emma. "Your father has just come into the room dressed in the most peculiar pair of red trousers which rustle like a bridesmaid's dress when he walks. This morning I found him doing keep-fit exercises on the landing. Is it the change of life, do you think? Did they mention anything about the male menopause in your sex education classes?"

Jade and Lallie flew into Dublin from Heathrow, stayed overnight in the Shelbourne and hired a car to tour the country. They went west to Galway, north to Donegal and then back down to Kerry. But either the houses were nothing out of the ordinary, plain Georgian mansions, or the owners were unwilling to have their privacy invaded by a film crew. In Dublin they called on Nicholas Johnson and Jade told him of their lack of success.

"Old and mysterious." He thought for a moment. "I'll put you in touch with a client of mine. Joachim Seefeldt. He lives in a castle, just outside Bannon as a matter of fact. Rather hard up. He might welcome the chance of some cash."

He dialled the castle number. Molly answered and when she heard what it was about, took it upon herself to arrange an appointment for them with Joachim who was due back that weekend for a cattle sale. "Films! That's more like it!" she said to herself as she put the phone down. "Bit of life about the place." She began to plan what she'd give them for lunch.

Lallie came away disappointed from meeting Nicholas Johnson. He was a paler, altogether less significant man than she'd imagined. His shoulders were stooped, his voice thin and fluting. No wonder Rachel had left him for Stefan. What was friendship compared with passion? Perhaps they'd got it wrong, perhaps they'd misjudged Stefan?

"We must show clearly the passion between them," she said to Jade, as they went shopping in Brown Thomas. "The film must show that by leaving Stefan, Rachel was renouncing passion."

"Passion?" Jade picked up a gold necklace and tried it on. "My mother was always passionate on stage."

"On stage, yes. But she never had another affair that lasted, did she?"

"No." Jade took off the necklace and put it back on the stand. "Perhaps she was a repressed lesbian."

"You think everyone's a repressed lesbian."

"True. Anyway, she was better off without it. Passion only muddles things. If she'd stayed with Stefan she'd never have become an actress. Do you know what I think?" She turned to Lallie. "I think she should have gone back to Nicholas."

"But he's . . . so conventional. A moderately successful lawyer uptight about his homosexuality. Now he *is* repressed."

"He'd have allowed her to get on with her work. He'd have helped her, looked after the practical side of things for her."

"Rather a utilitarian motive for staying with someone, don't you think?" said Lallie slowly.

"Nonsense! Passion can be very overrated." Jade went over to look at shoes.

So how would you rate our relationship? wondered Lallie, following her.

When Joachim arrived on the Saturday, Molly was buzzing with excitement.

"Now Molly," he said, "let's not count any chickens."

Privately he thought: overgrown gardens and peeling plaster – no one will want to film this place. However, it was too late now to put them off. He shrugged his shoulders and went to see his cattle, perfumed and beribboned, sent to auction.

Alan turned out to be right: the local farmers couldn't afford their prices. Only half the heifers were sold. The rest would have to be put back into the herd. The older cows would be sold to the meat factory, which wouldn't bring in nearly so much money as selling them at auction. Joachim set off for church the next day with a heavy heart.

Meanwhile Jade and Lallie were bumping their way over potholes down to Bannon. As the castle came into view, with all its different towers and turrets, Jade broke into laughter.

"Perfect! A fantasy castle. Just right for my mother!"

She stopped the car and gave Lallie a hug.

Molly was waiting excitedly at the castle door for them. She took them the long way round to the yellow sitting-room, across the square entrance hall with its curving staircase, through the library and the mirror-lined ballroom. She was determined to impress these visitors from London.

"Breathtaking!" murmured Jade, going over to one of the full-length windows that looked out on to the lawns. "You know, Lallie, this place has a wildness about it that's exactly what I was looking for. Let's keep our fingers crossed this Seefeldt chap is extremely hard up."

Joachim and Sam came out of church together. The service had gone much more satisfactorily this time.

"Wouldn't you know it?" said Sam. "Just because the Bishop isn't here. Ah ha!" he murmured, catching sight of Cornelius hovering. "Morning, Cornelius."

"Hello, Sam," shouted Cornelius, coming nearer.

Diogenes wagged his tail.

"V-v-vicar," said a voice behind them.

Sam turned round. Oh good, he thought, a new parishioner to impress Cornelius with.

"Good morning." He shook hands warmly with the short, bald man. "Newcomers to the area?"

"M-morning v-vicar. Y-yes, m-my w-wife and I hope to b-be r-regular attenders at y-your church from n-now on."

Sam beamed.

"I have to w-warn you though, I d-don't b-believe in f-flattering v-vicars. I've t-told every v-v-vicar in every p-p-parish I've b-been in to f-f-fuck off. And I shan't be afraid to s-say it to you."

Sam winced.

"Well done," said Cornelius, encouragingly.

The man went on his way.

"Sam." Cornelius shifted the newspapers under his arm. "I've been reading something that should interest you."

"Oh yes?" said Sam warily.

"Yes. Did you know Freud argues that religious belief is simply the search for a father figure? In other words, it's a neurosis."

"Freud? Are you still reading him?" Sam adopted a superior air. "We did touch on him of course when I was at theological college, but he was thought very outdated, even then."

"I'm surprised they let you read him at theological college," said Cornelius, put out.

"Oh yes," lied Sam. "But he was thought very old hat."

He climbed onto his lawnmower. Next Sunday he'd ask forgiveness in advance for the lies he'd be telling Cornelius after Mass.

"I can't think what you Anglo-Catholics are coming to!" exclaimed Cornelius to Joachim. "You seem ready to embrace any new trend that comes along. It's a dangerous tendency. You ought to stamp on it."

"I've some film people coming out from Dublin to see me." Joachim refused to be drawn into an argument over theology (it was Sunday, after all). He looked at his watch. "In fact, they should be there now. Want to come up and help me entertain them? I don't expect they'll stay long."

"Good idea." Cornelius bundled Diogenes and the newspapers into the back of Joachim's Land Rover. "The in-laws are visiting today so any excuse to delay going home is welcome. Elizabeth's mother is a witch if ever I saw one."

"On what do you base your opinion?" asked Joachim suspiciously. He started up the engine.

"She belongs to the beads and beans brigade. She brings us jars of homemade juices and jams, trying to poison us, for our stomachs are used to preservatives and chemicals. She spends a lot of the time when talking balanced on one foot like a stork (she claims to be practising yoga). When I came down with the flu, she sent round this perfectly vile concoction. It killed the plant I poured it onto. She's definitely a witch."

"They're in the yellow sitting-room, sir. Hello, Mr Fry," Molly added stiffly. She disapproved of Cornelius. "I've made extra for lunch, sir, seeing as you've got visitors."

"Oh I shouldn't think they'll stay," replied Joachim.

"As you wish, sir." Molly retired offended through the green baize door.

"Perhaps we could take them down to the pub for a jar?" whispered Cornelius, thinking that drunkenness might provide an acceptable excuse for not going home at all. "These film chappies like their drink."

He pushed open the door of the yellow sitting-room. "Oh," he said, taking in Lallie on the sofa. "Ah," he said, as Jade turned round. Ravishing. He studied her long blonde hair and boyish hips, not quite disguised by her calf length suede skirt. Diogenes gave him a warning nudge.

Lallie stood up. "Hello." She held out her hand. "I'm Lallie Greene. And this is Jade McKenna. She's the one making the film. Which of you is Mr Seefeldt?"

"Call me Joachim." He shook her by the hand. An intelligent-looking woman, he thought. "May I introduce a friend of mine, Cornelius Fry?"

Introductions over, Joachim offered everyone sherry.

"So you're looking for a place to film?"

"I think we've found it, Mr – Joachim, if you're agreeable." Jade clasped her knees. "It's a magnificent castle. Exactly what we had in mind."

Joachim looked surprised. "I'm afraid you'll find the place isn't as well kept as it might be. I don't live here all the time, you see. Some of the rooms on the upper floors are undecorated. And I have to say that the gardens are in a dreadful state."

"But it's extremely picturesque," interrupted Cornelius. "An absolute jewel. I'd draw up the contract now, if I were you. Yours isn't the first offer he's had. How much do you pay?"

"Cornelius!"

"This'll solve your money problems if you play your cards right," hissed Cornelius. "Stop selling the place short."

Who is that horrid little man? wondered Jade. She recognised him from somewhere.

"This film of yours," continued Cornelius. "It doesn't have a Muslim theme by any chance? I mean, you won't be importing Muslim actors into the locality, will you?"

"No. There's a Jew in it, though. A Russian Jew," replied Lallie, wondering if they'd just unearthed some ancient Irish prejudice against Muslims.

"That's no good. No good at all." Cornelius waved his hands about. "We've plenty of Jews round here. It's Muslims we're short of."

"Oh." Good gracious, thought Lallie, the ecumenical movement is making great strides in Ireland.

"Cornelius! Really! Do shut up," said Joachim.

"Lunch is ready, sir." Molly appeared in the doorway. This was part of her ploy. She never normally announced meals.

Joachim turned to Jade. "If you're really interested in filming here, would you care to stay and discuss it over lunch?"

Jade glanced at Lallie. "That would be great."

Lallie nodded. "Ages since we've had Sunday lunch. We usually make do with a sandwich."

Molly beamed. "You'll be wanting to be off then, Mr Fry."

"Not at all," he replied calmly. "I may as well be hung for a sheep as for a lamb. Or perhaps it is lamb we're having?"

"Our own venison, Mr Fry," said Molly coldly.

"Even better. I'll give Elizabeth a ring and let her know. My in-laws are in residence today," he explained to Lallie. "She'll understand my urgent need to get out of the house."

"*Did* your wife understand?" asked Lallie curiously, when Cornelius joined them at table several minutes later.

"Ahem! Not entirely." He shook out his napkin. "Never mind, it'll blow over." He winked at Jade sitting on his right.

She frowned. She was still trying to remember where she'd seen him before.

They were seated in the smaller of the two dining-rooms, looking out onto the terraced lawns. The room was entirely oak panelled and in one corner was a small door, no more than three feet high.

"It's called Puck's door," said Joachim, in answer to a question from Lallie. "He's a little elf who's said to appear whenever he's angry with the owners of the castle."

"Has he been sighted recently?" asked Lallie, with interest.

"The last time he was seen was in the nineteen twenties, apparently." Joachim poured out wine. "When the eldest son, John Walton (the eldest son was always called John, the Waltons weren't a family renowned for their imagination, I'm afraid), anyway, when he was disinherited for marrying an American. Apparently that annoyed Puck."

"A spirit with liberal views." Cornelius chuckled. "Ahead of their time, as they so often are."

"Surely you don't believe in spirits?" put in Jade.

"Ah my dear," Cornelius held out his plate as Molly reluctantly filled it with venison and red cabbage, "when you live in the country you begin to see that life is a lot more mysterious than city folk think. My mother-in-law, for instance, is a witch."

Jade looked alarmed.

"Now Cornelius," Joachim took up his fork, "spare us your family problems, please."

"Well," said Cornelius, through a mouthful of venison, "if this film isn't to have a Muslim theme which, if I may say so, is a great mistake on your part, what is it to be about?"

"My mother," said Jade simply. "Rachel McKenna. She was an actress."

"Ah yes!" said Cornelius. "A very fine one too. I saw her several times on the stage at the Abbey. I knew you reminded me of somebody."

"Since my mother had dark hair and I have blonde, it's generally presumed I take after my father," replied Jade, rather tartly.

"Was he famous too? I don't think I . . . "

"I don't know," Jade said firmly.

"Don't know? Oh, presumed. Oh, I see. Well, it sounds a very interesting subject," he continued hurriedly. "And you think this is the place to film it?"

"The early scenes, yes," replied Jade. "You see, my mother was brought up around here."

"Of course! Old Frank McKenna's place!" exclaimed Cornelius. "I got up a petition to save it. Didn't do any good. Another piece of our heritage gone."

"You knew him?"

Cornelius shook his head. "Before my time. My aunt sometimes spoke of him. She was taken to court by him once. Some dispute over right of way."

"I know where I've seen you." Jade waved a fork at Cornelius. "Outside Nicholas Johnson's office in Dublin."

"Oh. Mm." Cornelius blushed and shot a hasty glance at Joachim. "Money troubles, you know."

Molly brought in the apple pie while Joachim refilled their glasses and came to a decision.

"If you think the castle will suit your purpose, I'll be happy to let you use it. I'm not often here, so you won't be disturbing anyone – "

"Though of course your fee will have to take into consideration the inconvenience, wear and tear, damages and breakages," interrupted Cornelius.

"Cornelius!"

Cornelius raised his eyes heavenwards. "I suppose you think you only have to pray and gold coins will come tumbling down into your lap. This man went to church this morning," he added, turning to their visitors. "Quaint, isn't it? I bet two sophisticated beings like yourselves don't go to church."

"Cornelius, really!"

"Never," said Jade. "We're not religious. It's the here and now that interests me. Not what goes on after death, if anything does go on."

Mentioning death in Cornelius's presence was like showing a red rag to a bull.

"There you're making a big mistake. Montaigne, a wise man if ever there was one, said we should all train ourselves to meditate on death. Do you realise we in the late twentieth century are the first human beings to live without the stench of mortality constantly in our nostrils? Nowadays some people reach their fifties without seeing anyone die. In Dickens's time, it was the custom to take children to see dead babies laid out in their coffins . . . "

Lallie shuddered. She bent her head to her plate, an expression of pain on her face.

"Cornelius, please! This is hardly a suitable topic for Sunday lunch," protested Joachim.

But Cornelius was not to be silenced.

"Highly suitable, I should have thought." He looked round at them all. "You shouldn't try to avoid thinking about death, you know. It's part of us. Montaigne says we should all try very hard to have a good death."

"Excuse me." Lallie got up suddenly and left the room. They heard her go into the sitting-room next door.

There was a silence.

"Oh dear," said Cornelius contritely. "Did I go too far?"

"You did," Joachim replied.

"It doesn't matter," said Jade, torn between annoyance at Cornelius and irritation with Lallie for being so easily upset. "She's been overworking lately." Though actually, she thought, that isn't true. What *was* wrong with her then?

"I hope . . . " began Joachim.

Jade brushed his apology aside. "She'll be all right." She made no effort to follow Lallie.

Hard as nails, that one, thought Cornelius. Must be tough

being the daughter of a famous actress. And hadn't there been something about a sister? He tried to remember what it was.

Lallie slipped back into the room.

"Sorry," she said. "I suddenly felt, um, unwell."

"Let's go into the library for coffee," suggested Joachim. "Then I'll show you both round the place."

"Great!" replied Jade, frowning at Lallie.

"Now Cornelius," said Joachim in a low voice, as the two men led the way across the stone flagged hall to the library, "as the Pope would say, I expect you to observe a period of obsequious silence."

"Mea culpa, mea culpa, mea maxima culpa." Cornelius struck his breast. "How was I to know the woman would be so touchy on the subject of death?"

"Most people are," replied Joachim dryly. "It's generally considered impolite to bring it up."

Jade and Lallie wandered around the library admiring the collection of leather bound books, the baroque fireplace and the ornate plasterwork on the ceiling. Jade imagined a scene with her mother as a child taking refuge here from her father's bullying.

Cornelius stayed on the help show them round the castle.

"You got on well with that film maker," remarked Joachim afterwards. "You're getting to be quite a flirt in your old age."

"My dear boy." Cornelius spread out his hands. "Whatever are you thinking of? Anyone can see a mile off they're a couple of lesbians. You know, you really ought to spend more time out of churches, in the real world."

"Oh," said Joachim, colouring.

"Mission accomplished," said Jade as they drove back to Dublin.

"Yes," answered Lallie. "It's good."

"You might sound more enthusiastic."

"I am enthusiastic."

"I never said you weren't. Just that you didn't sound it,"

Jade bantered. As always when work was going well she was bubbling over with excitement and wanted everyone around her to share her high spirits.

There was a silence.

"I'm being quiet now," Jade said, "so you're supposed to talk. It's called having a conversation."

"Sorry. Don't feel much like talking," mumbled Lallie.

Jade sighed, drummed her fingers on the steering wheel, sighed again and finally switched on the tape deck.

"Grace, you do like me, don't you?" asked Leonard suddenly, at breakfast.

Grace stood in the middle of the room, holding a slice of toast.

"Of course I like you. You're my husband."

Leonard groaned. "That's what I was afraid you'd say." He sighed and folded his newspaper. "That's what women say when they're no longer in love with the man they live with. You're just putting up with me, that's what it is."

"Leonard," Grace set the piece of toast down on her plate, "I do like you. I wouldn't have married you – and stayed with you . . . I wouldn't be living with you now if I didn't like you – love you, I mean." Gosh this was difficult so early on a morning. She sat down.

"You're sure of that? You're sure you'd leave me if you didn't like me any longer? I mean, you don't feel obliged to stay, do you? If you feel trapped, I'd prefer to know."

"Leonard, what's brought all this on? You're not trying to get rid of me, are you?" she asked suspiciously. "You've not got your eye on a younger woman, by any chance? she added, remembering the red trousers and the keep fit exercises on the landing.

"No, no. Not at all. I just happened to pick up one of the girls' magazines that happened to be lying around and happened to read this article on how women of today often feel trapped in their marriages."

"I'm not a woman of today any longer, Leonard," she said, rather sadly. "More like yesterday. Or the day before yesterday. Anyway, what would I feel trapped by? The girls are practically grown up and you know how to iron you own shirts now. I could walk out tomorrow and you'd all manage perfectly well without me."

"I suppose so."

"Well, perhaps not perfectly," she added, a little piqued, "but you'd cope." A thought struck her. "You can't have 'just seen the magazine lying around' I always tidy the girls' things away after the holidays."

He looked sheepish.

"You see, darling," he reached across the table and took her hand, "I want to keep up with you. You seem to be changing so fast, taking an interest in . . . in new things. And you have become a little secretive lately, you know."

"Er, Leonard," she withdrew her hand, "since we're on the subject, I do have something to confess . . . "

"I knew it," he said dismally. "You're having an affair."

"No, no, it's this – I'm thinking . . . an *affair??* I'm thinking of doing some social work. An *affair?* Really! You know, visiting and so on. Actually, I've already started."

"Splendid idea." He looked visibly relieved.

Poor fellow, she thought tenderly. I really believe he did think I was having an affair.

Aloud, she said, "Who'd want to have an affair with me?"

"Plenty of people. You're a very attractive woman still." He came and stood behind her chair and placed his hands on her shoulders. "May I take this very attractive woman out to dinner tonight?"

She smiled up at him. "Certainly you may."

"Er – I don't have to wear the red trousers, do I?"

"Not if you want to impress me."

"Thank God. They were a bit over the top, weren't they?"

She patted his hand. "Just a bit."

Perhaps there was something to be said for being loved by and loving one's husband all these years. Marriage didn't scale the heights which she imagined an affair might reach. But there were little hills along the way.

"When I mentioned social work, your father didn't bat an eyelid," she wrote to Emma. "I really think you'll find him quite changed when you come home. He's becoming almost contemporary."

That afternoon Grace went round to visit Debbie. She took with her some of the girls' old baby clothes, the buggy Leonard had mended (now that he knew it didn't belong to her lover), and a few women's magazines.

"Ace!" Debbie pounced on the magazines as if it was Christmas. "I can never afford these." Her usual sullen expression vanished for a second.

Grace awarded herself a progress point.

"Shall we go for a walk?" she suggested. "I can carry the buggy downstairs."

"Good idea. The kids love going out but it's a lot of hassle on my own. Come on you two," She hauled the children off the bed and began buttoning them into flimsy nylon anoraks.

"Will they be warm enough?" asked Grace anxiously.

Debbie glared at her. "They'll fucking 'ave to be."

Grace could have bitten off her tongue.

They negotiated the stairs in stony silence, Grace dragging the buggy down whilst Debbie carried the two children.

"Sorry, Debbie," she said, when they reached the bottom. "Didn't mean to criticise."

"It's all right." Debbie fastened Lyn into th buggy. "I know they've not got proper outdoor things. The clothing grant was done away with."

Grace vaguely remembered having heard something about that in one of Thatcher's last budgets. She frowned. But wasn't that the same budget which had given Leonard that enormous tax cut? She looked at Jill shivering in her shoddy pink anorak, and felt like a thief.

"We'll walk quickly so they don't catch cold." Debbie grabbed Jill's hand.

They walked down the road, crossing it at one point to avoid a nasty looking mongrel, and went into the park. It was rather a wretched little park. Cartons, cans and dogs' excrement were scattered around the grey and dirty-looking grass. In one corner was a playground with a huge fence round it and a notice saying it was unsafe and not to be used. Spotting the swings, Jill started whining and tugging on her mother's hand. Debbie sighed.

"No you can't, Jill. No!"

"It doesn't seem fair, does it?" said Grace. "There ought to be somewhere for them to play."

"Round 'ere, you get used to life not being fair, Mrs Napier."

"Call me Grace."

"Can I? Can I really?" She seemed pleased. "I was wondering," Debbie went on, as they picked their way carefully over the grass, "if you'd mind doing me a favour, seeing as you've got a car? Would you call round to me Ma's and pick up some clothes? It's not far from 'ere, but it's difficult for me on the buses with these two. I left a skirt and a couple of shirts behind and I don't want that Penny getting 'er 'ands on 'em."

"Of course I'll do that, Debbie." Grace recalled the glint in Father Keogh's eye when he'd mentioned Debbie's family. "Er, do you and your mother get on? I mean . . . "

Debbie looked amused. "She won't bite you. So long as you make it clear you're not from the Electricity Board. She's all right, is me Ma. Just she gets hassled at times with all the kids and having no money."

"She has a lot of children, does she?"

"Six altogether. Four of us and two from her other husband." She sounded scornful. "Then there's Marie's kid."

"Goodness," said Grace sympathetically.

"Yer." Debbie stopped the wipe Lyn's nose. "You wouldn't catch me 'aving so many. I'm staying away from men till these two are old enough to fend for themselves. Then I'm going back to work. Maybe I'll even take some GCSEs. You can do them at night at the college down the road. Men just get in the way."

"Debbie . . . "

"Now don't you start with that patronising middle-class stuff. I'm all right – at least I would be if the council'd get off its fat arse and find me a place to live. I bet I know more about life then your . . . your what's-her-name?"

"Emma."

"Emma – with her fucking 'ockey matches and end of term dances. Sounds a right kid to me." Debbie put as much scorn into her voice as she could muster.

She's jealous, though Grace suddenly. I must be more careful.

"Emma's throwing herself into hockey at the moment because her boyfriend's left her for someone else. She's not very happy."

Debbie sniffed. "Men! They're all the same." She pointed to her children. "This one's father's an alcoholic and this one's into nicking videos. I won't 'ave nothing to do with them. Not good for the kids."

"Quite right," replied Grace, surprising herself.

They began to retrace their steps over the filthy grass. Jill cast one last longing look back at the playground.

"Do you know, Debbie, I found out a funny thing this morning. Leonard (that's my husband) thought I was having an affair because I'd been out visiting you and hadn't told him where I was."

"Christ!" Debbie looked at her in admiration. "Did he beat you up?"

"Well, no. That's not exactly . . . We got it sorted out in the end."

"Me Da used to beat up Ma sometimes," reflected Debbie. "When he thought she was going with other blokes."

"Dear me."

Debbie shrugged. "Aw, she never came to any 'arm. A few bruises, that's all." She glanced at Grace. "You don't mind 'im getting jealous then?"

"Well, to be honest, it doesn't happen very often."

"It'd bug me. Can't stand possessive fellas. How long have you been married?"

"Twenty years," Grace said.

"Jaysus! And you still love each other?"

"I think we do, Debbie. I think we do."

Debbie shook her head. "Some people have all the bleedin' luck. None of the women in our family could hold onto their men for long. It gives me a cosy feelin'," she added shyly, "thinking of you two lovin' each other after all these years."

"Your turn will come, Debbie."

"Na! Not me. You need a proper 'ouse and money to keep a man."

When Grace arrived home, she found a letter from Emma waiting for her. Emma wrote that she doubted she'd have time in the holidays to go visiting unmarried mothers in hostels as she'd be revising for her A-levels. She needed a C in Economics and a B in German.

"I was wondering when you'd feel the urge to go visiting," the letter went on. "Most of the girls' mothers have started it in the last year or so. We put it down to the change of life. It's rather trying but don't worry, it'll pass. Just remember not to get taken in by these people. Monique's mother actually started inviting them back to her home. Monique said you couldn't move in their house for alcoholics and the unemployed. She got a lot of her silver stolen and had to stop in the end. Remember, these people are hopeless. And if you do invite them home, don't let them anywhere near my record collection.

PS Will you ask Dad if I can borrow his red trousers?"

"Leonard," she said, later that night, in Luigi's, "I'm terribly worried about Emma."

He put the menu down. "Tell me quickly. What is it?" He groaned. "She's pregnant? On drugs? Failed her exams?"

"No, no, dear. Do hush." Grace was conscious of the wine waiter hovering nearby. "Order the wine and then I'll tell you."

"A bottle of 64," said Leonard at random.

"Very good, sir." With an air of contempt, the waiter took away the wine list.

"Now Grace, tell me."

Grace leaned conspiratorially across the table. "I believe Emma's turning into one of those radical right-wing persons."

"Is that all?" Leonard sat back in relief. "Mm . . . so our elder daughter's a yuppie, is she? Good. I've always wanted to see one of those at close quarters. I must observe her next time she's home."

"Leonard! It's terrible. Her last letter was so, well, so uncaring. She seems incapable of imagining what it's like to be poor."

"She'll grow out of it. God! This wine's awful!"

The waiter looked scathing. "It's what sir chose. Would sir like me to change it?"

"No. Never mind. Pour it out. We'll make do. It's probably a phase," he added, when the waiter had departed. "After all, when I first met you, you were toying with growing your hair long and going to live in a commune."

"Yes, well, I was trying to catch up with my own generation after years at home nursing my parents. Emma's position is quite different. As parents go, we're tolerant, open-minded, understanding. What has she got to rebel against?"

"I'm sure she'll find something."

Chapter Eleven

WHEN THINGS GOT VERY BAD PAT JACKSON WAS IN THE HABIT OF having a conversation with Margaret Thatcher. It was a habit she'd continued even after Major had taken over. Somehow it wasn't the same talking to a man.

"Is it my fault I can't make ends meet?" she'd say to her. "You're a mother. Could you have fed your kids on one pound sixteen a day? I'm not extravagant. We eat eggs and chips, macaroni cheese, a packet of hamburgers now and then. I haven't had proper meat since the day Sean lost his job. Never buy vegetables. Some days, when the money's run out and there's no one left to borrow from, I get by on tea and toast. And still I'm in debt.

"We owe five hundred pounds on the electric. The meter was robbed twice. They got away with eighty pounds one time, a hundred the other. What's that? Insurance? Don't make me fucking laugh. Then we got behind because they kept sending us estimates and then it was found they'd underestimated. How can you be expected to budget if they keep getting it wrong? So now it's been reconnected, illegally, and I'm a criminal.

"The DHSS is no help. They treat us like bleeding scroungers down there. If I didn't do a bit of home work now and then, like glueing on these earrings (oh yes, I saw you looking), the kids would never have any new clothes. As it is Sal has to hang around naked on wash day and I couldn't send Dave on that council holiday last year because he didn't have a pair of wellingtons.

"What's that? A job? My eldest girl, Marie, she's a real hard worker, but all she can get is cleaning. I'd take a job myself but I can't afford to. On supplementary benefit I get my rent and poll tax paid. Rebates wouldn't cover it. I'd be further in debt by the end of the month . . .

"Then there's Jimmy. Off God knows where. Joe with his YTS job coming to an end. Debbie in that bed and breakfast place (though we never could get on, her and me, we're too alike, independent). And now that Penny's taken to skiving off school whenever she has the chance . . . "

So it went on. Sometimes she got sick of hearing it herself. She went to see whether the bath had emptied. It hadn't.

The cold November wind howled round the streets of Munich. It tore through the courtyards of the Residenz and pulled at shoppers' hair in the pedestrian precinct making mothers irritable with their children. Joachim turned up his coat collar and crossed the bare open space of the Konigsplatz.

The farm was secure for another year, thanks to those film people. Was it part of a plan? Was it a sign that he should follow Cornelius's advice and choose happiness? Or was it a trap? He kicked at a stone.

At work things were beginning to hot up. He'd visited the Dortmund factory again.

"We've heard rumours, sir. Is it true they're going to ask for voluntary redundancies?"

How did these things get out?

"I'm not allowed to tell you anything at the moment."

Even this much, an evasion rather than a flat denial, was more than Wedelmeier would have approved of.

"The men'd be willing to go on short time, sir, even job sharing, if it came to it. We've families to support, sir, and loans to pay off. There's no work round here."

"I'll put the suggestion to the board."

Dutifully he informed the board of the workers' informal offer.

"It's no use, Seefeldt." Wedelmeier shook his head. "I know you feel strongly about those men but, let's face it, they've priced themselves out of the market with their demands. It's always that particular factory which is the first to threaten strike action. No, these rumours simply mean we must speed things up. James is dealing with the Bavarian end of things. We should be ready to move on that soon. And, incidentally, I've been rethinking what you said about our rival, HFW. Our accountants say it's worth making a bid for it."

"In that case why close down the Dortmund factory? We could afford to keep it open."

Hans Wedelmeier smiled. "We'll buy up HFW to prevent our competitors getting their hands on it, but we may decide not to operate it."

"You mean buy up a company only to close it down?"

"Standard practice nowadays, Seefeldt."

There's another world, thought Joachim, parallel to this, yet entirely different. And I'm rapidly losing the key to it.

Lallie walked up Kensington Mall and turned right, past the grey grim exterior of the Czechoslovakian Embassy, towards Hyde Park. She thought, I admired my father's gentleness, his patience with my mother. But I'm detached from him. I can stand apart from him and view him from the outside. Whereas I *am* my mother. It's with her eyes I look at the world. She's the shadow within me. I have to come to terms with her. It's time.

Lallie's world had always been, always would be, she supposed, women-centred. She turned into the park and began strolling towards the Orangery. Her closest relationships had always been with women. Men were the dark continent for her; it was if they had some part of them missing. She thought of Cornelius and his blundering: no woman would have gone on like that. And in all her relationships with women it was her mother she looked back to. She reached the Orangery and started to retrace her steps.

For Jade it was different. Jade had frankly detested her mother. Rachel's self-satisfaction, her prima donna manner. In *her* relationships with women Jade sought to escape her mother. Or rather, she sought a different kind of mother. One who'd pick up the pieces, Lallie thought, a little bitterly, and couldn't help adding, what about me then? Who'll mother me? If she fell apart now she'd cease to be any help to Jade and then what would happen? She must stop this brooding over the past. She must grab hold of life with both hands. Advance without fear. She permitted herself an ironical smile.

When she arrived back at their flat she found Jade bursting with enthusiasm over a new casting director she'd discovered.

"She's called Olivia. She's got tons of energy and a list of contacts as long as your arm. She's interested in working with us, if we can come up with the backing."

"That's great," murmured Lallie, wondering why she was always having to fake her enthusiasm these days.

"You should see her," enthused Jade. "Golden hair and a tan that'd knock you out. She spends six months of the year in California. We should have a holiday in the sun soon. You're looking a bit peaky."

She strolled into the kitchen. Lallie stood stock-still in the sitting-room, battling with jealousy. So it was happening again. She went through the familiar mantra. Love means allowing the other person their freedom. She couldn't hope to keep someone like Jade all to herself. It was the price you paid for living with a creative person. These sudden emotional attachments meant nothing, not even anything physical, usually (she remembered one incident in the past). She'd have to go along with it. Ride it out. Jade always came back in the end.

But why did it have to be like this? What had Jade said in Ireland? "Passion's very overrated." Lallie's parents, yes, there'd been passion there. Otherwise her mother wouldn't have survived as long as she had. Rachel and Stefan? Definitely. Lallie sometimes felt life with Jade was all on the surface.

Nevertheless, listening to Jade singing to herself as she moved about the kitchen getting supper ready, Lallie felt she'd happily swop personalities with her any day.

The block of flats where Debbie's family lived looked deserted. Grace had imagined pavements crowded with housewives pushing babies or shopping, children playing, out of work men hanging around in groups chatting. There was nobody in sight, apart from a small West Indian boy who sauntered past her whistling, hands in his pockets, black felt hat perched jauntily on his head. Grace looked up. One of the windows had a tablecloth strung across it in place of curtains. Loud, thumping music issued from another. It was bitterly cold up here on the top of the hill. The wind howled round the corner of the flats at her. Papers flew across the pavement. She shivered and went inside.

She took one look at the lift and decided to walk up. After a while she became aware of a steady tread on the stairs behind her. But the corners came upon her too quickly for her to see who was following her. She began to feel nervous. She imagined an attacker coming at her from behind, dragging her off, mugging her, raping her, dumping her body in some dark alleyway or, worse still, in that lift which smelled like a public lavatory.

She shuddered. Poor Leonard. A widower. He'd have to take all his meals at Luigi's. Then she thought, this is ridiculous. On the fourth floor she paused and waited for the person behind her to catch up. A tall, rather attractive-looking woman with short black hair came into view. Grace breathed a sigh of relief. The woman was dressed quite smartly. Perhaps the area wasn't as rough as it looked. She smiled at the woman and continued upwards.

She reached the fifth floor, pushed open the fire door and walked slowly down the stuffy, smelly corridor reading the numbers on the doors. Each doorway had a square of carpet in front of it that served as a doormat, some plain, some patterned, some ragged and stained. She came to a halt outside the Jacksons' flat. The footsteps stopped too. Grace turned round.

"Oh," she said, embarrassed. "Do you live here?"

"No. I'm visiting. Is it the Jacksons you want?"

Grace nodded.

Lallie stepped forward and knocked on the door. "The trick is to get your foot inside the door, at the same time making it clear you're not from the LEB." She paused and took in Grace's clothes. "You're not from the LEB, are you?"

"No. I know one of the daughters."

The door was opened by an exhausted-looking woman with dyed blonde hair. She wore a shabby skirt, no stockings and a pair of down at heel slippers. A cigarette dangled between her fingers.

"Oh it's you," she said to Lallie. "Come in." She glanced suspiciously at Grace. "Who's she?"

"I'm Grace Napier. I've a message for you from Debbie."

Pat clicked her tongue. "Like bloody Piccadilly Circus 'ere sometimes. You'd better come in too."

She opened the door wide enough for them to squeeze past into the narrow hall. Grace shivered as she followed Lallie into the bare living-room. The temperature inside the flat was several degrees lower than in the corridor and not much warmer than outside.

"Ay, nippy, isn't it?" Pat pulled her cardigan round her

thin shoulders. "I've been shopped. One of the neighbours squealed to the Electric that I'd been illegally connected and now we're off for keeps."

She stubbed out her cigarette in a saucer and fumbled in the pockets of her skirt for another.

"Sit down, you may as well."

She pulled out the two hard chairs for her visitors and went and leaned against the window-ledge.

"I'm on me own today. The kids are round at the Mammy's for a bit. They can't watch telly here and they kept whining about the cold. I'll fetch them back in a while. Then they can go straight to bed and keep warm."

"What are you going to do?" asked Lallie.

"I'm being taken to court an' if the judge is feeling filthy he'll put me in jail."

"Jail!" exclaimed Grace. "What good will that do?"

Pat shrugged. "Punishes me, dunnit? For being poor and in the shit."

"What will happen to the children?" Lallie asked.

"Care," said Pat, shortly. "Unless Marie can persuade 'em she's fit to look after them. The Mammy couldn't cope with them, that's for sure." She puffed on her cigarette. "Ah well, probably it won't come to that. I'll likely get put on probation, seeing as it's a first offence. And rapped over the knuckles and told not to be a naughty girl. As likely as not they'll reconnect us when the really bad weather comes, on account of the kids. They can't afford a scandal. But when summer comes, it'll be off again unless I agree to start paying them back bit by bit. What with, I'd like to know? They don't think of that, those judges, do they? They don't think that even five pounds a week for electricity means the kids going without food." She ran her fingers through her hair. "Jimmy'll see me right. He generally does. I used to refuse his money, proud like. Now I take it and no questions asked. Sorry I can't offer you a cup of tea." She grimaced.

"I've written a letter to the housing department." Lallie fumbled in her bag. "And filled in the form for you. Shall I read you the letter?"

"Aye, in a minute." She went and stood square in front of Grace, her hands on her hips. "What's Debbie want?"

Grace flushed. "I – I've got to know Debbie recently and she asked me to ask you for some clothes of hers she left behind. She couldn't come herself because of the children." She flushed again. Perhaps Mrs Jackson would think she was interfering between mother and daughter.

But Pat only shook her head and said, "I've a couple of her shirts, that's all. I took the skirt in for Penny to wear, so she can't have that. I'll look out the shirts for you now." She went out of the room.

She left behind an awkward silence. Finally Lallie introduced herself and commented on the chilliness of the room. They felt embarrassed, these two middle-class women sitting in their smart clothes in the bare room with its scuffed lino and damp patches on the walls. It's like a scene from some Victorian novel, thought Lallie, but then that's what this government wants, a return to Victorian values.

Pat came back carrying the shirts. "I wish I'd something more to slip her but you see 'ow it is. 'Ow is the kid anyway? No word from the council yet, I suppose?"

Grace shook her head. "No."

"Aye. They won't hurry themselves. They'll look out for the Pakis before us. She's better off out of here. This is no place for babies now."

"How do you manage for cooking?" asked Grace.

"Takeaways. There's a chipper round the block. I'm 'oping to get some gas off the Social Services so as I can boil water at least." She shook her head. "I knew it'd come to this. Your life's not your own on Social Security. They're always bloody snooping about. A girl down our corridor had a fella in to babysit for a couple of evenings and the DHSS were round like a flash to see if she was cohabiting. They treat us like criminals. The neighbours are as bad. Folks round here are terrified of others getting more than themselves. They want to know every little wrinkle and they shop one another at the drop of a hat. Well, no one can envy me now."

She glanced round the bare room.

"The DHSS told me I'd too many things. Me! I'd a couple of cushions and some of Sean's old clothes still. Sell them, they said, before you get a penny out of us. Doesn't seem fair, does it? Making me sell me 'usband's clothes."

She was interrupted by the sound of the front door opening. Penny appeared in the doorway of the living-room, bare legged, wearing a grubby shirt, an old skirt taken in at the waist and trainers with holes in the toes.

"What are you doing home in the middle of the day, eh? Answer me that, Miss." Pat stood, arms folded, in the middle of the room, facing her daughter.

Penny dragged one scuffed trainer along the lino.

"Got fed up, didn't I? We weren't learnin' anything. One of me mates socked the English teacher on the jaw and the headmaster came and gave us a talking to. We spent a whole class sitting there in silence. Dead borin' it was." She sniffed violently and her eyes watered.

"Listen my girl, you go right back there this minute and start paying attention or you'll never get a job."

"Yeah? That's what you said to Jimmy and Marie, and look where it got 'em." She broke into a coughing fit.

"Marie has a job."

"Yeah, cleaning people's toilets. Dead humiliatin'. I'd rather go on the streets."

Pat stepped forward and slapped her daughter hard on the cheek.

Penny stumbled back against the wall. Regaining her balance, she shot a look of hatred at her mother and dashed past her through the open front door. They heard her steps running down the corridor, accompanied by a hacking cough.

In the room there was an embarrassed silence. Pat ran a hand over her eyes.

"She's got bad blood in her that one and there's nought I can do about it."

She walked over to the window to see if she could catch sight of Penny. But her daughter had run off to some secret hideout and was nowhere to be seen.

"All the same, she's right," Pat murmured, half to herself, feeling in her pocket for another cigarette. "Fat chance she'll ever have of a job or a 'ome of 'er own. That school she goes to can barely control 'em, let alone teach 'em anything. The older ones – they were content to stick it out, even our Jimmy. But she sees further than they did at her age. She's grown up quick in this neighbourhood. She knows she's trapped."

She turned to face her two visitors.

"I shouldn't 'ave hit her. I never did used hit any of them. And she's not well, poor kid. You heard her cough. It's damp in this place. She can't seem to shake it off."

"I'm sure . . . " began Grace and then stopped. She could think of nothing helpful to say. Her life was as remote from Pat's as if they lived on different continents, instead of one and a quarter miles apart.

"We'll go now," said Lallie. "I'll leave the form for you here."

But Pat had turned back to the window, absorbed in her thoughts. Lallie and Grace let themselves out, closing the door softly behind them.

"It's a different world, isn't it?" said Lallie, as she and Grace trudged back down the five flights of stairs. "It's scarcely believable people live like this."

Grace nodded. "To think she might go to jail for not

being able to pay her bills!" She thought guiltily of the few times in her life when she'd overspent her allowance, buying clothes for Emma and Carolyn, or new things for the house. The worst it had ever led to was a row with Leonard.

"I know. If people like us get into debt there's always someone willing to give us an overdraft. There's no safety net for Pat." Lallie eyed Grace curiously. "How did you get to meet Debbie?" Grace explained. "So it's new to you too, then?"

"Quite new," said Grace.

On impulse and because she didn't feel like going home, Lallie suggested they have coffee. They walked round behind the flats and hunted for a café but found only a corner shop with bars on the windows, and a pub which neither of them fancied the look of. They ended up going for a walk in the park opposite. Quite a nice park, Grace thought, though it had rather more concrete than grass in it. She turned up her coat collar and stuck her hands in her pockets.

"Freezing, isn't it? I wonder where that poor child ran off to?"

"Back to school, let's hope," replied Lallie. "Though it doesn't seem to be much use."

"She wasn't even wearing a coat. And did you see her lips? All cracked and she had cold sores round her mouth. Nobody in this country should be forced to live without electricity. It's barbaric. It's a basic human right to be warm and to be able to boil water, isn't it?"

Lallie nodded. "There must be something we can do. Perhaps we should write to the papers, or speak to Pat's MP, or plead with the LEB. But then there're probably hundreds, if not thousands, of cases like the Jacksons up and down the country."

"I've an idea," said Grace, suddenly. "I'll give a party. A wine and cheese party. For the whole village. Some of them have been dying to see inside my house for years. I'll make them all donate ten pounds. That way at least her bill will get paid and she won't go to jail."

A wine and cheese party! Lallie didn't know whether to laugh or cry. Then she saw the eager expression on Grace's face and said, "Good idea."

"You're invited too, of course, and your . . . er?" Grace hesitated. Lallie wore a plain gold ring on the third finger of her left hand (it had been her mother's wedding ring). "Husband?"

"I live with a woman," said Lallie casually.

"Right. Yes." Grace swallowed. "Bring her too."

"I'll help you with organising it if you like," Lallie offered, as they walked in the direction of her bus stop. "It seems only fair." She smiled. "Wine and cheese. Fundraising the middle-class way."

"It's the only way I know," said Grace sadly.

Glimpses of God, thought Joachim. They're the most we can hope for in life, this world being but a shadow of another. And now he was beginning to lose even those glimpses. He was getting confused. Was it best for his sons (he was to see them soon) that they learn, like himself, to distrust the values of the country they were being brought up in? Was he right to encourage them to think of Ireland as their real home?

His own father, he was certain, had never been plagued by such doubts. For him, the generations had flowed into one another, like streams into a river, father handing onto son. They'd been a grand family once. No doubt the name had played some part in Katrin's acceptance of him; it was a name fit even for a hero's daughter, though Joachim had long since dropped the "von." His father had been a child at the court of the Kaiser. The family had owned estates in Westphalia and Saxony. They'd lost all but one in the war. Thirty years old when Hitler's war had broken out, his father had been sent to fight first in France, then in Greece, then on the Russian front. He'd finished the war minus one arm. He'd accepted that as normal. His ancestors included many generals.

Yes, the Seefeldts were a family full of history and tradition. But traditions only have value if they're passed on. The family, he thought. What do my sons care about it?

The doorbell rang. Joachim went to answer it.

"Hello."

He stood there, too stunned for words. A feeling so intense flooded his whole body that for a second he didn't know whether it was joy or pain.

"Christabel! . . . How did you . . . ? Why . . . ?"

She stepped inside and wrapped her arms round him.

"That feels good. Does it feel good for you?"

"Yes. Why . . . ?"

"Hush." She put a hand over his mouth. "No questions. No lies. Just accept it. I'm back."

He pulled away from her.

"Are you?"

"Yes."

She kissed him long and deep on the mouth. His body, long starved of love, took over from his mind. They made love in the hallway. Then he carried her into his bedroom and made love to her again. He found he'd not forgotten any part of her body. "My love," he murmured. "My own love." He got up and made them both coffee. When he carried it back to the bedroom she was sitting up on the bed, his robe wrapped round her, brushing her hair.

"I can hardly believe you're here. It must be a dream. Are you a dream?"

She laughed and shook her head. She reached out and took the coffee. "See? I drink. I'm not a ghost."

He sat down on the edge of the bed, picked up the brush and began brushing out her long hair.

"Are you back . . . ?" He left the question dangling.

Permanently he'd meant to add. The word didn't have much sense in the context of Christabel. He changed the question. "Why are you back?"

"I've travelled. Worked as a roadie. I got as far as New Zealand. I thought I'd forget you but I didn't. I usually forget people. You got through to me, touched me somehow. So I came back to see if you still wanted me."

"It was you I saw the other day then?"

"Probably. I've been back a month."

"A month!"

"I wanted to get something organised first. A job. And a place to live."

"You can live here."

"No, I can't. Not yet." She shook her blonde hair out of eyes and looked at him. "Let's take it one step at a time, shall we?"

"As slowly as you like, my love." He kissed her again.

"I haven't been faithful to you."

"I never expected you would."

"I half thought you'd have got back with your wife."

"No."

"I love you, you know. In my own way."

"I know. Why?"

"You speak to something in me. Call it passion if you like. Most of the men I meet are louses. Only after one thing."

He gave a fake leer at her beautiful brown breasts. "I'm only after one thing."

"No, you're not."

"No. I'm not." He smiled happily. "I'll live with you the rest of my life if you'll have me."

She set down her coffee cup. "We'll see. Now touch me again. I'd forgotten how good it was."

"I hadn't."

There was a strange light in Penny's eyes. "Come on." She giggled. "Give me some more. Come on. It's my turn."

Al passed her the crisp packet. She stuck her nose inside and sniffed at the blob in the bottom. She burst out coughing.

"Not like that! You're doing it all wrong. Kids!" said Sid contemptuously. Sid was thirteen. "Here, give it me."

He grabbed the packet from Penny, inhaled deeply from it half a dozen times, then handed it back to her. "Now try."

She inhaled, imitating him, and passed the packet to Al. "I can see witches." She giggled and leant back against the wall. "Witches and monkeys."

"I can see them too," blabbed Al. "Climbing all over the furniture."

They rolled on the carpet, giggling uproarously.

"Fucking kids!" snorted Sid. He was beginning to regret inviting them in. He grabbed the crisp packet lying on the floor and inhaled some more. He looked down. Al and Penny were still rolling around, giggling about Monster Mutant Turtles. He gave Al a kick. Al sat up with a yelp of pain.

"Great fat blob." Sid gave Al another kick in the stomach. "Great fat fucker."

For some reason, once he'd started, Sid couldn't seem to stop kicking Al. He was dimly aware of Penny's screams as she tried to drag Al away. Al got another kick from Sid and fell awkwardly on top of Penny. He was a big overweight boy of twelve, used to being bullied at school. He turned his head away and was violently sick all over Sid's mum's carpet.

"Aw, get out," said Sid, in disgust. "Get the hell out of 'ere. Both of you."

Penny grabbed Al's hand. They clambered to their feet and ran off.

"I should've known." Al panted. "He gets angry, does Sid, when he's been sniffing."

They stopped in the park to get their breath back, caught each other's eye and collapsed laughing on the grass. Passers-by cast them curious glances.

"What are you going to do now?" asked Penny.

Al shrugged. "Dunno. What about you?"

"I'm going home."

"Home? To your mum? Like this?"

"No." Penny giggled. "Not home to me ma. She hit me. I'm never going back there. No, home to my home."

"Home to your home," repeated Al, giggling.

They rolled around on the grass, kicking their legs in the air. "You look like a great fat tortoise." Penny stood up suddenly and began brushing down her skirt. "Shall I show you my home, Al?"

She looked at him shyly from beneath her uneven brown fringe.

"If you like." Al was quite comfortable where he was.

"Lazy sod! Come on."

Penny yanked him to his feet. She led him past the abandoned playground to one of the disused garages behind the flats. Nearby was a rubbish dump. Paint tins, car seats, broken glass, rusty prams lay strewn around. She clambered over some tyres and removed a piece of barbed wire and a plank that had once been loosely nailed across the garage door to prevent children and vandals entering.

"Well," said Al admiringly. "No chance of burglars here."

There was an old scrap of carpet on the floor, some empty sacks and an unopened packet of biscuits.

"This is where I live now," said Penny proudly.

Al looked around. "Not bad. With a bit of help, you could fix it up real nice. Can I come and visit you here sometimes?"

Penny rubbed one foot against her leg and considered. "All right, Al," she said eventually. "But don't go letting on to anyone else that I live here. I don't want hordes of 'em tramping round."

Like her half brother Jimmy, whom she adored, Penny was a loner. For the first time in her life she had a room to herself. She wanted to keep it that way.

"I won't tell no one," promised Al. "And I'll bring you something nice next time I come."

When he'd gone Penny sat down on one of the sacks and opened the packet of biscuits. She was quite content. There was nobody here to bother her or go on at her. Barring a few beetles and spiders (and she didn't mind those) she was quite alone. She looked around with satisfaction. A telly would be nice.

They were at a party. A bunch of hip film people sniping behind one another's backs and Jade in the middle wickedly lapping it all up, at her most entrancing.

"Olivia will be there," she'd said. "I'll introduce you to our new casting director."

"Whoopee. I can hardly wait," Lallie had replied, earning herself a glance of irritation from Jade.

Olivia the glorious, thought Lallie dully, shaking her hand. The trouble was, she could always see what attracted Jade and fell half in love with these women herself. Olivia was tall, slim and, to judge by the peals of laughter coming from her corner of the room, witty. She was wearing an off-the-shoulder green silk dress and a pair of jade earrings. Lallie wondered if there was some secret significance in this, then chided herself for being paranoid.

A small fat man sidled up to her.

"I hear there're plans for a new film?"

"Yes," replied Lallie shortly. She'd learned that in the film world you keep your mouth shut. This man was one of Jade's rivals.

"Talented lady, your Jade." He drifted off.

And me? What about me? she thought, rather drunkenly. Don't I have any talents too? But the truth was her gifts lay elsewhere – in careful research and painstaking documentation of historical facts. Without Jade they'd never have brought her much recognition.

She glanced over at Jade standing by Olivia's side. She'd lived too much through her lover these past eight years. Dazzled by Jade's talents and the success they brought she'd been content to abandon her own research, the dull routine of sitting in the British Museum day after day, in favour of shorter projects, quickly finished. It'd been years since she'd initiated a project of her own. Everything had been for Jade.

I don't belong here, she thought. This isn't my world. My world's back there, in Stockton. In that rickety old house which smelled of boiled vegetables. What have these glamorous film people to do with me?

But she knew she couldn't now, after tasting that glamour, go back to sitting tamely in the library uncovering facts about obscure historical figures. Glamour, fame, ambition, you always paid for them in the end. She'd cheapened her talents. She remembered her academic colleagues' astonishment when she told them she was going into film research. I've sold my gifts for a handful of coins and a few credits. No, she thought. I sold them for love of Jade.

And now Jade was talking to Olivia, the two of them alone, in a corner. Tears pricked the back of Lallie's eyelids. She clutched the wine glass tightly as though it might save her from making a fool of herself. She was being sentimental, sickening. If only she could get back to the small girl in the red and white kilt. Perhaps there lay the clue to where she'd gone wrong.

She walked over and touched Jade on the arm. "Ready to go?"

Jade glanced at her. "What's the hurry? It's early yet. Give me a few more minutes."

"I'll wait in the car. Good night, Olivia." At the door Lallie turned and saw Jade kiss Olivia lightly on the cheek.

"What was all that about?" Jade got into the driver's seat.

"What?"

"Leaving early and rudely like that." She started up the car.

"It wasn't rude. I have a headache."

"Did you even say goodbye to our hosts?"

"No," admitted Lallie.

The atmosphere was heavy with Jade's moral victory.

"Anyway, you met Olivia."

"Yes."

"What do you think of her? Talented, isn't she?"

"I didn't have much chance to speak to her."

"No, I saw you standing by yourself. You really must be more sociable at parties. It looks so bad."

"Yes."

"And try not to look so morose."

"No."

They got out of the car.

"Lallie! What the hell's the matter with you?" exclaimed Jade. They went up into the living-room.

"You keep on criticising me."

Jade flung her car keys onto the table. "If I criticise you, it's because I want to help you. You're so wrapped up in yourself these days. I'm trying to take you out of yourself."

"I keep seeing my mother . . . " Lallie's voice started to rise. "I want to escape. I want to be a different person – like you, like Olivia, like anyone else but me."

"Pull yourself together," said Jade coldly. She disliked scenes.

"I can't, I can't," gasped Lallie. She was finding it hard to breathe. "You love Olivia."

"I do not."

"You do. You do. And I don't blame you. Anyone would prefer her to me. I loathe myself." She began to sob.

Jade stepped forward and slapped her. Lallie stopped crying and stood still in the middle of the room, her cheek burning. Jade turned away from her and walked over to the window. There was a silence.

"I'm sorry. I didn't mean to . . . " began Lallie.

"I've never hit anyone in my life before," said Jade in a tight little voice. She kept her back to Lallie. "Olivia's neither here nor there. This is between us. Get a grip on yourself, Lallie. I'm going to bed. In the spare room."

She left the room without glancing at Lallie. Lallie sank down on the carpet. It would take time for Jade to forgive her for provoking this scene. She knew the pattern thoroughly by now. The cold withdrawal of affection, the stiff-lipped banalities they'd exchange at mealtimes, the absences from the flat. It would be like living with a stranger for a while . . . Ah, what a fool she was.

Waking in the night Joachim reached out an arm for Christabel and found . . . an empty space. He sat bolt upright and switched on the light. He got out of bed and searched every inch of the flat. She'd fled. She hadn't even left her phone number. It was starting all over again.

Jade had gone to bed hours ago. Lallie remained on the floor in their living-room, her hands clasped around her knees, thinking.

She knew now why she wanted so much to be Jade. To be Olivia. To be anyone else but herself. It was to get rid of memory. Again and again over the past few weeks she'd been seeing what she'd spent all these years avoiding. Her mother, sitting there in her wheelchair, running her poor bent twisted hands up and down the arms. If only she hadn't gone off to university and left her alone . . . if only . . .

Moved by some force outside herself, Lallie got up from the floor and went into the bathroom. Glancing at her face in the mirror, she put her hands on the basin to steady herself and opened a cupboard. She took out a razor blade still wrapped in its layer of cellophane. Sitting on the side of the bath she began making tiny cuts in her wrists. A criss cross of fine white lines appeared. Then spots of blood. Her wrists felt sore.

"My poor mother!" she sobbed, rocking backwards and forwards on the bath. "My poor, poor mother!"

She remained like that for over an hour, rocking and crying and making tiny cuts on her wrists. In the end, utterly drained, she threw away the razor, crawled into bed and fell into a deep sleep.

In the morning when she woke, she felt quite lightheaded. Almost cheerful.

"What's happened to your wrists?" asked Jade at breakfast.

"Nothing." Lallie pulled down the sleeve of her jumper.

"Let me see." Jade leant across the table, grabbed Lallie's arm and pushed back her sleeve. "What the hell have you been doing?"

"N . . . nothing," stammered Lallie. "It's nothing."

A shutter came down over Jade's face. She let go of Lallie's arm. "Don't you ever do that again." She looked at her without expression for a few minutes. "I can't cope with this, Lallie. You've got to see a therapist."

"No. They're . . . clumsy. They project their own neuroses onto their patients. I know how my mind works better than anyone. I can cure myself of this obsession with the past. All I need is time. And your help."

Jade looked away.

"Perhaps I'll go back to Stockton," Lallie added, desperate to sound positive. "Revisit some of the old places."

"Good idea," Jade said flatly. "I was going to suggest we spend some time apart."

Lallie felt her stomach turn over in fear. If she lost Jade who else did she have in the world? No father or mother or sister. No real friends, for now all her friends were Jade's. Separated from Jade she'd have no job either. She felt the ground give way beneath her. She clung to the edge of the table.

"I'm losing you, aren't I?" Try as she might, she couldn't keep the panic out of her voice.

Jade flicked over the pages of the book that lay beside her plate. "You're not losing me," she said, in a tight hard voice. "At least not if you pull yourself together."

She resumed her reading, an expression of boredom on her face.

I am irritating her, thought Lallie. I'm irritating her and I don't know what to do about it.

CHAPTER TWELVE

DEATH, THOUGHT JOACHIM SPEEDING ALONG THE AUTOBAHN TO meet his sons. Cornelius is right. We don't think enough about it. If he was to meet his death now, for instance, on this road. If a car were to pull out sharply in front of him, if the steering were suddenly to go, would he rejoice, knowing he'd put earthly things behind him and was going to meet his God? No. He would not. He'd want to see Christabel.

To die is gain, said Saint Paul. Was it ever possible – unless one was very sick – and even then . . . to feel the gain rather than the loss? Loss of the candles flickering in a dark church on a still Easter morning, of the first snowdrops beneath the evergreen oak, of his sons' faces when he took them to a match and their side won, of making love with Christabel whom it was likely he'd never see again. And yet all these things, it was promised, were pale images of another world. That world to which he was beginning to feel he'd lost the path forever.

He pulled up outside the apartment block. The boys were waiting for him, their jackets over their arms. Katrin nodded frostily in his direction. "Six o'clock sharp," she said and shut the door.

Joachim walked with his sons back to the car. There was a silence as the three of them got used to each other again, having become strangers over the past weeks.

Out of the corner of his eye he studied them. Peter, the elder, seemed to have had an encounter with a dye bottle. His blonde hair had gone black at the back and green around the edges. Joachim wondered what Katrin had had to say about that. He was dressed in a white jacket, white sneakers and purple trousers. In the lapel of his jacket he wore a diamanté broach Joachim vaguely remembered having given to Katrin. He wondered if his son was turning out to be gay or if it was the fashion now for German youths to dress like pimps. Above his left eyelid he'd painstakingly painted a black cobweb.

He was relieved to see that Werner, who was eight, was dressed more acceptably in sweatshirt and jeans. Presumably his mother still had some control over his wardrobe. Werner resembled Katrin. Joachim always had to remind himself it wasn't the boy's fault he had her square jaw and thick, black hair.

They all got into the car. Werner, as if by a prearranged plan, took the front seat. This was a change. Usually they squabbled for it. Werner twiddled with the knobs on the radio. Failing to find anything to his liking, he switched it off again and squirmed restlessly in his seat as they drove, in silence, in the direction of the football stadium.

Then the silence was broken as Werner's clear, high-pitched voice rang out. "Mummy's got a boyfriend. What are you going to do about it?"

Joachim put the car into fifth to give himself time to think. It groaned in protest. He put it back down to fourth.

"How do you know?" he asked cautiously.

"She calls him her business adviser, but we know."

Joachim glanced in the mirror. Peter was hunched up in the back, staring sullenly out of the window. His attitude plainly said *he* was taking no part in this conversation.

"What's he like, this boyfriend?"

Werner shrugged. "He's all right, I suppose. *We* think he's lazy."

"Why?"

"He makes Mummy bring him breakfast in bed."

"Oh." That seemed pretty conclusive evidence of a relationship.

"You've got to do something." Werner appealed to him. "He's taking her away for the whole summer."

So that was the situation. No wonder she'd been keen to hand over the boys.

"Not for the whole summer, Werner. Six weeks. And you're not being deserted. You'll be with me. Both of you," he added, glancing in the mirror again at the silent figure in the back.

"You've got to put a stop to it."

"Werner, how can I? Don't you think your mother deserves a holiday? There's nothing I can do to stop her going. Nor should I, if it makes her happy."

"She's not happy." Werner thrust his hands into the pockets of his sweatshirt.

"How do you know?"

"She cries a lot at night. When he's not there. We hear her through the walls."

Joachim felt a stab of pain and guilt.

"But Werner," he said more softly, "I don't see how I can help her. Your mother and I, we can't . . . she doesn't particularly like me any more. We've been over this. I expect you get fed up with the boys in your class sometimes too."

Werner drew his mouth into a pout. "You could try being nicer to her. Put your arm round her or . . . or something . . . "

Joachim winced at the thought of Katrin's reaction.

"It's no use!" Peter burst out suddenly from the back. "I told you you'd be wasting your time. He doesn't care about any of us."

"Peter, you know that isn't true."

"Oh, yeah? Then why are you always going away?"

This was a reference to their last meeting, cancelled because of the cattle sale.

"I explained about that, Peter. I'm sorry I missed seeing

you that weekend but I had to be in Ireland for the sale. And something else happened. Some film people turned up. They want to make a film in the castle. Isn't that exciting?"

There was an ominous silence. Out of the corner of his eye, he saw Werner turn round in his seat and exchange glances with Peter.

"Anyway," he went on hurriedly, "your mother and I thought it would be a good opportunity, while she's away, for you to spend some time in Ireland."

His sons groaned.

"It's lovely on the farm. You can go for long walks, fish, swim in the lake, help with the harvest. Who knows, you might even be taken on as film extras," he added shamelessly.

"We don't know anyone over there," wailed Werner. "All our friends are here. And Peter has a girlfriend. He doesn't want to leave her."

"Shut up, Werner," said his brother.

"Well, it's true. And I've got a job weeding people's gardens. I earned a lot of money last summer."

Joachim smiled at his son. "I'll pay you to work on the farm. And Peter can bring his girlfriend with him. Heaven knows, there's room." That's that settled, he thought.

There was a lengthy silence.

"Er. Don't you like Ireland?"

"No!" chorused his sons.

Joachim clutched the steering wheel and let out a long silent scream. Christabel. My love. Where are you? Come and rescue me from all this.

"'E sent someone round last night." Debbie zipped up Jill's anorak.

"Who did?"

"The owner. 'E sent this bloke round to 'ammer on our doors at two in the morning, scaring the living daylights out of us. All 'cos me and a couple of the others complained down at the DHSS about the kitchen. Mouse droppings on the cooker. The council's threatening to sue him. So 'e takes it out on us, 'oping we'll keep our mouths shut in future."

"That's awful, Debbie. Can't you go to the police?"

Debbie shrugged. "What good'd that do? He's their sort, not ours. They'd take 'is side. We don't even know 'is name. He's a crafty bugger, that one. Never shows 'is face round 'ere. Always sends someone else to do his dirty work."

Grace looked at her anxiously. "Hadn't you better move out of here for a bit? Go back to your mother's?"

Debbie tossed her head. "Na. I ain't afraid of 'im. Besides, me ma's up to her eyeballs, what with the electricity off and my kid sister scarperin' like that."

"Penny still hasn't come back then?"

"Nope. She won't 'alf catch it when she does. Three nights she's been away. Me ma's doing her nut. Sent Joe round 'ere yesterday afternoon to see if she was with me. 'Ere, you grab 'old of Lyn."

Together they negotiated the children and the buggy down the stairs. They were going to a jumble sale in the church hall. It wasn't due to start till three but when they arrived at half past two they already found a queue of people outside.

"Always have good stuff here," remarked the woman standing next to them. "Cast-offs from the nobs in the village. Quality stuff. Folks come from all over."

"Oh," said Grace, colouring.

At three o'clock precisely the doors opened. Grace paid the twenty pence entry fee for Debbie and herself. The moment the ticket was in her hand, Debbie rushed inside leaving the children with Grace. There was a general scramble to get to the trestle tables laden with blouses, cardigans, pans, all kinds of bric-à-brac. Debbie rooted along the stalls, seizing at once any item of clothing that looked as if it had a bit of wear left in it. By the end she had quite an armful of clothes but, after sorting through them with Grace, she discarded most of them, buying only a pair of plastic sandals for Jill, a dress for Lyn and a faded denim skirt for herself. They added up the prices. It came to two pounds fifty. Debbie joined the queue to pay.

Waiting for Debbie to pay, Grace stood at the back of the hall one hand on the buggy, the other holding on tightly to Jill, for she was afraid the child would run off and get lost in the crowd. She watched an old man in a threadbare suit finger a battered carpet sweeper. She longed to go over and tell him it was way past its useful life, but at that moment he put the sweeper under his arm and began fumbling in his pocket for coins.

"Hello, Mrs Napier." A voice at her shoulder made her jump. It was Father Keogh. She'd forgotten he'd be there. After all, it was his church hall. "I see you've made friends with Debbie Jackson." There was a hint of approval in his voice. "I don't suppose she's heard from the council yet?"

Grace shook her head.

"Pity." He stroked his chin. "Dreadful place, especially for these two little ones." He pulled a funny face for Jill, making her laugh, and held out his finger for Lyn to play with.

Grace began to warm towards him. On impulse she told him about Debbie's problems with the owner of the property.

He frowned. "I'll tell you what we'll do, we'll go to the Registry Office and look up the deeds. We'll find out the name of the owner and leak it to the press. Shame the bugger. It's the only way. I've done it before," he added.

"Leonard," said Grace, later that day, "what kind of a man would own a property like that and not care about the blocked loo or mice in the kitchen or plaster peeling off the walls?"

Leonard shrugged. "Someone who doesn't look too

closely at what his money's in. Someone whose aim is to get maximum return from his investment. Could be anyone. He's probably a perfectly respectable middle-class man with a wife who gives charity lunches. He's probably one of our neighbours."

"I don't care who it is," replied Grace firmly. "I'm going to blow their cover."

"I advise caution." Leonard pored over a sheet of figures. "By the way, I may be out of a job soon. They've started buying up shares again. The prices are going sky high."

"Have you found out who it is yet?"

"Hilltop Holdings, they're called. Funnily enough it's a firm Clive's had some dealings with. I must give him a call and get some information out of him."

"If you ask me, Clive's probably behind the whole thing. He knows what a good business man you are and how you're starting to turn the company round. He'd like it for himself."

"Grace, darling! How devious your mind is!"

"Devious? Nonsense! He's always wanted what you have," she added darkly.

"Clive has no reason to envy me." Leonard turned back to his figures. "Except," he looked up, "in so far as you're concerned, of course." He smiled.

Dear Leonard. How could he be so naive about his own brother?

She went to phone Lallie to make arrangements for their wine and cheese party. A polite, rather cold, upper-class voice informed her Lallie had left that morning for the north of England and wouldn't be back before the weekend. She decided to send the invitations out anyway.

Joachim opened the door, saw who it was and shut his eyes in relief.

"I thought you'd left me."

"I've been working. Waitressing in a nightclub. The hours are odd."

It might be true or it might be a useful alibi she'd cooked up. He decided not to enquire further. He pulled her towards him.

"Next time leave your phone number."

"You little devil! Put those biscuits back!" yelled the shopkeeper.

Frightened, Penny dashed out of the door and collided with the bulky form of Father Keogh.

"Now then." He put a hand on her shoulder to steady her. "What's all the rush?"

"I'm calling the police." The indignant shopkeeper appeared in the doorway. "She's stolen those biscuits."

"I never!" Penny tried unsuccessfully to squirm her way out of Father Keogh's grasp.

"I'm sure there must be some mistake," he said calmly. "Here," he fumbled in his cassock for coins, "there you are, paid for. Leave this to me, Fred, I'll deal with her," he added in an undertone.

"All right, Father," replied the shopkeeper reluctantly.

"Well now." Father Keogh took Penny by the arm and marched her briskly down the street. "There are a lot of people looking for you." He stood her at arm's length and scrutinised her, noticing her pallid complexion, watery eyes and the cold sores round her mouth. "I can't return you to your mother looking like that. What you need, young lady, is a hot bath and something to eat."

He bore her off, protesting, to the vicarage. Locked the front door and ran the water for a bath.

"What's your favourite food?" he shouted through the bathroom door.

"Caviar!" came the reply.

"Sure. What else?"

"Champagne."

"Come on, Penny. Play the game."

"Oh all right," she muttered. "Bacon and eggs then." Her words were swallowed by a bad bout of coughing. Listening outside the door, Father Keogh shook his head and sighed.

"If I didn't know you better," he said, as he drove her home, "I'd say that runny nose and cough wasn't a cold at all, but due to something else. Do you understand me, Penny?"

"Yes, Father." She sat in the front seat, hands in her pockets, chin thrust down.

"But I know you're too sensible to get hooked on anything as stupid as sniffing glue. You know what happens in the end, Penny? You'll be unable to think straight. Your memory will go. Your liver and kidneys will stop functioning properly. You'll end up a vegetable. Do you hear me?"

"Yes, Father."

"Promise me you'll stay off it."

"Yes, Father."

He glanced across at her. "We haven't seen much of you down at the youth club lately. You used to be so good at table tennis. You wiped the floor with the boys. How about giving it a try again?"

Penny shrugged.

"Four days it's been, Father," said Pat after he'd delivered her daughter to her and she'd been hugged and packed off to the kitchen to keep an eye on Sal and Dave. "I was out of my mind with worry. Where did you find her?"

"Down at the shops, almost getting herself arrested for taking a packet of biscuits."

Pat sighed and lit a cigarette. "Some days . . . "

He hesitated. "You know you could consider putting her into care for a while. It isn't that bad."

Pat drew herself up. "None of my family's ever been in care, Father, and we aren't going to start now. Not unless we're forced to," she added.

Father Keogh looked at her. "Have you been given a date for the court case yet?"

"Not yet."

"I can make enquiries for you."

She shrugged. "What's the point? It's not as if I've got a holiday planned, is it? Doesn't matter when the date is, does it?"

"Well, you know where to reach me if you need me."

"Yeah. Sorry, Father, if I spoke a bit sharp just now. I've a lot on my plate."

He sighed. "I know."

Pat gave Penny a good talking to and took her to and from school herself every day for a week.

After a few days Penny's "cold" cleared up and she began to get her energy back. With the electricity off there was plenty to do at home keeping Sal and Dave amused. She even spent a couple of evenings down at Father Keogh's youth club. She'd eavesdropped on the conversation between him and her mother and the talk of putting her into care had scared her. She made up her mind to toe the line for a bit.

But lying beside her mother at night in the cold flat, Penny found herself yearning for the garage she'd called home and the peace and quiet she'd found there.

CHAPTER THIRTEEN

LALLIE CAUGHT THE TEN O'CLOCK TRAIN FROM KING'S CROSS.

"Dante's visit to the Underworld," Jade had mocked, kissing her goodbye.

She'd no idea what she was going to do in the north, where she was going to stay or even why she was going back. She'd suggested it without thinking and Jade had pounced on the suggestion because she wanted to be alone for a few days, or if not alone, then with . . . but Lallie didn't want to think about that.

She'd brought her warmest clothes, remembering how even in the summer, the north-east wind used to howl round corners and tug at her blue velours hat as she walked home from school.

At Darlington she changed trains. Waiting for the train to depart, she watched women walk past on the platform in ill-fitting coats and shoes that were battered and scuffed. Up here faces were harder, clothes shoddier than down south. She sat in a carriage opposite two schoolgirls. Their voices had already achieved the flat, monotonous whine of their elders. Teessiders' accents sounded like one continuous moan against life. And who could blame them? She stared out of the grimy windows. Was it possible that up here in the north she'd rediscover a purpose for her life? A sense of her self that had somehow got lost lately? It seemed unlikely.

With a feeling of trepidation she got out at Stockton station and left her luggage with the station master. She had no idea where she was going. She wanted to walk and walk and see it all. Now that she was here she'd close her eyes to none of it. Something had called her back. She wouldn't rest till she'd found out what it was.

The station was surrounded by wasteland. The site of the first passenger railway looked devastated and forgotten. On her left was a row of terraced cottages and behind them stood a gas cylinder and a block of flats. She made her way down Bishopton Lane towards the high street, past boarded up shops and others advertising closing down sales. The pavements were filthy. Newspapers and crisp packets swirled around her legs in the wind. A group of men standing on the street corner watched sullenly as she walked by. In the past they'd have been old men, pensioners. Now they were young, out of work and prematurely aged, leading old men's lives.

Everything was smaller and dirtier than she'd remembered. Narrow little lives packed into narrow little streets. A child sauntered by swigging liquid from a vinegar bottle. Lallie passed a graffiti-covered bus shelter with all the glass knocked out and arrived in the high street sooner than she'd expected. Distances were shorter now than when she'd been a child and it had been a great adventure to take the bus into town with Tom and "go down the high street" of a Saturday afternoon.

The high street smelled of fish and chips and beer. Women laden down with shopping brushed past her wearing coats that didn't quite cover their skirts. Some wore stockings, some didn't. All of them looked as if their clothes would have fitted better on somebody else.

She stood for a moment outside the old Globe theatre to get her bearings. The Globe had been closed down and turned into a Mecca complex. "Bingo," read the sign, "The National Game." She made her way down the high street. Many of the shops had closed down. In their place, amusement halls had sprung up, advertising gifts galore and ten pound vouchers "to be spent in the supermarket of your choice." People were being encouraged to gamble their dole money on bingo and fruit machines in the hope of having more than bread and chips to put on the table for tea.

She went into a supermarket to buy a sandwich and noticed that half the brands she was used to in her local supermarket were missing here. The bare minimum was on offer. Whole shelves were filled with reduced price products. They'd passed their "sell-by" date, sometimes by as much as a month. The shops were having to adapt to unemployment or get out. The faces of the women shopping looked pale and unhealthy. Some of them were grossly overweight. Signs of bad diet and poor health care were everywhere. She passed the Town Hall. Over its incongruously jaunty Dutch exterior hung a huge banner: "15,219 Unemployed."

But the centre of town wasn't going to bring back her past. She needed to go somewhere where her memories were more personal. She turned the corner, past the Odeon cinema (now closed), into Yarm Road, the road on which her school had stood. It had been demolished soon after she'd left. A garish red brick pub now stood in its place. She paused to watch business men in grey suits sip their lunchtime pints on the spot where she'd studied and laboured and hated for seven long years. She walked on, past the grimy terraced houses, and turned right into Hartburn Lane. Snatches of a Dire Straits song echoed in her head. "Rain come down, forgive this dirty town. Rain come down and give this dirty town a drink of water." A lot of things needed forgiving here. She shuddered as she realised where her steps were leading. Back to the old house, the place where her mother had killed herself.

It looked even dingier than she'd remembered. A small semi-detached in a road of semi-detacheds. Paint was peeling from the front door. The curtains were crooked and grubby and a pane of glass was missing from one of the upstairs windows. The whole road had an air of decay about it, yet this was supposed to be a middle-class area. Perhaps the middle classes too were out of work.

She moved on aimlessly, back down Hartburn Avenue and into the park where her mother, when she was well, had taken Tom and herself to feed the ducks and play amongst the flower beds. A man was sitting on a bench by the pond. At his feet was a paper bag with a bottle inside it. At first she took him to be in his sixties but when she looked more closely, she saw he was probably no older than herself. His long ginger hair was tied back in a ponytail and there was a thick layer of ginger stubble on his cheeks. He wore a pair of dirty trousers and dark glasses. One lens was missing, which added to his sinister air. Through the white space where the lens should have been, she could see deep lines around his eyes. His face had a pinched and withered look. If he was the same age as herself he might well have been one of those boys from the secondary modern who used to lie in wait for the girls to come along and knock their hats off. She turned her head away and walked a few yards further on, to a bench facing the pond which had once seemed so huge and now looked so small. She sat down.

"I knew you'd come back."

Startled from her thoughts Lallie looked up to see a short, dumpy woman in her late forties or thereabouts standing in front of her. She was holding a small boy by the hand.

"Sorry?" Lallie stared at the woman's shoulder-length grey hair and worn face. She was dressed in a long cotton skirt, striped socks, clogs, a heavy pullover and a man's jacket. "I think you must have made a mista . . . " she began.

The woman gave a wry smile. There was a spirit in her eyes that contrasted oddly with the rest of her appearance.

"Don't you recognise me, Lillie Greene?"

The voice held a note that stirred some memory in Lallie, a note of challenge. She looked again. It was as if a blurred film was gradually coming into focus. But she didn't have it yet.

"Jenny Nattrass. Jenny Armitage to you."

The years spun away and Lallie was Lillie again, trembling as she knelt on a branch suspended over a stream, edging forward bit by bit, desperate to earn Jenny's praise.

She gasped. "Jenny . . . !" Was it possible? Not a woman

in her late forties then, but the same age as herself. "My God! Jenny!" She giggled like a schoolgirl beneath Jenny's amused, ironic gaze.

"I thought *you* were going to London and never coming back."

"I haven't, till now. But Jenny . . . you, after all this time! Married too. And a child." She glanced after the boy who'd wandered off to inspect the ducks.

"Not mine," said Jenny. "And not very married now either. I work at a drop-in centre for youngsters. It's attached to a hostel for the homeless. He belongs there. Well!" She sat down on the bench beside Lallie. "What brings you up here?" She ran a practised northern eye over Lallie's hair and clothes. "You've done well for yourself." The good old northern expression when confronted with the success of one of their own: half-proud, half-grudging, and not a little suspicious. "Kept your figure too, which is more than I can say for myself. What are you doing with yourself these days?"

"I work in films. I do research for Jade McKenna."

"Oh? Can't say I've heard of her. Well, films!" Again the appraising glance. "Who'd have thought it? Little Lillie Greene. What are you doing back here? Going to film us, are you?"

"Perhaps." It was good an alibi as any. "As a matter of fact, I've only just arrived. I've been walking around all morning, trying to get my bearings."

"Bit of a shock, I expect, seeing the old place again. You've lost your accent. You sound like a real southerner. Jack! Come away from there!"

The boy slouched back towards them.

"They found him yesterday, sleeping rough down in Portrack. I'm keeping an eye on him till the social workers decide what to do with him. Oh yes, things have changed around here, I can tell you. Well, you'll have seen for yourself – houses boarded up, half the shops in the high street closed down. These days anybody with any money moves out to the countryside and does up a cottage. Nobody lives in the town unless they have to."

She ran her clogs up and down over the pebbles.

"Stockton will be a ghost town soon, full of misfits like him." She pointed to the bored, grubby-faced child in front of them. "Why don't you make a film about that, eh? We could do with some publicity. Nobody bothers about us up here. We're the lost, the unwanted. I bet they've never even heard of us down in Whitehall."

It was a challenge in the old Jenny manner. She took a notebook out of her bag, scribbled on a piece of paper, tore it out and handed it to Lallie.

"Come and see us. Where are you staying?"

"The Swallow," Lallie said at random. It was the only name she could think of. The Swallow was the biggest hotel in the town, a tall, red brick building at the end of the high street. Again the ironic glance – you *have* done well for yourself. This time there was no need for Jenny to voice the words. They were written all over her face.

"Come and visit us at the centre," she repeated, gathering up her things. "Come and see how the other half lives."

Lallie watched as Jenny walked off, with Jack trailing behind, kicking up stones in his thin runners. Some of the old strength was still there, lurking behind the worn features. Jenny had never been like the rest of the women in Stockton, submissive and fatalistic. She'd always been a doer. Yet even she looked half-crushed by the hopelessness of the place.

Ironically, meeting Jenny made Lallie feel young and hopeful again. She rose from the bench and walked out of the park towards the bus stop. She'd catch a bus into town, pick up her suitcase from the station and book into the Swallow. It was brash and vulgar – a place for passing salesmen, businessmen attending conferences, the odd "posh" wedding. But it was comfortable. She badly needed to soak in a long, hot bath and wash off the grime of the town. And tomorrow – who knew? – perhaps she'd visit Jenny.

"They've decided on strike action at the Dortmund factory," Joachim dutifully reported.

Hans Wedelmeier remained unperturbed. "The Bavarian plant is almost ready for action. James's been speeding things up. We're quite safe. The other factories won't come out in support. They've been threatened with closure if they do. No, it's just a matter now of closing down the Dortmund factory as quickly as possible and paying off the men. And, now, Seefeldt, on a lighter note, have you chosen your new company car yet?"

"No."

Joachim turned on his heel and walked out of the office. Another black mark against him. He was in the grip of an inexorable machine. It was mowing down his workers and he was powerless to stop it. For its name was profit.

What was it God wanted of him? Lately he'd begun to feel hopelessly caught. Not only at work; with Christabel as well. She disappeared off for days on end. Where did she go? Who did she see? He was supposed to welcome her back, no questions asked. And he did. They were adults, after all. But he seesawed between joy and despair several times a week. This wasn't a proper life, she had him trapped in some kind of machine. Worse still, when he made love to her, it was his wife he was beginning to see, his wife's tearstained face. He clenched his fists. What does He want of me?

Perhaps he should leave his job and become a monk? He'd often thought of it. Join the brown robed brothers and hurry in open sandals through chilly streets to celebrate early morning mass. He'd put all the failures of his worldly life behind him.

Another fantasy, he thought bitterly. He had too much unfinished business in this world to think about the next. The farm, his men, his sons, Christabel, Katrin . . .

Grace picked up Father Keogh outside his church. He'd been celebrating Holy Communion. It would have been sheer hypocrisy to have attended herself, she felt, this being a weekday. He'd had nothing to eat yet that morning so he suggested they have coffee together before visiting the Registry Office.

It was a seedy-looking coffee bar in an area where Grace had never been before. Several of the people there seemed to know Father Keogh. An old man, his trousers held up by a piece of string, nodded to them on his way out.

"Thank heavens Penny's turned up at last." Grace stirred her coffee in the grubby cup and wondered if she could get away with not drinking it. She glanced across the table at Father Keogh. He looked pale and tired. What did vicars do between services? Write sermons? Visit the sick? She asked him.

"What do I do?" He brushed a hand over his eyes. "Anything that turns up. Yesterday the church silver was stolen. I spent the whole day trying to get it back."

"Gracious! But I thought it was locked away after services?"

"It is. That's how I knew this was an inside job. I put on my biggest collar, went down to the school where most of our choir comes from and spoke to the boys. They've a network of thieves operating in that school. By four, I had the name. The older brother of one of our choirboys. By five, I'd visited his home and retrieved the silver from under his bed."

"Heavens!" She gazed at him in admiration. "Did you call the police?"

"No." He finished his coffee. "I've spent years building up trust between the boys in that school and myself. If I'd called in the police, that would have meant the end of that trust. Next time the silver was stolen, it would have been gone for good."

At the Registry Office they discovered that Debbie's house, indeed all the houses in her street, was owned by a company called Hilltop Securities.

"Mm . . . a company is less easy to embarrass than a private individual." Father Keogh stroked his chin. "I'll have to think about this."

Hilltop, Grace was thinking, where have I heard that name?

CHAPTER FOURTEEN

JENNY'S CENTRE (TWO ROOMS IN A RUNDOWN VICTORIAN TERRACE) was light and bright. There was a green plant on Jenny's desk and plenty of helpful leaflets lying around. In one corner stood a coffee machine. From the back room came the sound of snooker balls. Teenagers wandered in and out between the two rooms, smoking, chatting, playing snooker, reading the job ads.

"We open the doors at nine," Jenny explained. "There's always a crowd of them hanging around outside. Some of them have slept rough. Others get kicked out of their hostels during the day. That's why we started this place up. Keep them off the streets. We work on the younger ones, try to get them back to school. With the older ones it's mainly a question of finding something for them to do. Voluntary work, odd jobs, training courses, we try everything."

"Who's we?" Lallie picked up a leaflet advertising a government training scheme.

"Steve and I. Steve's the guy I live with. He's down at the DHSS at the moment. Beard, denims, soft voice. A sixties child. Spent a couple of years in India. Never trained for anything. Always thought the jobs would be there when he needed them. Gives him something in common with these kids." She glanced up from the pile of letters on her desk. "What about you? Do you live with anyone?"

"I live with Jade. I told you about her. She makes films."

There was a silence. Then Jenny burst out laughing, laughter tinged with admiration. "Lillie Greene! You're gay!"

It somehow broke the ice, established Lallie on the same side in Jenny's eyes, an outsider. She began to let down some of the guards every northerner erects against strangers, especially ones from the south. She told Lallie more about her work.

"Society doesn't want to know about these kids. After six months on the dole, they lose all their self-confidence."

A boy of about sixteen strolled over to Lallie flexing his muscles. "Feel this." He thrust an arm towards her. "Come the revolution . . . " The challenge dangled in mid-air sounding pathetic. He wandered aimlessly away again.

A tall, gangling West Indian boy sauntered in. He wore a Wrangler sweatshirt, tight black jeans and Doc Marten's.

"Hi, Jonnie," said Jenny cheerfully. "How's it going? Hey, like your sweatshirt, kid."

He grinned and pushed back his cap.

"Things are fucking great, thanks. Got this job down the market. Wednesdays and Saturdays. Good money."

He sat on the edge of her desk, swinging his legs.

"You wait till I get my first Jag and you're still working in this crappy old dump. I'll come and fetch you once a week and take you out for a spin." He drove the imaginary car. "Fucking eighty mile an hour down the high street. I'll take you back to my mansion. A bloody enormous house with a big electric fence round it to protect my record collection. We'll have a couple of beers and watch a video. Any one you want, I'll have them all. We'll be brought food by one of my fans. Fucking gorgeous. Naomi Campbell type. Know what I mean?"

He sketched her body in the air, caught up in his fantasy. Lallie listened, caught up in it too.

"Fine, Jonnie," said Jenny who'd heard it before. "And how's real life? School, for instance? Why aren't you there now?"

His face clouded over. He got off the desk and began toying with the leaflets.

"Don't learn nothing interesting there. It's all bloody books, innit? What's the use?"

"Stick it out, Jonnie. Get some GCSEs. It'll help, believe me." Jenny reached for a local newspaper and read out the job ads. They all required GCSEs. "See what I mean?"

He was silent.

"Jonnie, has something happened?" she asked more softly.

He pulled his cap down and cast a sidelong glance at Lallie.

"It's OK. She's a friend."

That "friend" pleased Lallie.

"The old man came home roaring drunk last night. Beat up me mam." He clenched his fists. "One day I'll fucking take a swing at him, I swear I will." For a moment he looked violent, then the tension suddenly went from his body. "When I get the money together, I'm going to take her away from that dump and buy her a real house. Nothing grand, two up, two down, bit of a garden."

"That's a better dream, Jonnie. You know your mother could get a barring order."

"She won't. She loves that arsehole. God knows why."

"Hey, Jonnie! Come and have a game," called a voice from the back room.

Jonnie started forward, looked at Jenny and stopped. "Can't," he muttered. "Got sommat to do."

Jenny smiled. "Stick it out, Jonnie. Only a few more months to go."

"Only!" He grimaced and tipped his cap at them. "Good day, ladies." He went out whistling.

"Jonnie's father walked out on them when Jonnie was little." Jenny leafed through her mail. "For a long while it was just the two of them. His mother and he are very close. But his father came back recently to live with them. He's an alcoholic and inclined to be violent. She really should get a barring order."

Lallie watched the kids stroll in and out. One youth had tattoos on his neck and arms, another a shaved head and an earring through his nose. In small ways they were trying to make their identity felt. A thin girl with a pale, pinched face sat in a corner, smoking a cigarette. Straggly blonde hair hung down over her face. She wore knee length plastic boots and an imitation leather coat coming apart at the seams. Her fingernails were bitten back to the skin. Like all the rest she seemed listless, apathetic, as if she'd lost any sense of purpose in life. At nineteen, she was defeated.

"That's Susan. She's lost her job and hasn't a clue how to go about claiming the dole," Jenny muttered. "Her father died recently. Heart attack. He was forty-one. Happens to a lot of the men round here. Combination of bad diet and stress at being out of work. She's got no one now. I said I'd give her some advice." She went over to talk to her.

A short while later Jenny came back, sat down beside Lallie and sighed.

"These kids, they don't know what to do with themselves half the time. They think their problems would be solved if only they had money. Well, some of them would be, but not all. If you're poor today, you need courage. And a helluva lot of perseverance even to work your way through the social security forms."

Lallie thought of Pat Jackson running from one government department to another, filling in forms, working her way through the complexities of the benefit system so that she and her family could survive. She glanced over at Susan. A girl like that would have no chance.

Jenny grinned.

"Now I'll stop making political speeches. We'll have lunch and you can tell me why you've come back to visit us. Let's go to our alma mater. You know it's been turned into a pub?"

"Yes, I saw."

"Probably more use as a pub."

Lallie glanced at her in surprise. "You hated it too?"

"Not hate it, but it never taught me very much. And it just put obstacles in *your* way, brainbox."

"Ho, ho!"

"Well, you were."

They linked arms and walked down to the pub.

"Now, Lillie Greene, out with it. Why are you here?" Jenny perched expectantly on the bar stool, a plate of bread and cheese on her lap and a glass of beer at her elbow.

"No special reason. Just felt it was time I visited the old place again." Lallie stared at her beer. "In the old days we'd have been expelled on the spot for drinking this stuff." She took a sip and looked around. "Wasn't this the assembly hall?"

"Yep. You can still see the wood panelling." Jenny pointed to a wall at the back.

"All those speeches." Lallie sighed.

"All those prizes you won," retorted Jenny.

"I didn't do it on purpose."

"Yes, you did."

"Well, maybe. I wanted to get away."

"I know. You made that quite clear. So why have you come back?"

Lallie glanced down at her hands. "Memories. There's nobody left now, you know. Apart from my brother."

"Yes, I know. I heard about your mother. I'm sorry. I would have written if I'd known where to find you."

"It's all right."

"People used to say things. The grown ups, you know. As a kid, you don't understand. I never realised she was so ill. It must have been tough on you."

"Tougher on her." Lallie was silent for a moment. "Jenny, do you ever see any of the old crowd? Robina, for instance?"

"Robina Walker? Not for ages. She was running a catering

business in Middlesborough but she packed it in. Lack of customers. Why?"

"I thought of looking her up. Never mind. I suppose I'll have to pay a call on my brother and his wife, now I'm here." Lallie grimaced. "They've moved out to Great Ayton."

"Part of the mass exodus from the towns."

"My sister-in-law always was particular about where she lived."

"Lillie, I was serious about what I said yesterday," said Jenny, as they stood on the pavement outside the pub. "How about making a film, a short documentary, about this town and what's happening to it? Why don't you come over and see our women's hostel this evening?"

"Er . . . can't this evening."

"Tomorrow then. Come on, Lillie." Jenny placed a hand on her arm. "We're desperately short of money. The government's about to cut off our grant. We may have to close down the centre and then those kids will be back to wandering the streets again. We could do with some publicity."

"Jenny, I don't make films. I'm only the researcher. And it's not the kind of subject that would appeal to Jade."

"Then why have you come here, Lillie Greene?" Angrily, Jenny removed her hand from Lallie's arm. "Why come here if you don't want to help? We can do without people who only want to stand and stare."

She marched off down the street.

Lallie stood on the pavement remembering how it had felt when she'd been afraid to follow her friend's example and climb a tree or jump a ditch. The old familiar shame at having failed to rise to one of Jenny's challenges swept over her.

Penny began disappearing off from school again, a few hours here and there. Past experience had taught her cunning. She chose times when her absences wouldn't be noticed. Al came to visit her once or twice in her garage den. She had a mattress in there now and some empty paint tins for seats. He brought her presents. A bar of chocolate, a can of Coke, a radio. One afternoon he brought her some dope wrapped in clingfilm.

"It's better than sniffing glue, this stuff is."

She watched as he took some cigarette papers out of a tin, licked them and stuck them together. He drew a packet of cigarettes from his pocket, shook one out and split it with his thumbnail.

"This stuff's bloody good. You'll see."

He shook the dope onto the cigarette papers and rolled up the joint between his fingers. He struck a match, lit the reefer and inhaled deeply. He passed it to Penny who imitated him. She passed the joint back to him, leaned against the wall and closed her eyes. Al's radio was playing a song by Madonna.

"I can see bears." She giggled. "Big, cuddly bears. Come on, Al," she said after a while. "Give us some more."

He held the reefer aloft. "This time you got to pay for it."

Penny knew what he meant. She began unbuttoning her shirt.

"Aw, come off it!" he jeered. "I can get that at home any night watching my sister undress. She's sixteen. You should see the size of her knockers."

"Please, Al. That stuff's great."

Al shook his head. Bullied at school because of his weight, he was never slow to seize the opportunity to bully someone else in return.

"I'm not kidding."

Holding the joint aloft, he began to unzip his jeans with the other hand. She caught a glimpse of red underpants.

She retreated to a corner. "Won't."

"Aw, come on! It's no big deal. There's lots more dope where this comes from."

"I'll pay you for it. I'll get money."

"Huh! Where from? Your Mum's been cut off."

"From my brother. Jimmy'll give me some."

"Oh yeah? I heard he'd moved to Brighton."

"That's not true!" she yelled. Though it was true she didn't know where he was.

"Come on. You don't want me to tell your Mum you've been skiving off school again, do you? If you let me, I could fix up this place real nice for you." He took a step towards her.

She glowered. "I thought you were my friend."

"I am your friend. I just said I'd fix this place up for you, didn't I? I could bring you a telly. I've a mate knows where to nick them. We could come here every day after school. Come on!"

He was pulling her towards him. His hands were up her skirt, tugging at her knickers.

"And we'll get you better ones than these. Split crotch, like in the films."

He smelled nasty. Sweaty and sickly. She hated him. She began scratching at his face and hitting out, but he was too strong for her. He pressed her down onto the floor.

"Come on," he panted. "Give it me, I need it," he said, repeating words from a video he'd watched at Sid's place. "I want your fucking cunt."

He fumbled with his small hard cock, trying to put it inside her. He came before he'd succeeded, messily, spilling his semen over her school skirt.

"Sorry," he groaned, half ashamed now.

Penny only shrugged and said, "Give me that." She grabbed the packet of dope and rolled herself a joint. She lay back, puffing at it contentedly. "This stuff makes me happy." She giggled.

Al sat up and pulled up his jeans. "It'll be better next time," he promised.

But Penny was in a world of her own.

After Jenny left her standing on the pavement, Lallie went back into the pub and ordered two gins and tonic in quick succession. She drank one to her headmistress and one to her French teacher, who'd hated her and shown it. Then she mentally stuck up two fingers at both of them and went to ring her brother. Her sister-in-law, Evie, answered. Evie's astonishingly elongated vowels announced down the phone at her that she and Tom and the girls would be "simply delighted" to see her. Any time after six. Lallie put down the receiver and wondered whether, when it came to it, she would have the heart to go and see them.

By now rather drunk, she decided to walk up to Grangefield cemetery where her mother was buried. The wind was blowing strongly, tugging at her hair and skirt. The sky overhead was black. Typical north-east weather.

When she arrived at the cemetery, she saw rows and rows of graves stretching out in front of her. She hadn't realised there'd be so many of them. She weaved drunkenly in and out of them looking from right to left at the names on the headstones. The trees swayed and tilted above her head. After a while it dawned on her that none of the dates on these graves was later than 1920. The newer graves must be somewhere else. She wheeled drunkenly on, past the Jewish plot and the Hindu. Spots of rain began falling on her face and hands. It's hopeless, she thought, it'll take me days. She caught sight of a woman arranging some flowers round a grave.

"Excuse me. Is there a plan of the cemetery, do you know?"

The woman shook her head and indicated she couldn't hear her above the wind.

"A plan?" yelled Lallie.

The woman nodded and pointed to a shed on the left.

Lallie tapped on the door. A group of workmen were sitting in a circle, mugs of tea in their hands.

"Excuse me. I'm looking for a grave."

They indicated a man in overalls sitting in the corner.

"Serial number?" he asked.

"Haven't a clue." She leaned against the doorpost, her cheeks flushed from alcohol and walking. Rain dripped down the back of her neck.

"Come inside, love," said the man. "Don't stand there getting wet."

She swayed slightly as she stepped inside and would have fallen if one of the men hadn't sprung up.

"Steady on, lass. Take a seat."

She sank down. "I'll be all right. Just give me a minute." She closed her eyes.

"Takes them that way sometimes."

"Ay, give her a mouthful of tea."

Someone stuck a mug of strong tea to her mouth. She took a sip and felt better.

"Thanks. I'm all right now."

"About this grave, pet. Double or single?"

"Double." Her parents had been buried in the same plot.

She gave them names and dates and waited while they phoned through to the computer centre. Snatches of conversation drifted past her.

"He got three thousand for doing that job."

"Whew! Could do with a bit extra myself like. I took the wife and the niece . . . "

"Who?"

"The wife and the niece. To Redcar on Sunday. Cost us four pound for the three of us. Singles that was."

"Ay, shocking. Hear that Dick? Bill here was saying he took the wife to . . . "

"And the niece."

"He took the wife and the niece to Redcar and it cost four pound. Return was that?"

"No, singles."

"Ay, shocking."

"We've got the number of the grave, pet." The man in overalls put down the phone. "I'll take you there now."

Outside it was still raining heavily. Lallie turned up her collar.

"It's neat here," she said. "You keep the graves looking nice."

"Ay, leastways it hasn't come to opening up graves and burying folks on top of one another. Did you see that programme on the box last night?"

She shook her head.

"Chopping up old coffins they were and burying people in plots already occupied. Bloody scandal, that's what it is. Here's your grave now."

Lallie looked down and saw the simple headstone she'd chosen with Tom.

"Thanks."

Hurriedly she tipped him. He went off. She stepped forward and removed an ice cream wrapper lying in the grass on top of the grave. The grave seemed bare in comparison to the others. She should have brought flowers or a plant or something. She stood looking down. A dull heavy feeling came over her. The place was empty, deserted. A public cemetery wasn't the place for ghosts. Her mother wasn't here. She didn't know where she was (Lallie didn't know if she believed in an after-life) but her mother wasn't here. She turned and walked slowly away.

She hired a car and drove out to Great Ayton. She passed the factory site where her father had spent every day of his working life. She looked down at the huge industrial complex stretching out in front of her and was seized by a strange sense of awe. Here was a whole world throbbing with life, possessed of a power of its own which she didn't understand but which controlled the lives of everyone who lived in the area. And killed, she added to herself, thinking of her father.

Tom, his wife and their two daughters lived in a modern semi-detached on the outskirts of Great Ayton village. Evie, dressed in her best outfit, showed Lallie the fitted kitchen, the new curtains and the extension they'd had built on at the back, at the expense of some of the lawn.

"Tom and I have an en suite bathroom now. So much more convenient. Would you care for a cup of tea? Or perhaps a sweet sherry?"

"Tea please," replied Lallie. The gin had given her a headache. She wished she'd brought presents for her two little nieces. They sat side by side on the sofa in their Sunday best, faces scrubbed, patent leather sandals gleaming. She was a bit of a failure as an aunt, she reckoned, just about managed to remember Christmas and birthdays.

"Where are you staying?" Evie daintily poured out the tea.

"At the Swallow."

"Oh, Stockton! You'll find some changes there. They've ruined the centre with all those amusement arcades. I shop in Harrogate nowadays. Better type of shop. Do you remember Betty's? As good as anything you get in London, I'll be bound. Do you take sugar?"

Harrogate, thought Lallie. White-haired women in pearls and silk dresses, eating cream cakes in Betty's. "Better," she said, remembering Betty's cakes. "Better than anything we have in London."

"Pass Aunt Lillie a biscuit," said Evie, swollen with pride. "Oh dirty girl! You've messed your frock!" She shrieked and pounced on her younger daughter who'd spilled some juice.

"Never mind," said Tom placidly. "It'll come out in the wash."

He sat in the armchair, leaving the talk to the two women. Now and then Lallie caught him stealing a glance at her. He is pleased to see me, she thought. He's all the family I've got.

"You must come down to London," she said impulsively. "All of you." Though it was really only Tom she wanted. "Come and stay with me and show the children the sights."

"London. It's a long way." Tom's face broke into a smile. "Too many crowds for me."

"Oh Tom!" exclaimed his wife, exasperated. She turned to Lallie. "You see what he's like. It's as much as I can do to get him over to Torremelinos for a week in July."

They'd never come to visit. Perhaps it was a good thing. If they found out about Jade, they'd never come near her again. They'd not asked about her life in London. The world she moved in was out of their range, though she'd noticed Evie's surreptitious glance at her left hand.

"Do you ever think of our parents?" she whispered to Tom as she was leaving.

He shrugged and looked down. "Ay, I do. But where's the point in brooding? What's done is done." He placed his broad, strong hand on her shoulder. "Come and see us again, Lillie. We're family, we should stick together."

She felt, in his grasp and in his words, all the calm good sense of the northern working man. He was straightforward, a good man. Why had she turned out so complicated?

She drove out of the village and up onto the moors, to the spot above Osmotherly where they'd walked as children. She stopped the car and got out. It was pitch black. On her right she heard the wind blowing through the trees. A sheep bleated. The wind blew the sweet smell of ferns towards her. In the daylight one could stand here and look across vast spaces of flat moorland. Miles and miles of ferns and tough, springy heather bushes with sheep tracks running through them. She breathed in the cool night air.

Below her in the distance twinkled the Stockton lights. Gazing down at them she felt her heart twist inside her with pity and anguish. She'd forgotten what it was to feel deeply.

She must change her life. She must. Else the shadow of this place would be forever upon her.

The phone rang. He fumbled for the receiver. Christabel. At last.

"Joachim?"

"Oh. It's you."

"You must come." There was urgency in Katrin's voice.

One hand on the receiver, he groped for his watch. Three o'clock in the morning. "What the . . . ?"

"It's Peter. He's been picked up by the police. They raided a party. There were drugs, I think. They've arrested a group of them."

"My God! Where have they taken him? No, wait. I'll come round to your place."

They drove together through the empty streets. Joachim reflected that the last time they'd driven together at this hour of the morning was when he'd taken her to the hospital to have Peter. Glancing at her pale pinched face he saw his fears reflected there.

At the police station they came upon their son huddled in a corner, pale-faced, a bruise on the side of his cheek. Katrin hurried over to him.

"Peter, are you all right?"

"What do you think?"

He scowled and rubbed his hands down his shiny purple trousers. Joachim winced at his tone but Katrin didn't seem to notice anything out of the ordinary.

"What's happening?" he asked his son.

"They're letting me go. They say they may or may not press charges."

He glared at his parents fiercely, making no apologies, offering no explanations. A police officer came along and the necessary formalities were gone through.

Joachim drew Katrin to one side. "Does he often speak to you like that?"

She shrugged. "Sometimes. It's normal for boys his age, isn't it? His teachers say so anyway." The defences dropped a fraction. "He's got into bad company."

"I'm taking him home with me."

Katrin's expression was a mixture of relief and stubbornness. Proud, she wanted to resist, he knew, anything that smacked of defeat. She was punishing herself again by trying to shoulder all the burden. Somehow he had to break into this circle.

"I ought to speak to him. As his father," he said, using the kind of language she understood, the language of duty.

Reluctantly she agreed.

They dropped Katrin off and drove through the empty streets to Joachim's apartment. Peter sat hunched up and silent in the passenger seat.

"I suppose there's no point asking you why?" began Joachim, his eyes fixed on the road ahead.

"Cannabis is nothing special, Dad. No worse than the alcohol you get high on."

Joachim flinched. "It's not the first time then?" He took the silence to indicate an admission. "You're not selling the stuff?"

"Come off it, Dad." There was scorn in his son's voice.

He was failing to achieve the right balance. He made an effort and tried to remember that despite the purple jeans and ridiculous hair style, this was a young adult sitting beside him.

"When you get a job – "

"If."

" . . . a police record won't go down well."

"Depends what I decide to do. I'm thinking of joining a rock band."

Joachim snorted. "A fantasy world! You can't live life in a make-believe world of pop music, drugs and weird hairdos. Has your mother said anything to you about your hair, by the way?"

"Plenty. But then she's always nagging on about something. I've stopped listening to her."

"Don't speak about your mother like that." My God, he thought, I sound absurd.

Peter glared at him. "What do you care? And what's so great about the 'real' world anyway? Pollution, unemployment, cruelty to animals, divorce," he added meaningfully. "What's wrong with a bit of music?"

Joachim felt the ground being pulled from underneath him. He parked the car by the side of the road opposite his flat. He glanced up at the window. If there was a light on, Christabel would be there. There wasn't.

"Listen to me, Peter, I'm your father . . . "

"Yes, *Dad*?" The heavy emphasis on the last word and the irony in Peter's eyes as he turned to look at his father made Joachim feel, as he was meant to, the full force of his years of absence.

"OK," he said. "Let's sleep on it."

The door of the hostel was scratched and dented where panic-stricken women had hammered on it for shelter. It reminded Lallie of a wall she'd seen in Spain against which, so the guide had said, executions had taken place under Franco.

She'd gone back to visit Jenny at the centre and stood before her saying, "All right. You win. Show me everything that goes on here and I'll go back to London and try to raise some interest in making a documentary."

She'd spent the day at the centre and was now being shown round the hostel. It was for women aged eighteen and over.

"Though in a really desperate case, we'll stretch a point and take in a kid like Jack for the night," Jenny told her.

Lallie looked around the bare sitting-room with its stained, threadbare carpet and sagging sofas. A black and white television dominated the room. Two or three women sat around quietly chatting and knitting. A stout woman of about sixty with greasy, uncombed hair sat by herself on one of the hard chairs. Legs planted stolidly apart, dressed in a shabby black dress and yellowish cardigan, she played absentmindedly with the string of rosary beads in her lap. Deep furrows of misery lined her face. She rocked backwards and forwards muttering to herself. An advertising jingle came on, inviting her to apply for an American Express card. She stared vacantly at the screen. What kind of "homes" had they escaped from to make this seem like an acceptable refuge?

"What kind of women come here?" whispered Lallie.

"Women who've been beaten up by their men. Ex-addicts. Ex-prostitutes. The mentally unstable. All sorts of women who're too poor or too helpless to cope on their own."

"How long do they stay?"

"Some of them never leave. Some of them have been in care all their lives."

Jenny led the way down the corridor to the sleeping quarters.

Lallie looked at the rows and rows of cubicles. "You've a huge number of beds here."

"Not enough. Particularly in the winter. We often have to turn away the physically fit in favour of older women who'd otherwise die out on the streets. Homelessness kills, you see. And there's no way these women can make themselves heard. Homelessness isn't news unless there's a court case going on. We need your help, Lillie."

It was Jenny's old challenging tone. With a new note of desperation added. Jenny was actively pleading for Lallie's help, admitting she'd reached the end of her resources. Lallie squeezed her friend's arm. "I'll see what I can do."

"We're counting on you, Lillie."

On the train back to London, Lallie thought over the scenes of impoverishment she'd witnessed. Not just material poverty (she'd expected that), but lives severely diminished. An atmosphere of rejection and hopelessness hung over the town like a fog. Perhaps she *should* make a film about it? It would be an act of contrition towards the town she'd hated and despised for so long. The town which had killed her father when pollution spewed out from the factory chimneys got into his lungs. And killed her mother too by failing to provide her with a life that satisfied her.

Yes, a film might finally lay her mother's ghost. And it would be a public recognition that that abandoned town, with its lost and forgotten inhabitants, was somehow part of her own destiny and couldn't be lightly tossed aside. A film would unite the two parts of her life. Join Lallie with Lillie, finally.

But would she ever be able to persuade Jade to help?

CHAPTER FIFTEEN

JOACHIM WOKE TO THE SOUND OF HIS SON MOVING AROUND IN THE other room. He got out of bed, put on his trousers and went into the kitchen where he found Peter making coffee.

"Hello Dad. Sorry about last night. Got a bit aggressive, I guess. After-effects of the cannabis." He poured water into the filter.

Joachim sat down on a chair. The bruise on the side of his son's face had got bigger. It was purply green, yellow at the edges.

"Did they rough you up down at the station?"

Peter looked surprised. He doesn't give us much credit, thought Joachim.

"A bit." He grimaced. "It's the hair. Makes them furious. I don't think they'll press charges though. They aren't interested in hash. It's the big stuff they're after. Coke, heroin. There was none of that."

"I hope not."

"There isn't any harm in cannabis, Dad. It's just another way of relaxing. Coffee?"

"Thanks." He took the mug and stirred sugar into it. "I didn't realise you had ambitions in the music business, Peter."

"You never asked, did you, Dad?" Again the heavy emphasis on the last word. "Don't worry, I said it mainly to annoy you."

"Oh." He digested this for a moment, then said, "Your mother thinks you've fallen into bad company."

There was a silence.

"Have you? Answer me, Peter."

His son kicked at the table leg. "What does she know about it?"

"Try not to be hard on your mother, Peter," he murmured. "It's difficult living on your own."

Peter smirked. "We thought you had a woman here."

No point not being honest. "I do . . . sometimes. Not often." There was a pause. "Listen Peter, come over to Ireland with me for the summer. You could get to know how the farm works. It would be something different for you."

"Oh Dad! Ireland! That's your answer to everything, isn't it? Run away to your country retreat if you like. I'm not running with you. I'm German. I have to stay here and work out what that means."

Joachim, looking at his son's set and tense face thought, his anger is my anger. Bigger than his hurt over me, bigger than his disagreements with his mother, it's fixed deep inside him.

"What does it mean to be German? For you?" he asked softly.

Peter stood looking at him for a moment, the table between them. "It means accepting to live here and trying to work things out. It means admitting our collective guilt, facing up to the fact that grandfather was a Nazi," he muttered.

"Your grandfather never belonged to the Nazi party. He was conscripted into the army. There is a difference."

"He could have refused to fight."

"Yes, at the cost of his life. And he'd have thought that the coward's way out." God knew, he held no brief for his father. The old man and Joachim had never got on, so why was he defending him to his son? Perhaps there was something that ran through the generations. "Your mother's father was a hero," he added.

"Don't I know it?" Peter sighed. "*She* wants us to become businessmen. That's the other part of being German, at least as I see it. People of my generation have a duty to put a brake on all the materialism sweeping our country." He tilted his chin in a gesture unconsciously borrowed from his mother. "God knows what kind of monster this reunification's going to create."

"I shouldn't worry about that. Reunification's going to be a lot more expensive than they think."

"Is it?"

"Yes," said Joachim, glad there was something in this conversation he could claim to know about. "There's going to have to be a period of retrenchment. But if it's materialism you're worried about, why not take over the farm in a few years' time? There's nothing materialistic in the kind of life you'd have in Ireland. I always hoped you or Werner . . . the job situation's so bad nowadays."

"That's your dream, Dad. Not ours."

Joachim looked at his son. "So what do you intend to do?"

"I want to stay in Germany and study psychology. I want to understand what makes people kill and maim for the sake of some perverted ideal. I don't want to run away, like you, or despise people who're less than perfect, like Mum."

Their son had caught them exactly. Why had he never talked to Peter like this before? But it took more than a few hours on a Sunday afternoon to get to know someone properly. He'd always been so anxious to provide entertainment on his visits to his sons, he'd never allowed time just to sit down and talk. He looked at Peter. He needs me, he thought. He needs someone to talk to who is not his mother.

Then suddenly he said, this surprising son of his, "It's bloody silly you two living alone at opposite ends of the town. Come back to Mum. She needs you."

"Ah Peter." Joachim sighed. "It isn't as simple as that."

Lallie dumped her suitcase in the hall.

"Darling! Sorry I wasn't at the station to meet you." Jade came out of the sitting-room and kissed her. "I got held up. How did the trip to the ghastly Inferno go?"

"All right." Lallie, surveying her lover, found she looked, if anything, more beautiful than when she'd left. She returned the kiss and tucked her arm into Jade's. They went into the sitting-room. "Funny thing, I bumped into one of my old school friends up there."

Jade moved over to the drinks table and began pouring out gins. "Not the ghastly Ruth Martin with the over-productive womb?"

"No. Jenny. Remember? I told you about her."

"Vaguely." Jade handed her a drink and went to sit on the sofa.

Lallie judged that Jade had arrived at the limit of her interest in Stockton. She kicked off her shoes and squatted down on the carpet beside her. "How are the film preparations going?"

"Not bad. Rex is, as usual, being coy about coming up with backing. But Olivia's got some great ideas for a cast."

Olivia, thought Lallie dully.

"The plan is to get together a script (I've hired a scriptwriter, by the way), a budget and a publicity brochure for Cannes. If I manage to negotiate pre-sales to foreign distributors as we did before, Rex'll cough up. I – I'm going to be busy over the next few weeks. I'm working rather closely with the scriptwriter on this one, since it concerns my mother. Incidentally, I'm finding I'm becoming quite fond of her."

"Who? Olivia?"

"No, you idiot!" Jade flicked back a strand of blonde hair. "Rachel. That piece you wrote helped me get her in perspective, helped me see her as a person instead of just my mother. Maybe I should dedicate the film to you." She grinned.

Lallie's mouth tightened. "Sounds a bit like a goodbye to me."

Jade frowned. She pointed to the mantelpiece. "An invitation arrived for you."

Lallie got up to look. It was from Grace. "God! The wine and cheese! I'd completely forgotten. I promised I'd help organise it. I'd better phone." She turned to Jade. "Will you come with me? It's in a good cause – the Jacksons' electricity bill."

"How could I refuse?" answered Jade dryly. "After all, the Jacksons were old friends of my sister's. Her life was dogged by their unpaid bills."

She'll never help me with my film, thought Lallie.

"Doesn't your husband mind being invaded like this?" Lallie stood in Grace's shiny fitted kitchen cutting cheese into cubes.

"Oh, Leonard's quite tolerant really." Grace slid a tray of sausage rolls into the oven. "For a businessman."

She went upstairs, slipped into a cream silk dress and then came back downstairs and arranged a little table and chair by the front door, with a box for donations. Leonard staggered past carrying bottles of wine.

"You are a dear," she said.

He put the bottles down on the carpet and began opening a couple. "I'm not being entirely unselfinterested in helping you out this evening. I'm hoping to use the opportunity to get some lowdown from Clive about this Hilltop business. I can't work out whether they intend making a bid or not. It's most irritating."

Hilltop. Where had she heard that name before?

As Grace had predicted most of the village turned up,

eager for a glimpse inside her house. She caught sight of the woman from three doors down taking a close look at the wallpaper in the hall. "Regency stripes," she whispered to the woman beside her. "I was thinking of that for our dining-room, but seeing it here . . . Oh, hello, Mrs Napier."

What do I care, thought Grace smiling falsely, so long as they pay their ten pounds?

"No charge for you, Father Keogh." She beamed at the vicar and his wife, then kicked herself for her lack of tact as Mrs Keogh coloured up.

Father Keogh, never thin-skinned on his own account, said cheerfully, feeling in his back pocket, "I think we might rise to a pound."

Clive turned up in grey pinstriped suit and red tie, his shoes gleaming, his fair hair neatly combed and brushwaved. Jean had been left at home to babysit. Grace enjoyed stinging him for a tenner. She waved the extra donations box under his nose, to no avail.

"You're wasting your energy," he said darkly. "In six months' time that woman will have run up another massive bill for something else. I know these sort of people. They're hopeless."

"It's not her fault," Grace protested. "She wants to work but there're no jobs going. As you know."

"It's the price we have to pay," replied Clive comfortably. "It's the only way to modernise ourselves and become a competitive nation again."

"The price *we* pay?" exclaimed Grace. "I don't think *we*'ve paid anything. In fact, people like you and me have got richer."

"True," said Clive amiably.

"And for all Major's big promises of a more caring society, he's going on in the same old way. Only less efficiently. He hasn't even been able to get rid of the cones on the motorways. So much for that Citizens' Charter of his."

"I know. Time to bring back Thatcher, don't you agree?"
He sauntered off.

He *was* annoying.

Another of her neighbours arrived. "Hello Jackie. Yes, ten
pounds. And a small donation on top would be appreciated."

"Of course, my dear." Jackie, overdressed in sequinned
jumper and shiny gold trousers, stuffed another tenner into
the box. "Poor woman! You know, Grace," she leaned
confidentially over the table, "I've a very friendly bank
manager. He let me have an eight hundred pound overdraft
last year for a new winter coat. Shall I give you his name? He
might be able to help your friend out if she gets into
difficulties again."

"That wouldn't work in Pat's case," Grace replied. "For
one thing, she hasn't got the security of a wealthy husband
to guarantee the loan would be repaid."

Jackie looked taken aback. "You don't think that's why he
gave me the loan, do you? And I thought he was such a kind
young man . . . " She looked put out.

I'm making progress, thought Grace to herself, in what
are called the realities of life.

"Like me to take over on the door for a bit?" Lallie
appeared at her left elbow.

Simultaneously Clive reappeared at her right. "Darling, do
tell me, who's that ravishing young woman in the corner?"
He pointed to where Jade, in a pink jumpsuit, her blonde
hair loose around her shoulders, was deep in conversation
with Leonard.

"That's Jade, a friend of Lallie's here. They work in films.
Leonard's trying to persuade her to do some advertising for
him."

"Stunning!" breathed Clive.

"Isn't she? Single, too," Grace added mischievously, seeing
Lallie's attention had been distracted by another arrival.

"Oh? I may as well stroll over there and have a word with

her myself," he said casually. "We can always do with advertising." He almost licked his lips.

"Who is that man?" asked Lallie. "He reminds me of someone."

"That's my brother-in-law, Clive. Do you think you've met him before? He didn't seem to recognise you. I'm sorry, I should have introduced you – though I sometimes think it's better for people not to be introduced to Clive."

Grace went off to supervise the food. Her elder daughter, Emma, home to prepare for exams, had condescended to take a break from revising to hand round the sausage rolls.

"It's a phase she's going through, this concern for the disadvantaged," she heard her daughter assure a group of guests. "The change of life, you know. My sister and I are hoping it'll wear off soon."

"Emma!" Grace took her to one side. "I do wish you'd shut up. I went through the change of life, as you call it, years ago."

"Did you?" said Emma in surprise. "How can you account for this battiness then?"

"Emma!"

Lallie stared across the room at Clive who'd successfully cornered Jade and got rid of Leonard. Who did he remind her of? And why did seeing the two of them standing there talking give her an uneasy feeling? She shrugged. At any rate, it was a night off from worrying about Olivia.

"Uncle Clive seems to really fancy that woman he's talking to," remarked Emma, following her mother into the kitchen. "I wonder whether he'll ask her out for lunch and start an affair with her?" she added, for effect.

"I doubt it." Grace wrestled with some meringues that had got stuck to the baking tin. "Or if he does, he won't get very far. She's a lesbian. She lives with Lallie. Mind out of the way, darling."

"Mother!" exclaimed Emma. "You seem to be keeping

very bad company these days. An unmarried teenage mother, a criminal who hasn't paid her electricity bill and may go to jail, and now a couple of dykes!"

Grace paused in the middle of filling the meringues with cream and looked at her daughter. "Emma, I'm seriously considering taking you away from that school. It's turning you quite narrowminded."

"You can't," replied Emma smugly. "A change of school at this crucial stage would ruin my chances of getting decent A levels and going to university and getting a job afterwards. You'd never be rid of me."

Grace went back to filling the meringues. "I don't want to get rid of you. I love you. I just think you're becoming a little enclosed in your own class, that's all."

"You wait till Carolyn comes home." Emma popped half a meringue into her mouth. "She's even more radically right wing than me. She doesn't want to go to university or get a proper job. Her plan (has she told you this yet?) is to go to finishing school in Switzerland and then live in London doing odd jobs like helping out with children or cooking executive lunches till the right man comes along. She doesn't approve of working mothers. She nearly had a fit when I told her about your forays into social work. Luckily, you aren't doing it for the money."

Grace groaned. "How the generations repeat themselves! You sound just like your grandmother. What have I done to deserve such daughters? I brought you up to be nice, liberal-minded people and you've become a pair of right wing extremists. Here, you'd better eat the other half. You've spoiled my arrangement, I counted them out in pairs."

"I was banking on that." Emma grinned and stuffed the rest of the meringue into her mouth.

"A bit of a pain in the ass, that guy Clive," remarked Jade as they drove home.

"Oh? I thought you might have seen eye to eye on certain issues," replied Lallie coolly. She'd spoken briefly to Clive herself. "Such as the hopelessness of the hopeless?"

"Don't be bitchy, darling."

"Did you learn anything from Clive about the takeover bid?" asked Grace, packing away the last of the glasses.

"Yes. Bit of a shock really. Turns out Clive's more heavily involved with Hilltop Holdings than I thought. And they *are* seriously contemplating making an offer. I shall fight it, of course, for the sake of the shareholders." He sighed. "But it's damned unpleasant, fighting against your own brother. He doesn't seem to see it that way."

She put a hand on his shoulder. "Poor Leonard."

"I'm beginning to think you may have been right about Clive."

In the middle of the night Grace sat up in bed, her mind suddenly cleared of the alcoholic haze that had hung over it for most of the evening. Now she knew where she'd seen the name Hilltop before. On the documents she and Father Keogh had examined at the Registry Office.

She nudged Leonard. "Leonard, what is Hilltop Holdings exactly?"

"A holding company," he murmured drowsily. "It buys up other companies for its shareholders."

"Is it connected with Hilltop Securities, by any chance?"

"Hilltop Securities is a wholly owned subsidiary of Hilltop Holdings." He yawned.

"Does it ever buy property?"

"Sometimes." He rolled over and went back to sleep.

My God, she thought, Clive owns that slum Debbie lives in.

At almost exactly the same hour of the night, in a different part of the city, Lallie was also lying awake. She'd suddenly remembered where she'd seen Clive before. In a newspaper cutting, standing beside Rachel. An unnamed escort. She glanced across at Jade. Now she knew what had struck her as strange about seeing Jade and Clive together. They had exactly the same shape nose and exactly the same colour hair. Shit! What was she going to do?

Christabel had come back. After that scene with Peter, all Joachim felt was guilt. If he hadn't been so obsessed with Christabel maybe that incident at the police station would never have happened. Peter was right. He simply hadn't been there for his sons these past three years. All the little funny things they'd done as children, things Katrin and he used to laugh over when the children had gone to bed. Living apart from them, he hardly knew them any more. He remembered Peter's birth. That tiny wet miracle of a human being coming slithering out. Katrin's body lying torn and bleeding on the bed. Her arms reaching out to clasp her new-born child. They'd had all that together. All that richness. He looked across at Christabel. What had he swopped it for?

On his way to work, he watched a Jew in a black coat and hat hurry through the street, his hand resting on the shoulder of a small boy. The boy had a long pale face and ringlets that dangled down under his black hat. Conservative, patriarchal though it was, that father had something to hand onto his little boy. What was he handing onto Peter? A broken marriage. A broken faith.

He watched father and son enter the synagogue. How much was he to blame for the injuries inflicted on these people? The talk with Peter had shaken him. I wasn't there, he thought. Peter wasn't there. We weren't even born then. We had no part in it. He knew these arguments were in bad faith. The inherited guilt flowed through his veins as surely as if he'd been the son of a Nazi. He was part of that society, part of that tradition. We're all to blame, he thought.

What if he were to become a Jew then? Swap the role of persecutor for that of victim . . . ? No, Peter was right, you couldn't cheat on fate. He'd been born a German, raised a Gentile. He had to see through this twin destiny to the end. The bread must be broken, his life must be spent, poured out for love of God. He felt he was teetering on the brink of something big.

The day after Pat received Grace's cheque, Jimmy turned up.

"Where'd you get the dosh to pay off the electricity, Ma?"

"Some women raised it for me."

"Bleedin' charity!" He spat out the word. "Why didn't you ask me? I'd 'ave got it for you."

Pat shrugged. "Crime or charity – there's not much in it, is there? Once I knew I'd never be able to find the money myself, what did it matter where it come from?"

"You didn't used to be like that, Ma. Never give up on life, that's what you used to say." He laid a hand on her shoulder.

"Ay, well, perhaps I've more to put up with now." She moved away and lit a cigarette. "I couldn't risk the kids being put into care, Jimmy. Besides, I never know where you are."

"It's better that way, Ma, we've been over this before. I move around a lot. And if the pigs ever came and tortured you, you wouldn't be able to tell 'em anything."

"Torture! Jimmy, this is England, not some South American state. English cops don't torture people." Except the Irish, she added silently to herself.

"Well, rough you up, then."

"Why do you do it, Jimmy? Why not try going straight for a bit?"

"I'd go fuckin' crazy." His broad face crumpled into a grimace. "What's there to do? Sit round here all day watching the box? Nicking things keeps my brain ticking over. You feel you've fuckin' achieved something at the end of the day. I'm careful, I don't hurt people."

"And that cop you did time for for punching in the stomach?"

"He was beating up a friend of mine. *That* never got mentioned in the papers."

She looked at him. "Do me a favour, Jimmy. Don't take Joe with you. His training scheme ended last week and he's back on the dole. He disappears off all day. I don't know where he goes." Her eyes filled with tears. "Don't take him, Jimmy."

"It's all right, Ma." He came and put his arm around her. "Joe's never nicked nothing yet. I'll not be the one to teach him."

The door burst open and in flew Penny. "Jimmy! Jimmy! You're back!" Letting go of Dave and Sal, she rushed over to Jimmy and was swung up in his arms. "How long are you staying?"

"Dunno. Depends on what me mates have planned." He slapped her on the back, making her cough. "Come on, kid, let's go get something to eat for us all. We'll have a blow-out to celebrate my return." He glanced at Pat. "Cheer up, Ma. The electricity's back, I've got money, things are looking up. Listen, what about a real treat? A nice fat juicy steak? What about it?"

In the middle of the night Penny was woken by a tap at the front door. She heard Jimmy go to open it. There were snatches of conversation.

"There's a job on."

"Where?"

"Ealing. I've got the van. Get your fucking arse in gear."

Swiftly and silently so as not to wake her mother who slept in the same bed, Penny slipped out from under the sheets and ran into the living-room where Jimmy was pulling on his trousers.

"Take me with you, Jimmy."

He glanced at her. "You? You're just a kid. You'd get in the way."

"Please Jimmy!" She clasped her hands. "There's nothing for me here. I could cook for you. I'd do anything. Please, please!"

He bent down and put his hands round her thin waist. "It's no life for a kid. I don't want any sister of mine getting involved in the stuff we do. Besides, Ma needs you here."

"Get a move on, you cunt!" hissed the man at the door. "We haven't got all fucking night."

Jimmy straightened up and hurriedly fastened his belt. "Be a good girl and I'll bring you back something nice."

She turned her face away. Nobody understood. Not even Jimmy.

In the morning the flat showed nothing of Jimmy's recent presence, except his cap which he'd dropped in his haste to be off. Penny picked it up off the floor and stuffed it into her pocket. She forgave easily.

"He's gone," said Pat, half-relieved. "Let's hope this time he doesn't get himself caught." She slit open the letter in her hand. It was from the housing department. "Joe!" she shouted. "Come and help me with this."

Joe arrived in the living-room in T-shirt and underpants. He took the letter and sat down, scratching himself and frowning. He read it out loud, stumbling over the unfamiliar words.

"'The housing department has received your application for a transfer and is currently processing it. However, it is our duty to point out that your application does not possess a high priority.'"

There were several more sentences in official jargon. Joe read them over, then handed the letter back to his mother. "It means we haven't a cat in hell's chance of moving."

"You stay here." Pat fetched her coat. "Mind the kids and make sure Penny gets off to school."

"Where are you going?"

"Round to a friend to see what can be done about this."

She tapped the letter. "Those bastards down at housing aren't palming me off as easily as this."

Emma opened the door, took one look at the shabby woman on the doorstep, her stockings torn and the hem of her skirt showing beneath her coat, and shouted, "Mum! It's for you!" She left Pat standing outside and went back upstairs to her books.

"Pat! Come in." Grace ushered her into the kitchen. "Sit down. I'll make us a cup of coffee."

She heard Pat's story, read the letter and went to phone Lallie.

"We've got to do something to help her, Lallie."

"But what? I've never dealt with local housing authorities before, have you?"

"No."

"Let's get advice. We don't want to mess it up for her by getting their backs up."

"The Citizens' Advice Bureau?" suggested Grace.

"There's a local neighbourhood centre," whispered Pat. "They've trained people working there. Only I've been that many times already. I'd be ashamed to show my face there again."

"We'll go," said Grace. She arranged to meet Lallie that afternoon.

The truth was, Grace welcomed any excuse to be distracted from the problem of what to do about Clive. If it was only Clive, she wouldn't have hesitated to publicise the state of the properties owned by Hilltop. But there were Jean and the children to think of. The publicity would tear their lives apart. Every day she kept quiet increased her feeling of complicity. She was glad of an excuse to push Clive to the back of her mind for an afternoon.

Lallie, too, was glad of a few hours' escape from the flat. Ever since her return from the north she'd begun noticing small things – a new perfume on Jade's dressing-table, a new bracelet, different books by her bed (on Indian cooking and one called *Ways to Eastern Awareness*). She felt excluded. In the past Jade had shared every new interest with her. Now she was talking of filming something in India when the current film was completed. She'd told Lallie nothing about it, hadn't even asked her to do any research for it.

There were, as well, mysterious stretches of time unaccounted for, when Jade wasn't at meetings, or wooing backers, or working on the script, or doing anything else Lallie could think of. There was a wariness between them these days, like the silence before a big battle. She often felt Jade's eyes resting on her, as if she was weighing Lallie up. And because Lallie didn't want to think, yet, about what all these things added up to, she was pleased when Grace's phone call gave her an excuse to concentrate on something else for a while.

The neighbourhood centre was in a row of shops behind Pat's flat. It was a two-storey building, the top floor being given over to a second-hand clothing shop. The ground floor consisted of a small front room with a reception counter and benches for people to sit on as they waited to be called. A corridor led off this room to the interviewing cubicles, divided from each other by lengths of hardboard too thin to ensure privacy.

Grace and Lallie went up to the counter. They were given a number by a sulky-looking girl and told to wait their turn. They sat down on a bench and looked around. The room was stuffy and smoke-filled. People waited with bewildered expressions on their faces. Many nursed plastic bags bulging with documents. Their life stories, thought Lallie.

A fat woman on Grace's right was absorbed in recounting a story to her neighbour. Grace stole a glance at her. Her shabby brown coat had fallen open to reveal a dirty pinafore.

Her uncombed grey hair was tied back with a greasy ribbon. Her feet were swollen. She had on, not shoes, but a pair of down at heel slippers.

"Eighty-one 'e was," she was saying. "Ought never to've been left on 'is own. It was the vicar wot found 'im. Had to call the cops to break down the door. As soon as they got into the 'ouse they knows 'e was dead by the maggots dripping down through the ceiling."

Grace's stomach turned. She glanced at Lallie who raised her eyebrows and grimaced.

From the cubicles down the corridor issued a steady stream of tales of woe clearly audible in the waiting room.

"They say he doesn't qualify for child allowance any more and I'll have to pay them back," a West Indian woman was saying. "I don't want to have money I'm not entitled to, but my husband is dead and I've nothing except my social security money to live on. How can I pay them back?"

From another of the cubicles a man's voice could be heard, gently insisting, "I want an apology, that's all. I ain't asking for money. An apology's what I want."

"But Mr Davis, if I drafted a letter to your employers asking for nothing but an apology, I'd be letting you down. You lost two fingers working a machine you'd warned them several times was faulty. You're entitled to quite a lot of compensation."

"Don't want money. An apology, that's what I'm looking for. An apology."

From another cubicle came the sound of a woman sobbing. "I've nothing to give the kids to eat."

Grace looked round the waiting-room at the battered and defeated people. Where was any of this in the newspapers? Why didn't they protest? Why weren't these people marching on Downing Street in their second-hand clothes with their hungry children and shaming the government into doing something for them?

It's no use, Lallie was thinking. I have to ask.

"Your brother-in-law made an, er, impression on Jade the other evening," she began, sticking to the outer limits of the truth. "He seems an interesting man."

"Interesting?" Grace rolled the word around her tongue for a moment, testing it out in relation to Clive. She shook her head. "No. Not to me, at any rate. But then I don't suppose one's in-laws are ever very interesting, are they?"

"Jade's mother was interesting."

"Oh. Um. You think of yourself as married, do you?"

"Yes." Tears filled Lallie's eyes. She blinked and looked away. "Or used to." She swallowed. "About your brother-in-law. What does he do for a living? He was a bit cagey about it when I asked him."

Grace gave a short, harsh laugh. "He's a businessman. With fingers in numerous pies in the City. Has a law degree. That's probably why he's such a shady character. He studied in Ireland, at Trinity College. Leonard went to Cambridge," she added proudly.

Lallie felt something tighten across her chest. "Clive lived in Dublin?"

"Only as a student. He came back here to set up practice and marry Jean. Poor Jean." She sighed.

Their number was called.

The middle-aged woman with grey hair and a weary air listened patiently to their story and looked at the copy they'd brought with them of Pat's application to the housing department.

"I'll tell you frankly – she hasn't a hope in hell of moving. She's already lucky to have so many rooms. Do you know how scarce three bedroom flats are?"

"But it's damp!" protested Grace. "You can see it on the walls. Great grey patches. And the bath takes two days to empty."

"Tell her to complain to the council."

"She's done that. They don't take any notice. They keep passing her on to different sections."

The woman sighed. "I know. They're great buck-passers down there. They're about six months behind on all their repairs. Short-staffed. Look," she continued more sympathetically, "she can proceed with her application if she likes, but I'd be holding out false hopes if I said she was likely to be successful. She doesn't share a bathroom with another family, her children sleep no more than two to a room. I've seen couples with three children living with grandparents in a two bedroom flat who've not had an offer of a home of their own. There simply aren't enough places to go round. The average length of wait for a transfer in this area is thirteen years."

"It's unbelievable," said Grace.

The woman shrugged. "What's unbelievable to you, is life for the people round here."

Joachim lay in bed staring up at the ceiling. "I can't go on with this."

"I thought you loved me?"

"I do."

"Well then?"

"I can't go on."

Christabel sat up clasping her knees. Her long golden hair fell over her naked breasts. "We're going round in circles here. You love me. I love you. I know I'm not the most reliable of people but . . . "

"It's not that." He sighed. "There's something wrong. It's difficult to explain. I know there's something wrong."

"Look, I can be faithful to you, if that's what you want."

"It's not that. It's more than that. There've been times recently when I've felt . . . grace has been withdrawn. The safety net's no longer there. My love for you puts me outside the law."

"Shall we get married then? Is that what you want?"

"More than anything in the world."

"Let's do it then."

"I can't marry you, Christabel. Too much unfinished business."

"Your wife?"

"No, not my wife. My children." With his finger he traced the outline of her cheek. "I'm afraid of you, Christabel. I'm afraid of the passions you arouse in me. Painful, disturbing feelings. I'm like a child with you. I'm not used to that. I'm used to taking care of others – my sons, my men, Katrin . . . "

"I'm good for you then. Everyone needs a break from caring."

"Yes, but you confuse my mind. I can't think straight while you're around. I need to think of my sons. These are the crucial years. They'll never come again. If I muck it up for them now I'll never forgive myself."

"I've always given you space. Even if we married, you'd have plenty of time to see your sons."

"It's not only that." He hesitated. "My love, you fill me up. When you're around I don't need anyone else. I could happily forget all about my sons. I could happily forget about God. If I stay with you, Christabel, I'll lose my soul. I'll no longer need God. To love Katrin, I need God." He glanced at her. "You'll leave me in the end. I know you will. It's your nature. And the next time I won't be able to bear it. I'll have lost God, I'll have lost my sons and I'll have lost you."

"You're going to be unhappy for the rest of your life then? Repressing your feelings like this, you'll never grow, never develop as a human being. All that side of you, the feeling side, will be dead."

"I know."

"Don't you care?" She seized him by the shoulders. "Wake up, Joachim! Wake up! You've only got one life. Make the most of it. What's the point of saving your soul if you're dead inside?"

He looked up at her. She was his mirror image in so many ways. But she'd kept herself free. And he hadn't.

When challenged, Jade didn't bother to deny she was having an affair.

Lallie clenched her fists. "That damned Olivia."

"It isn't Olivia."

"Who then?"

"She's a scriptwriter."

"The one working on our film, you mean?"

Jade nodded.

So that was why she'd never got to meet her. Lallie grimaced. She'd been looking in the wrong direction the whole time. Olivia had only been a decoy.

"Lallie, it isn't important. At least it needn't be."

There was a silence. Lallie bit back the temptation to scream.

"Are you going to go on seeing her?"

Jade glanced at her nails. "That depends."

"On what?"

"On you, mainly. Look, Lallie, she's going back to India soon to see her family. It'll probably end there. It was nothing. An interlude. I needed to be with someone who made me laugh. I needed to get my thoughts straight."

"And?" Lallie wandered over to the window and looked out. Her eyes filled with tears. She swallowed and turned round. "What have you concluded?"

Jade shrugged and avoided her eye.

"You think I'm sick, don't you?"

"I think," began Jade slowly, "that you have an unhealthy obsession with your past which is making you bitter. I think you should see a psychiatrist."

"I don't need a psychiatrist. I need you." I freed you from your mother, she thought. Why can't you help me?

Jade brushed a hand across her mouth. "I'd like to help, Lallie, really I would. But I need you to be strong, like you used to be. I need you to be there for me. I'm no good with this sort of thing."

"With losers?"

"With sickness."

"I'm not sick!" yelled Lallie, sweeping a plate off the table.

They watched as it crashed to the floor and broke.

"I'm going out," said Jade.

"No, don't go! Please! Not like this!"

"I've work to do. And the sooner I go, the sooner I'll forget this scene."

She gathered up her bag and jacket and left.

Lallie bent to pick up the pieces of shattered plate. Tears rolled down her face.

"My dear Grace! What an unexpected pleasure!" Clive gushed down the phone. "Shall I fetch Jean?"

"Actually it was you, Clive, I wanted to speak to. I wondered whether we could have lunch together in town one day this week? There's something I'd like to discuss with you."

"Certainly, my dear. That would be delightful. Shall we say Thursday?"

She didn't much like his tone. She hoped he didn't think all his years of flattery had finally paid off.

They met in a tiny Italian restaurant off Trafalgar Square. The waiter, clearly a chum of Clive's, led them to a table for two tucked away in a corner.

"Well," said Clive, after the business of ordering was over, "I must say, this is most agreeable." He eyed her up and down. She'd put on her best linen suit to raise her morale. "You're looking ravishing, as usual." He placed a hand over hers. She withdrew it.

The waiter minced over to them with a bottle of white wine in an ice bucket. Another placed a plate of wild mushrooms in front of Grace and a tomato salad in front of Clive. He tasted the wine and nodded to the waiter to pour it out. "Have to watch the waistline." He took up his fork. "Playing squash three times a week just doesn't seem to help."

"Perhaps it's all the different business lunches you have to eat," suggested Grace, "pursuing all your different business ventures?"

The sharpness of her tone made Clive look up. "If you've come to plead Leonard's cause, you're wasting your time. The matter's out of my hands. Hilltop Holdings have made their bid. It's up to the shareholders now to accept or reject it."

She swallowed a mushroom. "I've not come about Leonard, though I must say that was the sneakiest thing I've ever heard of . . . "

"Business, my dear."

"Well, it's business I've come to discuss with you. Property business, to be precise."

"Still the best way of investing your money, take it from me." He lifted his glass to his lips. "I've a house in Kensington. Did I ever tell you about it? It's let to a visiting American professor and his family. I know where to find you good clean tenants if you're thinking of letting."

"It's not tenants who're the problem." She glared at him. "It's landlords who own run-down property and don't bother to carry out repairs."

"Dear Grace, what are you on about?" His tone was still jovial but his eyes had narrowed.

Grace rested her elbows on the table and tried to stay calm. "Hilltop Securities owns a house (a whole row of houses, actually, but I'm concerned with a particular one in which a friend of mine lives), it's in a disgusting state. The ceilings are cracking, there are mice in the kitchen and the lavatory's blocked. And you own it, Clive. Leonard told me you're the largest shareholder in Hilltop."

He shrugged. "I may own a property which needs some minor repairs done to it. I can't keep track of all the property we own. It's a holding company. We buy and sell very fast. I'll look into it." He drank some more wine.

Grace leaned across the table. "Clive, there's no way you don't know about the state of that house. There have been complaints from the council. Someone's even been round threatening the tenants and telling them to keep their mouths shut. Did you send him?"

"My dear Grace!" Clive spread out his hands. "I never knew you had such a vivid imagination! I'm sorry your friend has to live in such a frightful place. Incidentally, what are you doing having friends like that? Does Leonard know? But you must realise that no one at Hilltop has any direct involvement in the running of the property we own. It's all handed over to agencies. I promise I'll look into it. It sounds as though we should get rid of that particular property at once."

She wished she could tell whether he was lying. She wished she had more experience at this kind of thing. It was terrible, at her age, to be so naive.

"I could embarrass you. I could give your name to the newspapers."

Clive smiled. "I don't think you'll do that, will you, my dear? Think of what the publicity would do to Jean. Or to Leonard, come to that. Start flinging mud at one member of the family and it sticks to all the others as well."

He was forcing her to close ranks. How she hated him. He was making them all responsible.

And yet, she thought later that day, I suppose in a general way we always were responsible. We let these things go on. And even if I were to persuade the council to take Clive to court, there are hundreds more like him out there: anonymous shareholders of respectable companies making their profits out of other people's misery.

She sighed. It was all too complex for one person to undo. She'd started out with such good intentions, but it seemed good intentions weren't enough. The days of the old-fashioned do-gooder, her mother's generation, were past. She was up against forces too big for her. She was trapped.

The Jacksons must feel like this every day of their lives.

Penny had disappeared again. Pat went down to the call box on the corner to phone Father Keogh.

"Anyway, you can hardly blame me for being obsessed with the past," said Lallie, a few days later. "I'd have thought such an obsession (if it is one) would seem quite natural to you. After all, you're the one planning a film about your mother."

"That's different. My mother was gifted."

"Oh, I forgot. Only geniuses are worth remembering."

Jade frowned. "You know what I mean. It'll be a valuable record." She wandered over to the bookshelf and began idly flicking through some books. "Your years in the north were a complete waste for you, Lallie. You had nobody to understand you, nobody to share your ideas with. You should have put it all behind you by now. Instead you keep dwelling on it and it makes you miserable."

"I'm sorry I'm such bad company," said Lallie, stung. Then winced at the sound of her tone. "Perhaps you're right," she went on, more softly. "Perhaps I should just forget . . . and yet . . . I keep seeing . . . It's as if I needed to perform one last act of – of redemption." She hesitated. "I was thinking of making a documentary about Jenny's work up there. Will you help me, Jade?"

Jade looked up from her book. "That's not my kind of subject, you know that."

Lallie took a deep breath and ploughed recklessly on. "Then I'll make it myself."

Jade closed up the book and stared at her. "A film? You?"

"Why not? I've picked up a lot from you over the years. It's time I did something of my own again."

Jade continued to stare at her. Lallie could see in her eyes she'd ceased to be a lover and had become a rival.

In a park in Munich Joachim watched the sun set behind the

trees. The world was beautiful and he alone was the ugly spot, the stain. They'd walked in this park when the children were young, pushing Peter in his buggy, carrying Werner in a harness. Played football with them when they were older. He pictured Katrin stooping to fasten her sons' shoes. A good clean image. He watched Christabel walk towards him. His body thrilled at the sight of the swaying, dancing movement of her hips. Involuntarily, a smile rose to his lips. His life would be barren as a eunuch's without her. Full of clean innocent pictures. But barren.

Christabel sat down beside him.

"I've moved my stuff out. It's what you want, isn't it?"

He took her hand. "It's a tragedy, our story. I thought they didn't happen any more."

"It needn't be a tragedy. It's only you and your funny moral ideas. Nobody believes in them any more."

"I do."

"Does Katrin?"

"Yes."

She looked at him. "I can't give you up, Joachim. Go back to your wife. But go on seeing me. She need never know."

"Listen to me, Christabel. You are my height and my depths, you are the most secret part of my being. But I can't live divided. If I did what you suggested, I'd be cut off from God."

"Leave him. Step out of that moral framework you've imprisoned yourself in."

"Where else would I go?"

She sighed. "You are odd. You're the oddest man I've ever met."

"Will you think of me?"

She smiled. "I expect so."

For a time. Whereas he'd have all of his life to remember. To remember and regret. Depth was passing out of his life. From now on, his life would be all on the surface.

He sat and watched as she walked away. He'd thought it was only in films that hearts broke in two.

CHAPTER SIXTEEN

PAT STARED AT THE FAT FRIGHTENED BOY STANDING AT THE DOOR.

"What is it?" she asked in alarm.

"Oh Missus Jackson!" Al whimpered, his dirty face crumpling. "It's your Penny. She's been taken bad."

"What! Where is she?"

"It warn't my fault! Honest, it warn't!"

Pat seized him by the shoulders and shook him till his teeth rattled.

"Where the fuck is she? Take me to her."

She cast a backward glance at Sal and Dave watching wide-eyed. She went back into the flat and turned off the paraffin. "Not a wrong move out of either of you," she threatened. "Or you'll feel the back of my hand."

"Hurry up!" Al snivelled. "She can't breathe."

"Jaysus Christ!" Grabbing him by the arm, she hurried him along the corridor and shoved him into the lift. "Where is she? Where's she been hiding?"

"In one of the garages over the other side of the playground."

"Christ! So near!"

They ran, stumbling over empty cans and pieces of barbed wire, to the garage where Penny lay having convulsions on a dirty scrap of carpet. With each convulsion, her face turned a deeper shade of blue. Vomit trickled from her mouth. Pat glanced around and took in an empty beer can and several old rags lying on the carpet beside Penny.

"What was it?" she yelled, shaking Al again. "What the bloody hell have you been taking?"

Tears streaked his grimy face. "Fire extinguisher fuel. We put it in the beer can. Then she started like that, choking and gasping."

She knelt down beside her daughter. "You stupid, stupid kids! Go round the corner to the phone box. Dial 999 and tell them to send an ambulance." As he hesitated, she looked up and said, "If you don't do what I say right now, I'll break every fucking bone in your fucking body! Now go!" She gave him a push. He ran off.

Pat lifted her daughter up in her arms. The convulsions had stopped now. The little girl lay completely still, scarcely breathing. "Penny," she murmured. She wiped the side of her daughter's vomit-smeared mouth with a handkerchief. Penny opened her eyes but gave no sign of recognition. "Penny, why did you do this to yourself? I love you, you silly child. I fucking do." She buried her face in her daughter's dirty, matted hair.

It seemed to Pat an eternity till the ambulance arrived though in fact it took only a few minutes for it to get from King's. The sound of the siren blaring through the estate attracted people's attention. They opened their windows and hung out. Some even came out of their flats and gathered on the pavement to watch. Al, who'd had the fear of God put into him by Pat's words, had run off to hide after making the phone call. Joe emerged from one of the flats. When he saw his mother, he elbowed his way through the bystanders and ran towards the ambulance.

"Shit!" he exclaimed, catching sight of his sister lying still and pale on the stretcher.

"Joe, go back and see to Dave and Sal. I've left them on their own."

"No, Ma. Marie'll be home any minute to look after them. I'm coming with you."

Wearily Pat shook her head. It was beyond her resources at that moment to argue. They rode in the ambulance the few minutes down to King's and rushed through the corridors behind the trolley as far as the operating theatre. There they were ordered to wait outside in the corridor.

They didn't have to wait long. The doctor emerged from the theatre, looked at Pat and Joe huddled together on a bench and shook his head. "Asphyxia." He peeled off his gloves. "Your daughter's lungs were in terrible shape, Mrs Jackson. Has she been living somewhere damp?"

"Sedgefield Estate, doctor," murmured the nurse, glancing through her notes.

The doctor sighed. "Half our asthma cases come from that estate. I'm sorry, Mrs Jackson. We did our best."

Joe burst into tears.

Pat stood up. "I . . . "

The nurse put an arm round her shoulder to steady her. "I'll get you a cup of tea, Mrs Jackson."

"I want to sit with my daughter," whispered Pat hoarsely.

They moved the body to an empty room and laid it out on the bed.

"Who was with her?" asked Joe, tears streaming down his thin face.

"I don't know his name. A fat boy." Pat sat down by the bed and took Penny's still warm hand in hers.

"Al Cooper. The bastard!" Joe clenched his fists. "When I get hold of him, I'll fucking punch his head in."

"Joe, he's just a kid." She looked down at her daughter. "They were both kids. They neither of them bloody knew what they were about. If it's anybody's fault, it's mine, for bringing her into this world. Poor mite!" She sobbed. "She didn't have much of a life, did she?"

There was a tap at the door. It was Grace.

"A neighbour told me you were at the hospital. I came to see if there was anything I could do."

Pat stared dumbly down at her daughter's body laid out on the bed.

"Oh God!" breathed Grace. "I'm so sorry . . ."

"Sure, she's better off where she is," muttered Pat. She'd stopped crying now.

"How can you say that!" Grace fumbled for a handkerchief. "She had her whole life in front of her."

"Yes, and what a life!" replied Pat dryly. "Always on the look out for ways to escape. Now she's got what she wanted – permanently. Good luck to her, I say."

"You can't mean that. It was society – society that did it. We let her down," said Grace passionately.

Pat glanced up. "Society? I don't believe in society no more."

"You mean well, missus." Joe gently ushered Grace out of the room. "But you can't really know how we live."

Father Keogh appeared.

"One of your neighbours phoned. Mrs Jackson, I'm so sorry."

"Ah Father." She sighed. "Maybe she's better off where she is."

He put an arm round her shoulder. "Would you like me to say a prayer?"

"It can't do any harm I suppose, Father, can it?"

The door closed softly behind them.

Joe and Grace walked back down the empty corridor.

"I feel so useless," said Grace. "I've been no help to your mother at all."

Joe shrugged. "How could you expect to help? You were right. It's the whole of this rotten, stinking society that needs changing. Our Penny had no life. Lousy teachers, lousy damp flat to live in, shabby old clothes, not enough to eat. She never had any proper treats. No wonder she wanted to escape. Who wouldn't?"

She looked at the tall youth in shabby jeans and runners.

"How do you survive, Joe? You've no job now. Tell me. I want to try to understand."

"It's different for me. My Da was a good man, not like Penny's Da. I remember once, on one of his good days, he took us all on the bus to the sea. It's the only time in my life that I've been at the seaside. We built a castle in the dunes and walked for miles across the sand. The sea was so big. I'd never seen anything so fucking big in all my life, beautiful and powerful. When times are bad, I close my eyes and remember that day, remember there's something out there bigger than me, bigger than all this dirty little life. Penny had no day at the seaside to look back on. Nothing nice ever happened to her."

They stood outside in the carpark.

"Don't ever change, Joe. It would hurt your mother more than anything if you were to turn out like Jimmy," said Grace, with a sudden flash of insight.

He kicked a pebble around.

"I know that," he muttered. "She depends on me and Marie. We're all she's got left. That's what's keeping me from going and bashing Al Cooper's head in right this minute."

He clenched his fists and Grace could see, in the tautness of his young body, the barely controlled anger. Then he relaxed.

"Aw, he's such a wet. I'd probably end up killing him by mistake and get done for fucking manslaughter." He gave a short laugh. "Don't you worry about me, Missus. If I don't get a job soon I'll likely end up doing community work, taking kids for days out to the seaside." His face clouded over. "Now I've got to go back home and break the news to Marie."

He turned and began trudging up the hill to the flat.

Grace got into her car and started the engine. She felt nothing now. There were no more tears. It was as if all the feeling had been crushed out of her. She drove home.

She was greeted at the door by an unfamiliar smell and the sound of loud music and laughter coming from the study. She opened the door. Emma and several of her friends lay around on cushions on the floor, smoking and drinking beer. Heavy rock music thumped from Leonard's loudspeakers.

"Oh. Mum." Emma giggled and tried unsuccessfully to conceal a joint behind her back. "I didn't think you'd be back so soon. Want a beer?"

Grace felt pain explode inside her.

"What the hell do you think you're all doing, lying around here in the middle of the afternoon doping yourselves stupid?" she yelled. "Don't you realise how lucky you are? You're nothing but a bunch of idle, spoilt, middle-class brats. Get out, all of you! Go and do some work for a change!" She strode over and unplugged the record player.

"But Mum . . . " faltered Emma. "We were only listening to music and having a few drinks. It's our last chance before exams start. You've never objected to us smoking pot before."

"Emma! Either get upstairs and work. Or go out and do something useful with your life!"

Emma's friends had begun scrambling to their feet.

"I thought you said your Mum was easygoing," muttered one of them as he went out of the door. "Jesus Christ! Give me Attila the Hun any day."

Emma went out with them, slamming the front door behind her.

"Emma, I'm sorry," said Grace that evening. "A little girl died today. She belonged to that family I've been visiting. She never had a chance of a proper life. And when I came home and saw you, who have so much, lying around drinking and smoking yourselves silly . . . "

"Mum, it's all right." Emma put her arms round her crying mother. "Poor Mum."

Lallie walked down Kensington Church Street, past the late night supermarket where she and Jade used to shop on the way home from work, past the French restaurant where they'd eaten on the evening of Jade's return from Ireland. Everywhere there were memories, invisible threads tying her to this part of London. This place had been her life for eight years, had nurtured and sustained her. To leave now . . .

The rain began to come on more heavily. She took shelter inside the Carmelite church at the bottom of the street. Years since she'd been inside a church. She sat down on a pew and looked around. Each pew was numbered with a silver letter and the lights had bells over them in place of shades. Here and there along the walls were wooden doors with the names of priests written over them. Confessionals. Extraordinary to think all this was still going on, had done for years, regardless of changing fashions in the shops outside.

A tramp sitting in the pew across the aisle nodded in welcome. He was surrounded by plastic bags of every description. In the pews in front of her one or two women knelt in prayer. How safe it must feel to belong. But there was no place here for people like herself. Where did she belong then? Not in the north. Her visit home had shown her that. Not in London either, she was beginning to think . . .

The door opened and in came a young woman laden with carrier bags. She dumped them on one of the pews, genuflected towards the altar and knelt to pray. Lallie wondered what she was praying for. Boyfriend trouble? A sick mother? Or for the good of the world in general? Perhaps there were still people like that, who did their shopping in Barker's or Marks and Spencers' and popped into church on their way home to say a prayer for the starving in Africa. She felt obscurely comforted by this thought. If she were to have prayed at that moment her prayers would have been all for herself. For courage.

She thought back to her life before she met Jade. Casual

relationships, none of them meaning very much. Physical attraction, yes, there was always that, but afterwards . . . How much it took to build up a relationship. How little to destroy it.

She shivered. She was too old, too weary, to start over again. She supposed it would always be like this for her – relationships beginning or ending. Next time though, if there were to be a next time, she'd be more careful, she wouldn't throw the whole of herself into the relationship. No, she'd keep something back of her own. It was too painful otherwise.

She got up to go. The tramp waved goodbye. She waved back. She'd learn, she'd have to, to live alone again.

When she arrived back at the flat she suggested moving out, at least for a time. The relief on Jade's face was obvious.

Because she was in the process of moving, Lallie didn't hear of Penny's death till after the funeral had taken place. At Pat's request, Father Keogh assisted the Catholic priest at the ceremony. Grace looked after Debbie's children for the afternoon so that she could attend her sister's funeral. Grace sent a wreath. So did Jimmy. But he kept away from the funeral for he was wanted again by the police.

When everyone had shed their tears and said their few words and gone away from the cemetery, a pale, fat boy crept up to the grave and laid down his offering of wild flowers and daisies beside the rest. He crouched by the grave, blubbering. "I *will* be good, Penny. I will. I promise."

He must pour out his life. He must face up to the shadow. He went to see Katrin.

He told her he was resigning his job. He couldn't live any longer with the things he was being asked to do. "Money will be tight for the next month or so, but don't worry," he added, sounding more confident than he felt, "I'll find something else. If not here, then in Ireland."

"Why do you hate Germany so much? Why?" She sat upright on the hard chair, glaring at him, not a hair of her head out of place.

He thought of his conversation with Peter. "To be German is to know the meaning of original sin. There's something nasty inside us."

"Inside you, you mean," she said icily.

My God, why did she never hear what he was saying?

"I don't know why you and Peter take the war so personally," she continued. "Neither of you were born then. It has nothing to do with you. Why shoulder that burden? There're plenty of other things to worry about."

"Peter's right. The war's in our blood, Katrin."

Katrin sniffed. "Your father didn't even belong to the Nazi party."

"It's not a family thing. It's wider than that. We're a guilty race."

Why did she have to fight back all the time? Why couldn't she simply agree for once? He had the feeling they were like two machine parts that would never properly interlock. She always missed the point.

"Katrin," he went on more softly, "are you happy these days?" He fingered a book lying on the table. "Werner – the boys – told me you have a . . . a friend."

She stiffened, wary. "Well?"

"Does he make you happy?"

She looked away. "Happy? What does that mean? I get by. I survive. Happiness," she lingered on the word. "No, I shan't ask for so much again."

She was frozen into her hatred of him. She'd been hurt once, in her pride. No, more than that. He must be fair. Her heart had been wounded and, never being very large, had closed in on itself. Christabel danced before him, laughing as she turned to look at him, her long hair blowing across her mouth, her eyes ablaze with life. Though he'd given all that up, he couldn't go back. He couldn't live with Katrin. She shut out life. She didn't know how to open her arms wide enough. She took little bits here and there, and that was enough for her. But it wasn't enough for him.

"I'm sorry," he said. "I'd hoped you were happy with this man. You deserve it."

He stood up to leave. She started up too, seemed about to say something. Then frowned and stayed silent.

"Don't worry about Peter," he said, his hand on the latch. "Despite appearances he has his head screwed on. I think we never gave him enough credit."

He went out of the apartment block and began walking towards his car. A feeling of deadness came over him. There was something wrong.

He retraced his steps. From behind the door came the sound of sobbing.

"Katrin! Let me in."

She unlocked the door and flung herself into his arms.

"Katrin, Katrin." He stroked her hair. Her sobbing was dreadful to his ears. "Stop. Please stop."

He led her into the living-room and sat down on the sofa, his arms still around her.

"What is it, Katrin? Tell me. Is it this man?"

"No. He means nothing to me." She was calmer now, dabbing at her cheeks with a handkerchief. "I thought I could replace you, but I can't. He likes coming here because it's comfortable. He's rather badly off. But I – I don't believe he really cares for me."

"Katrin," he said slowly, fingering a strand of her hair. "Tell me truthfully, what would make you happy? Would you like us to try again?"

"You're the father of my children." The simplicity of her words belied the anguish on her face. "I love you, Joachim. I've never stopped loving you even – even during that horrible time. Only I kept thinking of Papa and I couldn't seem to say it. Teach me to say it again, teach me to love." She looked at him and he saw in that moment she was utterly bereft.

"I will," he replied and heard a door slam shut in his heart.

He'd been on the wrong track. He couldn't leap upwards in one bound. It took years and years of patient obedience. Intuitions of God were worthless unless accompanied by an effort of the will. Was it possible for him to will himself to love Katrin? To train himself to want less so that Katrin could have more? Will and discipline, words so foreign to his way of thinking. How pleased his father would have been to have heard him utter them!

They weren't naturally made for each other, he and Katrin. She couldn't bend her nature to his, so he must bend to hers. What was marriage, after all, but a preparation for loving God? Learning to yield one's will to that of another, to alter, to bow, like a blade of grass?

But a small part of him would sob always for Christabel. He couldn't help that.

That night, Joachim and Katrin made love.

Lallie rented two rooms in Dulwich from a friend of Grace's. She moved in her few pieces of furniture but didn't bother to arrange them properly. She was about to return north to meet an executive from Tyne-Tees television and discuss with him the possibility of making a documentary.

The evening before she went north she met Jade for dinner in the Vietnamese restaurant opposite their old flat. The owner knew them both well and, embarrassingly, gave them a secluded corner table. The conversation was strained. The scriptwriter was due back from India the next day. Lallie had chosen the date of her departure deliberately . . . She picked up the menu. She was in a dilemma, too, about Clive. This might be the last chance she'd get for a while (ever?) of speaking to Jade alone. Should she tell her of her suspicions about Clive?

"Here." Jade drew a letter from the pocket of her leather jacket and tossed it over to Lallie. "It arrived this morning from Stefan. I thought you might be interested."

Glad of a diversion from troubling thoughts, Lallie read through the letter.

"Dear Miss McKenna," it ran. "I was very interested to learn of your plans to make a film about your mother and also that I am to figure in it.

"As you no doubt know, I am now a well-known poet, invited frequently to North America to give readings. But at the time I knew your mother I was struggling to gain an audience for my poetry in the West. I hope your film will reflect my struggles during those years.

"I look back on that period of my life with a certain amount of anger. Not only was I fighting for recognition for my poetry, but also there was your mother who, I regret to say, turned out to be not at all the companion I'd hoped for. I felt – still feel – she used me for her own purposes. I'd hoped she would be my companion and share with me the struggle on behalf of my work. But I'm afraid she had ideas of her own. She took what she wanted from the relationship. Then she left.

"Yes, she was entirely unsuited to be the wife of a poet. She lacked passion. I realised later she was incapable of it, that self-sacrificing spirit needed for life with an artist. She'd been feigning all along. She was, essentially, shallow. An ideal person to be an actress.

"Let me give you one example. I wanted Rachel to take my religion, to become a Jew for my sake. I wasn't particularly observant myself at that period but, in our religion, it's the women who are responsible for handing on the religious traditions to the next generation, for seeing that the rituals are observed in the home. This is what I wanted Rachel to do. And for a while she did try studying our faith. But the ritual scared her. Her so-called 'love' for me wouldn't even carry her that far.

"Take my advice – don't idealise your mother. Such

idealisations make for bad art (this was something your sister never understood). Show her as she was, as I have tried to describe her in this letter.

Yours faithfully,

Stefan Chertkov.

D.Litt. h.c. (Harv.)."

"Typical, isn't it?" commented Jade as Lallie handed back the letter. "Putting the boot in like that. He never could stand rivals."

"No," agreed Lallie. Yet she couldn't help thinking something in that letter rang true. Maybe it was the part about Rachel lacking passion, being a taker rather than a giver. She looked at Jade. Old Frank McKenna's genes. Perhaps there was something to be said after all for Stefan's side of the story.

"We missed the Jewish aspect," Jade continued. "But I shan't alter anything now. It would mean having to rewrite a huge chunk of the script. Anita would go crazy."

So that was her name. Lallie flushed and bent her head to her plate.

Jade bit her lip and hurried on, "I'll miss you when you're in the north, Lallie, you know that?"

Lallie nodded, keeping her eyes fixed on her plate. Easy to say those words now the break had been made. Jade was always fond of people who laid no demands at her door. That's where I went wrong, thought Lallie. I asked for help when I shouldn't have.

She blinked away the tears and looked up at Jade. A person like her needs laughter and fun, not gloomy old me. I'm not right for her. Though she may be right for me. She sighed. She'd have to do it on her own then, work out her feelings about the past, her mother, by herself. She fingered the wine glass. When it came down to it, had she ever had a relationship closer than the one with her mother? Would she ever find another like it?

Jade walked her to the tube. Lallie had to get down to the

Elephant and Castle. From there she'd catch a bus. Dulwich wasn't the easiest place to live without a car. At the top of the steps leading down to the tube Lallie hesitated. She'd still not done anything about Clive.

"Jade, there's something I want to tell you before you go. Remember Clive? The man you talked to at Grace's party?"

"That prick? I remember him all right. Rang me up two days later, wanting me to have lunch with him. I told him where to get off."

"Well, I . . . "

She faltered. Jade's image of herself had been built up over the years around the myth of her unknown father. Her unknown, glamorous father. Her kind, unselfish hero. Lately Jade had begun to think more favourably of Rachel – or the Rachel Lallie had given her. But the myth of her father remained a powerful one. It would be brutal, wouldn't it, to shatter it?

Anyway, what was her guess based on? A similarity of looks, a couple of newspaper cuttings, a coincidence of dates? No, there was more to it than that. Rachel's refusal to have anything to do with Jade's father suddenly made sense. Clive was a bully – Lallie had spotted that at once – and Rachel had had enough domineering men in her life. But how could she tell Jade her father was someone she'd loathed at first sight?

"You were right," she continued. "He turned out to be thoroughly rotten. A slum landlord."

Jade laughed lightly. "Is that all, darling? I thought for a moment you were going to tell me something important." She kissed Lallie on the cheek. "Still, it's nice to know I can be right about people sometimes." She squeezed her arm. "Take care." She turned and walked away. She'd always hated lengthy goodbyes.

Lallie watched as Jade walked down the street and turned the corner without looking back. Then she went into the tube station and bought her ticket. She sat on a bench to wait for the train. A new part of her life was beginning. She must make something good of it. For her mother's sake.

She heard the distant rumble of the approaching train. As it roared into the station she stood up, tense and ready.

Joachim phoned Cornelius from Germany.

"Cornelius, I've come to a decision. I'm selling up in Ireland and settling in Germany for good."

"This is very witty of you, Joachim." Cornelius chortled down the phone. "You surely can't be serious? What sort of a farmer are you if you let a bit of wet wheat put you off?"

"It's not that . . . Cornelius, I've decided to get back with Katrin. To try and make a go of it again."

There was silence at the other end.

"I expect you totally disapprove?"

"I totally disapprove," agreed Cornelius.

"It's not a question of happiness."

"Obviously not."

"It's to do with promises and keeping faith."

There was another silence.

"So you're going for the big one then," said Cornelius.

"What do you mean?"

"Sainthood. Martyrdom."

Three weeks after Penny's death Pat received the following letter from the housing department.

"It has come to our notice that, due to the recent demise in your family, you are now occupying accommodation which is larger than the guidelines permit for a family of your size.

You will appreciate that we have on our waiting list families living in desperately overcrowded circumstances. I am therefore instructed to inform you that you are being transferred to a two-bedroom flat which has fallen vacant in your block.

Yours faithfully,

PD Smith, Housing Officer."

That was that then. Pat folded up the letter. Whatever

happened to you in life, there was always some bugger waiting for you with a rule book.

"It doesn't work, this going in blind," Grace said to Leonard, a few days later. "There're forces ruling people's lives I don't begin to understand. I'm going to enrol on a course. Get a professional training," she added, silencing her mother's voice of disapproval for the last time. "So that next time I'll know what to do."

"Good idea. I might join you. Looks like I'm going to be out of a job pretty soon," Leonard growled.

"That's nice, dear. We can be students together."

"Oh my God!" screamed Emma. "Tell me which university you're going to so I can leave it off my list. Hey! Stop it!" she yelled, as Grace and Leonard began pummelling her with cushions. "Behave! You're not students yet!"

"I don't understand, Sam. How can he do it?" Cornelius glared across the table at his friend. "How can he go back to that frightful woman?"

"Ah, Cornelius, who can tell what goes on in another man's soul? For it's the soul we're speaking of here." Sam took a sip of coffee and fingered his collar. "I'm a simple man, too easily distracted by the noise of the world – organising fêtes, repairing the church roof, lusting after cars." He grimaced. "All these things prevent me from hearing God's voice as clearly as I should. But the finger of grace has touched our friend."

"How do you know?" asked Cornelius, exasperated.

"I've prayed beside Joachim in church for many years now," replied Sam simply. "You learn a lot about a person by praying with them – and I've seen in Joachim the silence of a soul in communion with God. It hung around us in the church as we prayed." He looked away. "It's an eloquent silence, that silence of consent. I envy Joachim." He was silent for a moment. "I tremble for him too. It's a fearful thing, to be marked out by God."

CHAPTER SEVENTEEN

SOME WEEKS LATER JOACHIM FLUNG OPEN THE WINDOWS OF HIS library and stepped out onto the lawn. The last time he'd do this. Neither his sons nor his sons' sons would live here. Soon there'd be a new owner and a new family line. The futures of Alan and Paddy and their families would be made secure. The castle would be repaired, there'd be money for farm machinery, money to plant trees and experiment with new crops. The film people would come and perhaps others would come after them. The roof would be mended, the castle redecorated.

It was only right. He stood on his lawn looking out over the fields which he would never again see harvested, to the trees where he would never again walk on a Sunday afternoon. A deer came leaping out of the woods and bounded gracefully across the ploughed field to the trees on the other side. He glanced towards the crumbling garden wall and the stone summerhouse with its gaping hole where the roof had been taken off. It was only right.

But as he turned back into the castle, his loss weighed heavily upon him.

He went through the castle room by room, noting which pieces of furniture would have to be packed up and shipped across to Germany and which could be auctioned off with the castle. In the dining-room he paused. He thought he'd caught a glimpse of a tiny elf-like creature standing on the table, arms crossed, scowling fiercely at him. He brushed a hand across his eyes. The creature was gone.

In the afternoon he walked over the fields to Cornelius's house.

"I shan't disguise to you that I think this is sheer folly," said Cornelius, opening the door. "That woman will ruin your life." He led the way into his study. "Oh, not in the conventional sense. She won't spend all your money or be unfaithful to you. But your life will become impoverished." He flopped into a chair and gazed challengingly at Joachim. "Her unloving nature will dry up your heart."

"I have chosen, Cornelius," replied Joachim quietly, "to stay and heal my marriage." He wandered over to the window and looked out for a moment. Then he turned and faced his friend. "I'm resigning my job. I'm going to look for something more worthwhile to do. She's agreed to that much."

"Yes, but to give up your farm! Your visits to Ireland! The one thing in life that brings you happiness. Surely that wasn't necessary?"

Joachim had never heard Cornelius speak with so much feeling before. He sat down.

"Peter was right when he said Ireland's an escape for me. I must stop escaping. Face up to being German, a father and married to Katrin."

"Is this what your religion teaches? To give up the only thing you value?"

"Not a giving up. A gain, I suppose. There are certain kinds of love that poison your life. Oh, not immediately. But in the end."

"Pschaw!" Cornelius snorted. "Don't mouth your religious platitudes at me." Diogenes licked his paws excitedly. "What's this?" he sneered. "A theophany? A sudden conversion to a belief in the sanctity of the marriage bed? You don't sometimes think," he continued, putting his fingertips together, "that your religion's just another escape?"

Joachim shook his head. "Faith is comforting, yes. But

beyond that it's . . . terrifying. Most of the time I don't want to hear his voice."

"Joachim, is this really what he wants you to do? The New Testament is one of the most profoundly anti-marriage texts I can think of. And I cannot see how he can be a God of love if he demands you give up all that's dearest to you. Christabel. Ireland. What kind of love is that?" he added contemptuously. "Even Katrin could do better."

Joachim came and sat closer to the fire. "Perhaps it isn't love, perhaps sometimes it's the opposite . . ." He stared into the flames. "It's better not to talk of God, I think. Yes, silence is better."

The silence of the mystic. Cornelius remembered Sam's words. He shook his head. "I can't fight silence."

The two friends sat for a while by the fire in sadness, watched by Diogenes.

"You and Elizabeth could visit us in Germany."

"We could," agreed Cornelius, thinking that when he next saw his friend he would perhaps be much changed. "On the other hand, we'd bring back memories and you may not want to be reminded. Of all this, I mean." He waved a hand in the direction of the window and the fields lying beyond.

"I shall keep the memory of this place – and you, Cornelius – like an icon in my heart. I shall take it out and look at it from time to time. It will be my final act of rebellion," he added softly.

"I'm glad to see you're not yet a saint!" retorted Cornelius.

The two friends embraced.

"You realise," he said, as he showed Joachim to the door, "the church here is going to get terribly Low. Sam will never manage the vestments and the incense on his own."

He watched as Joachim set off back across the fields to his castle. Diogenes nuzzled into his leg. He bent down to stroke the dog. "Yes, old fellow, you feel it too." Joachim turned. Cornelius gave a last wave and went back inside his house, Diogenes at his heels.

Watching his friend disappear into the house, Joachim felt his heart twist inside him with anguish. A silence hung over the fields, like the silence of a figure on a cross. Would he be able to bear it? He looked up at the grey sky. The clouds began to part. A watery Irish sun emerged. Yes, the bread was being broken, the wine poured out. But he could still hope that one day the veil would be rent. He could still hope to soar.

EPILOGUE

1998

"THE PEACE OF THE LORD BE WITH YOU ALWAYS," INTONED THE new Archbishop of Canterbury.

"And also with you."

"Let us offer one another a sign of peace."

The Archbishop of Canterbury exchanged the kiss of peace with some bishops and other church dignitaries, then moved forward to the front pew of the cathedral where the Prime Minister was waiting for him. The Archbishop looks tired, thought the Prime Minister, as if he's been in the job for years. Taking the prelate's hand, he smiled.

"Good luck, your Grace."

The Archbishop, who neither liked nor trusted politicians and who'd had his moments of disappointment over this one, paused. Maintaining his grip on the Prime Minister's hand, he looked into his eyes.

"That rather depends on you, doesn't it, Prime Minister?"

"On God, surely," the Prime Minister retorted.

For the first time during the enthronement ceremony, the Archbishop of Canterbury smiled. His weary eyes beamed.

"The peace of Christ, Prime Minister."

He let go of the Prime Minister's hand as the choir began singing the *Agnus Dei.*

Pat Jackson, sitting with Sal in front of the television, exclaimed suddenly,

"Bugger me! Now I know who it is, it's Father Keogh!"

"Who is?"

"That man, the Bishop with the funny hat, the geezer shaking hands with Tony Blair. I couldn't place him at first. That explains why he's not been around much lately. Bloody hell! A Labour government, an Archbishop of Canterbury from this neck of the woods. Whatever next?"

"Don't worry, Ma. Nothing changes 'ere. You'll see."

Pat returned to her work, glueing silk into jewellery boxes for eighty pence an hour. She sat on an upturned crate. Her furniture had been repossessed. Jimmy had brought round the telly yesterday evening. She knew better than to ask where it came from. Sal was right, nothing changed. All the same she couldn't help wondering, seeing their Father Keogh all dressed up as an archbishop, talking to the Prime Minister . . .

That was that, then. Grace looked at the TV screen. That had finally sealed it. Labour in government. Father Keogh in Canterbury. Now perhaps people like Clive would finally get their come-uppance. She switched off the television and opened her casework file.

Lallie was listening to the car radio. She was on her way back to Stockton to film part of the TV series "The New Britain", looking at revitalised communities in the inner cities following on the new regional development programme of the Labour government. She'd stumbled on the Radio 3 broadcast of the Archbishop's enthronement by accident. She remembered Pat Jackson talking about Father Keogh. The church was coming in on their side then. At last.

In a hotel room in London, on a business trip, Joachim sat mesmerised in front of the television screen. There, seated just behind the new Archbishop, was Sam Cleary, now apparently the Most Reverend Sam Cleary, Bishop of Meath. Tears pricked the corner of his eyes. Impatiently, he brushed them away. What was the matter with him? Things were all right, weren't they? Peter was completing a doctorate in psychology. Werner was doing well at school. Katrin had got a part-time job working with refugees seeking asylum in Germany. The family was back together again.

The Bishop of Meath stood up and moved forward to the front of the cathedral to read from *Revelations*, a passage specially chosen by the Archbishop. Joachim stared at Sam's familiar face. Tears rolled down his cheeks. He was homesick for Ireland. For Christabel. For life lived on more than a mundane level. It had all been more difficult than he'd expected.

"They shall neither hunger any more nor thirst any more," read Sam. "The sun shall not strike them, nor any heat; for the Lamb who is in the midst of the throne will shepherd them and lead them to living fountains of waters. And God will wipe away every tear from their eyes."

He'd known passion once. That was something to hang on to. He knew what he was capable of. Some people never found out. He'd desired Christabel like he sometimes, too rarely, desired God. A flame in the deepest part of his being. Should he have gone with it? Wherever it had led? He rose from the bed and went to get a handkerchief to blow his nose.

In Canterbury cathedral the choir and congregation moved into the first verse of Newman's great hymn.

"Lead, kindly Light, amid the encircling gloom,
Lead thou me on;
The night is dark, and I am far from home,

Lead thou me on."

Joachim lay back on the bed and shut his eyes as the music swept over him. He would go on. He had to. One day the dawn would break.